An ORPHAN'S STORY

Cathy loves writing because it gives pleasure to others. She finds writing an extension of herself and it gives her great satisfaction. Cathy says, 'There is nothing like seeing your book in print, because so much loving care has been given to bringing that book into being.' Cathy lives in Cambridgeshire.

T0318059

CATHY SHARP

An
ORPHAN'S
STORY

HarperCollins*Publishers*

HarperCollins*Publishers* Ltd
1 London Bridge Street
London SE1 9GF

www.harpercollins.co.uk

HarperCollinsPublishers
Macken House, 39/40 Mayor Street Upper
Dublin 1, D01 C9W8

First published by HarperCollins*Publishers* Ltd 2025
1

A catalogue record for this book is available from the British Library

ISBN: 978-0-00-868016-9 (PB)
ISBN: 978-0-00-868017-6 (TPB)

This novel is entirely a work of fiction. The names, characters and incidents portrayed in it are the work of the author's imagination. Any resemblance to actual persons, living or dead, events or localities is entirely coincidental.

Typeset in Sabon Lt Pro by HarperCollins*Publishers* India

Printed and bound in the UK using 100%
Renewable Electricity at CPI Group (UK) Ltd

This book contains FSC™ certified paper and other controlled sources to ensure responsible forest management.

For more information visit:
www.harpercollins.co.uk/green

CHAPTER 1

The bedroom curtains were open and the moonbeams
streamed through, lighting the colours of the patchwork
coverlet on his bed. Arthur watched it for a few
moments, his young face intent and serious. He could
hear the argument in the bedroom next to his. It had
been going on for a long time and it worried him.
Giving a little moan of distress, he curled under the
blanket, trying to block his ears. He hated the sound of
sharp voices; they made him want to cry, bringing back
memories that frightened and hurt him. These past few
weeks the quarrels had happened frequently and he
didn't understand why or what was going on. Was he
the problem – would they send him away again?

Arthur's memories of his past life were hazy, perhaps
because he'd learned to block out those things that
distressed him. He remembered being frightened when
he was sent out to Canada from England on a huge
ship, remembered Julie, Davey and Beth, the other
children, who had been kind to him on the voyage.

The voices in the next room were louder now and
Arthur trembled as he listened to the endless quarrel.

'What about me and Arthur?' Emily's voice rose shrilly. 'You can't just abandon us. I can't manage the shop and the child and everything else alone. It isn't fair, Ken. Besides, I don't see why you want to join up – it isn't our war.'

'My parents came out from Britain, as did yours, Emily,' Kenneth Henderson spoke calmly. 'This war just drags on and I feel it is my duty to offer my services. Unless we all do what we can, the world will be overrun by this madness.'

'I've read the Allies are beginning to turn the tide,' Emily retorted. 'If you wanted to go, Ken, why now – why not two years ago – when it first started? It's 1943 and—'

'I don't believe it is nearly over,' Ken repudiated her assertion. Listening from his bedroom, Arthur thought he seemed to hesitate, then, 'I've made up my mind – I *have* to go.'

'And what happens to me if you get killed – and Arthur? You can't expect me to bring him up on my own?'

'You wanted the boy, Emily. I went along with the adoption for your sake.'

'Oh yes, blame me,' Emily countered bitterly. 'It was you that said maybe we should offer a home to one of the evacuees!'

Now they *were* quarrelling about him. Arthur threw back the bedcovers, jumped out of bed and ran down the wooden stairs and out into the large back garden. In the dark of night, he could see nothing, hear only the strange grunts of animals, and smell the sweetness of the night-blooming flower they called Midnight

Candy. It was cold and his feet were bare, but it was better than listening to them. His eyes stung with tears and he scrubbed at them with the back of his fist. What was happening? Why were they suddenly so angry with each other? He didn't understand and it worried him.

Arthur had been nearly six when he came out to Canada, and two years had passed since he began to live with his new parents. He would be eight soon. He was no longer a small innocent boy but an inquiring child and had begun to understand the things that had happened to him. Until he was nearly five, he'd lived with his mum and dad in a nice house in London; it wasn't a big house, just two rooms up and down with a lean-to scullery at the back, but it had been warm and dry, and smelled clean, and Arthur had been wrapped in a cocoon of love. Then something bad happened. His big, cheerful father, who worked on the docks, was killed in a terrible accident – Mum had told him they'd been loading ammunition onto a ship and it had caused an explosion, sending his dad to Heaven.

Arthur had cried himself to sleep that night and many nights afterwards. It seemed impossible to him that his father would never smile at him again, never pick him up and carry him on his big shoulders or tickle him to make him laugh. He'd wanted his mother to hold him and kiss him and tell him it would be all right, but she hadn't. She'd pushed him away, told him not to bother her, and so he'd crept away to cry his heart out alone. That was when his world fell apart.

Mum had cried all the time for weeks and weeks, and then she'd started to act funny. He vaguely remembered that she staggered about in the night and

3

knocked things over, and she got upset over all sorts of things, screamed at him, and shouted for nothing, and a couple of times she'd hit him. Then a lady from the council had come and taken him away, first to an orphanage and then to the ship. She'd told him his mum had died and was now in Heaven with his dad. Arthur had cried and cried but his tears didn't change anything. He'd been put on a ship taking him to Canada, because there was no one left in England who wanted him.

A sob broke from Arthur as he remembered his friends from the ship; they had been so kind to him, especially Julie. He hadn't understood that once they got to Canada he would be separated from them.

When Emily Henderson came for him, she'd told him she would be his new mother. Arthur had gone to her trustingly but it was all so confusing. He hadn't understood why he'd been taken from his first mother and given to another all this way from his home, but it had been all right – at least for a start.

When they arrived at the shop that sold all kinds of clothing, it had smelled clean and nice and Arthur had met Ken there – his new father. He wasn't a bit like Arthur's big cheerful first father. He was thin and serious and he wore gold-rimmed glasses. However, he'd smiled and given Arthur a boiled sweet, telling him he was welcome to their home and promised that if he was good there would be sweets every Saturday.

The house he was taken to later that night was nice. It was much bigger than the terraced house his first mum and dad had lived in, and smelled of polish. His bedroom was twice the size of the one he'd known for

4

the first five years or so of his life, and it was full of nice things to play with – like model cars, a teddy bear, and lead soldiers. He knew they were lead because he was told not to suck them, because lead was bad if you put it in your mouth. All the things had belonged to Ken – his new dad – and Arthur wasn't sure if he was supposed to play with them or just look at them on the shelf. They weren't his, they belonged to Ken and Arthur wasn't sure Ken liked him very much. He would smile and nod, but he never hugged Arthur or threw him into the air the way his father had.

When he'd been at the house for two weeks, he started to play with the toys very carefully. Ken played with him sometimes – especially with the clockwork train set. It was fun and Arthur enjoyed it, but it didn't happen often, because his new dad was very busy with the store. His new mum told him that people needed clothes all the time and so his dad had to be there to look after things. He seemed to work very late at night, too. Sometimes, Emily went in to the shop to help but that was only after Arthur started to go to school.

It was very strange at the school for a while, so different from the one he'd known in London. At his old school he'd done sums and writing but other than kick a ball in the playground, nothing more had been asked of him. Here at his new school in Canada it was very different. There were lots of different lessons – painting, and model making in woodwork class, and nature walks, as well as history and learning about other countries. There were more organised games than had happened at his old school, and in the summer – which was lovely and sunny and seemed much longer, they had picnics and even swimming in the river. The winters were very cold and there was a lot of snow, but that could be fun too, making snowmen in the garden with Emily.

Arthur loved Emily. She was pretty and kind and sometimes she kissed him. He thought she liked him but wasn't sure. His real mum had loved him until his dad died and then she'd stopped caring about Arthur. So it was hard for him to know what to expect of his new home.

His new parents had bought him new clothes as he grew – and he'd grown a lot that first year. He'd been given the best food he'd ever eaten and soon filled out, becoming taller and heavier than he'd been when he arrived. His new mum had taken him lots of places, to see Walt Disney pictures at the cinema, to football matches with Ken; it wasn't the same kind of football as he'd watched at home once with his dad, but it was fun, and a few times during that lovely summer, they'd gone for a car ride, away from the busy streets of Halifax into the wilderness. They'd taken food in a picnic basket and a blanket to sit on – and once they'd seen a bear. It had wanted their food so they'd left some sandwiches and retreated to the car because Ken said you didn't argue with a bear.

Arthur had been happy. Gradually, he'd begun to forget his first mum and dad. He was fussed over by his second mother and her friends, and even Ken seemed content to have him around. Arthur had begun to understand about the war in Europe. It was all because of a man called Hitler, so his teacher said. He learned that London had been bombed but Arthur wasn't sure what that meant until he saw a newsreel when he was taken to see Mickey Mouse at the cinema one Saturday. It looked terrible to see houses on fire and Arthur realised that he was lucky to be here.

Most of the first year had been good. It was some weeks after the news of the terrible bombings in London started that things began to change. Arthur had listened to the quarrels in the next bedroom, without truly understanding them. It seemed that Ken wanted to join the British Airforce and go to fight Hitler and Mum didn't want him to go.

Arthur liked his Emily-mum better than his Ken-dad. He'd been treated kindly by both, but he'd never been quite certain of Ken; his smile wasn't right, it didn't touch his eyes only his mouth. What he'd heard that night had made him even more uncertain – was it only Emily who had wanted to adopt Arthur?

His thoughts were interrupted suddenly as a light beamed across the garden, highlighting the lawns and neat shrubbery, and his mum came out in slippers and a housecoat. 'Arthur! What are you doing out here, love?'

Arthur walked to her, his head down. 'I heard you arguing . . .' he said, gulping back his desire to cry. 'Is Ken going away?'

'I don't know,' Emily replied and, looking at her, Arthur could see she had been crying, her face all red and patchy. He slipped his hand into hers.

'I'll look after you if he goes, Mum,' he said and felt her fingers close round his tightly. 'We'll manage . . . won't we?' He longed for a reassuring hug and to be told they would be fine, but Emily was upset and angry.

'We'll have to,' she said, more sharply than she normally did. 'He makes me so cross sometimes. Why must he volunteer? And why must it be back there? *This* is our home now. It's so stupid.'

Arthur looked up at her fearfully. 'Will you send me away?'

She looked down at him blindly, hardly seeing him for a moment, and then her face registered shock and distress. 'No, of course not, Arthur. You are my little boy. I love you. Please tell me you know that I love you.' She bent to ruffle his hair, which had turned golden like ripe wheat in the hot sun of the previous summer. 'I always wanted a little boy, you know. When I couldn't have one, I wanted to adopt – but Ken wouldn't let me until we heard you were coming all the way from England.'

Arthur smiled up at her. 'So I *am* your little boy,' he said. 'I always will be – won't I?'

'Of course you will,' she reassured him. 'Come in now and I'll make us both some cocoa.'

Arthur let her lead him back into the house. Ken hadn't come down and it was just them. He watched as his mother moved about the large, spotless kitchen and then brought big round cups to the table, filled to the brim with creamy cocoa. She put the biscuit tin in front of him and he helped himself to a chocolate one.

'We'll manage,' she told him then, her expression hard and determined. 'If Ken goes away, we'll manage, the two of us together.'

CHAPTER 2

In London, Rose Parker looked up as Harry Smith entered the kitchen of the house where they now lived together. Her own house had been lost in the bombing raids and Harry had offered her a home. At first, she'd stayed as a guest but now they lived as man and wife, though her real husband Reg was still around somewhere. However, she would never return to him after the way he'd treated her. The last time Rose had seen Reg, he'd beaten her and left her for dead on the pavement.

She was busy making toast and the smell of it was enticing, as was the pile of golden buttery-looking slices already waiting. Harry had shaved and washed and she caught the fresh clean scent of his shaving soap as he came and sat down at the kitchen table. It was one of the things she liked best about Harry since she'd moved into his house; he always kept himself spruce and was never surly in the mornings. She supposed that was two things, but there were quite a few things about Harry Smith that Rose approved of. Her husband Reg was entirely different. She'd always had to nag him to wash and shave and he would only really clean himself up once a week – and, in the mornings, he was a surly bear. She'd decided their marriage was over when he'd beaten her that last time – and Harry swore that if he ever came near her again, he would kill him.

'Mornin', love,' Harry said, looking at her fondly as he reached for a slice of toast. It was mixed butter and marge but tasted good as he bit into it. 'You're pleased with yerself?'

'Yes, I am, Harry,' Rose told him with a beaming smile. 'I had a letter from little Alice Blake this morning. Her aunt has invited me down to stay for a few days – if I fancy it.' Alice was the daughter of Dave Blake and Dora – Rose's friend, who had sadly died from a direct hit by a bomb which had left her young children motherless. Dave was away serving in the Navy and his children, Alice and Davey, had been reunited after many months apart when Davey's mother had sent him to Canada.

'You'll go,' Harry said instantly. 'You're due a break from the factory. Take the time and enjoy yourself, Rose. I know how much you love that girl.' Harry was the manager of the munitions factory where Rose worked as a line supervisor and if he said she could take time off for a visit it was official, even though they were working flat out to keep up the quota needed. The British troops were under the cosh, according to the newspapers, and everyone at the factory routinely put in extra hours to churn out the ammunition they so sorely needed. 'I know you were very worried about Alice when we didn't know where she'd been sent.'

Alice had been sent to stay at a farm, as were many kids in London at the start of the war. Unfortunately, the farmer's wife had died and the little girl had been sent on to an orphanage, where she'd been desperately unhappy.

'Yes, I was. She's a little darling,' Rose said. 'I thought her mother was wrong to send her to the country when she did – but at least Alice lived and she might have died if she'd been with her mother when that bomb hit. She was happy at the farm, but that orphanage she was taken to was wicked.'

'You'd have taken her yourself if Dave hadn't thought she'd be best with her aunt,' Harry said and smiled at her. 'Why don't you go down this weekend, love? You can have all my sweet rations. I don't need them. Buy as much as you can for the kids – and if you need any money, just ask.'

'You're a good man, Harry,' Rose told him and smiled. She'd hesitated to move in with him, because folk did love to gossip and she'd feared Reg's anger if he'd come home and found her living with another man. He'd heard rumours last time he was home which is why he'd attacked her in the street. She might have died there for all he cared, but she'd told him they were finished and she hoped he wouldn't come looking for her again. After what he'd done to her, Reg deserved no consideration from Rose and Harry had gone to the police and reported it as he wasn't one to let things go. If Reg returned, he'd find a way to make sure Rose was safe. 'I think I shall if you don't mind, love,' she said now.

'No, you get off and enjoy yourself with them kids,' Harry said and hesitated. 'I ain't forgot about adopting a lad – but when I inquired, they asked if we were married. I said no and they pulled long faces.' He scowled, clearly annoyed over it. 'Makes me want to spit – there's all them kids needin' a home and they pull a face cos we ain't wed.'

'Perhaps I should ask a lawyer if I can divorce Reg,' Rose offered. 'I reckon we should just lie about it, Harry. I doubt they have the resources to check.'

'We could get married, then we'd have our proof . . .'

'Don't you think the registrar might check that I was still wed to Reg?' Rose looked at him doubtfully. 'That's bigamy and we might be in trouble.' She hesitated, then, 'Let's see if we can foster a kid first. I saw an advert in the paper asking for foster parents. We might have more luck that way.'

'Yeah, we might,' Harry agreed but looked doubtful. Unbeknown to Rose, he'd tried more than one agency and they'd all asked the same questions. Seemed they thought children orphaned by the Blitz were better off in children's homes than with a couple living in sin.

They'd thought for a while that Rose might have another child but she'd had a miscarriage and the chance had just slipped away. The fact that she had conceived but couldn't hold the child inside her had distressed her, and although she didn't say much, they both knew she longed for another child.

Why couldn't that bugger Reg Parker just disappear? Rose had thought him dead once before, when a telegram came saying he was missing – but he'd turned up like a bad penny and caused her a load of trouble. If he dared show his face round here again, Harry knew he might do something desperate. He wasn't normally a violent man, but Reg didn't deserve forgiveness in Harry's estimation.

'Do you want me to look into it?' he asked

'Yes, I do,' Rose agreed and gave him a peck on the cheek as she put another piece of hot toast in front of him. 'It's half margarine this morning, because we've nearly used our butter ration, but there's a pot of your favourite marmalade.'

'I don't mind marge,' Harry told her. 'Besides, I can't taste it with marmalade. It's just another thing we 'ave to put up with, love.'

The war had caused hardships of all kinds, rationing being only one, but Harry reckoned it had done him a favour. If it hadn't been for the war, Rose wouldn't have left Reg and come to live with him. Her house had gone, along with most of Silver Terrace; thankfully, she hadn't been in it. Faced with being homeless she'd moved into his spare room just as a friend, but after Reg had beaten her to within an inch of her life, she'd decided to give Harry a chance and he couldn't have been happier. It was the best time of his life, war, or no war.

Rose saw the man as she stopped to buy a pie and chips after she finished work for the evening. She recognised him and turned away, not wanting to speak to him, but he crossed the road and came over to her, planting himself in her way.

'Too posh to speak to an old friend now, Rose?'

'I wasn't aware that we were friends,' Rose retorted sharply. 'I thought you'd moved on – thought it was too hot for you round here since the last time you were arrested?'

13

'Now, Rose, that's not kind, is it?' Mick George grinned at her. He was good humoured enough and kind in his way, though a confirmed crook. 'I only wanted to ask after Davey and Alice. I know you hear from them.'

'Yes, I do,' Rose's tone softened a little. Mick had always been sweet on the kids' mother, Dora Blake, and they'd had an affair after she quarrelled with her husband Dave. 'They're very happy living with their aunt, thanks, Mick.'

'Glad to hear it,' Mick said. 'I still miss Dora, you know.' He put his hand in his pocket and took out a ten-shilling note. 'Buy them kids something from me, please, Rose.'

Rose hesitated. Any money Mick had would be dishonestly come by. To take it would be nearly as bad as accepting stolen goods. 'I don't think I should,' she said. 'But I will tell Davey that you asked after them.'

'Alice loves Tom Thumb drops,' Mick persisted and thrust the money into her hand. 'Go on, what harm can it do, Rose?'

'Oh, very well,' she replied. 'Just this once – but don't ever ask again, because I won't take it.'

'I know yer as straight as a die,' Mick said and grinned now that he had his way. 'That money was honestly come by. I've been working in a club fer youngsters – so yer can ease yer conscience, Rose Parker.'

Rose nodded and walked off without answering. She didn't believe him, but she genuinely believed he'd loved Dora and was grieving for her loss. If it helped him to give Dora's kids something, then she couldn't throw it back in his face. She wouldn't tell Harry, though, because he'd hit the roof. He had no time for the likes of Mick.

Smiling, she walked to the little shop at the corner of her road. Inside, it smelled of paraffin, candles, carbolic soap, and something else she wasn't sure of. The shelves were stocked with all kinds of things, despite the rationing, varying from bootlaces, knicker elastic and disinfectant to jars of sweets, vegetables, cheese, and ham. Ah yes, she thought that was probably what she could smell – a strong disinfectant. It might have been a broken bottle but Sid had probably had rats in again; they got everywhere since one of the sewers was broken by a bomb; that was months ago but it still hadn't been repaired. It was just another thing they had to put up with these days.

'I want to buy all my sweet rations today, Sid,' she said to the shopkeeper, letting her gaze travel along the rows and rows of jars on the shelf behind his head. 'Have you got Tom Thumb drops – and sherbet lemons?'

'Yes – just had the sherbet lemons in this morning.' He reached up to get the jars down and carefully checked her coupons before weighing the sweets. 'You want equal measure of both?'

'Yes, please,' Rose said. 'They're for Dave Blake's kids. I'm going down to visit them at the weekend.'

'You'll like that, then,' Sid replied and drew a line through her coupons as he finished measuring out the sweets. The Tom Thumb bag was much bigger because the drops weighed lighter than the bigger sherbet lemons. 'Take these from me, Rose.' He handed her two sherbet dips with liquorice dippers.

'That's good of you, Sid,' Rose said. 'I've got Harry's coupons here – what can I get for them?'

'You could buy a chocolate bar for each of them and some toffee. I've got some nice toffee pieces. I could make up two small bags if you like.'

'Yes, that's a good idea,' Rose smiled as he meticulously marked the coupons as used and then weighed the toffee and handed her two small bars of Fry's chocolate. He gave her a big brown paper bag to put everything in and Rose paid him for the sweets and walked to the door, but just as she was about to go out, he called her back.

'I've had some tins of red salmon come in,' he told her, giving her a conspiratorial wink. 'There ain't enough for everyone – but if you want, I can let you have two tins.'

'Oh, thanks, Sid,' Rose said and looked at the label as he handed one over and then the other. 'It came all the way from Canada – fancy that.'

'Yes.' Sid smiled and nodded. 'Harry's partial to red salmon, I believe.'

'Yes, he loves it in a sandwich but we haven't had any for ages.' Rose nodded. 'I'll leave him one for his tea, but I'll take the other down for Alice's aunt. I doubt if they've seen it since before the war where they live.'

'I was lucky to get it,' Sid replied and took the ten-shilling note she handed over, giving her a few coins change. 'I try to look after me best customers, Rose.' He touched the side of his nose and smiled.

Rose didn't ask how he'd come by the salmon. As far as she knew he was an honest shopkeeper – but a lot of people weren't averse to an occasional luxury, even if it might have fallen off the back of a lorry. What you didn't know, couldn't hurt you, that's what she said. Not that she'd have bought it from someone she knew to be dishonest; after all, Sid might have got it perfectly legally. Sometimes these things did manage to get through and it was the sharp shopkeepers that snapped them up – first come, first served when there was stuff off the ration.

Rose hurried on. Her pie and chips would be getting cold. She would pop them in the oven to warm and they'd be fine when Harry got in. He was always half an hour or so later than her, because he had to supervise the hand-over to the next shift. Later that evening he would go back and have a walk round. He didn't have to, but he liked to make sure everything was fine at the factory before he went to bed and he would probably put in extra hours while Rose was away . . .

'Aunt Rose! Aunt Rose!' Alice flew down the garden path to hug her as she arrived. 'I've been looking for you all the morning.' The house was larger than Harry's in London, the walls a mixture of red brick and pebbledash with small, white-framed windows. The front garden had a lawn and a few rose bushes and some lavender that smelled wonderful when in full bloom.

'I told her you wouldn't be here until after lunch but we couldn't get her away from the window,' Davey said as he followed his sister down the path at a slower pace. 'Did you have a good journey?'

'Yes, thanks, Davey,' Rose said as he took her basket and her bag, carrying them into the house for her. Their

Aunt Marie came bustling through into the hall to offer her a welcome, smiling as she saw Rose.

'It's lovely to see you, Mrs Parker. I'm glad you've come down for a few days – you'll be glad to get away from the bombs and the noise, I dare say?'

'We haven't had many bombs for a while now,' Rose replied. 'I think Coventry and some of the coastal towns have been getting the worst of it just recently.'

'I wish they'd all stop so we could go back to the way things were before this wretched war,' Marie grumbled. 'It's awful what has happened to folk these past months, losing their homes and their lives, too. We're better here than you are in London, but nowhere is completely safe while that madman is allowed to run riot.'

'I read where some of his own generals tried to kill him,' Rose observed. 'Pity they didn't succeed. I reckon we could come to terms with the Germans if it weren't for him.'

'Mebbe . . .' Marie said but looked doubtful and shook her head. 'Come in, Rose, and let's try to forget there's a war. I've made some tea – and there's fresh prawns I bought at the harbour, caught this morning, and salad from my own garden – the tomatoes are beautiful this year and I've lots of them. You can take a few back to London when you go.'

Rose thanked her, glancing around the large, old-fashioned kitchen with its oak dressers set with chunky blue-and-white crockery, the big, scrubbed-pine table, covered just now with a thick cream lace cloth and set with some of the blue-and-white plates and cups and saucers.

Rose went to her basket and then handed the big brown paper bag to Davey. 'These are for you from Harry and me – and Sid from the corner shop sent you the dips.' Davey exclaimed joyfully and set about sharing out the goodies inside. Rose smiled and passed the large tin of red salmon to Marie.

'Goodness gracious me,' she said. 'I haven't seen any of that since the war started. How on earth did you find it?'

'The man who runs the corner shop sold it to me,' Rose told her with a smile. 'He let me have two tins because I'm one of his best customers. It came all the way from Canada.'

Davey perked up at that and wanted to look at the tin. 'We had a canning factory not far from us when I lived with Corky and Rodie,' he told them. 'We used to have fresh salmon, mostly, if Corky went fishing or one of his customers brought one in to sell.'

'That was nice then,' Marie said. 'You like your fish, don't you?'

'I like tinned salmon best,' Davey said 'But Bert cooked all kinds of things when I looked after him – we had skunk a few times . . .' He laughed at the look on their faces. 'It tasted good, but Bert didn't tell me what it was until after I'd eaten it.'

'That was when you lived in the wilderness,' Rose said, nodding at him. 'You liked Bert, didn't you?'

'And his son Albert,' Davey replied. 'Albert helped me by taking me to look after his father. He brought us supplies but then he was killed at sea – and then Bert got ill and died, and I went to live with Corky for a while.' He looked sad for a moment as he remembered the sailor who had looked after him and gave him his first home in Canada.

'Yes, I remember,' Rose said. 'It was Corky who arranged a passage home for you, wasn't it?'

'I wanted to get home for Alice,' Davey told her. 'I liked Canada. I'll go there again one day – and maybe I'll take Alice and Dad and – and Judy, too.' Judy was his father's new wife and the children loved her, though they only saw her now and then because she worked as a nurse. Aunt Marie said she was needed by all the men wounded in the terrible war.

Rose smiled and nodded. She'd always liked their dad, but he was away fighting again, though he'd made plans for a fishing boat of his own when he returned at the end of the war. Until then the children were happy enough here in this lovely old house with their aunt. Rose thought you could tell it was ancient by the vibes of permanence that seemed to come from the walls; Marie had told her that most of her family had lived and died here, and it was a happy feeling, especially in the big warm kitchen.

Marie was pouring boiling water into a big brown pot. Rose washed her hands at the deep kitchen sink and the children did, too. As well as the lovely fresh prawns and the homegrown salad – which was crisp and delicious – there was crusty bread and some farm butter. Rose had never tasted butter fresh from a farm before; it had a softer feel in the mouth and a lovely melting taste. Marie had also made a big seed cake and some strawberry jam tarts.

'We'll have the salmon for tea on Sunday,' Marie said, looking pleased. 'We do very well for fresh fish, Rose,

20

but there's not much going in the way of tinned stuff so it will be a nice change, and it's Davey's favourite.'

'I like your fish and chips, too, Aunt Marie,' he said. 'And these prawns are yummy!'

'That's all right then,' his aunt said smiling. 'Eat up then, children, and you can take Rose for a walk on the beach – well, the bits of it that aren't mined.' She nodded to Rose. 'Davey knows where it's safe to play and so does Alice.'

'Oh, I'm sure they do,' Rose said and gave them a loving look. 'I'm looking forward to being shown around . . .'

CHAPTER 3

When Ken first went off to fight for the right to be free and to save the world from tyranny, Arthur thought he liked being alone with Emily best. She looked a bit red-eyed for a while and she was angry with Ken for leaving them, but she still cooked nice things for them to eat, and though she was busier a lot of the time, she still took Arthur to school and fetched him home, unless he went to play with friends. However, she spent a lot of time in the evenings doing what she called 'accounts' and after a few weeks, she began to look harassed. One evening, when Arthur asked her to get him a drink, she looked cross and told him he was old enough now to get himself a drink.

Arthur managed to fill the big kettle from the sink and carry it to the large black range, but when it boiled, he found it difficult to hold it steady when he tried to make coffee, and inevitably he spilled a few drops on his hand, which hurt. When Emily realised what he'd done, she cried out in distress.

'I'm sorry, Arthur,' she told him. 'I thought you meant a glass of cordial or water. I'll make the coffee . . .' She fussed over the red mark on his hand, running cold water over it and then applying a salve.

'I'm sorry I can't help you,' Arthur told her, tears in his eyes. 'You've got too much to do now Ken isn't here.'

'He always did the accounts for the shop,' Emily told him, 'and I can't make them add up right, Arthur. It seems to me that we're losing money from the till but I don't know how.' She shook her head. 'It must be my adding up – I can't believe that anyone would steal from us so it must be my fault.'

'I'm good at adding up,' Arthur told her, but she just smiled and looked away. She didn't believe him. He peeked in her big black book when she was getting their meal. There were lots of columns of figures, some in red and some in black ink. Arthur wasn't sure what they meant, but he painstakingly added the first two columns and pencilled in the totals at the bottom. They were different to the totals Emily had written down. However, he didn't understand what the figures represented.

When Emily and he had finished washing the dishes, she went back to her checking of the accounts and after a few minutes, she called to him.

'Arthur – did you touch my accounts?'

'I added up the two columns on the first page. I wrote it in pencil . . .' he faltered, looking at her nervously. Would she be cross that he made it different to hers.

'If your total is right, that's why the rest of them went wrong.' Emily looked at him. 'I didn't know you were clever at sums, Arthur?'

24

'My teacher says I'm top of the class and I always get them right.'

'Come and show me how you did it,' Emily invited. Arthur went to her side and showed her the scrap of paper he'd used. Instead of trying to add the whole column as she'd done, he'd added two figures together and then added the next figure to his total and so on all down the page, ticking each one as he'd done it.

'That's the way my dad taught me,' Arthur said and smiled as Emily checked the figures with him and saw her mistake. 'Dad was very clever with numbers – but he liked working outside and not in an office.'

'I think you're *very* clever,' Emily said and gave him a hug. 'Will you help me get these silly accounts right, Arthur?'

'Yes, Mum,' he said and grinned. 'My dad said I was a genius with numbers – not sure what that means, though.'

'It just means you're exceptionally clever at something,' Emily said and sighed. 'I've been going over and over these silly things and couldn't see where I'd gone wrong.' In truth, she'd made more than one mistake, but with Arthur's help she saw them, but her worried look still didn't go away. Something else was wrong.

Emily sat checking endless figures long after Arthur had gone to bed. She was annoyed with herself for making a silly mistake, but maths had never been her forte. She liked to sew and bake and make things nice in the home. At the shop she was good with helping the customers choose their new clothes and people liked her – but she wasn't trained to keep accounts or run a large business. She was just a very ordinary woman who could look after a home and care for those she loved. She supposed that was why Ken had found her boring and he must have felt that or he wouldn't have stopped loving her.

She knew he had tired of her when he spent longer and longer at the shop in the evenings and went away on fishing trips at weekends with his friends. Sometimes Emily wondered if he'd ever loved her. She'd loved him with all her heart when they were wed, but for a while now she'd felt hurt and angry at his neglect. They'd been happy for a while – at least, she had – but Ken had changed, little by little, and it had started just after Arthur arrived. He'd become more and more distant until most nights he didn't even bother to kiss her before rolling over and falling asleep. Now he'd deserted her and left her to look after a failing business, because the figures didn't lie, even if she had made mistakes. The shop takings were barely enough to cover all the wages and expenses, let alone Ken's expensive habits. He'd taken his new car with him when he'd left, together with most of his possessions. Emily knew in her heart that he wasn't coming back.

What was she going to do? Somehow, she had to make a living for herself and Arthur.

Sighing, she picked up the letter from England. It was from her Great-Aunt Becky. Her aunt was a widow of some twenty-five years, having lost her husband to the Great War, as it was called. It was that war that had brought Emily's mother to Canada. She'd married a

Canadian soldier stationed in England and come back with him to his home. Aunt Becky, as she called herself in her letters to Emily, was alone and not feeling well. Emily was her only relative and she'd written to say that she would like to see her.

I know there is a war on at the moment, Emily, my dear, but if you could think of coming to visit me one day, I should love to see you.

Before he left, Ken had told her he was going to join the British Royal Air Force. She'd had just two letters to tell her he'd arrived in England and had joined the RAF and nothing since. If Emily went to visit Aunt Becky, she could arrange to meet him, and . . . Emily's thoughts went no further because, in her heart, she knew her marriage had been failing for a while, and had no idea of what came next. She folded the letter and put it away before deciding to retire. Emily couldn't afford to visit Aunt Becky – if it was even possible with a war on; she had a failing business to run and bring back to profit if she could. She sighed as she snapped off the light in the kitchen and began to climb the stairs. Perhaps she should approach the bank for a small loan . . .?

Arthur thought things were all right again for a few weeks. The worried look was still there sometimes in Emily's eyes, but she smiled when she saw him looking at her and he knew she tried to put her troubles aside. The summer weather had come now and at school they played lots of games and did things Arthur liked. On Sundays Emily made a picnic and they sat under an awning in the garden to eat it, but they didn't go out into the wild places that Arthur loved the way they had when Ken was here. As time passed, Emily looked more anxious again, and it wasn't doing the accounts that was worrying her, because Arthur asked if she needed help and she shook her head.

'It's all kinds of things, Arthur,' she told him. 'I can't buy the things I need for the shop because a lot of the woollens and tweeds came from places like Scotland and Italy, and they're in this senseless war, too. It just seems harder and harder to make the shop pay.'

'Can't you buy things here in Canada?' Arthur asked and she looked at him doubtfully.

'I could – but our customers like the quality of the goods from Scotland and we sold lots of Italian leather and there was lace and— Oh, all kinds of things we can't get.' Emily sighed. 'Ken looked after all that. He knew what was wanted and where to source it – or I thought he did.'

Arthur felt upset because his Emily-mum seemed unhappy. As the weeks turned into months, he thought she looked more and more anxious, and then one day he came home from school and found her sitting at the table with her head in her hands, and, as she looked up, he saw she had been crying. Arthur ran to her, gazing up into her face. She looked pale but her skin was blotchy with red patches and he knew she'd been crying for a long time.

'What's wrong, Mum?' he asked, hugging the bit of her he could reach. 'Did I do something wrong?'

Her hand stroked his head, and then she sniffed and wiped the tears from her cheeks. 'No, you make life bearable, Arthur,' she told him with a watery smile.

'It's too much for you to understand, love, but I have to close the shop and Ken will be so angry with me for making a mess of things—' She raised her head suddenly, a flash of anger in her eyes. 'But it's his fault. He must have known it was happening before he went – and yet he still left us to cope on our own . . .'

What did that mean? Arthur didn't understand what was happening, but he knew it was bad. Emily wouldn't close the shop unless she had to – but why?

'Is there anything I can do?' he asked, looking up at her anxiously and his forlorn expression brought a smile to her face.

'Bless you, Arthur, I know you would if you could – but it's money, you see, and this time there is no mistake – the bank says we owe them five thousand dollars and they won't let me use the business account any longer.' She looked at Arthur, her hand ruffling his blond head. 'I can't repay them so they'll take the assets. I'll be lucky if they leave me the house because it's in Ken's name and I've been told that he put it up as surety. It depends how much they get for the stock.' Again there was a flash of anger in her eyes. Arthur had always thought Emily pretty, her hair a light brown and her eyes soft grey, but it was the light in those eyes and her soft smile that made her beautiful. At the moment they were missing. She looked pale and tired, and there was an air of defeat about her.

'Could we go and live somewhere else?' Arthur suggested and she looked down at him, pensive and silent, clearly thinking.

'I don't have any family here in Canada,' Emily said. 'Ken has an uncle but he's a surly old bear. He wouldn't lift a finger to help us – and I don't want to ask him for help.' She was silent for so long that Arthur rubbed his head against her arm, willing her to come back to him. Emily looked down at him and sighed deeply. 'I can only see one thing for it, Arthur. My Aunt Becky lives in England down in Hastings and runs a fish and chip shop . . .'

Arthur's spine tingled. He'd come from England and he associated it with bad memories. 'Can't we stay here, Mum? I can go to work . . .'

Emily laughed and kissed him. 'Bless you, my darling. You can't work. You have to go to school and you're clever – your teacher said so. We won't be near the bombs, Arthur. We'll be down near the sea and it will be nice – and we might get to see Ken. If he'd only written to me and told me where he was stationed . . .' Emily shook her head. 'If we go to England, I can find out where he is.' A look of determination came into her face. 'He'll be angry with me for losing the business, but *I* didn't take a loan from the bank. It was his fault, not mine – and even if I didn't run it as well as he did, I did my best.'

Arthur realised that she was very angry now, but not with him. It was Ken who had let her down. He didn't truly understand about bank loans and a lot of the stuff, but he knew that it meant trouble. It seemed that they would be going back to England – and that meant he would go on a ship again. Arthur didn't like ships; they made him feel ill. He remembered London and the house he'd once lived in, but he didn't know where Hastings was and he wasn't at all sure he wanted to go back to England, but there was nothing else he could do. Emily wasn't his real mum, he knew that, but she'd been kind to him and he didn't want to be left behind. Arthur hated to see her so unhappy and pale. It wasn't fair that she'd been left to cope with whatever had happened. It must have been happening for a while. Arthur was bright enough to understand that it couldn't have all gone so wrong in the short time that Ken had been gone.

Ken had gone off and left Emily to cope. He hadn't cared what happened to them. Just the way Arthur's mum had neglected him and then let the council woman take him away. A chill ran down his spine and he was uneasy, though he didn't know why the thought of going back to England should frighten him.

Although Ken had been kind enough at first, Arthur had always sensed that he didn't truly love him, the way Emily did – but surely Ken loved her? Or perhaps he didn't? Arthur couldn't understand why he'd gone. He didn't think Emily knew either.

'The bastard!' Emily exclaimed suddenly, as if it had just become clear to her. 'The rotten bugger. He knew this was coming. He had to have known!' Emily was suddenly sitting up straight and her air of distress had gone. She was blazing with energy and anger. 'When I find him, he'll wish he'd never been born. I shall find him, Arthur. He had no right to act so righteous and make out he was off to be a hero knowing that he'd made a mess of things here.' She put her arms about Arthur and hugged him tight and he could feel her anger building. 'I'll show him. I'll go to Aunt Becky. She always sends me a card and some money at Christmas. I can stay with her for a while –

31

work in her fish shop, or – or something.' She smiled down at Arthur. 'Don't you worry, love. We'll be all right. I promise you. I'll make a proper life for us and it's no good Ken thinking he can come crawling back when I succeed.'

CHAPTER 4

'It's all right fer some.' A spiteful voice reached Rose's ears as she stood watching the line of women workers. They were packers and the material they handled was extremely volatile and at the most dangerous stage of its journey through the munitions factory. 'Get in wiv the bloody manager and yer can skive orf to the sea fer a holiday.' The sniggers that followed made Rose furious but she swallowed her ire.

'That box is incorrectly packed,' Rose said and walked to the line, taking a box off and repacking it expertly herself. 'Please pay attention, Gertie. That's the second box of yours I've had to repack this week. If you want to keep yer job, keep yer mind on the work. An incorrectly packed box might cause an explosion if it was dropped.'

'Bloody 'ell,' Gertie Bright muttered. 'Why don't yer pick on someone else fer a change, Rose Parker? Anybody would think yer were the bloody Queen 'erself.'

'Gertie, please leave the line,' Rose said sharply. 'Sylvia, take her place.'

Gertie came sulkily towards her, Rose signalled to one of the other line managers, who was on a break. 'Please take over for ten minutes, Mrs Griggs.'

'Come this way, Gertie,' Rose instructed, leading the way to the office where Harry was working on some lists.

'Wot yer pickin' on me fer?' Gertie demanded as she was ushered inside the office. 'Just 'cos I might 'ave said somethin' . . .'

'I don't mind what yer say about me,' Rose said and closed the door behind her as Harry looked up inquiringly. 'Gertie is on a warning, Mr Smith. She has already had two warnings for incorrectly packing explosives – should I let her go or give her a week's suspension?' Suspension meant loss of earnings and Rose was well aware that Gertie could ill afford to lose a week's pay.

Harry looked at Rose and then at the other woman's indignant face. Gertie looked red but also there was the beginning of fear in her eyes. She wouldn't want to lose her job, because, although there was plenty of work going, it would probably be back to scrubbing floors for her.

'I didn't mean nuthin'!'

Harry's gaze hardened. 'What has she been sayin'?'

'Nothing that matters,' Rose replied. 'This is purely a work matter, Mr Smith. Is it suspension or the sack?'

'I leave it up to you, Rose,' Harry said. 'I think a few days suspension – with a warning that if it happens again, it is instant dismissal – but it is your decision.'

Rose nodded. 'Very well, Mr Smith. Gertie this is a formal warning. You may take two days suspension –

and if you're careless again it will be instant dismissal. You know as well as I do that these things must be packed safely. Otherwise an innocent handler could be killed if there was a tiny spark.'

'Yes, I do know, Rose.' Gertie looked deflated. 'I'm sorry.'

Rose nodded to Harry and ushered her out of the office. Gertie looked at her sullenly. 'I might not bother comin' back . . .'

'That's your decision.' Rose raised her eyebrows. 'If you want your cards, let us know.'

She turned and walked back to the line, taking over from her deputy. 'Everything all right?'

'Yes, fine, Mrs Parker.' Mrs Griggs nodded and walked away.

Rose stood watching the women work. She noticed a few of them gave her dirty looks, but they kept their heads down when the next box came down to them, placing the dangerous material securely within the thick wadding. No one was saying much, though that wouldn't last. The joking and wisecracks would start again soon, because they were a tough lot of women and knew that the work they did was dangerous. Rose knew there would be more spiteful remarks meant for her ears but she would ignore them. She'd called Gertie out for slackness and not because she'd made a snide remark, whatever the women might think. Rose remembered too well the carelessness of another line supervisor at the beginning of the war that had led to a fire and her death as well as others; it wouldn't happen on her watch if she could help it.

She'd known that her second little holiday to the sea

this summer would be noticed and had been prepared for some gossip, and jealousy, but Harry had been keen for her to go again, and she enjoyed her visits with the children. They and their Aunt Marie would have her there every weekend if they could. She also knew that some workers felt she was privileged, because she lived with Harry, but within the factory, Harry was boss. She called him Mr Smith, consulted him on serious matters and received no favours. Her trip to the sea had been noticed and she'd expected some reaction to it – but it had been worth it. Rose smiled inwardly as she remembered how good it had been walking on the beach with the kids, enjoying fresh seafood and fun and laughter, away from the pressures of work.

It would have been easy to let her mind wander to those delightful days spent with Davey and Alice. Alice had clung to her, not wanting her to leave, but Davey had just told her to give his regards to Harry. He was so grown up now. His trip to Canada and the months he'd spent there had changed him, turning him from a bright, energetic lad to a confident youth. Davey certainly knew what he wanted of life. Had he been old enough, he would have been off to sea like his father, and in another year or so he would do just that. Rose banished the happy thoughts. She was here to do a job and must keep her mind sharp, not let it wander on a sunlit beach.

'Poor Gertie,' Harry said that evening as he drank his half pint of bitter after he'd eaten supper. It was the only alcohol he allowed himself, even though he was officially off duty until the next morning at seven.

36

However, Harry was never not on duty, ready to rush back and take over if a crisis should occur. 'She was fit to burst but you put the fear of God into her, Rose.'

Rose smiled at the memory. 'She got off lightly, Harry. If I hadn't known she has three kids at home and no one to help her, I would have dismissed her then and there. Had I not noticed she'd left a section un-wadded, that box could have gone up if someone tipped it or dropped it.'

'Yes, I know, love,' Harry told her with a nod of approval. 'That's why I wanted you as line supervisor. Your sharp eyes don't miss much.' He looked at her thoughtfully. 'What did she say?'

'Nothing much,' Rose replied. 'You know what they are, Harry. I live with you but we're not married – therefore I receive favours. It was bound to get them grumbling, me havin' a few days at the sea for the second time this summer, when they're all workin' flat out.'

'They're entitled to a holiday, but most of them prefer the extra pay.' Harry nodded his understanding. 'They don't see it that way, of course. Don't let it get to you, Rose. You know I love you and I would marry you like a shot if I could.'

'I know – and I don't care what they say,' Rose told him. 'I'd have given her an earful if I was still on the line, but I have to keep discipline now I'm a supervisor so I bring them to you.'

'That's my Rose,' Harry said and studied her for a moment, then, apparently satisfied, 'When are you going down again then?'

'Not for a while,' Rose replied. 'I know I could take

the time off and be damned to the gossips – but you need me here and the kids are fine where they are. I wish they were here with us, but there's nothin' to be done about it – and it's a good life for them there. Their aunt dotes on them and the fresh air is wonderful. I wish you could come too, Harry.'

'I can't leave the factory,' Harry said. 'They rely on me to keep it going.'

'I know – but you'd love playin' with the kids, Harry.' She sounded wistful and he looked at her.

'We'll have our own one day,' he said, giving her a look filled with love. 'I reckon you could get a divorce after what Reg Parker did to you, love. We might be able to adopt a lad then.'

'Yes, I'd like to help some of the poor kids what are livin' on the streets,' Rose told him. 'I've seen a few of them hangin' round the market at the end of the day, hoping to be given some fruit that's on the turn or a stale bun. I often buy a bagful for them.'

Harry nodded. 'You've got a soft heart, Rose,' he told her. 'One day we'll have a family, I promise you.'

Rose turned away but not before he'd seen a flicker of pain. Rose had two grown-up sons from her first marriage, but she seldom heard from them; they'd both left home young to get away from their bully of a father. When Rose had found herself pregnant with Harry's child, she'd been over the moon, but she'd unfortunately lost it. They hadn't spoken about it. Rose was perhaps a little old to be having a second family but she'd hoped so much to have another child. The loss had pulled her down for a couple of weeks, but then she'd been back at work, acting as if nothing had happened, never speaking of her loss, but they both knew it was unlikely the chance would come again. Rose's only hope of another child would be adoption or fostering.

Her eldest son had a child, but despite inviting them to visit, Rose had never yet seen the boy, despite the gifts of money she'd sent ever since his birth. She suspected they blamed her for their father's bullying or perhaps they simply didn't want to risk seeing Reg.

'I might be allowed to foster an older child,' she said after a long silence. 'I couldn't do my work and look after a young 'un but an older child, one that goes to school.'

'Yeah. I'll look into it,' Harry said, but he already had. The answer was always the same. 'We prefer our foster parents to be married.' He glared at nothing in particular. 'Let's see about that divorce, Rose. I'll speak to a lawyer on Monday. It's my afternoon off.'

Harry scowled as he left the lawyer's office that Monday afternoon. What a waste of time that had been! He'd explained the situation; he'd even taken the telegram from the Air Ministry that had reported Reg as missing but the lawyer just shook his head over it.

'You know that Mr Parker returned – and it was recorded because he was believed to have attacked Mrs Parker and was reported to the police. You have two choices, Mr Smith – Mrs Parker can sue for divorce on the claim of brutality or, if he doesn't turn up alive again, you can wait seven years and have him declared dead.'

'Bloody hell!' Harry exclaimed. 'Wait seven years –

no way!' He thought for a moment. 'How likely are we to get a divorce through if we claim physical violence over a number of years culminating in an attack that could have left her dead in the street?'

'You have witnesses?'

'Not to the attack – but it is on record that she was badly beaten.'

'But no one saw him actually do it . . . I know it was him, Mr Smith. You reported it and Mr Parker was seen in the area and heard to threaten his wife with violence if he caught her – but that is not the kind of proof a divorce court would ask for.'

Harry had just stared at him. Everyone knew it was Reg Parker who had attacked Rose but she needed witnesses, because otherwise it could be construed that she was blaming her husband simply to obtain a divorce.

'So what do we do?' Harry asked.

The lawyer looked at him doubtfully. 'I will consult with others, Mr Smith. I am not certain – but we might be able to push it through if it isn't contested. It depends. We would have to serve papers on Mr Parker, of course – and there's the rub. Do you know where he is?'

'No idea,' Harry said, fuming inwardly. Rules and regulations! Reg Parker was a bully and deserved to be thrashed, but although Harry could arrange that if he ever showed up, he couldn't just have him killed. If he and Rose were to marry, they had to do it right – with no rumours or prison sentences hanging over them. 'It's all of a piece, ain't it?'

'I am very sorry,' the lawyer replied. 'There are

occasions when the law is an ass and I feel that this is one.'

He'd been sympathetic and helpful, but couldn't offer a solution. If Reg Parker turned up and accepted the papers there was a chance that they could get the divorce through – especially as he might be in trouble with the law – but even if he were sent to prison that left Rose just where she was, unmarried, and according to people in positions of power, unfit to foster or adopt a child.

Harry seethed with fury but there was nothing he could do. His love for Rose was deep and unbounded. If it would help, he'd kill Reg himself – but that wouldn't solve their problem. Reg must die of natural causes or agree to a divorce and neither of those was likely.

Harry was a hard worker. He'd always saved his money and he had a nice bit saved. Maybe, if they went away where folk didn't know them, they could pretend to be married. Harry would even change his name for Rose's sake. Was it possible to get hold of a fake marriage licence, go through a ceremony even though Reg wasn't dead? That was bigamy and an offence that carried a prison sentence. Rose wouldn't like the idea much, but with all the bombs, fires and one thing and another, it might be possible to get new papers for them both. Of course, he'd go to prison if it was ever discovered – but Harry would risk that to make his Rose happy.

He felt a shadow of guilt at the back of his mind. The work they both did was important. Rose had recently prevented a nasty accident that might have happened if she hadn't noticed the careless packing. Harry kept the factory running smoothly against all the odds. Could either of them simply walk away for personal gain?

Rose wouldn't have it. He shook his head as he called in at the florist on the corner of Commercial Road. Flowers wouldn't make up for what she'd lost – but for the moment it was all he could do. He'd never thought he would be glad to see Reg Parker again, but now he wished it would happen. If Harry could find him, he'd force him to accept the divorce, even if he had to beat him black and blue to do it.

CHAPTER 5

Something was very wrong. Arthur sensed it the moment he got back from school that late summer afternoon. There was no sign of tea and Emily was sitting in the front parlour, just staring blankly at the wall. On the table in front of her were some papers that had been crumpled. She looked sort of defeated and so sad that Arthur went to her instantly, touching her arm.

'What's the matter, Mum?'

Emily looked up wearily, her eyes red rimmed, but she tried to smile. 'Is it that time already?' she said jerking up and glancing at the clock. 'Did you walk home alone?'

'Yeah, I was all right,' he replied. 'It isn't far, Mum – but why have you been crying?'

'There's nothing for you to worry about, love,' Emily said but he shook his head.

'I'm nearly eight now, old enough to help, Mum. You can tell me – there's no one but me to look after you.'

Emily gave a watery chuckle. 'Very well, I may as well tell you. I've had another letter from the bank

43

and it seems they now own the house. All I have left is a couple of hundred dollars that I saved myself. I've been thinking whether to try and find work here or go to my aunt in Hastings in England . . .' Emily sighed deeply. 'Today someone called here and asked after you. He said a Miss Vee wanted to know if you were all right . . .' An oddly defiant look came to her eyes. 'I don't know her but I've heard of this lady, Arthur. She has a lot of money and influence in this area and – well, if I'm forced to work long hours and I can't find a decent home for us I think they might take you away from me and give you to her.' Emily knew that Miss Vee had already adopted one little evacuee girl and had helped another, older girl. She worried that the woman might suggest Arthur would be better off with her – and perhaps he would.

Arthur looked at her, feeling frightened. 'They can't do that!' he protested but knew that they could, because it had happened before. 'Please, Mum, don't let them do it! I don't want to be taken away from you!' It couldn't happen again. It mustn't! He wanted to stay with Emily.

Emily raised her head and now she had a look of determination again. 'No, Arthur, I won't let them take you,' she promised. 'We're going away – back to England. I wasn't sure what to do, but now I've made up my mind. Tomorrow, I'm going to the booking office to find us a passage on a ship as soon as I can. They'll no doubt tell me I'm mad to travel with a war on, but there must be a way. We'll go away and then you won't have to leave me ever.' She got up and went into the homely kitchen with its oak dressers

44

and blue-and-white crockery, still talking as much to herself as to him. 'This is just a house – though it's better than I ever had before and I'll be sad to leave it – but I can put my things in store and when I have a home again, I'll send for them.'

Arthur didn't say anything. It was a nice house, clean and pretty, but it had never truly felt like a home. He was apprehensive and he wanted to cling to his Emily-mum and feel her arms around him, but he knew that her mind was on other things.

'I shall need a reason to travel,' Emily went on, but Arthur sensed she was thinking aloud. 'They will ask me why I want to travel to a country that's at war and being bombed, but I'll say my elderly aunt is unwell – yes, that's what I'll tell them if they ask. I'll say my aunt needs me – she's been in hospital.' Her eyes snapped with a flash of anger. 'If I manage to find Ken that's just where he'll be when I've finished with him. I'll never forgive him for this, Arthur. Never!'

Arthur sat down at the kitchen table as she opened a tin of red salmon and made sandwiches for them both. He loved salmon sandwiches with cucumber. It was a luxury he'd never tasted before he came to Canada and he wondered if they would still have it for tea when they got to England; he doubted it, because all he remembered were narrow streets with lots of terraced houses all back-to-back in rows, and not a tree or a lake in sight. He still wasn't happy about making the return journey to England, but it was better than being taken from Emily, for whom he had a grateful affection. She wasn't truly his mum, but she was kind and thoughtful most of the time. It made him angry and sad by turn that people could just take him away and pass him on to someone else – as if he were a parcel or a second-hand coat.

Emily looked at him and smiled. 'Eat your tea up, love. I've got apple pie and ice cream for afters. We'll be all right, I promise you. I think we'll be better off with my aunt. I've never met her, though she says she saw me as a child, but she writes me kind letters. She will let us stay with her until I get on my feet. I need to trace Ken and I need to work – but I'll find something I can do.'

Arthur lifted his anxious gaze to her face. 'Perhaps she'll let you work in her fish and chip shop.'

'Perhaps she will – but I'd only do it until I can find something better,' Emily said, her face stormy. 'My parents brought me out here when I was small, Arthur. They came to find a better life – and they did. They were never rich, but Dad had a good job and he had savings when he and Mum were killed in a road accident . . .' She blinked hard, clearly distressed at the memory. It was as though she was remembering rather than talking to him as she went on, 'I was married to Ken by then and he asked me to invest my dad's money in his business. It was small at the time and he used the money to expand. He told me we would be rich – but now we have nothing . . .' She swallowed hard. 'He never told me the shop was in trouble – I've no idea where all the money went . . .' Emily shook her head angrily. 'He had no right to waste what was mine!'

'I'm sorry, Mum.' Arthur went to her at the other end of the table and hugged her. Emily smiled and hugged him back. 'It isn't your fault, love, and it isn't mine.'

'Ken did a bad thing,' Arthur said, looking at her. 'Will we live with him again when you find him?'

'We shall not!' Emily said with an angry look. 'I want to find him and I want an explanation of what he did with all the money – that shop was doing well, so what happened? That's what I'd like to know.'

'What went wrong, Hank?' Mrs Veronica Bittern, widow to the late Billy Bittern – and known to her friends and family as Miss Vee – looked at the officer of the law. 'I thought it was a thriving business? I know that shop carried expensive merchandise and I was sure it was profitable. Why would it close down?'

Hank Wrangler looked at her and frowned uncertainly. 'I'm not sure I should tell you, Miss Vee – I know the bank foreclosed and Mrs Henderson will lose everything.' He hesitated, then, because she was looking at him in a certain way and he couldn't resist that look. No one refused Miss Vee when she gave them that look. 'I've heard that her husband was a gambler . . .'

'Now he's cleared off and left her to face the consequences. Well, that's terrible,' Miss Vee said, frowning. 'I suppose there's nothing to be done about the foreclosure?'

'I believe it's a substantial debt, Miss Vee. I dare say Mrs Henderson will be looking for a job and a place to live – unless they allow her to stay in her home for a while.'

'I could offer a job and perhaps a home,' Miss Vee replied, wrinkling her smooth brow in thought. She was well dressed in an elegant grey dress, medium-heeled black suede court shoes, and her hair was coiffured and trimmed neatly. She looked what she was: a wealthy widow who had come to terms with life and her loss, and found a new happiness by adopting her much loved daughter, Beth. Beth was an evacuee from England and had come out on a ship with Julie and Arthur at the beginning of the war, and also a boy named Davey who had disappeared on the last night of the voyage. 'I might even be able to purchase their house and lease it back to her.'

'Now, Miss Vee – what would Mr Malcolm say?' Malcolm was her brother and had previously worked as purser on the ship that brought Beth out. It was he who had brought Beth to her. Vee knew that both Beth and Julie would be anxious for Arthur if they knew his mother was losing her home.

'Mr Malcolm doesn't need to know. I am perfectly capable of managing my affairs, Hank.' She gave him a straight look that would have put fear into a lesser man. Hank was young, strong, and confident, but even he would own to a slight feeling of apprehension when Miss Vee was displeased. 'I don't plan to *give* Mrs Henderson her house. She won't even know who owns it. I'll arrange it through the bank. And I'll make sure I get a good price.' Vee nodded and smiled. 'You've done an excellent job, Hank, thank you. I'm sorry that she wasn't responsive to your questions about the boy when you visited her home, but I daresay she's worried sick. I shall visit myself – but I'll arrange for her to stay in her home first. Once she is settled, I can invite her and Arthur to meet Julie and

Beth. It is a pity we didn't find them until after Julie's wedding to Jago.'

That had been a happy affair for all of them. Jago had a disability in the form of a club foot but he was a handsome, strong man and made little of it. His love for the little evacuee girl shone out of him, and despite Julie's young age, no one had doubted their marriage was right for them both. 'Julie really wanted to see him there, but I will arrange a little party for their meeting.'

'No wonder so many folks love you, Miss Vee,' Hank responded with a grin. He was a handsome man and the son-in-law of Selmer, who had managed Vee's store for years. Malcolm had taken over now and Selmer had retired to spend his life enjoying himself, which meant he went fishing a lot. He visited Miss Vee a couple of times a week and they sat on the porch in the shade, talking about her parents and the old days, and drinking beer or a glass of mint julep. 'My father-in-law sees you as next to God – and there's times I think the Almighty comes a close second with him.'

'Now that's blasphemy,' Vee reprimanded but laughed. She was well aware that her old friend had loved her for years. Had she not still cherished her late husband's memory so dearly she might well have married him, but these days they were both past needing marriage; it was enough just to be good friends. 'Thank you, Hank. I know you've spent a lot of your free time on tracing Arthur's foster parents for me. I am so glad you did, because now I can look after his mother – make sure she and Arthur don't suffer. I shall just keep a friendly eye on them. No need for either of them to know.'

He nodded, understanding that she was telling him to keep what he knew to himself and also dismissing him. He laughed as he replied, 'I surely will, Miss Vee – and if you need anything more just let me know.'

'Oh, I shall, Hank,' she told him with sparkling eyes. 'I most certainly will.'

CHAPTER 6

Arthur couldn't believe how quickly it had all happened. One day, Emily was talking about leaving on a ship for England and within a week she'd packed everything into big tea chests and had it stored with her furniture until they returned.

'We can only take one case each,' Emily told Arthur. 'Perhaps a satchel on your back for small things you want to take with you, love. I wish we could take more but once I start earning money, I'll buy us new clothes. I'm not sure what the weather will be like there so we'll take some of our summer things and some winter.'

'When do we leave, Mum?' Arthur asked, feeling bewildered by the suddenness of it all.

'I was lucky. There's a convoy leaving this weekend. We have the only cabin available for passengers. Most of the space is taken by crew members and cargo, but it's a private chartered vessel and there is a cabin that the owner sometimes uses. He isn't travelling this time – so we got it.' Emily's brow wrinkled. 'You know there is a war on, Arthur, so very few people can travel and it's dangerous, but the captain was a close friend

51

of my father and has arranged everything for us. He told me he thinks it unlikely he'll be attacked, because he's sailing with a convoy of other merchant ships and their escorts. It isn't one of the bigger ships that carry essential war materials and they're the ones the enemy normally tries to take out, them and the destroyers.' She paused. 'But if there is an attack we have to stay below deck and he says it will be frightening.'

Arthur nodded. He'd learned a bit about the Atlantic run in school, and he knew that ships of all nationalities were being attacked if they took goods to Britain. It meant that they might be attacked from the sky or below the waves.

That was a bit scary, but Arthur's world had already been turned upside down. Emily was acting strangely these days; she often seemed to go off in her own thoughts, forgetting about him for ages. He didn't know what to do to help her. She was upset and angry but she kept telling him her anger wasn't for him. It was for Ken who had let her down and she was going to let him know what she thought about that when she saw him. Sometimes, Emily was in a happy mood, laughing and teasing him, telling him that it would be a good life in Hastings, which was a seaside town in Sussex. Arthur had never heard of it – but Emily said it was nice there and spoke vaguely of woods and cliffs and a beach. She hadn't been there but she thought they would soon find a home and be happy.

Arthur wished they didn't have to leave Canada. He liked where they lived and he'd enjoyed going to school – and he loved the wilderness, where the bear had wanted their food. Arthur hadn't been frightened of the bear. Ken was but he'd liked it. He loved the mighty trees that rose so high into the sky you could hardly see their tops, the colourful birds, and small animals that had scampered into the woods as they approached. He hoped the woods in Hastings would be near them, because he loved their cool shade and the way they whispered to you if you listened. In London, he'd never seen a lot of trees and the only animals were a stray cat or a dog wandering the streets.

So Arthur whispered a prayer at night that, somehow, they could stay here in Canada, where he'd learned to be happy, but now here they were, staying at a cheap lodging house until they could board the ship. Emily's house was locked up and the key left under a flower pot by the front door, empty of their possessions. It was clear there was no going back. Arthur was being returned to London, to a life he could only now vaguely remember as being unhappy.

Emily knew Arthur wasn't happy about the move and she was sorry, but she was at her wits' end to know what to do for the best. She could stay in Canada and try to find a new home and a job, but if she didn't make a success of it, she might end up losing Arthur. At the moment, he was Emily's only reason for living and she'd longed for her own child. She loved Arthur and wanted to do her best for him – for them both – but she wasn't sure she was strong enough or clever enough to do it. Her talent was in keeping house, not sitting at a desk, or working behind a shop counter, though she could do that if she had to.

Aunt Becky's letter was in her bag. Emily had brought

it with her so that she could find her when they got to England. She'd been a tiny baby in arms when her parents returned to Canada so had no memories of the country, but it would be easy enough to find Hastings. She only had to get on a train or a bus, she thought, not allowing her doubts and fears to surface. It would be an adventure. Besides, when she had saved enough money she could return to Canada, if she wanted.

Not for the first time, her anger against Ken made her clench her fists. He'd had no right to go off and leave them that way – and that wasn't the half of it! She knew now where the money had gone; he'd gambled it away on horse racing. If Emily could have got her hands on him then, she might have killed him. He deserved it!

She shook her head determinedly. She wouldn't let him make her miserable. He was a cheating devil and she would make him pay when she divorced him, but for now she had to think about the future. What would Aunt Becky be like? She'd asked Emily to come for a visit , but would she want them to live with her permanently – or at least until Emily could stand on her own feet and make a life for herself and Arthur?

Emily could only pray it would be all right when they got there.

Arthur was sick for the first two days, despite the luxury of the cabin they travelled in. Emily had been delighted when she first entered it, because it was posher than she'd expected. The mahogany wood surfaces gleamed with polish and it smelled clean and fresh – or it did until Arthur started bringing up bile every few minutes.

There was a little porthole to look out of and that made it a little better than on his voyage to Canada. After three days Arthur felt much better. There was a door that led out on to a tiny deck outside their cabin and once Arthur began to find his feet and feel less sick, he was able to sit out there with Emily. It was actually quite pleasant then and he didn't feel ill anymore.

There were lots of other ships within hailing distance, the smoke rising from their stacks. Sometimes he would see men working on the decks and he'd wave at them, some of them waving back when they saw him.

The nice sailor who brought them food and stayed to chat with Emily told them Arthur was getting his sea legs and would be fine now. Emily hadn't been ill at all and now that she'd left Canada behind her, seemed more cheerful. She laughed and talked to the sailor and he told her she was brave to go to England to look after a sick relative. Arthur thought it was a shame to have told Jock a lie but Emily said it was necessary and it was only a white lie. Arthur remembered his real dad had said lying was always wrong, but he didn't tell Emily she was naughty. It just made him a little uncomfortable when his new friend Jock was so friendly and kind.

On the fourth day, Jock brought him a wooden whistle he'd made for him. Arthur tried it and found it made all sorts of notes if you put your finger over different holes. He told Jock he was clever to make it and that made him laugh.

'I reckon you're a clever little lad,' he'd told Arthur. 'Not every boy can make a tune on a whistle.'

'He's really clever with numbers,' Emily said. 'I kept making mistakes with my accounts but Arthur found it in a trice.'

'That's a bright boy,' Jock said. 'You must be so proud of him, Emily.'

'Yes, I am,' she replied and smiled at him. 'Arthur helps me a lot, don't you, darling?'

Arthur nodded. It made him vaguely uncomfortable when Emily giggled and flirted with Jock. He didn't know why, because he liked the sailor. Jock was much nicer to Arthur than Ken had been and it was very bad what Ken had done to Emily. Arthur hoped he would never have to live with him again – Emily said they wouldn't but he wasn't quite sure he could really trust her. Yes, she was kind, and loving – but since Ken left, she'd changed somehow, become . . . different, a bit distant at times. Or perhaps it was just all the upheaval making him uncertain, afraid that once again he would lose everything.

The voyage was blessedly peaceful. Arthur had feared they might get attacked by planes and sunk, and, even though he'd learned to swim in Canada, he wasn't sure he could swim in the middle of the sea. When he went out on the little private deck that was normally used by the ship's owner, Arthur looked up at the sky and scanned the waves for any sign of an enemy plane or submarine, but he never saw anything.

'The gods are looking after us,' Emily told him, laughing and ruffling his hair when she saw him looking up. 'I told you it would be fine, didn't I?'

Arthur smiled. When Emily laughed and teased him, he was happy again. He loved her in his way and she was always telling him she loved him. Sometimes, he believed her, but since she'd told him that the law officer had come looking for him and was going to take him away and give him to someone called Miss Vee, he'd had this uncertain feeling in his tummy. He'd been frightened when he'd come to Canada, but, gradually, he'd learned to have confidence in his new life – now it was changing again. Even though he was with his Emily-mum, he couldn't help the feeling of terror that came over him when he thought he might be taken away yet again.

They were back in England. Not in London but in Liverpool. It was busy and smelly in the dockyards, where the ship manoeuvred to its place amongst the other big ships, so much going on all at once that Arthur craned his head to watch crates being loaded and barges darting in and out to guide the ships in.

It was a while before everything was in place and they could disembark, seagulls whirling and crying overhead as they walked from the deck to the docks. It felt a bit strange to be on solid ground again after their time at sea, and they were surrounded by people working and calling out to each other. Arthur clung tightly to Emily's hand, fearful of being separated in the confusion.

As they left the docks and found a bus stop, Arthur could see signs of what he thought must have been bombing raids; there were buildings that were blackened by fire and spaces with just debris where they'd been torn apart by the blasts. Everywhere, there was activity and an air of determination. Cheerful voices called out to one another in a thick accent that Arthur couldn't understand, but everyone seemed friendly. When they got on the bus, the conductor was a young woman who addressed Emily as luv and chattered away as she issued their tickets.

'We're a long way from my aunt's,' Emily told Arthur. Jock had given them a packed lunch when they left the ship and they ate it on the bus. 'We shan't get there tonight. I think we'll have to catch a train to go all that way, but I wanted to get away from Liverpool. It's too dangerous to be in a port like that.' He knew she meant in case there was another bombing raid.

Arthur just looked up at her and munched the egg sandwich he'd been given. It was good but his stomach was churning. The Liverpool docks reminded him of London and he didn't want to remember – not the last months when his mum had changed, becoming so different and scary. Why did people change like that? Arthur wondered. His mum had always been kind, smiling, and loving – and then she'd changed. Emily had changed a bit too, though not as much as his mother had after Dad died. Arthur missed his real dad. He'd been a good one – and he'd never changed. He'd just died . . .

Arthur swallowed hard at the memory. His eyes stung but he blinked away the tears. Emily was still with him. She wasn't his real mum and he wasn't completely sure she loved him, but she was familiar; he loved her, and she was all he had. He didn't know what he would do without her.

They stayed that night at a boarding house in somewhere called Chester. The next day Emily left

Arthur in their bedroom and told him not to move until she returned.

'I'm going to send my aunt a telegram to tell her we're here, so that she's ready for us when we arrive,' she told him. 'Then I'll check the times of the trains and buy us something to eat.'

Arthur nodded, but felt nervous. He didn't want her to leave him alone in this strange place but she had that look he was coming to know in her eyes and he knew that he had to do as he was told. He sat on the bed and played with his wooden whistle. He could make several tunes now. None of them were known to him, but he'd discovered that he could do all sorts of things with his new toy. It was a nice sound he made and it kept him from thinking what he would do if Emily didn't return.

A young woman entered the bedroom while Emily was gone. She'd come to clean the room and she smiled to hear him playing his tune.

'Mum gone out then?' she asked and Arthur nodded.

'She'll be back soon,' he said and the girl inclined her head and smiled.

'You play a nice tune,' the girl said. 'Who taught you?'

'No one – I just play,' Arthur replied and she smiled again but he didn't think she believed him.

The girl left and he was alone once more. He put down his toy and went to the window, looking out. It was raining and the sky was grey. The sun had been shining when they left Canada. His stomach was rumbling, because they hadn't had much for breakfast – just a piece of toast and margarine with a scraping of marmalade.

Arthur sat down again. What would he do if Emily didn't come back? He didn't know anyone here. Perhaps he should go to London? He recalled his school vaguely. If he went there perhaps someone would help him . . .

He had just picked up his whistle again when the door opened and Emily entered. She was smiling as he got up and ran to her.

'I've sent the telegram,' she told him. 'Aunt Becky wanted us to go and stay with her as you know. She said so in her letter. I can work in her fish and chip shop if I want – but there are jobs in factories. So many men have gone off to the war that there is bound to be a job if you're prepared to work hard.' Arthur thought she was talking to herself again rather than him, trying to reassure herself that she'd done the right thing.

'It'll be all right, Mum.' Arthur looked up at her. 'I'm hungry.'

'So am I,' Emily replied. 'I bought some rolls and a nice man in a shop let me have some ham, but I could only get margarine. I'm sorry I was so long, but I had to go and get ration books for us. I had to wait in a queue and then they were a long time deciding what I was entitled to as I'm not a British citizen. It was easier to get yours, because you still are, even though you're Canadian, too.' Emily sighed. 'I thought it would be so easy as my parents came from Britain, but the girl at the council says I might not be able to stay here indefinitely. I've had to register and I may have to apply to the Government for a permit to stay longer than a few months.'

Arthur stared at her, feeling bewildered and hopeful. 'Does that mean we might have to return to Canada?'

'It might,' Emily told him. 'I suppose I could have got work there but I was determined to find out why Ken hasn't written to me. I know he's behaved very badly, but I still need to know if he's alive.' Arthur listened but didn't speak. There was something about all this he didn't like, didn't understand.

Emily looked thoughtful. 'If he isn't alive,' she added, talking to herself again. 'I'd be free and could marry a British man and then I could live here.' She looked at Arthur. 'Your papers make it legal for you to stay here.'

Arthur didn't know what she meant. It was obvious she was deep in thought again. Was she thinking she might leave him here if she returned to Canada at the end of her permitted stay?

'I'd come back with you, wouldn't I? If you returned to Canada?' Arthur asked anxiously.

Emily blinked then smiled. 'Yes, of course,' she said, putting her arm around him. 'You're my little boy, Arthur. If I return to Canada, you'll come with me.'

Arthur nodded and hugged her leg. He was glad she'd said so but he wasn't quite sure he believed her; his real mum had loved him once. How could you ever be sure people wouldn't change their minds?

CHAPTER 7

Rose looked at Harry anxiously. She'd sensed his mood ever since they left work that evening and she had to ask, 'What's wrong, Harry? Is it something at work?'

'Yes,' he said and sighed. 'I've just been told they're closing the factory and relocating to the country, somewhere it will be safer. It makes sense, Rose. The bomb that landed two streets away last week was too close for comfort. Had it landed just a bit nearer it could have sent the munitions factory up – and maybe half of London.'

She nodded her head. 'I'm only surprised they didn't do it sooner,' she replied. 'Have they told you where it's to be located?'

'In a secret location, that's all they've told me yet. They'll be taking us all down by bus – those that want to go.' Harry rubbed the bridge of his nose. 'From what I can see, we'll lose at least half of our workforce. The women who have children or dependent relatives at home will want to stay here. Quite a few have children staying in foster homes in the country but the train service from London is good, making it easier to visit.

Until we know where we're going, a lot won't feel like giving up their lives to work in an obscure country location.'

'What do you think about the move, Harry?' Rose asked him. 'I know you feel responsible for the factory – but do you want to leave London?'

'I have to go where they need me,' Harry told her. 'I signed on for the duration and I can't let them down – but will you come with me? You don't have to, Rose. There's other war work you can do here – and there's the house, too. What do we do about that?' He looked at her uncertainly, as if he wasn't sure she would change her life again just to be with him.

Harry owned his house. Rose understood that a lot of his life's savings had gone into making it a beautiful home and it would be a risk leaving it empty at any time, but with the bombing raids and people desperate for homes after losing theirs, it could cause a lot of problems.

'I'll come with yer,' Rose decided after a few moments' silence. 'We can either leave the house as it is or store the furniture and let it out for a couple of years. If we get a lawyer to do a proper lease, we'd get it back then. If we just let it ourselves, we might not.' There were strange laws about what a person could and could not do when the house was let; tenants had rights for life as long as they paid their rent, so if they refused to leave you couldn't make them legally. Of course some landlords just threw them out and changed the locks but Rose didn't fancy that; if they let their home they could get if back if they needed it themselves – as long as it was done properly.

Harry looked relieved. 'I was afraid you would say you didn't want to leave London. All your friends are here and you're a real Londoner, Rose,' he smiled.

'Yeah, that's true and I wouldn't do it fer everyone,' Rose said and laughed. 'Harry, you're a dafty. Course I'm not going to leave you to go on your own and me not know where you are. What do you want to do about the house?'

'I think we'll store the furniture for now and let it on a short lease,' Harry said. 'If we find a decent place we can fetch our stuff down – but if not, we'll live in digs for a while. I suppose the ministry will find us accommodation, but if we don't like it, we'll move into a place of our own.'

Rose nodded. 'That's a good idea,' Rose agreed. 'There is one thing, Harry – if we're given rooms in a boarding house, they won't give us a double. We'll be in separate rooms – maybe different houses.'

'I hadn't thought about that,' Harry said and frowned. 'We can't have that, Rose. I don't suppose . . .'

'Say we've got married?' Rose questioned. 'I wouldn't mind – but there's a few big-mouths who would soon let the landlady know it was a lie.'

'I've been thinking . . .' Harry looked a bit odd, almost guilty. 'Reg could already be dead. We might never know the truth . . .Why should we have to wait around for his pleasure?'

'You mean we should tell everyone he's dead and just go ahead?' Rose frowned. 'There might be big trouble if he suddenly turns up.'

'Supposing I sent you a telegram saying he'd been killed in action? You could use it as proof if anyone got nosy and we'd have our own lives. We could tell folk we got married – and then we could adopt a child.'

Rose looked at him hard. Harry had obviously been giving this thought for a while. 'I know you mean well . . .' She saw the apprehension in his eyes and knew that he expected her to refuse. It was what she should do, of course. They would both be guilty of bigamy if she agreed – and yet it tempted her. Some of the women's jibes about being a kept woman had got to her, despite her thick skin, and she wanted to adopt a child. Rose had her grown-up sons but they never bothered to visit these days, despite her inviting them. That saddened her but she knew Reg had driven them away and neither of them wanted to risk seeing him again. If she dismissed Harry's idea of a fake wedding, it meant that they might never have the settled life they both wanted. Besides, they did dangerous work and it was never certain there would be a tomorrow. 'How would yer do it?' she asked tentatively.

'I have to go up to Scotland to a special meeting,' Harry told her. 'The factory will close this weekend and everyone will get letters telling them where to be if they want to keep their jobs. I can get hold of a genuine telegram and send it to you through the post. You can show it to people – and then when I get back from my trip, we'll have a registry office wedding . . . invite a few friends, make it look real.'

Rose nodded. 'It might work – but you would need to send a real telegram as well – cos folks round here are nosy and they'd say they hadn't seen the telegraph boy.' She frowned. 'How are you going to get a genuine telegram, though?'

'That's the easy part,' Harry said with a rueful look. 'I've got several in my office at the factory. Some folks can't read them, Rose – they ask me to do it for them and then when I try to give the telegram back, they refuse to take it.'

'But don't they say your name – like Mrs Parker?'

'I could get that altered,' Harry told her. 'I've got one addressed to Mrs R Barker – you remember Ruth who was injured in a blast at the factory, Rose? She lost her husband some months prior to the accident and, afterwards, she was too ill to work so she went away to stay with some cousins at the coast somewhere. I could change that B into a P with no trouble.'

'I remember,' Rose nodded slowly. 'But it don't seem right, Harry. If you falsify it . . .' She shook her head and was silent for a moment, remembering. 'Ruth lived three doors down from me in Silver Terrace . . .'

'That's why it's perfect. Most folk won't remember the number of your house, Rose.' Harry moved towards her, his eyes pleading with her. 'I'll only do it if you agree, love – but it would solve our problems.'

Rose drew a shaky breath and then inclined her head. 'Yes, it would,' she said. 'Go on, then – in for a penny in for a pound. If we get found out, we'll say it must have been a mix-up at the War Office; them buggers make enough blunders so who's to know?'

Harry laughed in delight, grabbed her, and hugged her. 'That's my Rose,' he said. 'You won't regret it – and if ever we learn that Reg is alive, we'll apply for that divorce, but we'll move out of London to do it.'

'With my bleedin' luck he'll turn up like a bad penny,' Rose grumbled. 'Never mind, we'll face that when we come to it. So when do you have to leave for this meeting, then?'

'Next Monday,' Harry said. 'I'll announce the closure to the factory workers on Friday evening. I've been authorised to pay two weeks' holiday money on top of their wages. That should stop a storm of protest; they'll then have about three weeks to make up their minds what they want to do – and in that time you and me can be wed.'

'I hope this new factory is bigger,' Rose said. 'We're going to need more production to make up for the lost time.'

'I think it's already up and running,' Harry said. 'I'll just be one of the managers there, Rose. It won't be as much responsibility.'

'That will make less worry for you,' she said and smiled. 'You've been wearin' yourself to a frazzle, Harry.'

He nodded, looking thoughtful. 'It has been more than enough,' he agreed. 'I know you don't talk, Rose, but this secret place . . . I think they're making a new sort of weapon in part of it. That's why it has to be so far away in the country. I'm going to find out more about it when I go to this meeting, but I probably shan't be allowed to talk about it.'

'I just work and do what I'm told,' Rose replied with a grin. 'Sounds as though they ought to pay us all danger money, Harry?'

'You'll probably all get extra money for the relocation – though I've been told to stress that they are key workers and must show loyalty and duty to their country.'

'That will go down well with some of 'em,' Rose said and laughed. 'I can't wait to see their faces . . .'

Harry had gone off to Scotland, leaving Rose to arrange for their furniture and possessions to be taken into store. She was using a remover from out of town, because there was less chance of it all going up in flames there. The worst nights of the Blitz were behind them, but still the bombs fell, though not with the same intensity. Rose had often wondered how the munitions factory had survived the constant bombing night after night during the Blitz. They had all taken their lives in their hands every day, working on the production lines, and it would be far safer for them in the new location – not that this had made any difference to the uproar Harry's announcement had caused.

Rose shuddered at the memory of Gertie Bright's screech of outrage. She was used to the foul mouths of many of her workmates but the torrent that had poured from the angry woman made even Rose blink. Gertie had called them both every disgusting name she knew, and that was a lot, blaming Harry and Rose for keeping the move a secret.

'I've only known a few days, Mrs Bright,' Harry had told her. 'I was ordered to tell you tonight – and the extra wages you'll receive should make up for any inconvenience. You'll either choose to come with us or find a new job. While it's considered your patriotic duty to make the move, it's understood that some may not be able to—'

'What about me bleedin' kids? Am I supposed ter bring them wiv me?' Gertie demanded.

There were murmurs of agreement. Harry gave her a straight look. 'Had you let your children go to foster homes in the country for the duration you would not now be faced with this dilemma.'

'Shut yer mouth, yer bleedin' sod!' Gertie exploded. 'What I do wiv me own kids is my business. I'd never 'ave seen the bleeders again if they'd had a taste of country life. Where I live now is a bleedin' stink 'ole since me 'ouse got bombed.'

Harry looked at her for a few seconds, then said, 'You won't be relocatin' then, I take it? You may collect your cards with your wages – and the same goes for anyone else who wishes to find other work in London.'

Gertie had subsided into a grumbling, red-faced but deflated opponent. She looked defiant but scared and Rose felt sympathy for her. She was subdued, still flinging the occasional accusation, but clearly beaten and uncertain of her next move. Questions had been fired at Harry one after the other from worried women. Where would they stay? Where were they going? How would they let their husbands know where to find them?

He did his best to answer: 'I don't know where the factory is situated yet. I do know it's an isolated situation – and I think we won't be allowed to name it to anyone. We'll be given accommodation when we arrive. And I imagine all mail will be forwarded to us at the new location. I'm sure you know that you can't pass on any information in your letters because we're all subject to the Secrets Act and information carelessly disclosed helps the enemy. This place was a cardboard box factory before the war and perhaps that's why we've escaped the bombs – but it will be safer where we're going.'

Gradually, the grumbling had subsided, but several women had asked for their cards when leaving that night. They had already decided they would not be leaving London and all they knew, for this new location; some said they would have to think about it.

Harry had gone off to Scotland, unsure of just how many of his workforce would turn up on the day. Now Rose was busy arranging their move, and on her way to visit a friend in what was left of Silver Terrace.

'You're goin' then?' A sharp voice from behind her, made Rose turn to look. The woman was one of Gertie's cronies and had been a leader of those who sneered at Rose for living in sin. 'Know where an' all, I shouldn't wonder.'

'I have no more idea than you, Bren,' Rose replied. 'Yes, I'm goin'. Harry's letting his house through an agent and we'll come back at the end of the war.'

'Not if yer Reg catches yer,' Bren replied nastily. 'He'll flay the skin off yer back.'

'I'm divorcing Reg,' Rose said. 'Harry and I will get married as soon as we can. I don't see what business it is of yours – but Reg forfeited my respect when he attacked me.'

'Getting' all hoity-toity now, ain't we?' Bren jeered and walked off down the road, planting her feet heavily as she went. She was a tall, solidly-built woman and a bully. She and her husband had rows every Saturday night, when they both got drunk. A big man himself, he'd been driven from the house more than once by Bren, with a frying pan, and received as many black

71

eyes as he gave. His work on the docks was considered vital and therefore he still lived at home with Bren and his six children.

Walking on, Rose ignored the woman's taunts. Bren had made it clear she wouldn't be relocating; perhaps she enjoyed her regular fights on a Saturday night too much. Rose laughed to herself at the idea.

'Something funny?' Hearing the voice to her left, Rose turned and saw Mick standing there. 'You look cheerful, Rose. I thought you'd be screamin' in protest at bein' dragged from London?' He'd heard the news then, but that was no surprise. Mick knew everyone and a lot looked up to him and were grateful for the occasional tin of peaches they found standing on their doorstep, a gift from their local bad boy. He made no secret he dealt in stolen goods but as he often gave to those in need, he was tolerated and even liked by some.

'Why should I?' Rose said frowning. 'It's still too dangerous round here, Mick.'

'If it's got yer name on it, it'll find yer,' Mick replied and grinned at her. He shrugged. 'I reckon they've flung the worst at us and couldn't break us. Daft closing that factory now.'

'I . . .' Rose was saved having to answer as the siren went off and everyone started to run for the nearest shelter.

'It's just a false alarm, ' Mick said and then paled as they heard the blast a few streets away. 'I thought they'd done with us! Still, it don't make no difference. If it ain't yer turn, yer OK.'

He went off whistling. Rose proceeded on her walk. She could see smoke issuing into the sky and heard the wail of police and ambulance vehicles and the clang of the fire engines on their way to the scene. Maybe it would just be one this time. It was as if they were being warned that, though the Blitz was over, the bombs could start again at any time. There were another two bangs down by the docks and then the sound of the ack-ack took over.

As she watched the smoke climb higher, Rose gasped. She reckoned she knew where it was coming from. Breaking into a run, all thought of her intended visit to Silver Terrace gone from her head, she arrived to see the factory she'd worked in for many years in flames.

'My God!' Rose breathed in horror. 'That could have been us . . .'

There would be no saving the factory; the fire had already taken a fierce hold and several fire engines had screeched to the scene and were trying to prevent the flames spreading elsewhere. Although most of the materials they'd used in assembling ammunition had been cleared out, there had clearly been enough of something left to obliterate the building.

'Seems we was lucky . . .' Gertie's voice sounded strangely humbled. 'I ain't sayin' they done right by us – but we'd be dead now, gal.'

'Yes, Gertie,' Rose agreed. 'I doubt many of us would've got out. It must have been a direct hit.'

'Yeah, reckon it was,' Gertie said. She gave a sharp laugh. 'Them buggers would mess their britches if they knew how close they'd come to taking out half of London in one go – and all they got was a bleedin' empty factory!' She clutched at herself and both she and Rose started laughing. They laughed and laughed until the tears ran down their cheeks and then Gertie hugged Rose and they were holding on to each other. 'Yer don't want ter take no notice of me mouth, gal. Me brain don't know what me tongue's up to 'alf the time.'

'I never do, Gertie,' Rose said and wiped her face. Her action left streaks down her cheeks where the soot had blackened her skin. Gertie started laughing again.

'Yer face,' she said, took a white handkerchief from her pocket and rubbed it over Rose's cheek. It came away black and Rose laughed.

'You want to look at yourself, Gertie,' she said. 'What say we have an 'alf of pale ale down the pub to celebrate?'

'You payin'?' Gertie demanded and Rose nodded, making Gertie grin.

'Come on then,' she said. 'Might as well 'ave a send orf afore yer go.'

The siren for the all-clear went half an hour later. Rose sighed with relief when she got in and found the gas was still working. She could make herself a cup of tea. Pale ale was all right, but there was nothing like a cuppa after you'd had a nasty shock. Hearing the knock at the door, she opened it to see the telegraph boy on his bike. He handed her a buff envelope.

'It's all right, missus,' he said with a cheeky grin. 'It ain't bad news.' Then he cycled off whistling.

Rose opened the telegram from Harry and read it. He would be back at the end of the week. She frowned as she remembered the telegraph boy's cheerful words.

She'd forgotten the boys always said that if it wasn't an official telegram; they always knew. However, it couldn't matter. Rose's neighbours might have been watching from behind their net curtains, but none of them were on the street to hear.

Now, she had to decide how to behave. Her estrangement from Reg was well known so tears wouldn't look right. She thought about it for a moment and then nodded. She wouldn't say anything, but then, when someone asked – and they were bound to, she'd say what she felt – bleedin' good riddance!

It was what her workmates would expect so it was what she would say. They might be shocked when she and Harry married quickly but she wouldn't be around to hear the gossip. Rose felt a little sick inside, because this wasn't right. It was a lie and lies always caught you out – but just maybe they would get away with it, even if it meant that after the war, they would need to go somewhere else to live.

CHAPTER 8

In Lower Sackville, Canada, Mrs Vee Bittern looked at the young officer of the law in distress. 'I couldn't believe it when the bank told me she'd handed in her keys a few days after your visit, Hank. I asked if they knew where she'd gone, but they couldn't help me. I wish I'd told her what I intended now. I can't imagine why she went off like that.'

He shrugged his broad shoulders and looked concerned. 'That's disturbing, Miss Vee, but we'll look for her in the lodging houses . . .'

'I doubt if you can help this time,' she informed him with a grim smile. 'I did a little digging myself and she told a neighbour that she was going to England to look after a sick relative.'

Hank stared at her in disbelief. 'Doesn't she know there are still bombs falling over there? There's rationing and all kinds of shortages . . .what the hell made her do it? And how did she get passage?'

'That's what I'd like to know,' Vee said. 'I feel guilty – responsible. If my asking you to find Arthur has made her take flight . . . Oh, that poor woman, and little Arthur. I can't bear to think of them alone over there at such a terrible time.' The horror of what might happen to a woman and child, alone, with only a sick relative to help them, made her shudder.

'I can't think that she believed it was an official visit; I simply told her that his friends from the ship wanted to see him and that's why you'd asked me to look for him.'

'She must have been at her wits' end because of all that business with the bank loan she knew nothing of, apparently. It was wicked of her husband to go off and leave her with a debt they had no hope of paying – and a child to care for. It must have felt an impossible task.'

'Maybe that's what she thought,' Hank suggested reflectively, 'that if the authorities knew she had no means of support, they would take Arthur away from her. She ran away to stop us taking the child.'

Vee pressed a hand to her eyes, shaking her head. She sat down in the comfortable elbow chair at her large, mahogany desk, trembling inside at the thought of what might happen to Emily Henderson and Arthur.

'How terrible. If anything happens it will be my fault . . .'

'Don't take it to heart, Miss Vee,' Hank told her. 'For all you know she might have been planning to take the child before I spoke to her – and it was with good intentions you asked me to find them.'

Vee lifted her head, her eyes wet with sudden tears. 'I know, Hank, but it upsets me – that little lad. Will he be safe? To be sent all the way out here alone and now taken back when it's far more dangerous . . .' She sighed and then drew her shoulders back, in command once more. 'I must do what I can to discover if he's safe and well cared for, Hank. I know it isn't official business – but can you find out if there is an agency or a force that would be able to trace him for me?'

'I can't do it officially, Miss Vee. What I can do is try to find a private agent to work for you personally.'

'Yes, yes, that's what I meant,' she agreed instantly. 'I'd like to make sure that the child is safe – but Emily needs help, too. She must feel as if she's been abandoned.'

'She was, to all intents and purposes,' Hank replied seriously. 'She has a good case for divorce – but I doubt she'll find her husband. He could be anywhere by now.'

'Emily told her neighbour he'd gone back to England to join their RAF and fight for the old country – his family were all British. I think Emily's father was Canadian but her mother may have been British, so her neighbour thought.'

'She is a Canadian citizen, though,' Hank said. 'I'll get a few names for you – and now I must go or my chief will be sending a posse for me . . .'

Vee laughed as he left, pausing to speak to Aggie on his way through the kitchen and appropriate one of her warm tarts. She continued to sit at her desk, thinking, then she opened a drawer and took out a letter from England, which had recently arrived. Malcolm had visited the family the previous year, after being wounded and nursed back to health by the woman who was now his wife. Vee had thought her brother would never marry but he'd met Sheila. She'd been helping to care for their Great-Aunt Annie, who had since died. One of her sons had written to Vee, thanking her for the gifts she'd sent to his mother and to other members of the family.

'*Mum really appreciated your help, Cousin Vee. I'm on leave at the moment before returning to duty, but if ever I can be of service, please let me know.*'

Vee ran her finger over the lines of copperplate letters. Joe was in the Air Force and his writing was some of the most beautiful Vee had ever seen. She pondered for a moment. He'd given her an address to write to and she'd sent him a card a few weeks previously – but now she wondered. Joe could certainly help if he knew of anyone who might trace a child alone, although Arthur wasn't alone. Why had that thought popped into her head? Vee frowned and put the letter back into the drawer. Perhaps she would just leave it to Hank for the moment. He'd never let her down – and yet, she was asking a lot. Here in Canada, his word carried the full force of the law, but over there . . .

A shudder went through Vee as she thought of a newsreel she'd seen a few weeks previously: damaged buildings, burned homes, and people struggling to survive, that's how it had come over. She knew food parcels had been sent to Britain from Canada on more than one ship, because she'd helped collect the money to fund them.

What on earth had possessed Emily Henderson to go there when she had only to ask and a job could have been found for her right here in Canada?

CHAPTER 9

Emily approached the fish and chip shop apprehensively. Her aunt had sent her a welcoming letter when she'd told her they were coming but it was going to be a very different life to the one she'd known. It was midday and the shop was clearly busy; a queue had formed and was right out of the shop, spilling on to the pavement outside. Taking a deep breath, Emily went and stood in the queue, patiently waiting until they reached the front; it would have caused outrage if she'd walked straight past the women and children queuing.

It struck her as strange at first that there were hardly any men around and those few were clearly old, in their teens, or proudly wearing a uniform. She found it very different from back home, but it was better here at the coast than in some of the places they'd stopped in on the way. She'd hated the dirty towns that looked so drab, the streets narrow terraces with scarcely a sign of a flower or a tree. Here it was better, fresher with the breeze blowing in off the sea. Chilly, in fact, she thought with a little shiver, despite her dress and cardigan under her raincoat. It was drizzling again and had been most of the day. Arthur was wet, water dripping off the end of his nose. She thought he looked miserable and half-wished herself back home – but she didn't have a home now, thanks to Ken. When she caught up with him, he would know it!

She reached the end of the queue and asked for threepence worth of chips, paid, and gave the packet to Arthur. He smiled faintly and began to eat. They hadn't eaten much on their journey. Emily was saving her money – just in case.

'May I speak to Mrs Becky James?' she asked politely of the girl behind the counter. 'I'm her niece . . . or great-niece I suppose.'

'She ain't here,' the girl said with a sniff. 'That's why we've got such a long queue this morning. I can't manage it with just Tom out the back.'

'Where's my aunt?' Emily persisted, pushing the harassed-looking girl. 'I need to find her. I sent her a telegram to say I was coming. Doesn't she live over the top now?'

'You're holding up the queue,' the girl said and glared at her. 'I ain't got time to find her address for you – I've got more than I can cope with here.'

'Supposing I give you a hand?' Emily said. 'I could go through the back, wash my hands, and come back and help you serve.'

The girl stared at her for a moment and then nodded. She jerked her head towards a door behind her and lifted the flap on the counter. Emily went through, taking Arthur with her.

Through the door was a kitchen, where a lad of

about sixteen was peeling potatoes. Two buckets of cut chips were waiting to be taken through. He grinned at Emily. 'Has the lad come to give me a hand?'

'He'll help if he can – but no sharp knives,' Emily replied, responding to the youth's cheeky grin. 'I'm going to help in the shop.'

'Yeah, Ruby's going nuts trying to serve on her own.'

Emily went to the sink and washed her hands. She took a white apron off a hook, removed her raincoat, and looked at Arthur. 'Be good for a while. I need to help Ruby and then we'll go home.'

'Can yer get me a bucket of potatoes, Arthur?' the youth said. 'I need to wash them first, and then peel, else the chips get dirty.'

Arthur nodded. 'I can wash them,' he announced, 'if you like.'

'There's a good lad.'

Emily left them and went through to the shop. Ruby looked at her and nodded. 'I'll do the portions,' she said bossily. 'You can put the salt and vinegar on, wrap and take the money.'

'Yes, all right,' Emily agreed. 'You'll have to tell me how much.'

'Look on the board and listen,' Ruby replied grudgingly. 'I'll tell you just for a start.'

Emily took her place. She listened to what the customer asked for, then, when the portion was passed to her in a sheet of newspaper, Ruth told her how much and she asked the customer if they wanted salt and vinegar. Several wanted to put it on themselves so she let them, then wrapped the parcel and took the money. Ruth was dishing up so fast that there were two waiting when she got finished with the first.

She saw that one had fish and chips and the other just chips. 'Do you want salt and vinegar?' she asked and was surprised when a deep voice answered, 'Yes, and plenty of salt please – and it will be two shillings for my order, miss.'

Emily looked up and saw the young man in a blue-grey uniform. She hadn't noticed him come in. She glanced at the board, which had all the prices written clearly. 'Yes, one and ninepence for the fish and chips and threepence for extra chips.'

'You're a quick learner,' he said and Emily blushed at the approval in his blue eyes. He was in his twenties, she thought, younger than her and very attractive with a cocky smile.

'It's on the board,' she said and handed him his food in return for a coin she just about recognised as a florin. No change needed. She wasn't quite used to the English money yet, though she was learning fast.

'I need to be,' she told him. 'I only arrived from Canada a couple of days ago. I've come to visit my aunt.'

'See you around,' he said, nodded and went out.

Emily didn't have time to think about him. He was attractive and had a nice smile but Ken had let her down so badly. She'd loved him, trusted him, and he'd lied to her, again and again. Emily needed to know why. At this moment she didn't think she would ever want to live with him again; she could never trust him, but she had to see him, to finish it.

She thought that if something had happened to him,

she would find herself a bloke she could really trust –
someone who would help her make a home for Arthur.
Emily didn't think she'd want to marry again – and she
couldn't afford a divorce anyway. That cost money and
she had very little. Hardly enough to pay for a week's
bed and board, if she wanted to keep the fare home to
Canada, just in case she had to leave.

For the moment, she was struggling to keep up
with Ruby. It seemed Ruby had the easy bit, but Emily
wasn't going to complain however hard she worked
her. The girl was sullen and if she took a dislike to
Emily, she wouldn't tell her where Great-Aunt Becky
lived. Emily didn't have the address of her home, only
the fish shop.

'Why don't you know where she lives?' Ruth asked
suspiciously. 'If she is your aunt, you should know
where she lives.'

'I just had this address,' Emily admitted. 'Aunt Becky
used to live over the shop. I didn't realise she'd moved.'

'That was three years ago. Dunno why she didn't
give you the address.' Ruby stared at her. 'She said you
were coming – all of a fluster over it, she was.' She
sniffed loudly. 'I suppose I'll give it to you. I'd never
have got through if it hadn't been for you.' Her manner
was still grudging.

'Thank you.' Emily kept the sharp retort she felt like
making inside. 'Where is my aunt? Why isn't she here?'

'Don't know,' Ruby said and sniffed. 'She gave me
the keys last night and said she had something to do
this morning but would come in later and I was to
carry on until she got here – but she ain't come.'

'Did you know what to do?' Emily asked, looking at the fryer behind the counter. Ruby was wiping it over in a desultory way.

'Yeah, course,' Ruby answered scornfully. 'It ain't the first time I've opened up, but we used to have more help. Tom's father was always out back and he did a lot of stuff. He's a deep-sea fisherman but don't always work every day – he's at sea now, doing special work, so Tom says. He's taken over his dad's jobs but he ain't as fast and don't know it all yet.'

Emily nodded and accepted the scrap of paper Ruby had scribbled the address on. She looked at it. 'Old London Road – is it far from here?'

'You can get the bus over there,' Ruby said and began to take off her apron. 'And when you see her, you can tell her I'll be leaving unless she gets more help. I can't manage this place on my own – even if she isn't feeling up to much.'

'Is my aunt very ill?' Emily looked at her anxiously. 'She said she hadn't been too well in her last letter, but I thought it was just a cold or something.'

'She don't tell me much either,' Ruby retorted with a sniff. 'You'd best get off. The bus will here in five minutes.'

Emily went to the kitchen door and called Arthur. He came to her at once, and she picked up their cases, thanking Ruby and hurrying the boy out of the shop towards the bus stop. She had only just got there when one turned up and, seeing Old London Road on the front, she pushed Arthur up the step and found them a seat. When the conductor arrived, she asked for one and a half fares and her florin was accepted and a threepenny bit change given. Emily handed it to Arthur, smiling.

'For sweets,' she told him. 'Once I'm earning, I'll give you threepence a week pocket money, Arthur, and you can earn more doing little jobs.'

'Thanks, Mum,' he said, pocketing it and fidgeting a little on his seat. 'What shall we do if Aunt Becky doesn't like us?'

'Oh, I'll find work,' Emily said but she'd wondered about that, too. It wasn't going to be easy supporting herself and Arthur. She'd never been good at fending for herself and that was why she'd come all this way, because she needed someone to help her. It was, she supposed, why she'd married so young. Ken had seemed strong and supportive, the sort you could rely on, but he'd let her down and while that made Emily angry, it also frightened her. She wasn't sure she could manage on her own.

The house was at the bottom of quite a steep hill; there were houses on either side, very different to the ones Arthur had got used to in Canada, and far more solid looking than the one he'd lived in when he was a small child. These were mostly double-fronted and well-built with neat curtains at the windows but no front gardens. The bus stopped almost outside Aunt Becky's house and they only had to walk a few yards with the heavy suitcases. Emily knocked at the front door and waited but there was no answer. She knocked again three times but still no one came and she looked again at the scrap of paper in her hand. Yes, this was the right address; she asked Arthur to look and he confirmed it.

'She knew we were coming . . .' Emily looked so worried and Arthur wriggled. He wanted the loo but knew there was no chance of it yet. 'I suppose we'll just have to wait for her.'

She'd put the cases down and sat on one, Arthur on the other. It wasn't very comfortable and they were both hungry, tired, and thirsty, too. Emily glanced at her watch, got up and went to see if there was a way round the back. Arthur crossed his legs. He would have to go soon or he would wet himself.

'Hello?' a voice caught their attention and a woman came out of the house opposite. She waved at them, waited until a bus and a car had passed, and then came across the road to them, looking at Emily. 'Are you Mrs Emily Henderson?'

'Yes, yes, I am,' Emily said eagerly. 'I was looking for my aunt – but I think I must have the wrong house.'

'No, Mrs James lives here,' the woman said. 'I'm Mrs Anne Rowe and I know her well. But I'm afraid I have bad news for you – she was taken to hospital early this morning with a ruptured appendix.'

'Oh, no!' Emily exclaimed. 'Oh, that's terrible. Poor Aunt Becky. She must have been in so much pain.'

'I think she has been for a while . . .' Mrs Rowe hesitated, then said, 'Look, why don't you come and have a cup of tea with me, and I'll see if I can help you? I know you've come all the way from Canada, haven't you?'

'Yes, we arrived two days ago, but it took me a while to get things sorted,' Emily replied. 'Thank you. I should be grateful for that cup of tea. I may need to find somewhere to live . . .'

'Oh, I have a key to the house; Becky gave it to me,' Mrs Rowe said. 'I just wanted to make sure you were her niece – and this is your little boy?'

Arthur winced at the way she looked at him. He wasn't a small boy but he was in pain. 'Can I use your toilet please?' he asked as soon as they walked inside her house, which smelled of lavender polish and looked as if nobody lived there because it was so neat and tidy.

'Oh – yes, of course,' she said. 'It is up the stairs and the first door to your right. Can you manage on your own?'

'Yes, he'll be fine,' Emily answered for him. 'He's eight now. Be careful, Arthur. Don't touch anything you shouldn't . . .'

Arthur nodded and ran up the stairs. He was bursting to empty his bladder and only just managed to get his trousers down before the stream of hot urine escaped. Inevitably, some of it splashed on the polished lino. He stared at the small puddle, not knowing what to do; he dared not leave it there and he couldn't see any toilet paper, so he grabbed the towel and mopped the floor with it. It was white and the yellow stain spread through the fluffy threads. He looked at it guilty and took it to the hand basin, dipping it under the tap and rinsing it until the yellow faded. After that he didn't know what to do with it so he left it in the basin.

Feeling guilty, he crept downstairs and followed the sounds of the grownups' voices. They were sitting in a posh front room. It smelled of lavender again and there wasn't even a cushion out of place.

'You were a long time?' Emily looked at him. 'Are you all right, Arthur?'

'Yes, thanks, Mum.' He wanted to confess but the lady who had kindly invited them in was staring at him and he couldn't speak.

She got up then and went to make tea, bringing a tray back a minute or so later. There were three cups on it, a sugar bowl, milk jug and teapot, all fine porcelain, with dainty silver spoons. Arthur sat on his chair, frozen with fear as he watched her pour liquid into the cups and offer Emily the sugar basin. There were tongs and lumps of sugar and Arthur shook his head as he was offered the bowl. He couldn't do that; he would drop them and send it all flying. Emily saw he was nervous and put one lump in for him. She picked up the cup, leaving the saucer on the tray.

'Hold it with both hands and you'll be fine,' she whispered and he took it, feeling so guilty. He'd done a wicked thing in that posh bathroom and his guilt made his hands shake. Emily would be shamed if she knew.

Arthur sipped the tea. It tasted awful; the worst he'd been offered since they got here. He liked the coffee they'd had back home much better and after two sips he put it back on the tray.

'I'd offer your little boy a biscuit but I only have rich tea and I doubt he'd enjoy them. We haven't had chocolate ones for ages now.'

'No, I didn't realise how bad the rationing was until we got here,' Emily said. 'We mustn't take your biscuits. If you would give me my aunt's key, we'll go and find somewhere to rest, because we're both tired.'

'I suppose it's all right,' Mrs Rowe said. 'She gave it to me last night in case you came while she was at the doctor's. She was going this morning – but then she must have been very ill in the night and called him out. I saw them take her away in the ambulance early this morning.' She got up, went to the highly polished sideboard, and took out a heavy, dark metal key, handing it somewhat reluctantly to Emily.

'Thank you.' Emily stood. 'Say thank you to Mrs Rowe, Arthur. We'll go and deposit our cases and then we'll get something to eat.'

CHAPTER 10

Arthur couldn't wait to get out of the neighbour's house. He carried the bags while Emily brought the heavy cases. She soon had the door open and they went into the house. A pleasant smell of flowers met them as did a friendly clutter of things, walking sticks in a big vase in the hall, coats hanging from a stand, boots just inside the door, and a canvas bag slung over the banisters. They went to the open door at the end of the hall and discovered the kitchen; it was also untidy, the large kitchen table cluttered with baking trays and crockery that ought to have been replaced on the big painted dresser at one end. The sink was full of unwashed dishes and saucepans still contained the remains of a meal on the drainer. It had obviously been abandoned, probably because Aunt Becky had been too unwell to clear up.

Emily looked about her. She had dumped the cases in the hall and gave a sigh. 'It looks as if I'll have to tidy up a bit, Arthur. First, though, we'll see if there's anything to eat . . . I think that door may lead to a pantry . . .'

She opened a door and nodded, smiling as she went

inside the pantry. Its shelves would, in normal times, probably be stocked with preserves and tinned foods but there was only one small cluster of what looked like pickles and some jars of jam. However, on further exploration, Emily found half a dozen eggs, bacon and a large bag of potatoes; there was also a bag of plain flour and a half a pound of butter, still in its greaseproof paper.

'I'll make us some mash, a fried egg, and a slice of bacon. I can replace them with my ration books when I shop,' Emily said. 'I think I'll cook first and then tidy up when we've eaten.'

'I can put those dishes on the dresser, Mum, and clear some of this mess for you.'

'Let's see what's in those saucepans,' Emily said and peered inside. The large one was filled with meat and vegetables. Obviously, a stew intended for Aunt Becky's supper. Emily sniffed it and nodded.

'This is still fresh. I can reheat it this evening for our supper.' She put it to one side, and finding cooked potatoes and some cabbage in the other two, she told Arthur they would have them fried instead of making mash. 'We can't afford to waste food,' she said. 'Be careful with those dishes, Arthur. They aren't ours. We're just guests until we can find a home of our own.'

Arthur carried them very carefully and set them out on the dresser. Already, the kitchen had begun to look better. It wasn't dirty, just untidy, and that was because Emily's aunt was ill.

'Do you think Aunt Becky will be all right, Mum?' he asked as he looked round for another job. 'How long will it be before she comes back?'

'I don't know. I shall go to the hospital this evening and see her,' Emily said and frowned. 'I can't take you with me, Arthur, so you'll have to stay here on your own. Will you be all right? Or should I ask Mrs Rowe if you can go there while I'm gone?'

'No! Please don't – she won't want me,' Arthur blurted out and Emily looked at him. 'I didn't mean to, Mum, only I wanted to go so bad and some went on the floor and . . .' He gulped. 'I wiped it up with a towel and then rinsed it in the sink.'

'Arthur, you didn't?' He nodded, hanging his head, and then, to his surprise, Emily started to laugh. 'Oh, Arthur! Well, it was my fault. I should have asked before I rushed to catch that bus.'

'I'm sorry, Mum. I didn't mean to shame you.'

'You haven't.' Emily smiled and ruffled his hair. 'But why use a towel? Wasn't there any paper?'

'I didn't see it. There were just fancy dishes with soap in and a sort of doll thing.' Emily nodded. 'I couldn't leave a puddle on her floor.'

'No, you couldn't,' Emily agreed. 'Come on, Arthur, find some knives and forks for us – this is nearly ready.'

Arthur opened the dresser drawer and found a collection of knives and forks, none of them matching. He picked the ones he liked and brought them back to the table. The knives had bone handles but the forks didn't. 'These were all I could find, Mum.'

'At least Aunt Becky doesn't live in a palace like over the road,' Emily said and brought two plates of steaming hot food to the table. 'I'll have a good look round later this evening, but after we eat, I think I'd better go and find out how my aunt is.'

The bacon was streaky and crispy with fat, the egg sunny side up, as Arthur liked them and the bubble and squeak was just as he remembered from his childhood – the cooked potatoes and cabbage crisped outside in the bacon fat and soft inside. It was delicious and they were both starving. They ate every scrap and then Arthur helped Emily wash up with hot water boiled in the kettle.

Emily went out into the hall, opened two more doors, and then told Arthur he could go into what looked like her aunt's sitting room. 'I think she uses this one,' she told him. 'The other looks like the front parlour and feels cold. I doubt it's used much. You can wait here for me, can't you?'

Arthur looked round and nodded. There was a lot of clutter – books, envelopes tucked behind ornaments on the mantelpiece, and a bag of knitting wool beside a comfortable chair. It was a room he felt at ease in, but he was uncertain about being left there alone.

'What shall I do, Mum?'

'Look and see if any of the books interest you.' She went to the bookcase and took out an Atlas. 'There you are, Arthur. That should keep you going for a while. I'll be back as soon as I can, love. I'm sorry to leave you alone – but I don't have much choice.'

Arthur made himself smile. 'I'll be all right, Mum,' he said, though inside he was begging her not to leave him alone in a house he didn't know.

'I'll come straight back,' she promised, 'but I must see if I can visit Aunt Becky.'

Arthur nodded. She kissed his cheek and went into the hall. He heard her putting on her coat and then opening the door. She called goodbye and then the door shut with a bang behind her. Arthur ran to the window and looked out, watching her as she walked to the bus stop, checked the numbers, and then set off walking again. He stared after her for as long as he could see her and then went back to the Atlas he'd discarded on the floor.

He sat down beside it and flicked through the pages, not really seeing the pictures or maps. The house seemed big and empty now that he was alone so he took out his wooden whistle and played his tunes, the ones that came into his head. After a while his feeling of being abandoned began to fade as he reasoned that his mum was only going to the hospital and would return soon – but he was bored.

They hadn't been upstairs yet. Emily had been too busy clearing up in the kitchen and preparing their meal. She wouldn't mind if he went exploring – would she? Arthur ventured into the hall. There was one other room they hadn't been in; he opened the door opposite and peeked in. It was a dining room but looked as if it was never used. He closed the door and turned towards the stairs. Should he? Dare he? He shuffled towards them, still undecided, then he heard something upstairs – a slight noise . . .a mewing sound?

Arthur started up the stairs. He could hear the plaintive sound clearer now. Surely that was a cat? He paused, listening, and then walked towards the door from behind which the sound seemed to come. Opening it, he was startled as a hissing, ginger, furry thing shot past him and ran down the stairs. He stared after it and decided to follow. How had it come to be shut in an upstairs room?

The ginger cat had made straight for the kitchen. It sat by the door, giving Arthur a hostile, wary look as he entered. He hesitated but it mewed plaintively so he went to the dresser and fetched a small dish. There was a bottle of milk in the pantry. Arthur fetched it and poured a little into the dish. For a moment the cat eyed it suspiciously but then got up to investigate, sniffing, and then began to drink. It finished the milk and looked hopefully at Arthur but he dared not give it any more milk. Remembering the stew in the saucepan, he fetched it and spooned some into the dish. The cat once again eyed his offering with suspicion but ate all the meat, licked the jelly, declining the vegetables, before returning to its place next to the door.

'Do you want to go out, Puss?' he asked and the cat mewed.

Arthur tried the door and found it was locked, but the key was hanging on a string by the doorpost so he inserted it and unlocked the door. The cat shot past him and out into the long garden, disappearing over the wall at the end. Arthur went outside. He saw a saucer by the back door that had obviously held food in at one time and realised that it was probably where Aunt Becky fed her cat. The lawn looked as if it needed cutting and the borders were a bit overgrown and untidy, the flowers tumbling over and petals shedding over a grey concrete path.

Arthur wondered why the garden was neglected. Was it because Aunt Becky had felt ill for a while but just carried on? He remembered the way his birth mother had started to neglect things after his dad died and for the first time in a long while his eyes filled with tears. He felt sad because he'd loved her and still didn't understand why she'd let him be taken away. Wishing he hadn't let the cat out, because even though it wasn't very friendly, it had been company, he returned to the empty house.

He picked up the dish and the spoon he'd used and put them in the washing-up bowl. There was a little warm water left in the kettle so he poured it over them and left them to soak, then he wandered back into the hall. He ventured up the stairs once more and into the room the cat had been imprisoned in. Seeing a sash window that was opened a little at the bottom, he wandered over and looked down into the back garden. There was a shed close to the house and he realised the cat had jumped from the shed roof to the window, but then found itself in a closed room. Perhaps it was normally left open for him?

The room looked as if it might be Aunt Becky's, because a pair of slippers were placed beside the bed, which had been left open, the sheets pulled back. She must have got up in the night and gone downstairs to get help. Arthur hadn't seen a telephone so that meant she must have gone outside to summon a neighbour. He frowned as he thought of Aunt Becky having to struggle outside to call for help. Perhaps that was why she'd told Emily she could come, because she'd known she wasn't well – only they hadn't been here in time to help her.

Leaving the room, he closed the door again. It felt wrong to intrude. He was undecided whether to continue exploring, but after all, Aunt Becky had said they could come and the other rooms must be for them. He opened another door and discovered another double bed, this time immaculately made up with a shining satin coverlet. The next door led to the bathroom and Arthur decided to relieve himself again. This time he wasn't in such desperate straits and managed without getting any on the floor. He washed his hands at the sink, drying them and leaving the towel tidy on the rail.

The last room was a single with a bed, a chest of drawers and a chair beside the bed. On the bed was an old teddy bear. It had been much loved and was missing an ear and an eye. Arthur went to sit on the bed he felt sure was meant for him. On the wall opposite the bed was a picture of Jesus blessing people, and on top of the chest was a box. He lifted it down and took it to the bed, sitting down to open it. Inside was a set of toy soldiers, made of metal and painted red and blue. Some had tall hats on their heads, some carried guns and some had horses to ride.

Arthur took them all out and lined them up on the bed, but they kept falling over so he fetched them down to the floor and squatted with them, forming battle lines, and making the horses charge against each other. He played with the soldiers for a while, replacing them carefully in their box when he'd finished.

How much longer would his mother be? Arthur returned the box to its place and went back down the stairs. He got himself a cup of water and drank it, and then went out into the garden. There was no sign of the cat and he sighed, feeling the loneliness settling round him again. It was warm outside still and he wished he had a ball to kick around, but the only balls he'd had were back in Canada, in storage with all the other stuff they'd left behind. Sighing, he went back inside.

The suitcases were still in the hall. Arthur tried to lift his but he couldn't manage to get it more than a few inches before he had to drop it again. He had a thought and decided to open it, which he did by snapping up the hinged clasps. He took out a few of his clothes and carried them upstairs. The drawers of the chest in the little room were empty so he placed his first load in the bottom one and went back for more. Some of the things were Emily's. She'd packed a heavy coat and some shoes in with his things, so he put them to one side and carried the rest of his stuff up in two loads, placing them all in the chest of drawers. He had two storybooks and he put them on the chest with the box of lead soldiers. Then went back down. He replaced his mother's things in the case and found he was now able to carry it upstairs. Taking it to the bedroom he believed would be Emily's, he left it just inside the room, then returned and carried his satchel up to his own room. He unpacked a few treasures, including a model car and some colouring pencils, a notebook in which he liked to draw things, a grubby handkerchief, a bar of half-eaten nougat, and his collection of pebbles. Apart from that there was a crumpled shirt, a pair of clean underpants and his pullover. He added these to his drawer, took the nougat with him to eat and returned to the hall, eyeing his mother's case. Deciding he'd better not unpack that, he left it for her to take up on her return, and went into the sitting room.

Once he'd eaten the nougat, he decided to explore

the room again. The ornaments on the mantel amused him for a while; there were all kinds of bits and pieces, including screwdrivers, nail files, a tarnished silver jug, a model of a dog in brass, several dark photographs in wooden frames and a tin of peppermint sweets, as well as three small silver brooches, all of animals or birds, and some feathers that might have come from a hat. Arthur smiled as he saw the eclectic collection; he thought he was going to like Aunt Becky.

He wandered back to the bookcase. Here too there were all kinds of books and on the bottom shelf he found a copy of an adventure story. It was called *Treasure Island* and he took it out, feeling pleased as he saw it had some pictures inside. Arthur liked books with pictures, even though he was able to read any book. He settled down and was soon immersed in the story, his loneliness forgotten for now.

He was lying on the floor with the book by his side, having fallen asleep, when Emily finally returned. It was late and it was dark and she switched on the electric light, startled at first to see him lying there, but then she smiled as she realised he was sound asleep. She hesitated for a moment, unwilling to disturb him, but it had to be done and she was drained, her eyes gritty with tears after the news she'd been given. Aunt Becky was very ill and the doctors were not sure she would recover.

'She must have ignored the pain for a long time,' the senior nurse had told Emily. 'It was touch and go whether she would come through the operation, but she did – now we have to wait and see whether she'll recover. She's in her sixties, and will be quite frail for a time, if she makes it through the night.'

Emily had wept on her way home. She didn't know her aunt well, just from a few letters and cards, but she'd been counting on a home with her for a while, and now it seemed that might not happen. Besides, Aunt Becky was all she had in the world, apart from Arthur.

Arthur seemed to become aware of her, opening his eyes and smiling up at her. Emily's heart turned over and she felt a rush of tenderness. She did love him, truly she did – she just didn't know if she could cope alone. It would be hard work, bringing up a child and holding down a full-time job . . . yet she must, somehow. The alternative didn't bear thinking of.

CHAPTER 11

Rose wore a smart suit for her wedding to Harry Smith. It was dark green with a boxy jacket and a pencil skirt and she had a cream lace blouse under it. Both of them had been bought from a second-hand clothes stall but they were good quality and fitted her well. She'd had them cleaned, even though they looked new and had obviously come from a well-off first owner. She'd wanted something new but there was nothing smart or pretty in the shops, which were now only allowed to sell the new utility style. So Rose had chosen good second-hand, and she was pleased she had when she saw the look in Harry's eyes.

'You look wonderful,' he whispered as she came down the stairs.

Rose smiled, wishing that they were truly getting married rather than going through a sham just for appearances. The word had spread that Rose had had a telegram and Rose had encouraged the gossips to think it had been one of *those*, letting them glimpse the black edging on the telegram that Harry had given her. Although a few looked down their noses at how swiftly her second marriage had been arranged, the women she got on with nodded their understanding. Harry was making an honest woman of her rather than continuing to live in sin.

As if he sensed her suppressed doubts, Harry took both her hands in his, looking her in the eyes. 'As far as I am concerned, this is the real thing,' he told her. 'You'll be my wife, Rose, and I'll never let you down while I live.'

'I know that,' she replied, the sheen of tears in her eyes. 'You're a good man, Harry. I only wish I'd married you years ago.'

Harry smiled and kissed her softly. 'Come on,' he said, handing her a small posy of flowers. 'This is just so we can be together, Rose. Don't worry about it, it will come right.'

Rose nodded and squeezed his hand. 'It *is* right, Harry,' she said. 'I just hope that bugger doesn't come back and cause trouble.'

'If I see Reg again, he'll wish he'd stayed away,' Harry retorted grimly. 'He's dead to us, Rose. Forget him.'

Rose nodded and they left his house together. Their cases were packed and ready for the journey to a destination only Harry knew as yet but had told Rose was in the south of the country and a coastal area. They would have a few days holiday in a small hotel at the seaside and then move into the boarding house that had been allotted to them as temporary accommodation. Harry had promised to find them a place of their own as soon as he could but they wouldn't be returning to his house until the end of the war.

Harry had decided to let it through an agent. If he'd left it empty, someone would have broken in, because it was hard to find accommodation of any kind in London now, so many homes had been destroyed in the area.

'If it's still standing at the end of the war, we'll decide what to do for the best,' Harry had told Rose. 'We might want to make a new life elsewhere.'

Rose was sad to be leaving; it was by far the nicest house she had ever lived in, but she wasn't sure she wanted to come back to London. There were a lot of memories, both good and bad. She'd had friends here once, but many of them had gone, some dead, some, simply tired of struggling through the Blitz, had chosen to move away when their houses were lost.

'Come on,' she said as she saw a look of sadness in Harry's eyes as he locked the door, perhaps for the last time. 'We've got the future to look forward to, Harry.'

'Yes, we have,' he said and his smile lit his eyes. She took his arm and they set off for the registry office, walking to the end of the road where they caught the next bus.

Several of Harry's friends had turned out for the wedding, wearing their best suits and a rose in their buttonholes, but the only faces Rose knew were those of Gertie Bright and Maisie Townsend, both of whom had worked at the factory with her, and neither of whom had signed on to relocate. Gertie threw a handful of confetti over Rose and wished her luck. Maisie gave her a lucky horseshoe tied with blue ribbon.

'Have a good life, Rose,' Gertie said, looking suspiciously close to tears. 'I'm going to miss yer, gal.'

'You'll find another job, Gertie,' Rose said. 'There's plenty of work going.'

Gertie sniffed and looked at Harry. 'I might change me mind and come wiv yer,' she said in a muffled tone. 'Me eldest girl says she'll look after the little ones and her pa will still be 'ere.'

'If you do want to come, be there at eight Thursday morning for the bus. It will pick you up at the bottom of Curdle Lane and we'll find you a room when you arrive.'

'Thanks, Mr Smith,' Gertie said and sniffed. 'Fell out with me bleedin' 'usband, ain't I? He said he'd kill me if I even thought about it – so I reckon I'll go. Can't let the bleeder think he's the boss . . .' She gave a cackle of laughter. 'He'll get short shrift from our Shirl, I can tell yer – tongue like a knife that girl's got, and handy wiv 'er fists. He'll be beggin' me ter come 'ome afore long.'

Harry grinned. 'Up to you, Gertie,' he said. 'Come and have a drink and a bit of cake down the pub. It's only a butter cream sponge but there might be a pork pie going.'

'Yer on,' Gertie said. 'Mine's a pale ale and a pie.' She looked at Maisie. 'Are yer comin' then?'

'Yes, please do, Maisie,' Rose said but the other woman looked at her oddly and shook her head.

'No, thanks. I just wanted to see if you went through with it.' She looked at Rose again. 'I don't believe Reg is dead,' she muttered and walked off, leaving Rose to stare after her in dismay.

'Now what did the daft bugger mean sayin' that?' Gertie said. 'You 'ad the telegram, didn't yer, Rose?' Rose nodded. 'Well then, take no notice.'

'I don't intend to,' Rose replied but in her heart she felt guilty. She was glad Maisie wasn't coming with them to the new location.

'You mustn't let that woman get to you, Rose,' Harry said when they were on the train, in an otherwise empty first-class carriage, heading for their holiday at the coast. She'd been quiet for a while and he reached for her hand, holding it firmly. 'Maisie doesn't know anything. We don't know where Reg is or if he's alive, so how can she?'

Rose hesitated, then, 'She might, Harry. I think they might have been having a fling. I know Reg had other women and I think Maisie might be one of them. She hinted at it once at work but I ignored her.'

'Her husband would kill her if he knew.' Harry frowned. 'She can't know for sure, Rose. If she did, she would have come right out and said it.'

'Yes, I know.' Rose looked at him and then nodded. 'It threw me for a while, Harry, but I'm not going to let it bother me. We'll stick to our story and no one can prove otherwise.'

'No, they can't,' Harry said. 'A lot of records are going missing these days, burned, or lost during bombing raids and in the chaos that happens afterwards. Maisie is just a shrew. Forget her.'

'Yes, I shall,' Rose said and leaned towards him, kissing him softly on his cheek. 'I'm going to be happy.'

'Good,' he said, but they both knew Reg's shadow would be there for a long time to come.

'So,' Rose said, determined to change the subject. 'Where are we going then, Harry?'

'It's a place on the south coast called Hastings,' he replied. 'The factory is located a few miles away, tucked inside a forest so that it's hard to spot from the air. I thought we'd take our holiday close by so we can have a scout round, see if we can find ourselves a house to rent.'

'That's a good plan,' Rose agreed. 'We can explore the area.'

Harry nodded. 'Most of the workers will be accommodated at Bexhill and there's a bus that takes them there and back, but we might choose to be a bit further out, if I got a little car.'

Rose gave him a quizzical look. 'I didn't know you could drive, Harry?'

He laughed. 'I've had a few goes at it, but I didn't bother back home. I could walk anywhere I wanted and there was always a bus, but I reckon I could afford a little car and then we could go for drives out on our day off, once I've got my licence.'

'We might,' she agreed, then gave a little giggle. 'Splashing out, ain't we?'

'Might as well spend the rent money for the house,' Harry quipped back at her. 'Our accommodation will be paid for the first few months, to compensate for the move, and I've got a few bob put by, Rose.'

Rose glanced at the 22ct gold ring on her wedding finger and the small diamond band that went with it. Her old wedding ring, which she'd put at the bottom of her handbag, was 9ct, as were most of the rings the women she knew wore – unless they were silver.

'That was a big sigh?' Harry looked slightly anxious.

'I was thinking of Dora,' Rose said. 'How things

change, Harry. Dora's gone and Dave has married again and the children live with his aunt . . . Now we're married too and leaving London.'

Harry nodded, clearly understanding that she felt further away from the kids she loved now that they had left London. It would certainly mean a longer journey to see them and she would have to change trains a few times, but it was still something she could do now and then.

'You'll see them again,' he said, reaching for her hand.

'You mean Alice and Davey?' Rose smiled and shook her head. 'I wasn't thinking of them, Harry. It's just . . . leaving London makes you think back.'

'Not regretting it?' he asked anxious for her.

Rose shook her head. 'No,' she replied. 'No, I don't regret any of it since I met you, Harry.' She smiled at him. 'Don't worry. I have a good feeling about things. I believe our lives will get better soon. The war can't go on forever and when it ends, we can go anywhere we like.'

She'd written to both her sons, telling them she understood Reg was dead and that she'd married a good friend. Perhaps now they might get in touch and even bring her grandson to visit one day.

CHAPTER 12

'I've seen Aunt Becky and she's sitting up in bed – she sends you her love and said there are more toys in the cupboard under the stairs.' Emily sounded more cheerful, more like she used to when Arthur first went to live with her.

Arthur looked at her. Her hair was loose, brushed softly round her face and her eyes sparkled. 'I'm glad Aunt Becky is getting better,' Arthur said. 'When is she coming back home, Mum?'

For the past few days, Emily had left him alone in the house every evening while she went to the hospital. During the mornings, she took him into town, down to the sea front to the fish and chip shop, and he helped Tom in the kitchen, washing potatoes and watching as the youth peeled and sliced them into fat chips. Each day he had a bag of chips and crispy bits off the fish batter for his midday meal, and in the evenings they had whatever Emily could afford to buy for tea. Mostly, it was something on toast: grilled tomatoes, a little bit of cheese, eggs, when they could get them, or beans. Arthur didn't complain, but Emily grumbled about the meat ration, and splashed it all out on some ham, four ounces of streaky bacon, and sausages at the weekend.

'I don't have time to make stews or pies,' she'd told him. 'We'll just have to make do with what I can buy.'

It was a strange life and Arthur missed going to school, though in the afternoons his mother sometimes took him on the beach. She bought bread and made sandwiches with lettuce and cucumber sprinkled with salt and they tasted wonderful as they sat in the hazy autumn sunshine.

'Aunt Becky says there is a good junior school somewhere just a short bus ride away,' Emily said to him now. 'As soon as I get time I'll see if they can take you, Arthur. It will be better for you to be at school than stuck in the kitchen washing potatoes.'

'I won't know anyone,' Arthur said nervously. 'I wish we were still at home, Mum.'

Emily looked at him and then sighed, sounding weary. 'I need you to go to school, Arthur. It's against the law to keep you away – and, besides, I have to work longer hours. Ruby does have help in the evenings – but only for three nights; the other three she works alone in the shop but Tom's father helps out when he can in the kitchen and they have another girl. Aunt Becky used to work two shifts some days. It's no wonder she wore herself out.'

'When will we be together?' Arthur asked, feeling doubtful. 'If I'm at school all day and you go to work in the evenings?'

'Only three evenings,' Emily said. She ruffled his hair. 'It's only for a while. I'll see if I can find someone to help so that I don't have to leave you every evening, love. I am sorry you've been so much alone since we got here.'

'It's all right, Mum,' Arthur said in a small voice, but it wasn't. He hated being left alone in this house, which creaked when the wind blew and sounded creepy, especially when his mother came in after dark. The last two nights she hadn't got in until gone ten and Arthur had begun to feel very frightened. He was so scared, because he didn't know what to do if she never came back.

'I know it isn't all right,' Emily said. She sat down quite suddenly on the settee and burst into tears. 'I truly am sorry, Arthur. I didn't mean it to be this way. It will be better when Aunt Becky comes home. She won't be able to work for months, so she'll be here for you – and you will like her, I promise you.'

Arthur nodded, but bit his lip. He was close to tears but didn't like to see Emily cry. 'Don't cry, Mum,' he begged, pressing up against her knee. 'I love you and I'll be good. I'll go to school when you tell me and—'

'I know you will.' Emily said and ruffled his dark gold locks. You've always been good and I do love you. I promise we'll do things on Sundays, go to the beach or the woods and to the cinema on a Saturday afternoon, too.'

Arthur nestled his head against her, feeling safe as she stroked his hair. If only it could always be this way, but he knew that in the morning they would go to the shop and in the evening, he would once more be alone . . .

Emily looked down at the sleeping child. She'd investigated the cupboard under the stairs for him and found a train set, which they'd set up on the floor of his room and an old football, also some skittles and a set of building bricks. Arthur hadn't been interested in anything much apart from the football; the train set, once put together was boring as the clockwork train just went round and round in circles. It didn't make up for playing with other children or swimming in the shallow water at the edge of a sparkling lake when they explored the wilderness.

'Oh, Ken,' she muttered as she left the room, leaving the door just ajar the way Arthur liked it. 'Why did you do this to me?'

She was so angry with her husband. Just before she'd left Canada, Emily had learned that he'd been unfaithful to her. A letter had come addressed to Ken and she'd opened it; it had been from his other woman – and it seemed he'd deserted her too, because she was demanding to know why he hadn't been to see her. She lived some distance from Halifax and Emily had understood then that his fishing trips with friends, or his trips out of town to source new goods for the shop, had been combined with pleasure for Ken. How could she have been such a fool as to trust him all that time? The signs had been there but perhaps she hadn't wanted to know.

Ken was a gambler and a cheat and Emily meant to get even. She would find out where he was stationed and then she would hunt him down and shame him, demand compensation for the money he'd stolen from her. It was stealing when he'd used it for his mistress and gambling, not for their business! Her first anger had turned to a cold knot of hatred. It was Ken's fault that she was here, working at a job that she didn't much like but would pay the bills, until she could find something better.

Returning to the kitchen, Emily washed dishes and cleaned. She was almost dead on her feet and at the moment she couldn't see things getting much better. Aunt Becky's recovery would be slow and when she did come out of hospital, she wouldn't be able to do a lot – it would be more a case of looking after her. Well, at least she would be company for Arthur, if that was any compensation.

Emily knew that Arthur was miserable. She'd dragged him halfway across the world for this! If she'd known what it would be like, she might not have come. Back in Halifax she could have found a place to rent and a job – perhaps a better one than she had here. Emily wasn't sure why she'd done it now. At the time she'd thought it would be better for them both, and she'd panicked when that law officer came asking about Arthur, but now she wasn't so sure. Supposing Aunt Becky remained an invalid? Emily hadn't bargained for that and wasn't certain she could cope. Oh, she liked her aunt, but she was still young, and she wanted a bit of life.

A little smile touched her lips as she thought of the young man who had insisted on walking her home from the hospital the last two nights. She'd met him as she'd left her aunt's ward, remembering his cheeky smile from the first time she'd served him at the fish shop.

'It's the beauty from the chippie,' he'd said, grinning as they almost bumped into one another. 'What are you doing here?'

Emily had explained and he'd told her he was visiting his grandfather, who didn't have long to live. His smile had dimmed and Emily had warmed to him because of his obvious concern for the man he loved, so she'd gone with him for a cup of tea at a café on their way back to her aunt's house. They'd talked and talked and the time had vanished. Emily felt guilty for leaving Arthur and she'd told Pete – as he'd asked her to call him – that she had to get home to her son. Of course that led to explanations, and Pete was angry with the way she'd been treated. He'd given her an address she could write to and find out where Ken was stationed. Pete was in the RAF too but on extended leave because of wounds to his leg and thigh.

'Lucky to be alive that's me,' he'd told her. 'Jerry had a good go but couldn't get rid of me.'

Emily had laughed and sympathised but she'd liked him. He was a few years younger than her but it didn't matter; the attraction was there from the start. So much so that she hadn't been surprised when he'd been waiting outside the hospital for her the following night. He'd seen her to the door again and then given her a kiss.

'That's for luck,' he'd said when she'd laughingly protested. 'I'm going for a medical in the morning – if I pass, I'll be back to work soon.'

Emily nodded. 'Then I wish you luck.'

'Humm,' he said, drawing it out. 'I'm not sure what I want now, Emily. I was praying they would pass me as fit – but if they do, I shan't be around for a while to see you home.'

Emily laughed. 'I can walk myself home, even if the last bus has gone.'

'Yes, but who will you find to walk with?' His blue eyes quizzed her. 'I'd like to think you'll wait for me – I'll be back for a few hours when I can.'

'Daft! I'm a married woman—' Emily said.

'Not for much longer,' Pete retorted. 'Ditch the rat, Emily. You can't still care for him.'

'No, perhaps not . . .'

'Then, I'll be seeing you . . .' Pete had walked off whistling.

Emily laughed and entered the house, feeling exhilarated. It was all nonsense, of course. The young airman was flirting, nothing more, but it was nice to be flattered and courted again. It seemed a long time since any man had paid her compliments.

Her smile had left her when she saw Arthur curled up on the floor. His face was grubby and she could see the marks of tears on his face. He'd smiled at her trustingly, as he woke and looked up at her, and her heart caught. She should have come straight back to him instead of flirting with Pete – and she would. Arthur was more important. It was just that she was scared and lonely . . .

On Sunday they went to the beach. It was a very pebbly beach and parts of it had barbed wire to keep them out, because there was still a fear of invasion and the beach had been mined, even though the RAF had won the battle in the air. However, there were places where the sea came in far enough and it was safe to paddle in the salty water. The breeze was strong and it was cool

119

despite a hazy sunshine, but Arthur loved being there with Emily. She'd hired deck chairs and taken a packet of sandwiches with them.

Arthur sat and munched jam sandwiches and drank orange squash from a thermos flask. Emily had stood it in a little rock pool and so it was nice and cool to drink and they took turns to drink from the little cup that screwed on the end. After the sandwiches they shared an apple. Emily cut it into slices and it was juicy and sweet. They watched the spray against the breakers as the wind got up and it became quite rough, but neither of them wanted to leave. It was a perfect time for them, and they hadn't known much of that lately.

At a quarter to five, Emily told Arthur they had to go. 'I'll just have time to make us some tea,' she told him and ruffled his hair as he bent to put on his sandals. 'I've got some bacon to cook and we'll have it on toast.'

He smiled at her happily. There was still one more treat to come before she went off to visit Aunt Becky.

Emily was cooking their tea when the doorbell rang. She looked at Arthur in surprise, wondering aloud who it could be, and then went to open it. Arthur heard her exclaim as she recognised whoever it was. He thought she sounded happy and excited, and then she returned with a man he'd never seen before.

'This is Pete,' she told him. 'He's a friend of mine, Arthur. Say hello to him.'

'Hi, Pete,' Arthur said. The man was smiling. He looked all right but Arthur wondered how his mum knew him. He didn't think she knew anyone in England. 'Are you in the RAF?'

'Yes, I am, Arthur.' Pete grinned at him. 'You're a clever lad to recognise the uniform.'

'I've seen it at the cinema,' Arthur told him. 'In Canada they showed pictures of men in uniforms like yours and said you were battling for Britain?'

'We did and we won,' Pete told him. 'I like the pictures, too. How about you and me and Mum go one Saturday afternoon?'

'Oh, Pete,' Emily exclaimed. 'I work until two on Saturdays and then again for a couple of hours in the evening sometimes. I have other things to do in the afternoons.'

'Nothing more important than a trip to the pictures with us, though?' Pete said cheekily and Arthur saw his mum blush and then laugh.

'No, I don't suppose there is,' she admitted, and then looked at him curiously. 'I thought you went for a medical?'

'I did and they've given me a couple of weeks more leave before I report back – what say we take a little holiday, have a few days off to explore the countryside.'

'If only I could,' Emily said. 'I have to work most days, Pete – and I need to visit Aunt Becky in the evenings. I really only have Sundays and Tuesday afternoons off.'

'Then we'll go out on Tuesday,' Pete said. 'I can borrow a friend's car and we'll take a trip, wherever you fancy.'

'I'd like to go somewhere we can walk in a park or

the woods,' Emily replied. 'We can take a picnic and a flask.'

'Oh, we might do better than that,' Pete told her with a grin. 'I reckon we might get some ice creams and cakes, perhaps go to Lyons' Corner House when we come back?'

'That would be a treat, wouldn't it, Arthur?' Emily looked at him and he saw the excitement in her face. She looked so pretty at that moment.

'Yes, Mum.' Arthur munched on his bacon on toast. He noticed that Emily had made one for Pete too, so she must like him. That was all right. Arthur liked him, too.

'Are you going to the hospital later?' Pete asked her and she nodded. He looked at Arthur. 'What happens to you, young man?'

'I stay here on my own. I'm all right.'

'You'll be going to school the week after next,' Emily told him. 'It won't be so bad then, Arthur.'

'Why don't we take him with us?' Pete suggested. 'I'll take him to the pier and we'll play on the penny slot machines for an hour and then come and fetch you.'

'I thought the pier was closed?' Emily frowned.

'A bit of it's open this end,' Pete told her. 'Or we could just have an ice cream in the café if you'd rather I didn't take him on the pier.'

Arthur could see Emily was hesitating. He waited with bated breath and then she nodded. 'Would you like to go with Pete, Arthur?'

'Yes, please,' he said quickly. He would rather do anything than stay here alone again.

'All right,' Emily agreed. 'Thank you – it's good of you, Pete.'

'Nah, Arthur and me are going to be mates, aren't we?'

Arthur nodded. Pete seemed all right. He was glad he'd come, because his mum looked happy. She was smiling, her eyes bright, alive, and the way she used to be, instead of tired and worried.

CHAPTER 13

Rose looked around the room she and Harry had been given at the boarding house in Bexhill. It was clean and adequate, with a chair to sit on and look out of the window towards Beachy Head but there was no view of the sea, just an expanse of grass at the top of the cliffs. She and Harry had taken a walk to gaze out at the sea; the water had looked dark green and the foam was creamy as it broke against the sheer cliffs. The wind had been very strong so they hadn't lingered, because even this early in the autumn it had been cold.

They'd found a small café and gone in, shivering, for a cup of tea. The woman had laughed when she saw them rubbing their hands.

'You're not from these parts?' she'd asked. 'London, I'm guessing. You won't be used to our sea breezes.'

'It's more than a breeze,' Harry had countered. 'Damn cold on the cliffs.'

'It will get a lot colder,' the woman had promised. 'Just a nice breeze at the moment.'

'It's two coats colder than it was in London,' Rose

had replied, making the woman smile and nod as she'd served their tea.

That had been at the start of their few days' holiday, but since then they had been too busy at the munitions factory to bother with sea-gazing on the cliffs. They'd found a nice little pub within walking distance of their accommodation and went there sometimes in the evening, and on a Sunday for lunch. Their landlady gave them breakfast and a room but their meals were provided at the canteen all the workers used. As these were normally filling but not very tasty, they ate at a café or took a pie and chips back to their room in the evenings. They were not supposed to do that but Harry said she could only throw them out once. Neither of them was keen on living that way and he was searching the newspapers for a house they could rent locally, but so far hadn't found anything suitable.

'There's a four-bedroomed place in Hastings,' Harry spoke from behind Rose as she was tidying some things away. 'We could afford it, but it would mean getting up an hour earlier in the mornings and we'd be back later at night.'

'We don't need anything that big,' Rose told him. 'We'll manage here for now, Harry. Something will turn up.'

He nodded and walked to join her. 'Leave that for now,' he said and took her in his arms, bending to kiss her softly on the lips. 'Are you all right, love? I know this isn't much of a life. I'd hoped we would find something better by now.'

'It's only been a couple of weeks,' Rose said and hugged him. She knew he was only concerned for her sake. 'I can put up with it for a bit longer, Harry. I've known worse. You should have seen some of the places I lived before we got the house in Silver Terrace.'

'I know – but I wanted to give you a good life.'

'And you have. I'm all right, Harry,' she assured him and then laughed. 'Gertie didn't last long, did she?'

Gertie had surprised them by getting on the bus with the other workers who had relocated, but at the end of the second week she'd asked to be released, and Harry had let her go, after she signed a paper to swear not to reveal the location of the factory. He'd made her do it, because he knew Gertie to be a terrible gossip.

'My girl says she can't manage wivout me,' she'd told Rose. 'To tell yer the truth I only come fer a bit of peace. Me old man is a right bugger at times. I thought it would do him good if I left him for a bit – and it seems he's been like a bear wiv a sore 'ead so I'd best get back. I'd stay 'ere if I could – it's been like a bleedin' 'oliday.'

Rose thought she would miss Gertie. She'd got a tongue as sharp as a viper's sting but she was fun when she wanted to be. Besides, since coming to their new location, Rose hardly ever came into contact with the women she'd supervised in London. She'd been put in charge of a different section. Harry was working with most of them, though they'd been split up into various groups. Rose had been assigned to similar work as she done before, supervising a line assembly, but Harry was overseeing a different part of the factory. She understood that it was where they were making a new kind of weapon but he didn't talk about it so she wasn't sure.

They parted when they were through the gates each morning and met in the evening, or sometimes in the canteen, though Harry often had tea and a butty brought to him in his office. Rose never lingered over her lunch break. She had no real friends here but Harry, though she got on well enough with the local women, who seemed more respectful and were much easier to supervise than those she'd worked with in London.

It was a bit of a strange life but busy. Rose missed having her own home, but she wasn't going to complain. She would much prefer to be here with Harry than back in London with Reg and found that she was beginning to feel as if she were truly wed to the kind man she'd come to love. Harry had taken her in when she needed help and looked after her when she was ill. How could she not love the man who had been so good to her? He'd given her the only real happiness she'd ever known. All that was missing was a child they could adopt as their own, but that couldn't happen until they had their own home. She thought that when it did happen, and if they were lucky enough to get a child, she would cut her hours at the factory. They had drawn workers in from all over the country and seemed to function well; it was far better equipped for safety and proper working conditions than the old one and Rose didn't think it would matter if she worked fewer hours.

'Shall we go to the pictures next weekend?' Harry asked her. 'There's a decent film on in Hastings and we've both got Saturday and Sunday off.'

'Yes, why not,' Rose said. 'We can get something to

eat there too – maybe go to a café or get some fish and chips.'

'We'll do that,' Harry agreed. 'I like the fish down here – tastes better somehow.'

Rose laughed. 'It's them sea breezes,' she said. 'They make you hungry.'

The film was *The Maltese Falcon* starring Humphrey Bogart and Harry really enjoyed it though they'd seen it before. It wasn't Rose's favourite; she liked a comedy or a musical best, but she enjoyed the outing. They had a bag of chocolate toffees to share and an ice cream from the girl with a tray when she came round in the interval. An organ was played in between the main film and the cartoons and some people in the audience sang along to the popular tunes, which made for some laughter and a nice atmosphere.

They'd gone to the matinee performance and quite a few of the audience were children, young boys, and girls. Rose was surprised in a way, but the B-film had been a cowboy so they had probably enjoyed Roy Rogers. Her attention was caught by the sound of laughter and she turned her head to look at the young woman, her husband, who was wearing an RAF uniform, and the boy with them. He looked to be about eight or perhaps nine and seemed happy. Rose was reminded of Davey Blake and a wave of nostalgia swept over her. Sometimes she missed Dora and those kids so much.

'It was a good film, wasn't it?' Harry asked and she looked up at him, tucking her arm through his and smiling.

'Yes, it was, love,' she agreed. 'I liked the trailer for

that film that's coming soon – *Arsenic and Old Lace*. That'll be a laugh with Alec Guinness.'

'Yeah. We might come and see that, too,' Harry agreed. 'Shall we get some fish and chips? I can smell them and they smell good. We could eat them in that bus shelter over the road.'

There were some glass and brick shelters here and there along the promenade, to protect folk from the fierce winds, Rose reckoned. She agreed, because the smell from the fish and chip shop was making her hungry and they would go cold before they could get home on the bus.

The shop was busy. Rose saw the young family she'd noticed leaving the cinema were buying some chips. 'One large cod and three portions of chips,' the man in uniform said and paid for them.

'We could have done with some help this evening,' the girl behind the counter said to the young woman, a bit sullenly, Rose thought.

'I'll be in on Monday as usual,' the boy's mother replied and they went out.

Harry bought cod and chips for them both, asked for plenty of salt and vinegar and was told to put his own on before they were wrapped in newspaper. They carried them across the road to the shelter and discovered the family there.

'Oh . . .' Harry hesitated but the airman grinned at them. 'Budge up a bit, Arthur. Make room for the lady and gentleman.'

'Are you sure you don't mind?' Rose asked.

'Of course not,' the woman replied. 'There's plenty of room – and it's too cold to eat them on the beach.'

'We find it cold here,' Rose said. 'We're not local.'

'I'm Canadian,' the woman replied and smiled. 'I'm used to cold winters – but this wind does go through you.'

Rose nodded and they sat down to eat their supper with their fingers. The food was piping hot and she had to blow on the fish before eating as it burned the tongue if you weren't careful, but, oh, it did taste good. There was something about eating seaside fish and chips from the newspaper. Normally, she would have had them straight out onto the plate at home. Sometimes, back home, she'd taken her plate round the chippie and put greaseproof paper over it to carry it home, but paper was short these days; you couldn't always get greaseproof and some chippies asked you to take your own newspaper with you.

The family had finished eating their meal. Rose watched as the mother wiped her son's greasy fingers on a handkerchief and then round his mouth, before wiping her own hands. They stood up to leave. The boy looked at Rose and smiled shyly. Her heart caught as she glimpsed an underlying sadness before he turned away. She wanted to give him something and reached into her pocket finding a sixpence.

'It was nice meeting you,' she said as the woman turned to say goodbye. 'I'm Rose. May I give your son sixpence for sweets?'

The woman hesitated, then smiled. 'I'm Emily and I work at the fish and chip shop most mornings and three nights a week. Thank you – Arthur doesn't get many sweets. Say thank you to the nice lady, Arthur.'

'Thank you, Rose,' he said and smiled shyly once

more as she handed him the coin. 'You're a nice lady . . .'

Rose just smiled. Something about his voice made her wonder. It wasn't exactly East End of London, but there was something different about the way he spoke – it wasn't quite as Canadian in accent as his mother's. She had a feeling that Arthur had lived in London but didn't know why she thought that, because it wasn't likely if his mother had come over from Canada recently. Watching them walk away to deposit the paper in a waste bin, she felt wistful somehow.

'Nice lad,' Harry remarked as the mother's family disappeared from view. 'Reminded me of Davey Blake – had a bit of London in his accent, didn't he?'

'That's what I thought – but his mother is Canadian.'

'If she is his mother. They didn't look much alike, did they?'

'He called her mum twice . . .' Rose looked thoughtful. 'He didn't speak to his father.'

'Yes, he did,' Harry contradicted. 'He called him Pete. I heard him.'

'I missed that then,' Rose said. 'Do you think Pete's his mother's brother then? I thought he was his father but if he called him Pete . . .'

'I doubt it. He comes from a different class. You could hear it in his voice – got that cut-glass edge to it. I bet his family's well off. Not sure about her, though. You can't tell with foreigners.'

'Harry! She was all right.'

Harry laughed. 'No disrespect to foreigners, Rose, but you know what I mean. She's different somehow. Seemed all right, though.'

132

'Yes, she was friendly. I wonder why Arthur's so sad?'

'Was he?' Harry looked at her. 'He seemed to enjoy his supper. What made you think he was sad?'

'Just a look in his eyes,' Rose said and then laughed. 'I probably imagined it, Harry. I'm soft over kids.'

'Yeah.' He reached for her hand and squeezed it. 'We'll find a home and then we'll adopt. We can apply as soon as we get our own place – and you can give up working such long hours just as soon as you like, love.'

'I'll keep on for a while after we get settled, but do less hours,' Rose told him with a smile. 'He was a nice little lad but he has a home. We'll take a child who has nothing, Harry.'

'Aye, we shall,' he agreed. 'Do you fancy a pale ale before we get the bus back, Rose?'

'I don't mind if I do,' she agreed. 'Let's go to that pub up the road where they have a sing-song round the piano. I feel like a bit of music.'

'Right,' he said and took her paper to deposit it in the waste bin.

'We might as well have a bit of fun while we can.'

CHAPTER 14

It was better once he started school. Arthur felt shy and awkward the first couple of mornings, but after that he made a few friends to play with in the lunch break. He didn't go home to lunch as some children did who lived close by. Emily was at work and she packed him sandwiches to take in and eat, but after the first week a teacher told him he could have cooked lunches if his mother paid for them. It cost two shillings and sixpence a week, but when he told Emily she said it was a good idea.

'It's no more expensive than sandwiches and you'll have something warm inside you – and I shan't have to cook every evening.'

Arthur didn't mind the school meals, which were things like toad-in-the-hole, bacon pudding with cabbage and carrots, or shepherd's pie, and sometimes a vegetable pie with no meat. It wasn't as good as when Emily cooked for them but it was warm and filling and he liked the afters; especially jam roly-poly and treacle tart.

Arthur's friends, Jimmy and Bob stayed for lunch too

and they were always hungry and ate everything, even suet pudding, which Arthur didn't much like. He usually gave them his portion if they wanted it. Afterwards, they went into the playground and had a game of rounders or simply kicked a football about. Neither of them lived near Arthur. He would have liked them to come round to his and play on Saturday mornings but they lived on a council housing estate further out of town and Emily said it was too far to take him there and fetch him when she got home from work.

'Aunt Becky isn't getting on as she should,' Emily told him after some days had passed. 'I had thought she might be home before this but she seems very weak. I'm going to ask the doctors about her when I see them.'

'Is Pete coming this weekend?' Arthur asked her when she fetched him from school that Friday evening. 'He's nice, Mum. I like him.'

'Yes, I do too,' Emily confirmed. 'He's gone home to see his parents this week so I don't know when he'll be back. Then he has another couple of days before he reports to his base. I don't suppose we'll see much of him then.'

Arthur was sorry about that, because Emily had seemed happy when they had outings with Pete. They'd gone to the woods and to the beach, for a trip round the bay in a boat, too, as well as the cinema. They had laughed a lot, and it had been like being with a real family. Arthur had vague memories of having fun when he'd had his own family, but they didn't seem real anymore. Was there ever a time when he'd felt secure and loved? He thought there was, but it was so long ago and other memories had blocked them out. Some of them so painful that they made him cry if he thought about them – like the way his mum had changed towards him. The memory haunted him and made him uncertain of whom he might trust.

Emily said she loved him. He thought she did and he loved her but was frightened of losing her. Sometimes, when she wasn't so busy, she would talk to him, even play with him for a few minutes, but most of the time he was alone at home. So he liked school. He liked sitting in class and he'd found he was ahead in most of the lessons; in Canada he'd been a good student but only somewhere in the middle when it came to tests, but at his new school he came top several times.

'How did you learn that so quick?' Jimmy asked him one day when he'd been praised for getting all his sums right.

'I'd already done those at school in Canada,' he'd told him when it came to fractions and Jimmy was lost. 'I'll show you how I do them if you like.'

'Nah, I'd rather play football,' Jimmy said. 'I'm going to be a footballer when I grow up. My dad says I don't need a lot of learning for that – just be good at kicking a ball.'

Jimmy's dad was a deep-sea fisherman. He took his boat out in all weathers to bring back the fish the nation so desperately needed. Rationing of meat was tight and a good catch was worth a fortune, or so Jimmy said. Arthur knew it was more difficult to buy food in England than it had been in Canada because Emily grumbled about it constantly.

'I knew they had rationing here, but I never realised it would be so hard,' she told Arthur when she couldn't buy any fresh eggs and was forced to use the powdered stuff she despised. 'I can't make cakes like I used to, Arthur. And I'd love a poached egg on toast.'

'Marmalade's all right, Mum,' Arthur said, because he didn't like to see her so worried.

She ruffled his hair, making him squirm away. 'You're a good boy, Arthur. I suppose it's no worse than you were used to when you came out to Canada, but I'm accustomed to lovely fresh food. I hate it when I go to the shop and they tell me all they have is a piece of whale meat. I don't know how folk eat that – it's so oily.'

'We had it at school in a pie and I ate a bit of it but Jimmy finished mine up. He'll eat anything. He says he doesn't get much at home.'

'Poor kid,' Emily said and smiled at him. 'Never mind. I'll have our rations tomorrow and if we're lucky we might get a slice of ham each.'

'I like ham,' Arthur agreed. What he liked best about the weekends was that Emily had some time to spend with him. They'd found some jigsaw puzzles under the stairs and were doing one together on the floor in the parlour. It was fun, but then Emily had to go back to work and he hated being alone all evening. It seemed so long and he was lonely, left to amuse himself for hours on end. 'Can we go to the pictures again, Mum?'

'We'll see,' she promised vaguely. 'I don't earn much and you need some more clothes for school. It's going to be cold in a couple of months and you'll need a pair of long trousers and a couple of jumpers – perhaps an overcoat, too, if I can afford it.'

Arthur finished the jigsaw puzzle by himself that evening. He'd finished reading *Treasure Island* ages ago but there weren't any other books he wanted to read on the shelves. At school there was a library with lots of interesting books but he wasn't allowed to bring them home. He was reading *King Solomon's Mines* in class, but they wouldn't let him take it out of school. The teacher told him he should go to the local library in the town but Arthur didn't know where it was and his mother didn't either.

'I don't have time to hunt for it, Arthur,' Emily had told him. 'When Aunt Becky comes home I'll ask her where it is – and I might be able to spend more time at home then. The doctors said she'll need looking after for a long time. So perhaps I can do less hours in the shop, get someone in to help Ruby.'

Bored and restless, Arthur took his English exercise book out of his satchel and drew some lines, crossing them twice so that he had nine squares. He began to play noughts and crosses, but it wasn't much fun on his own. He drew some squiggles and then tore the page out, screwed it up and threw it at the fireplace. Why had they come to this horrible house? When it was windy it creaked upstairs and his spine prickled with fear – was there someone up there?

This evening it was calm and there wasn't a sound in the house. Arthur hardly ever saw the cat. He knew his mother fed it sometimes, but often it didn't appear for days. Emily said she couldn't spare much food for a cat and it would have to catch mice for its supper. It wasn't a friendly cat and didn't allow Arthur to stroke it, but it was company of a kind – when it came.

Arthur was hopping from one foot to the other, trying to keep busy when he heard the door knocker. He stood absolutely still for a moment – had Emily forgotten her key?

He went slowly towards the door. His mother had told him not to open it but whoever was there knocked again. Cautiously, Arthur turned the handle and opened it a little. He gave a gasp as he saw who was there and opened the door wide.

'Hello, Arthur. Is your mum home?' Pete asked, smiling at him.

'Mum's at the shop until seven and then she goes to the hospital until half-past eight. She'll be home about nine, unless she misses the bus then it will be nearer half-past.'

Pete grinned at him. 'It's nearly eight thirty now. How about I come in and wait for her?'

'Yes, please,' Arthur welcomed him in. 'We could have a cup of cocoa if you like.'

'I bought these.' Pete showed him a bag of sugar-coated buns. There were three and they looked delicious. 'We can have ours with our drink and leave the last one for Emily when she gets back.'

'Cor, lovely,' Arthur said, leading the way into the kitchen. He fetched out the cocoa tin and some mugs while Pete put the kettle on. While it boiled the two of them sat at the kitchen table and ate their buns. The pink icing was so sweet and delicious but Pete made the cocoa lovely too, whipping it up in a bowl before adding the sugar and hot milk so it was all frothy.

'Where did you learn to do that?' Arthur asked admiringly.

'At home. My mother always does it like that,' Pete said. 'Have you got a dog or any sort of pet, Arthur?'

'There's a cat that visits sometimes,' Arthur told him. 'We don't know who it belongs to but we give it milk and a few scraps. Mum says it'll catch mice if it's hungry. I'd like a dog but Mum says we can't feed it.'

'No. A lot of folk had to put their animals down at the start of the war, because they knew it would be impossible to feed them – but rabbits eat grass and lettuce leaves. You could grow the lettuce in the back garden, Arthur. Would you like to have a pet rabbit?'

Arthur looked at him in surprise. No one had ever asked him anything like that in his whole life. Emily gave him things when she could afford it but she couldn't afford to buy him pets even if she'd thought of it. With a pet to fuss and play with he wouldn't be so lonely.

'I think I would,' he said uncertainly. 'Could I keep it in the back garden?'

'You could, in a hutch,' Pete said. 'You could also have a couple of hens if you wanted. They'll eat any scraps and you might get some eggs if you're lucky and they start laying.'

'Mum would like that,' Arthur said. 'Do you think she would let me have them?'

'Why don't we ask her?' Pete said as they heard the sound of a key in the lock. Then Emily walked in. She stood looking at them for a moment and then sat down in a chair and burst into tears.

'What's wrong?' Pete asked, getting up and going to put an arm about her shoulders.

'It's Aunt Becky,' Emily gasped. 'She died this evening . . .'

'Oh no, I'm so sorry,' Pete said. He took out a clean handkerchief and handed it to her. She mopped at her cheeks, sniffing as the tears slowed. 'I don't know what to do! This house is hers and the shop. I'm not sure whether I can go on living here.'

Pete looked at her seriously. 'She knew you were living here?'

'Yes, of course. She told me she was glad I'd come and hoped I'd make my home with her – but I'm not sure who owns the house now.'

'It belonged to her?' Pete questioned and Emily nodded. 'What about the shop?'

'I think she rents the premises – but the business is hers.'

'Who's her next of kin?'

'I'm not sure. I think I might be . . .' Emily sighed wearily. 'I should have stayed in Canada – but I didn't have a home there either . . .'

'Do you know if she made a will?' Pete asked and Emily shook her head.

'We didn't talk about anything like that. I thought she'd get better and come home – they say it was a stroke, quite sudden.' She gave a little sob and then shook her head. 'I suppose I should find somewhere else to live.'

'No, not yet,' Pete told her firmly. 'It may be that it

could be yours if you're the next of kin but you won't know until you discover whether she had a will or not. I think you should stay here for the time being. You must look through her papers, see if you can find anything relevant and only move out if you're forced to leave.'

'Are you sure?' Emily faltered. She held out her hand to Arthur who went to her and held it tight.

Arthur hadn't met Aunt Becky, but he felt sorry that she'd died. It was always sad when people died. Arthur had cried when his dad died in that accident. Perhaps if Aunt Becky had come home he wouldn't be on his own so often – but she wouldn't now. He blinked hard, listening to what Pete was telling his mum.

'Yes, I'm certain you should stay here, Emily. It will take ages to settle even if you aren't the beneficiary,' Pete told her confidently. 'Why should you give up a comfortable home to live in digs if you don't have to? If you are your aunt's beneficiary, you'll have your own home, and the business, Emily. That's worth some investigation at least.'

Emily stared at him, looking a bit stunned. 'I hadn't even thought about that,' she breathed. 'If I don't find a will, what should I do?'

'Then you must go to a solicitor. You would have to prove who you are and your kinship to your aunt and I suppose they would advertise to see if there were any other claimants. All that would take time and even if it turned out there was another relation you might still get some of it.'

'Then I should stay here until things are settled?'

'Who else would look after things? You'll need

143

to arrange the funeral – and you'll need your aunt's papers for that. Have you any idea where she keeps things like that?' Pete glanced around. 'Is there a desk or anything?'

'There's a chest of drawers upstairs. I haven't looked in her bedroom, only just to dust it a couple of times.'

'She keeps some things behind the books,' Arthur said and they both turned to stare at him.

'What sort of things, Arthur?' Pete asked. 'How do you know?'

'I looked for something to read,' Arthur told them. 'There wasn't much but the books are two deep on some shelves so I took them off and I found some keys and a tin box. I-I left them there when I put the books back . . .' he faltered as he saw their faces. 'I didn't do any harm but I had nothing to read.'

Pete frowned but didn't say anything. Emily stood up and walked into the sitting room. Pete and Arthur followed.

'Where are they, Arthur?' his mother asked.

Arthur went to the bookcase and took down a row of books. Fitted into a recess at the back and flanked by more books was a square black tin box. The keys were a little further along the shelf, hidden by a dictionary. Emily picked up the box and the keys.

She looked at Pete for encouragement. 'Should I open it?'

'Yes. Of course. It may contain money and you'll need some for the funeral.'

Emily nodded, looking anxious as she inserted the key and opened the box. Lying on top of some papers was a small amount of white five-pound notes. She took them out and counted them. There were twenty. One hundred pounds.

'She must have saved that for a rainy day,' Emily said shakily. She lifted out the papers beneath. The first was a marriage certificate, the second was Aunt Becky's birth certificate, that of her husband and son came next, another folded document, and then a handwritten will.

Emily handed the will to Pete with a hand that trembled slightly. 'What does it say?'

He'd been reading the folded document. 'This is a letter of condolence. Did you know her son was killed in the Great War?'

She nodded. 'Yes, my mother told me. Aunt Becky wrote to her when he died. She was devastated, I know.'

Pete opened the envelope and read slowly and steadily through the document, then he looked at Emily and frowned. 'She has left the house and business to her niece Emily Henderson, and a few pieces of jewellery to various friends – and she has signed it, but . . .' He shook his head. 'Unfortunately, it isn't witnessed, Emily.'

'What does that mean?' she asked, looking up at him anxiously.

'It means that you'll have to go through a solicitor and apply to the courts for your inheritance. Your aunt made her wish plain enough and she doesn't mention anyone else but because the will isn't witnessed and wasn't done through a solicitor, you'll have to go through a lot of rigmarole to get the property. The solicitor will advertise to see if anyone else claims and the Crown Court has to agree that you are entitled

145

to the property. Although your aunt made a will, her failure to have it witnessed means she's intestate in the eyes of the law and the Crown Court can then claim her estate – though normally they wouldn't do so if there is a living relative.'

Emily stared at him. 'I had no idea there were laws like that,' she said. 'It isn't right when Aunt Becky obviously wanted me to have her property.'

'No, it isn't fair. Still, a good solicitor will make sure you get it – but it does take time, Emily.'

She nodded, still looking bewildered and red-eyed. 'I'm not sure how I feel . . . I just wish she'd got better and come home.'

'Yes, of course you do.' Pete smiled at her. 'I'll find you a good solicitor, Emily. I know someone in London who does this sort of thing – a friend of my father. He won't charge you anything until it's all settled.' He looked at her. 'Is there anything more in the box?'

'Yes – a post office savings book . . .' Emily opened it. 'There's five hundred pounds deposited!'

'That's better than ever,' Pete said. 'It will pay all the expenses of applying to the court and perhaps some over.' He looked thoughtful. 'You keep the notes, Emily. You might need them in the meantime; the solicitor can pay all the funeral expenses out of this money.'

'But – supposing someone else does claim?' Emily said looking at the money in her hand as if she was afraid of it. 'I've never had this much money in my hand . . . I never saw my parents' money . . . it was just a number in a bank until Ken took it for the business.'

'You've been cheated once,' Pete said. 'Your aunt meant you to have this, Emily. Keep the money and

146

we'll apply through the courts for what should be yours.'

Emily sighed. 'Yes, I shall – and thank you for helping me, Pete. I would not have known what to do without you.'

Pete nodded and sat next to her. He put his arm about her shoulders, turned her towards him and kissed her gently. 'I care about you and Arthur.' Smiling, he held out his hand to Arthur. 'We were talking about getting him a pet rabbit and some chickens – to lay eggs for you. I think you should do it, Emily. Put down roots here. I can't see that anyone else is going to come and take it away from you – so stay here, at least until the war is over.' He hesitated, then, 'If I come back in one piece, we'll talk about the future then . . .'

Emily blinked away her tears. She smiled at Arthur and ruffled his hair. He pulled away and she laughed. 'Would you like some pets in the garden? But you will have to look after them yourself.'

'Yes, please, Mum!' Arthur said. 'Pete said I could grow lettuces, too.'

'Tell you what – I'll come tomorrow and dig over a bit of the garden at the end,' Pete offered. 'I'll bring some seeds too. It's a bit late in the season but you'll get a few lettuce and some winter greens if we put them in now which will feed the rabbit and chickens; and you'll have peelings and stuff the hens will eat.'

'You can't want to spend the last day of your leave digging the garden,' Emily said but he just laughed.

'I'll be with you and the boy. You go in and tell the girl at the shop what has happened first thing and then come back. You can hire another girl to do some of your shifts now, Emily. You're the boss.'

Emily looked doubtful, but nodded. 'I think we should close the shop for a few days,' she said. 'Show some respect for my aunt. I'll give them all a holiday. I know there's enough in the till to pay them a week's holiday money.'

'That is a good idea,' Pete told her. 'You won't feel like working until after the funeral is over.'

'No, I don't,' she agreed. She turned to look at Arthur. 'Time for your bed now, love. You still have school tomorrow.'

'Let him have a day off,' Pete suggested. 'You can send a note when he goes back after the weekend, explain that his aunt died and you needed him here.'

Emily looked undecided, then smiled. 'All right – just one day won't hurt.'

Arthur kissed her goodnight and then went to Pete and offered his hand. 'Thank you for helping Emily – and for thinking of the rabbit,' he said. Pete looked at him for a moment and then pulled him into a fierce hug.

'Go on with you, young rascal,' he said. 'Upstairs to bed now. I'll see you in the morning.'

CHAPTER 15

Arthur opened the door to Pete the next morning. He'd been up early and he knew his mum had been awake half the night because he'd heard her moving about downstairs. She was still a bit red-eyed when he went down for breakfast and they ate in silence, but once Pete arrived, bringing with him not only a beautiful white rabbit, but also a hutch and wire to make a pen for the hens, as well as his gardening tools, Emily was smiling again.

The rabbit was in a box with straw inside and Pete handed it to Arthur, telling him he could take it out and let it run around on the kitchen floor. 'You can stroke it and pet it,' he told Arthur. 'The pet shop owner said it was used to that, because kids came into his shop to look at it most days.'

'What's its name?'

'It's a girl and her name is Bella – because she's beautiful.'

Pete smiled as Emily offered him a cup of tea, but shook his head. 'I'll have something later,' he told her. 'There's quite a bit of work to do if we want to get things right for your rabbit, Arthur. And the chickens, of course. I've left them in a crate in the car, or rather the truck. I borrowed it from a friend so I could bring everything I needed.'

Everything Pete needed included fence posts, rolls of chicken wire, a bag of compost, tools and various other bits and pieces. He spent most of the morning, digging and hammering in fence posts so that he had a pen the chickens and rabbit could run in. Although he warned Arthur not to let the rabbit run unsupervised as she might dig a hole and escape.

Emily called him in then and they all had cheese on toast with slices of streaky bacon on top. Pete demolished his and called it a banquet. He went back outside after a short rest, taking Arthur with him to help with the positioning of the hutch, and to show the boy how to sow lettuce seed in the little patch of vegetable garden he'd made. There were some little plants for winter greens that Pete thought might produce some food for them as well as the rabbit and chickens. He'd also brought a bag of corn which he said the chickens would like, but told Arthur to use it sparingly.

'It wasn't easy to get,' he told him with a grin. 'A friend of mine got me the hens and this from his father's farm but he sneaked it out so I don't think there will be any more. Scraps should be enough for them anyway, and they'll find some food of their own in the grass.'

'What does Bella like?' Arthur asked. He'd fetched the rabbit out and let it move around on the grass but Bella didn't seem to want to go far and was content munching a patch of long grass.'

'She will save you mowing the lawn,' Pete said, laughing at the fat rabbit who seemed content just to sit and munch. 'But she'll love lettuce leaves and carrots, too. You can buy special food from the pet shop but I doubt your mum has money for that, so stick to scraps and pick dandelions if you see them. She might like them.'

'Did you have a rabbit when you were a boy?' Emily asked, coming up with mugs of tea for the workers, who had finished their industry and were just admiring their handiwork.

'I had every pet you could imagine, rabbits, frogs – a snake once to my mother's horror – dogs, cats, and a pony. I was lucky.'

Emily nodded. Arthur hung on his every word as he told them stories of his childhood and pets. Now that the work was done, they all went inside. Arthur had tucked Bella into her cosy hutch and the chickens were exploring their run and the little shelter Pete had built them at the bottom, which had straw for them to lay their eggs, if they did.

'If they don't lay after a while, we can always eat them,' Emily said and Arthur looked at her sharply.

'You can't eat Martha, Jinny, and Sally,' he said, horrified.

'So you've named them already?' Pete smiled but he'd noticed Arthur's look. 'Don't worry, Arthur, I'm sure they'll lay some lovely eggs for you – and Emily was only joking, weren't you?'

'Yes, of course,' she said quickly, but Arthur thought she had meant it. He knew food was short, and their rations didn't always go far, but the chickens were pets,

151

a gift from Pete to him, and it made him uneasy that his mother might kill them for food.

'Well, I'd best get back and clean up a bit,' Pete said. He looked at Arthur. 'Would you mind if I took your mother out this evening? She doesn't need to go to the hospital now and it's my last free evening for a while. I know it means you'll be on your own—'

'I'll fetch Bella in with me,' Arthur said and smiled. 'I don't mind – and thank you for all you've done today.'

'It was a pleasure, son,' Pete told him. 'I enjoyed myself.'

Arthur felt a warm glow inside. Pete was nice. It was almost like having a father again.

After Pete had gone, Emily made some Spam sandwiches with pickle. There were some jam tarts left from the previous day, even though Pete had eaten three with his tea. Emily said Arthur could have the last two but he left one for her and after asking if he was sure, she ate it and smiled at him.

'If the solicitor says I'm entitled to this house and the business, would you like to stay here, Arthur? I had thought we might go back to Canada once I'd sorted things with Ken, but I'm not sure. I could sell it all and go and yet . . .'

'You like Pete, don't you?' Arthur asked and she nodded. 'He might not want to go to Canada.'

'I doubt if he would,' she agreed. 'I'm not sure that ought to be a reason to stay. Pete seems very nice but you can't always be sure about people, Arthur.'

Arthur nodded. He knew what she meant. She was still angry over what Ken had done behind her back.

'I like Pete,' he said. 'If we went to live with him when the war is over, I wouldn't mind – but if we didn't, I did like it in Canada.'

'Better than here?' Emily asked and he nodded. She looked thoughtful for a moment, then, 'Yes, I think I do, too. It is nice here, though, Arthur – we have the woods to walk in and the cliffs to look out from, which is a lovely view – and the beach is a bit stony except when the tide's out, but it's still good to go there, isn't it?'

'It's lovely when we have time together,' Arthur told her and she looked at him hard and then smiled.

'Yes, it *is* nice then,' she said. 'I'll have to go on working at the fish shop for a while, Arthur. I'm not sure how much of a profit we make after we pay wages, but, if it *is* mine, I won't be working in the evenings, but I might continue in the mornings for a while.'

'And I'm at school then and I have friends at school,' Arthur said and she nodded thoughtfully.

'Well, we'll see,' Emily said and sighed as she looked at him. 'I know it hasn't been much fun since we got here, but it will get better.'

'It was fun today,' Arthur said and her smile showed she agreed. 'I think Pete is sweet on you.'

'Is he now? And where did you get that expression?' Emily asked but her eyes had lit up. 'I do like him, Arthur – but don't get your hopes up, love. It may be just a pleasant interlude. For one thing, I'm older than he is, not much but a few years.'

'You don't look it,' Arthur said and she burst out laughing.

'Oh, Arthur,' she cried. 'Don't say things like that!

You'll get me thinking of it all being wonderful – and I have a lot of problems to work out before I can get involved with Pete or any other young man.'

Pete gave Arthur a packet of fruit gums when he came to collect Emily that evening. He looked very smart in his uniform and Emily was dressed in her best frock with a little red jacket that had pleats at the back. Arthur waved them off and then fetched Bella from her hutch. He brought her in and gave her a piece of apple he'd saved for her, watching as she nibbled contentedly, his fingers stroking her soft fur. At first, he let her wander on the floor and then he picked her up and sat down with her on his lap. He kissed her soft fur and talked to her.

'I think Emily likes Pete more than she says,' he told Bella, 'and he is fun. I wouldn't mind living with him, but it wouldn't be until after the war. I think he lives out in the countryside up north, he said, but I don't know where.'

Bella munched. She seemed quite content to be stroked.

'I don't know if we could take you and Martha and the others back to Canada,' he confided to her. 'Perhaps it would be best to stay here . . .' He nuzzled his face into her fur. She stilled for a moment but then seemed to relax, sensing he meant no harm to her. 'I've never had a pet before. I wouldn't want to leave you behind.'

Bella was quite content and Arthur laughed. He decided he would take her up to his bedroom. She didn't make much mess and he would clear it up if she did. He walked upstairs, confiding his hopes and fears to his pet and then stopped at the landing as a hissing sound startled him. The cat had appeared and had its back arched, looking at him and the rabbit in what Arthur felt was hostility.

'Go away, cat!' he said, kicking in its direction but not at it. 'Bella isn't for you.'

The cat sprang at his leg, its claws raking his bare leg above his sock, and then rushed down the stairs. Arthur let it go. It could just sit in the kitchen and wait until his mother came home. His leg was smarting where it had clawed him and he wasn't going to give it any milk.

Emily found the cat on the kitchen table when she got back. It had eaten some bread she'd left there and knocked over a jug with flowers, spilling water over the crockery and the remainder of the bread. She shooed it out of the kitchen without giving it milk. The damned thing was a nuisance, really. She'd fed it for a start, thinking it was her aunt's cat, but had since learned that it was a stray that went round a lot of the houses looking for food. She wasn't sure how it had managed to get into the house. It was a pity Arthur hadn't put it out, because now they had no bread for their breakfast the next morning and that meant a trip to the shops. Fortunately, there was one just down the road, but it didn't sell lovely crusty loaves like the one the cat had ruined.

She yawned as she cleared up the mess. She would have to tell Arthur he mustn't leave the cat in the kitchen, because they couldn't afford to waste food. Pete seemed to think that she would get her inheritance, but Emily couldn't believe she would be that lucky. Someone would probably turn up to claim a part of it, though her aunt had told her more than once that she was her only relative – and there was the handwritten will. If only it had been witnessed.

Making herself a cup of tea, Emily thought about her evening. Pete had kissed her properly for the first time and she'd known he wanted more. She did, too, but wasn't ready to trust again. First of all she had to find Ken and have it out with him. Why had he lied to her and cheated her all those months and years? It hurt to remember that she'd been such a fool, believing all his lies.

Sighing, Emily went upstairs. She peeped into Arthur's room and saw the rabbit was on his bed. He hadn't turned his light out but was sound asleep. She smiled and went to kiss him. He murmured something but didn't wake.

Emily put out his light as she left. He was a lovely child and she knew she was lucky to have him. If she got the inheritance her aunt had intended her to have, she wouldn't have to fear losing him. She was still torn between staying here, where she had a business to run and a house of her own, or returning to Canada – that was if she was allowed to stay.

A smile touched her mouth as she'd told Pete that she might be sent back at the end of her permitted stay. 'Well, you know how to make sure you can stay, don't you?' Emily had shaken her head. 'All you have to do is marry an English chap – like me.' He'd grinned at her and she'd given him a playful tap on his arm.

'You know I can't do that – I'm still married to Ken.'

'Curse him,' Pete said. 'I've told you, ditch the rat, Emily.'

'I would, but that takes time,' she said thoughtfully.

'I dare say you can get an extension to sort out your affairs here, but . . .' He'd looked at her oddly. 'I want you to stay somehow, Emily. Don't let them send you back – fight it. Arthur was born here and you had an English parent. You could get citizenship if you tried. Speak to the solicitor about it when you see him.'

'You said he'll write to me as soon as he works out what it's best for me to do regarding Aunt Becky's property?'

'Yes, definitely,' Pete replied. 'I rang him and gave him all the details so he'll go into it and then write to you.'

Emily nodded. 'So, until then, I just carry on?'

'You do – and I'll be back when they give me leave, Emily.' Pete had kissed her again then. 'You're my girl, Emily, don't forget that, because that's the way it's going to be.'

'I'm not sure I could divorce Ken here. I might have to go back to Canada to do it . . . I'll speak to the solicitor,' she'd replied and then he'd hugged her and told her that's what he'd wanted to hear.

Emily smiled as she settled down in bed and drank her tea. The future looked much brighter but she still couldn't believe it would all happen just like that. Life had a habit of kicking you in the teeth when you least expected it . . .

CHAPTER 16

Life settled down for a while after Pete returned to his base. Arthur went to school on his own now. He and Emily caught the same bus but she got off before he did and went to work. In the afternoons, he caught the bus home and his mother would be there, preparing their tea. Arthur had school dinners so it was mostly something on toast or chips, sometimes with an egg or a sausage, but on Saturdays and Sundays they had a nice cooked lunch. Emily saved all the peelings from the potatoes at the shop. She boiled them up and fed them to the chickens. So far, the hens had produced one or two eggs a day, which meant that Emily could sometimes make cakes, too.

'That was a good idea of Pete's,' she told Arthur as she gave him a bowl of potato peelings to feed the hens with, and some cabbage leaves for his rabbit. His own plants had begun to grow, but Emily said it was the wrong time of year to plant them and doubted he would get much, but she bought huge cabbages from the market and the outside leaves lasted most of the week. There were also peelings from the carrots and any other vegetables they had at the weekend.

The evenings were no longer so lonely for Arthur and he looked forward to spending them with his mother. Emily now took him to the library on Saturday afternoons after she finished work. Arthur went in with her on Saturday mornings and helped in the kitchen with peeling the potatoes. When the shop closed, he and Emily went shopping for groceries and called in at the library so that he could choose books to last him all week. Emily sometimes brought one home for herself, too.

Mostly, she just sat and listened to the wireless while she mended things or stitched a new dress or knitted a jumper for Arthur. She would talk to him about her day and he would tell her about school. Sometimes they made plans for what they would do when Emily could afford it.

'Ruby is more polite to me these days,' she remarked the week after Aunt Becky's funeral, which took place while Arthur was at school. Emily said she didn't want him to attend, because he didn't know Aunt Becky and it was better for him to be at school. It seemed that Ruby was uncertain what would happen now that her boss had died, but Emily had told her it was being sorted and she would know in good time. 'She knows I was Aunt Becky's only relative so she probably thinks I'll be her boss.'

'Do you like working there?' Arthur asked. 'Are you happy here, Mum?'

Emily had looked at him oddly. 'It's all right for now,' she said after a pause. 'What do you want to do, Arthur – if we had a choice?'

160

'Don't know . . .' He shrugged his shoulders. 'I like my school. I came top in sums this week and last but it was nice where we were before.'

'Back home in Canada?' Emily nodded. 'I'm not sure what to do when it's all settled. I could sell everything and go back. I think that might be best . . .'

'Would we have to go on a ship again?' Arthur asked. 'I get sick on ships.'

'Only for a little while,' she said and reached out to ruffle his hair but he darted out of her way. He didn't like that much but she always did it. 'I'll think about it, Arthur.' She hesitated, then, 'I might have to go up to London soon, to see the solicitor. Do you think you could manage here for a couple of days on your own?'

Arthur stared at her, dismay all over his face. 'All on my own?'

'Oh, Arthur, don't look at me like that.' Emily sighed. 'I'd come back as soon as I could. I just don't want to take you out of school so soon after you started. Besides, who would feed the chickens and Bella if you came with me?'

Arthur considered for a moment, then, 'The lady over the road – the one with the posh house?'

Emily laughed and shook her head. 'I doubt it, Arthur. I don't think she's forgiven you yet.' Arthur blushed and looked down. 'I explained it wasn't your fault – and her toilet roll is under that lady with the crinoline skirt.'

'That's a daft place to put it,' Arthur said. 'If I'd known it was there, I wouldn't have used the towel to mop up.'

'I know – and I'm not blaming you,' she said

smiling. 'I just don't think she would want to feed your pets. When you have pets, you have to look after them, Arthur. You don't want them to die of neglect.'

He shook his head. No, he didn't want them to die, but he didn't like the idea of being left on his own. 'I might get hungry on my own . . .' he said weakly.

'You can find a piece of cake or make yourself a sandwich,' Emily said. 'I'd leave plenty of food for you. You know where the fish shop is and I'd give you money to buy chips – besides, you have a school lunch; you wouldn't starve.'

Arthur thought about the range in the kitchen. It kept the house from going cold, its warmth penetrating through the ceiling into the bedrooms so they were never freezing even as the weather turned much colder. It was nearly November. He wasn't sure he could keep it going. Yes, he struggled to bring in a scuttle of coke for his mother in the mornings and another at night – but Pete had had to show her how to bank it up and rake it out in the mornings. It was different from the one she'd used at home in Canada.

'I don't like being alone at night,' he said in a low voice. He was frightened of being alone in the dark but felt that made him a coward and was ashamed.

'You would be perfectly safe here,' Emily began and then sighed. 'I suppose I could take you with me. The lady next door would come round and feed the chickens and Bella.'

His face lit up and he ran to hug her. 'I'd work harder at school to make up my lessons!'

Emily kissed the top of his head. 'Well, we'll see. I haven't heard from the solicitor yet but I think I may have to go and sign something, and I may be able to kill two birds with one stone.' Arthur looked up at her inquiringly. 'Ken is in London – or stationed not far away. I'm going to write to him and suggest we meet. He owes me an explanation and a whole lot more . . .'

Arthur lay in bed thinking about what his mother had told him. He hoped she wouldn't let Ken come back to live with them; he'd made Emily so unhappy, and it was his fault they'd had to leave their home and come here. He'd told Emily he liked it all right here, and his school was nice, but he didn't like where they lived as much as the light and airy house they'd had in Canada. This house had small windows and was dark most of the time, and it creaked when the wind got in the eaves. Sometimes, when Emily went out in the evenings to work as she still did three times a week, he got frightened of the noises from upstairs. He'd shut Aunt Becky's window so the cat didn't come in that way now and they hadn't seen it for a while. Arthur didn't trust that cat around his pets.

He wished that Pete hadn't had to go back to fighting the enemy. It had been nice having him visit and Emily had smiled a lot. She wasn't as unhappy as she had been when they left Canada, but she still looked worried. She'd told him that if the solicitor said she wasn't entitled to live here they would have to look for rooms.

'I don't think I could afford to rent a house,' she'd said, more to herself than him. Then she'd looked all cross again and he'd heard her cursing Ken. He didn't think she liked him very much now so perhaps she would tell him to stay away from them.

Arthur's cheek was damp as he finally fell asleep. Life was so uncertain and he sometimes longed for the kind of homes his friends at school had. They seemed to be so sure of life and their place in it while he wasn't sure of anything anymore.

The letters came three weeks later. Two of them waiting on the mat when Arthur and Emily got in. His mother had fetched him from school for once and they'd gone to a shop to buy him a new pair of shoes.

'Your old ones aren't worth repairing,' Emily said. 'Besides, you've grown and I think they're pinching your toes.' Arthur hadn't complained of the discomfort; shoes cost money and Emily still didn't have much. She only took the wage she'd earned from the beginning and banked the rest of the takings after the expenses were met. It wasn't her money yet and she was very particular about writing it all down in a book.

When Emily saw the letters lying there, she pounced on them with glee and tore the first open, reading the contents as she continued into the kitchen. Then she turned to Arthur with a smile on her face.

'Pete was right,' she said, sounding excited. 'This is from the solicitor. Mr Baxter thinks I shall almost certainly get it all. He has to advertise for a few months but if no one comes forward in that time he will apply to have me named as Aunt Becky's heir – and he says that he can arrange for an extension on my time here because of the legal necessity for me to sign papers when the time comes.'

'So you don't have to go up to London yet then?' Arthur asked hopefully.

'No, not to sign anything, but . . .' Emily had opened the second letter and took a deep breath as she read it. 'This is from Ken and he wants to meet in London – this weekend.' She looked at Arthur, a slightly pleading expression in her eyes. 'I can't take you with me. I need to have it out with him, Arthur. I shan't be away all night. I'll catch the early train and be home by nine at the latest. You can manage on your own for one day, surely?'

Arthur's mouth felt dry. He wanted to shake his head and scream at her, 'You promised! You promised!' but he knew it wouldn't help him. He could see that she'd gone off into one of her deep moods and wasn't listening. She was just talking at him, the way she had done when she was so upset at having to give up her house in Canada.

It was that rotten Ken again, upsetting her. Arthur wished he hadn't written to her. Why did she have to go to London to meet him? Why couldn't he come here?

He must have spoken aloud, because Emily looked at him. 'I don't want him to come here, Arthur. If he heard about Aunt Becky's house he'd be after it. He stole from me once before and I don't intend he should do it again.' A hard expression came into her eyes. 'I just want the chance to tell him exactly what I think of him.' She reached out to ruffle Arthur's hair and smiled. 'Are those shoes more comfortable, darling?' He nodded. 'That's good. I thought we might have some nice ham with chips tonight – if you'd like that?'

'Yes, please, Mum,' Arthur said and she bent to hug

him. He buried his face in her dress, holding back the tears. New shoes and the promise of a nice tea were good but they didn't make up for a broken promise.

Arthur swallowed his fear and held back his tears. He wasn't a coward and he didn't want to cry again, but Saturdays were special. Usually they did something nice in the afternoon, like changing the library books and perhaps having an ice cream in Lyons' Corner House. This Saturday he would be alone from early in the morning to late at night . . .

'Why don't you go and fetch Bella in?' his mother asked as she started to prepare their meal.

Arthur nodded and went out into the garden. What he saw there made him scream in terror and run back into the house.

'I am so sorry, Arthur,' Emily said, stroking his hair as he sobbed into her shoulder. She held him on her lap, arms around him, hugging him as the horror of seeing his pet rabbit lying on the lawn with its throat bitten out and blood all over its white fur. 'I don't know how Bella got out of her hutch. Are you sure you latched it securely before you went to school?'

Arthur nodded vigorously but didn't speak. She wasn't sure whether he was traumatised or just hurt and angry, so she stroked his shoulders and kissed the top of his head. He was still a young boy and to see something as vicious as that was horrible for him. She'd felt squeamish herself as she'd picked the dead rabbit up and placed it in the hutch. The fastening was just a loop latch with a piece of wood pushed through it. Secure enough, it seemed, and yet if it hadn't been pushed all the way through it might have fallen out; it was lying on the grass.

Surely no one had come into the garden and done such a nasty thing? Emily reviewed her neighbours in her mind and dismissed the idea – it must have been an animal of some kind.

'Do you think a fox got in?' she asked aloud and then cursed herself as Arthur stiffened in her arms.

'It was the cat,' he stated in a muffled voice and then raised his head and looked at her. 'That nasty cat – it hissed and scratched me the first time I took Bella upstairs. I shut the window in Aunt Becky's room so it couldn't get in—' He broke off on a sob. 'Why did it do it, Mum?'

'I don't know,' Emily replied but she'd seen evidence that whatever had killed the rabbit had eaten some of the flesh from its throat. However, she didn't want to tell Arthur that. 'Do you want to bury Bella in the garden? I've got a shoe box she can go in . . .'

Arthur wiped his cheeks with his fist. 'Yes, please, Mum,' he said in a whisper she could scarcely hear. 'We can say a prayer for her.'

'Yes, my darling, we will,' she said softly.

As she released him and prepared for the rabbit's burial, Emily knew she couldn't go away that weekend and leave him here alone, not now – not with that awful sight so fresh in his mind. She would have to take him to London with her. Ken had told her not to, but she'd find somewhere to leave Arthur, just for an hour or so while she told that wretched man what she thought of him.

CHAPTER 17

The train station in London was crowded and smelly when Arthur and Emily arrived at Charing Cross. She looked around and saw there were a lot of men in uniform saying goodbye to sweethearts and wives. It was eleven thirty in the morning and Emily had arranged to meet Ken at two thirty that afternoon.

'Are you hungry?' she asked Arthur and he nodded vigorously. 'I think there's a Lyons' Corner House somewhere on the Strand. Shall we go there and have something to eat?' It was where she was meant to meet Ken later. Emily still wasn't sure where she could leave her son while she met the man she now thought of as her former husband, had made up her mind to tell him she wanted a divorce.

Arthur nodded vigorously. He clung to her hand as they emerged into the busy street. She entwined her fingers with his, squeezing gently, and he looked up and smiled. Emily's heart turned over.

'When I meet Ken, do you think you could go for a walk round, look in shops and things? Then find your way back to the café?'

Arthur hesitated and then nodded. Emily smiled. She knew he was a bit nervous in a strange place but he was grown up now; he went to school on the bus by himself and he walked by the sea sometimes until they met after she finished work on Saturdays. He would be fine on his own for a while. True, it was a bit chilly but he could find a bus shelter to sit in if he was cold. She'd thought she might find a hotel room and leave him there for an hour or so but they were all expensive in this part of London, or those she'd checked on were.

'I'll walk with you for a bit when we've had our food,' she promised. 'You can always ask someone if you get lost, Arthur. Just ask for the Lyons' Corner House on the Strand. Anyone will tell you.'

Arthur nodded again, but didn't speak. Emily held his hand and walked determinedly in the direction of the famous restaurant. It wasn't full because the busy lunch hour hadn't yet started. They found a seat, ordered a pot of tea, an orange squash, and tomatoes on toast for two. Also, an ice cream for Arthur to follow.

The Nippy smiled at them and swiftly wrote their order on her pad. All the waitresses were called Nippies and were very smart in their black-and-white uniforms, which were more modern these days, the girls now permitted to bob their hair, and they were all chirpy young things, smiling and rushing around so efficiently. The service was the same in every Lyons' restaurant and the girl was soon back with their tea and the toast followed almost instantly.

'It's nice here,' Emily observed looking round her. 'You'll find this easily enough, Arthur – won't you?'

'Why can't I come with you when you meet Ken?' he asked looking at her anxiously.

'Because it might not be very pleasant and he told me not to bring you,' Emily replied. 'He's going to be very angry when I've finished with him, Arthur.'

Arthur bit his lip and nodded. Emily ignored the pleading in his eyes. She understood he might be a bit nervous on his own in a strange city but he'd been born in London so he ought not to be too frightened. Perhaps she would have done better to leave him at home, but he'd been so distressed over the brutal slaughter of his pet rabbit.

'I shan't be long,' she told him now. 'I'll give you some money and if you want you can go in a café and buy a drink – or perhaps the Zoo.' Emily had no idea where the Zoo was or if it was open. 'I'm not sure if that is open but you might find a museum or something.'

'I'll just walk around unless it rains and then I'll find somewhere to shelter.'

'Yes, and before you know it, I'll be waiting for you outside this restaurant. You won't forget where to come, Arthur?'

'No, Mum. I'm not a baby,' he said and smiled suddenly.

'Of course you aren't,' she replied. 'You go to school on your own and come back on the bus so you'll be fine, won't you?'

They'd wandered around for a while after they'd eaten, admiring the imposing buildings, and learning the place names. Arthur knew the way back to Lyons' better than she did. He was a quick, intelligent boy and his reading was very good. She felt better about leaving him on the streets when the time came to meet Ken.

'Now this is for you,' Emily pressed a half crown into his hand. 'Don't lose it, love, and don't spend it unless you want to sit down and have a drink – but it's yours. You can spend it when we get home or save it in your box – but if you need anything, you've got it.'

'Thanks, Mum.' Arthur's smile lit up his face and made her feel happy. It was a lot of money to give a boy of his age, but she didn't often give him pocket money; she didn't have much to spare. There was Aunt Becky's hundred pounds, which she'd tucked away safely, but she didn't feel right about spending it yet, whatever Pete said about it being hers. However, she felt better knowing Arthur had some money in his pocket. 'I'll meet you back here by a quarter to four at the latest.'

'Yes, my love,' she said. 'I shall be waiting for you.'

She bent to kiss the top of his head and then walked away, crossed the busy road and then turned to smile at Arthur. She waved her hand and went into the restaurant. Looking round, she saw that a man in uniform was staring at her and her heart jerked as she saw Ken. He looked smart and attractive in his blue-grey uniform and she remembered why she'd fallen in love with him in the first place. He could be charming when he chose and he was smiling at her now. He stood up as she approached and pulled out a chair for her.

'You're looking very well, Emily,' he began but she'd remembered now and was angry.

'No thanks to you,' she replied sharply. 'I think you've got a lot of explaining to do, Ken.'

'I know I owe you an apology. I should have told you the business wasn't doing well.'

Emily shot him a look of scorn as she sat down. 'Do you think I'm stupid enough to believe your lies – after what you did?' He looked shocked and then slightly uncertain. 'Oh yes, I know. I know about the gambling – and her!'

'I know I was foolish and let the debts get out of hand but it wasn't all gambling, Emily. The business started to fail and I tried to win enough money to prop it up but I just got in too deep . . .' He didn't mention the woman; he must have known that nothing would excuse his cheating.

He was lying and nervous. She could see a fine line of sweat on his upper lip and his eyes wouldn't meet hers. His hands were restless, fiddling with knives and spoons on the table as she stared at him, waiting for an explanation.

'What makes you think there was another woman?' he asked at last.

'She sent you a letter.' Emily reached into her purse and took it out, handing it to him. She saw the flush rise up his throat and into his face as he refused to take it and felt sick as she replaced it in her bag. What kind of a fool was she to have been so blind all those years?

'She never meant anything to me . . .' he excused himself weakly.

'That only makes it worse,' Emily said coldly. 'Did you ever love me – or did you just see a trusting little fool you could use? How do you intend to pay back the money you had from me?'

Ken looked at her then. 'I don't. I can't – and it

was invested in the business, Emily. Whatever is left is yours.'

'That means I get nothing,' she said. 'The bank took everything except what was in my own name – and that was little enough. I want a divorce, Ken. I have plenty of evidence. I've had enough of your lies. I hope you won't contest it?'

He was silent for a moment, then, 'No, you can't have your divorce.' He smiled at her, turning on the charm that had so often won her in the past. 'We can make it work, Emily. I'll do better next time, I promise – and with what your aunt left you, we can start again once this war is over . . .'

'What do you mean?' Emily glared at him. How could he possibly know Aunt Becky had left her anything?

'Well, you always said you were her only relative and she had her own business. Who else would she leave it to?' He gave a little shrug, as if it were the most natural thing in the world to assume she would get her aunt's property.'

'She left me nothing, so don't get your hopes up,' Emily retorted. She was furious as she understood why he'd agreed to meet her. Somehow, he'd learned of Aunt Becky's death – well, she'd advertised the funeral to let her aunt's friends know.

'Come on, Emily. I wasn't born yesterday,' Ken said with a nasty little twist of his mouth as he saw her reaction. 'I'm your husband so you owe me some of it. I'm entitled to half at least. A solicitor will tell you that.'

'Over my dead body!' she said.

Emily rose to her feet. He put a hand out towards her. 'Won't you at least stay for a cup of tea? We can talk about it . . .'

Her face registered disgust. 'No. I've said what I came to say – or most of it. You've behaved badly, Ken. I couldn't believe what a rotten trick you'd served me, but now I'm over you. I just don't want to ever see you again.'

She got up and walked away, leaving him staring after her. She was seething inside and stood in the street for a moment seeing nothing. Then she looked about her, hoping to catch sight of Arthur but he'd wandered off somewhere. Emily cursed herself for not telling him to wait outside. She hadn't realised she would get it all out so quickly and she'd told Arthur to come back by a quarter to four so there was almost an hour to wait.

Tutting to herself, she walked away. She would go window shopping for a while and then return and meet her son. He would be anxious and probably be back here by three thirty. Turning in the direction of Leicester Square, she walked, lost in thought.

Arthur wandered aimlessly for a few minutes, staring up at the imposing buildings all around him. He'd never seen anything as impressive in his young life; it looked to him as if people lived in palaces here, but the roads were congested with all kinds of traffic and it was so noisy. In that moment he longed for the peace of the wild places he'd visited while living in Canada, where the only sounds were of rushing water or a bird's song.

His earlier memories of London were nothing like this long, completely overwhelming street. Arthur could vaguely remember the back-to-back terraces, the dirty little alleys and the piles of rubbish lying in the gutters around his parents' home. His mother hadn't liked him playing in the street, but he thought he'd been happy kicking a football around with his friends and for a moment wished he was there again, but then he remembered the cool freshness of the air as he paddled in the clear waters of a lake and changed his mind.

He looked at a clock in a tall building with a spire and saw it was only fifteen minutes after three. That meant he had half an hour to wait before he met his mother. Wandering further along the Strand he saw posters for a musical show and looked at the smiling faces depicted.

Were people ever that happy? he wondered. Arthur wasn't happy. He was uncertain about his Emily-mum. Sometimes he believed she loved him but at others he thought she could easily forget him, just the way his first mum had. He felt a coldness in the pit of his stomach. Supposing she wasn't there when she'd said she would be?

London was a frightening place to be if you were nine years old and had just half a crown in your pocket. Feeling sudden fear he retraced his steps towards the corner where he'd left her, a sickening thud in his ears, his breath coming faster in great gulps as his fear mounted.

'Arthur!' Hearing her voice, he spun round and saw her emerging from a shop with some bags in her hand. 'Oh, I'm glad I've found you, darling,' she said. 'We can catch an earlier train if we hurry.'

He ran to her and she caught his hand as they

176

turned towards the station, their hurrying feet making a little clipping noise. Arthur laughed; his foolish fears forgotten. She hadn't gone off without him after all . . .

'I've told Ken I wanted a divorce,' Emily said as they sat on the train going south. 'He admitted what he'd done but he wasn't helpful and tried to persuade me to take him back but I shan't. I shall speak to the solicitor about a divorce and so we'll be well rid of him.'

Arthur nodded, looking at her thoughtfully. 'What shall we do now, Mum? Will you go back to Canada when you get your inheritance?'

She hesitated, then, 'I'm not sure, Arthur. I know you liked it there but it's nice where we live, isn't it?'

'Sort of,' he agreed. 'I like it when we go to the beach and school is all right . . .' He didn't voice the but that was in his mind. The house they lived in was better than anything he'd known in his early childhood, but . . . he didn't like it when he was there alone, because it was dark and dreary.

'It is different,' Emily agreed. 'I think it will do for the time being, Arthur. We've got Christmas to look forward to now and they do say this horrid war may be over in a few months so perhaps things will change for the better then.' She smiled at him, wanting to change the subject. 'I finished my business sooner than I'd expected so I went shopping for surprises for Christmas.'

Arthur smiled back. He liked it when his mother was happy. Perhaps it would be better now.

'Is Pete coming home for Christmas?' he asked and Emily laughed.

'I hope he'll get leave. He promised to visit if he does.'

Arthur nodded. If Pete came to visit it would be all right. 'You should ask him to stay with us for Christmas,' he said and saw a faint blush in his mother's cheeks.

'Yes, I might just do that,' she told him. 'It will be better now, Arthur. Once the shop is mine, I can hire another girl and I shan't have to work in the evenings and one day we might go somewhere else to live. Yorkshire perhaps . . .'

'If you marry Pete?' Arthur asked and saw her blush even deeper.

'He hasn't asked me yet,' she said and laughed.

'But he will,' Arthur said and smiled as her eyes lit up. It was what she was hoping and Arthur thought it would be nice because then they could be happy again.

He began to imagine a future with Pete as his dad. They would have dogs and cats and perhaps live in the countryside away from dark houses and cats that murdered his pets.

CHAPTER 18

'What do you think about it then?' Harry asked as they looked round the house they'd come to see. 'Will it do, Rose?'

The three-bedroomed semi-detached house had been built about thirty years previously; it had high ceilings that had cracked a bit but the rooms were light and airy, wall-papered with an embossed paper that had been painted over with emulsion, probably because the plaster had cracked on the walls, too. The window frames had peeling paint and the kitchen was just a stained sink with a wooden drainer. They would need to buy a gas cooker and the sink looked a danger to health. However, there was a perfectly good inside toilet with a washbasin, though no bathroom.

Rose considered for a moment, then, 'I wouldn't want to live here for the rest of my life, but if we replaced that sink, put a bit of fresh lino down, and brought our own stuff from London, we could make it comfortable.'

'That's what I thought,' Harry agreed. 'We'll only be here for a few years, Rose. I wouldn't buy it but the rent is reasonable for this size house.' He glanced around the kitchen. 'I'll help paint this – and I can replace that sink myself. No point in asking the landlord. He'd say yes to get us in and then we'd still be waiting in a year's time.'

Rose nodded. It wasn't as nice as Harry's own house in London, but she'd lived in worse when she was married to Reg. She smiled up at him. 'I reckon it will do for now, Harry.'

'We'll soon have it looking spick and span, love – and it's the best we've seen so far. We're a short bus ride from the factory and it isn't far into Hastings.' He looked at her for confirmation. It's situation between the two was, in truth, the only thing going for it, but with a bit of elbow grease it could become a home. 'So I'll tell him we'll have it, then?'

'Yeah, go on,' Rose agreed. 'When do you think we can move in?'

'This weekend. I've got a day off Sunday so I can get started on that sink and you can buy some paint on Saturday and we'll get the kitchen cleaned up. Then we'll arrange for the furniture to be brought down in a couple of weeks – give us time to do whatever we need to make it fresh and clean.'

'It's not that bad, really,' Rose told him. 'I think it's just tired – and the plasterwork isn't good, but we can fill the cracks and paint over it and they won't come back for a while.'

'I might find someone to skim the ceilings,' Harry replied. 'One of the men at work used to do it. I'll ask if he feels like earning a few bob on his day off.'

'We'll have to measure up for the curtains,' Rose

said. 'I reckon I've got some packed away that might fit the back windows but I'll need new for the front.'

'You do what you want, Rose,' Harry said. 'We've got a bit saved so don't worry about a few pounds.'

She nodded and smiled. Harry was a generous man. He treated her as if she was truly his wife and had told her that everything he had was hers. Rose reckoned she'd been lucky he'd taken a shine to her. When she thought back to the years she'd suffered at the hands of a careless, selfish husband, she wondered that she'd been fool enough to put up with it. Harry had shown her how good life could be.

She scarcely ever allowed herself to give Reg more than a passing thought these days. Once upon a time she would have felt she owed him some loyalty, but not anymore. He'd forfeited her respect when he'd beaten her and left her to die on the pavement. It was thanks to the hospital and to Harry that she was still here.

Looking round her once more, Rose felt a tingle of excitement as she began to plan the colours she would use, to bring warmth and comfort to this rather soulless house.

'We'll be in for Christmas,' she told him happily. 'That means we can have a Christmas tree – and our own special dinner.' She would put some trimmings up and buy cards to send to her sons, and her grandchild, giving them this address. Perhaps they might bring her grandson to see her.

'Can't be too soon for me,' Harry agreed. 'I'm fed up with half-cooked breakfasts and burned toast.'

Rose laughed. 'I know you hate runny eggs and I do too when they're like they were this morning; the white wasn't cooked. Horrible. Waste of good eggs. When I think how nice they would've been fried or scrambled I could weep.'

'Aye, I've never been one for a boiled egg,' Harry admitted, 'but when the white isn't cooked . . .' He made a face at her and then laughed. 'I didn't marry you for your cooking, Rose, but you're a good one – and a king to our landlady.'

Rose didn't mind working at the factory. She enjoyed the laughter and chatter at break times when everyone relaxed for a while, but the work they did was demanding and could be dangerous if just one person on the line was careless. It meant Rose was constantly alert, monitoring the line, making sure that everyone did what they should.

In the evenings she liked to relax with Harry. They mostly went for a drink at the local pub, though there wasn't always any beer to be had. Like everything else it was in short supply, but the company was cheerful and they sometimes had a sing-song round the piano. At other times, they settled for a cup of tea and a sandwich rather than face the tasteless food their landlady served up each night. Rose was looking forward to getting their ration books back so she could do her own shopping. Even with all the shortages, she knew she could serve up better meals than they'd been getting recently.

She had started to make a list of all the stuff she needed to make her home comfortable. In her belongings stored in a warehouse just outside London, she had an old-fashioned sewing machine. Once their possessions were delivered, Rose intended to take a few days off to make her curtains and finish whatever decorating was left by then. It was going to be a busy few weeks, because at the moment they'd been asked to work extra hours to get the orders out that the army desperately needed to continue the fight.

Rose didn't often bother to read the newspaper reports of the war, but she sometimes listened on Harry's wireless, though she preferred to listen to Henry Hall or concert music. She knew that the Allies had made good progress in their invasion of Italy and that some British ships had been sunk or damaged off the coast of Brittany, but she was more interested in what happened closer to home. Towns and cities in Britain were still being bombed, despite the heavy raids on Berlin by the Allied forces. It all seemed such a waste of life to her. She didn't hate the Germans the way some people did – it was that ruddy Hitler and his cronies who were causing all the trouble in Harry's opinion and she agreed with him. If someone could just get rid of him it could be all over in a trice – at least, that was what most folks thought.

It would be nice to get back to normal life, she thought. To be able to buy what you fancied for supper rather than what you could get. It wasn't easy to buy new stuff these days and Rose was glad she had her own furniture safely stored away. She'd been able to buy some of the paint she'd needed but there wasn't much choice, just cream, yellow, a pale blue, and whitewash for the ceilings.

'It's the war, missus,' the hardware shop assistant had told her. 'We're lucky to have anything to offer you. They want the factories for more important stuff these days.'

Rose had smiled and nodded. She, of all people, knew that, but she wasn't going to tell him she worked at the munitions factory.

'I tell you what I have got though,' the man had said suddenly. 'We've got a lot of wallpaper in stock from before the war. Not many folk are bothering about decorating right now but I've got some you might like.'

'Yes, I'd like to see it,' Rose had replied and he went through into his back room and brought out a roll of cream paper with a Regency stripe in green and little gold leaves between the stripes. 'That's pretty – how much have you got?'

'I reckon there's twenty rolls left of this – and there's a rose-patterned one but I thought you'd like this best.'

'I do,' Rose had confirmed. 'I think I'm going to need at least a dozen rolls but I'll reserve it all please. I might have enough to do one of the bedrooms as well.'

He'd looked pleased. Rose had paid him and left, carrying as much as she could manage. Harry would fetch the rest of her purchases on Saturday evening after he left work. She had enough materials to start decorating that Friday evening and the prospect pleased her. She and Harry would soon have the place looking good.

The new sink and draining board were in place and the tap was working. Rose had arranged for a new cooker to be installed that Saturday morning and she'd bought a kettle. She lit one of the gas rings and put it on to boil so they could have a cup of tea. As yet they had no chairs so they sat on the stairs to drink it.

'You've got yellow paint on your nose,' Harry told her, but the look in his eyes was gentle and caressing.

'You've got a black mark on yours,' she retaliated and took out her hanky to rub it off. Harry caught her hand and kissed it.

'Enjoying yourself?' he asked and she nodded.

'Not as much as I shall when we move in,' she said. 'Did you ring the warehouse, Harry?'

'Yes, I did – forgot to tell you, sorry,' he apologised. 'The bloke said they had a bit of fire damage last month. He thinks our stuff is all right, but we'll need to go up and show him the paperwork because a lot of theirs was lost in the blaze.'

'I hope we didn't lose much,' Rose said. 'Are they insured for loss in a fire, Harry?'

'Not sure. Normally they would be but you can't insure against bomb damage. Anyway, you won't know until you go, Rose. It will have to be you – because I can't get away.'

'Oh, well, I can take a day off next week,' Rose said thoughtfully. 'I don't mind, Harry. I might pop into London and see a couple of friends.'

He inclined his head in agreement. 'That's what I thought, love. You do that and if you discover we've lost stuff, you might find something in Joe's – that's if he's still there.' Rose looked at him questioningly. 'He runs that second-hand place down the Commercial Road.'

'Oh yes, I remember.' She sounded doubtful. 'We don't want junk, Harry.'

'No, certainly not, but he sometimes had a few nice bits – Georgian, he said they were, and you won't buy anything new that's good at the moment. That utility stuff isn't my kind of thing – too basic for my liking.'

'I agree,' Rose replied with a frown. 'We had some nice things, Harry – did you buy any of them from Joe's?'

'That gate-legged table came from him, and the Windsor chairs we had in the kitchen. Oh, and the pair of little tables – he called them wine tables. A lot of it was my grandfather's stuff – the oak dresser and the kitchen table, as well as the horse brasses and the wall clock.'

'I do hope they haven't been fire-damaged,' Rose said. 'I chose that firm because they were out of London, but they've let us down.'

'I don't suppose it was their fault,' Harry said cheerfully. 'Fire can start anywhere – besides, it's only things. If the lot has gone, we'll find something different.'

'Yes, you're right,' Rose agreed. 'I'll go up next week then and see what I can sort out.'

The caretaker looked at Rose's paperwork carefully and his frown disappeared. 'That's fine, Mrs Smith. Nothing of yours has been damaged – the fire didn't get that far. Our firemen are wonderful – the way they coped during the Blitz was miraculous.'

'So everything is as it should be?' Rose asked and felt relieved as he nodded. 'So when can you deliver it for us?'

'Next weekend,' he told her after checking his notes.

'Our Keith does the delivery but he works as a hospital porter Monday to Friday; it's his bit for the war. He's strong enough but the army wouldn't have him because of his flat feet. I'll send him and the boy – Jake is fifteen but he's strong.' He gave her an apologetic look. 'We don't have much manpower these days. Most of the staff joined up and we're down to older blokes like me, who served in the last war and aren't fit to be called up, or young lads who can't join yet.'

'I know how it is,' Rose said. 'Where I work it's just the same – women and older men.'

He smiled, pleased that she hadn't raised objections. 'Most folk put their stuff in for the duration,' he remarked as he asked Rose to sign his release form. 'Are you settling down there, Mrs Smith?'

'I'm not sure yet,' she said. 'We've found a place to live. We were in lodgings for a while, but now we've got a house.'

He nodded and she paid the bill for storage and the delivery and left, feeling relieved. She walked to the station and caught the next train into Liverpool Street Station. From there she would take a bus. She wanted to walk by their house and see if the tenants were keeping the windows clean and then she would visit a couple of people before she made her way home.

Rose visited a couple of friends in what was left of Silver Terrace. She noticed that the rubble had been cleared and when she spoke to Joyce Green, who lived right at the end, the only bit that Hitler's bombs had missed, she asked if they were going to rebuild the terraces that had once been there.

'Dunno,' Joyce said with a shrug. 'Can't see they would bother yet – bloody Hitler might knock 'em down again.'

'Yeah, he might,' Rose agreed. 'Still, I reckon things are improvin' from what the papers say.'

'Maybe . . .' Joyce looked at her oddly. 'How are yer gettin' on wherever yer are these days?'

'Oh, we're all right – busy, you know.'

'Still with that Harry, then?'

'Yes.' Rose looked at her. 'Why – what's on your mind, Joyce?'

'I just wondered . . . this came for yer . . .' She handed Rose a rather grubby envelope. 'Dunno why they keep deliverin' letters to Mrs Parker down this lane. You'd think they'd know better.'

'You know what things are like,' Rose said casually and pocketed the envelope. She'd glanced at the writing and recognised it at once and her heart was racing. 'Thanks for takin' it in for me, Joyce. Maisie used to, but she moved away.'

'That's right – and the new folks don't know yer. I told postie I'd give it to yer, Rose. I hope it ain't bad news? Yer look as white as a sheet.'

'Do I?' Rose shook her head, taking a mental hold on her nerves. 'Must be me age, Joyce. Or the London air.'

'Yeah – or somethin' . . .' Joyce gave her a sly look and Rose knew then that she'd opened the letter and stuck it back down. She knew who it was from. 'I heard yer got married in a rush afore yer left London.'

'I had a telegram to say Reg was dead and we'd parted for good a while back so I thought I might as well get wed.'

'Telegram, was it?' Joyce said, giving Rose a queer smile. 'Well, I reckon it takes all sorts. Whereabouts did yer say yer were livin' now?'

'I didn't,' Rose told her. 'We're not allowed – it's a secret location.'

'Yeah? Well, it would be . . .'

Rose put down her cup after sipping it twice. 'Well, I'd better go. I'll see you, Joyce – thanks for the letter.'

'No trouble,' she replied, then, 'I hope things turn out all right for yer, Rose.'

Rose nodded and left. She was conscious of the other woman watching her all the way down the road. Only when she was sitting on a bus heading for the railway station did she look at her letter. It was Reg's writing and it had been posted in London three months ago – so after she married Harry – and it had been opened!

She opened it and read the few lines Reg had scrawled.

Yer a bitch, Rose Parker. I know wot yer done and I'll make yer pay.

It wasn't signed but she knew it was Reg. Her heart raced wildly and for a moment she was panic-stricken. Reg was alive and he'd heard about her marriage to Harry. She was a bigamist and could go to prison for it!

Rose couldn't breathe. She felt overwhelmed with guilt and fear and her vision blurred as she stared from the bus window seeing nothing.

'Charing Cross . . .' The conductor touched her shoulder. 'Here, you all right, missus?'

Rose stared up at her blindly. 'What? Oh, sorry . . .'

She got up hurriedly and left the bus. It was a while

before her train was due so she found a café and bought herself a cup of tea. Her hands were shaking as she sat down to drink it, a loud ringing in her ears. Reg had discovered that she'd married Harry. He was going to make her pay . . . She felt sick and anxious, but as she drank her tea the panic began to recede. Reg would have to find them first – but would he be crafty enough to set the law on them?

Rose knew they'd taken a risk when they married. She'd been unsure but it had felt nice to wear Harry's ring on her finger and pretend that Reg had simply faded away, never to return.

Would Joyce talk to others about that letter? Rose was certain she knew what was inside it. Had Reg asked about her when he returned to London to find the factory gone? Who else had seen him and knew that the telegram had been a lie? She'd been feeling so much happier, setting up in their new home, but it could all come tumbling down about her ears.

Rose took a deep breath. She mustn't let herself worry for nothing. Reg hadn't signed the letter. Joyce couldn't know for sure that it was from him, because she wouldn't know his scrawl. She might think it, but she had no proof – and there was still a war going on. The authorities had too much to worry about to chase after a woman who might or might not be a bigamist. Who knew what might happen in the future?

Harry frowned when he looked at the brief letter. 'We always knew it could happen, Rose,' he said calmly. 'We'll just stick to our story if the cops come after us –

but don't worry about Reg. If he dares to show his face here, I'll handle him.'

'It fair took the wind out of my sails,' Rose told him. 'It ain't Reg I'm so worried about, Harry. It's what they'd do to me if the coppers arrested me. I'd go to prison for bigamy.'

'No, you won't,' Harry said. 'I won't let anything bad happen to you, love.' He took her hands and kissed her. 'This is my fault. I shouldn't have persuaded you to do it, Rose. I'm sorry if it upsets you.'

'I'm all right now,' she answered stoutly. 'It was just getting that letter – it was a shock, Harry. I thought Reg would stay well away from London.'

'So he should if he knows what's good for him,' Harry said and his fists curled. 'I'd like to give that bugger a taste of his own medicine. After what he did to you, he's a dead man if I find him.'

'Now don't talk daft,' Rose said and kissed him. 'I don't want you gettin' into trouble, Harry. I reckon if we don't go back to London, we'll be all right.'

'You won't go there alone again,' Harry promised and hugged her. 'Reg won't find us here – and don't worry about him reporting us to the police. He's wanted for too many things himself to do that. No, he'd use his fists on you like he did the last time if he got the chance, but he won't.'

Rose laughed and gave him a little push. 'You look so fierce, Harry. I almost believe you'd kill for me.'

'Believe it,' Harry told her. 'I'd do anything to protect you, Rose. You just remember that, love.'

'Yes, I shall,' she said and squeezed his hand. 'I reckon I'm lucky to have you, Harry Smith.'

'I love you, Rose.' He looked at her anxiously. 'This hasn't spoiled things for you – moving into the house and all that?'

'No. I shan't let it,' she replied. 'I'm looking forward to it – and to Christmas. We'll enjoy ourselves as much as we can, Harry, and not think about what might happen.'

Rose reassured him, but there was now a slight shadow hanging over her that she couldn't shake off. She had no doubt that Reg was alive and gunning for revenge. If he ever found her, he would make them suffer for what he saw as her betrayal.

CHAPTER 19

'Come on, Arthur,' Emily said, smiling at him as he dragged his feet that morning as they walked along the broad street. The wind was bitterly cold as it blew in from the sea, and her breath made little clouds on the frosty air. 'We're going to Mastins – I hear they have a Christmas grotto.'

'What is that?' Arthur asked, skipping to catch up with her. He knew that Mastins was a big department store in a street with a lot of tall buildings, apartments with balconies at the front. He'd been there with Emily to buy some things she'd needed soon after their arrival in Hastings.

'You'll see,' she promised and took his hand as they crossed the road after a bus had passed by. A few cars were parked outside the apartments but there wasn't much traffic otherwise, not like the roads in London had been when he'd wandered around on his own. 'I'm going to buy you something nice for Christmas, Arthur – but I thought we might look round the Christmas grotto first.'

Arthur looked up at her. She looked much happier

than she had for a while and he knew it was because she'd had a beautiful Christmas card and a letter from Pete. He was going home for two days at Christmas and then he would come to Hastings and visit them before returning to his base.

They went into the family-run firm. It smelled nice, Arthur thought, a scent of soaps, perfumes, and new things. His mother didn't linger but moved in the direction of a sign saying *Father Christmas Grotto*.

'I don't believe in Father Christmas,' Arthur said, hesitating. 'It's just a story people make up for children.'

'Yes, perhaps it is,' Emily agreed, 'but it's nice to have a little fun now and then. Shall we see what they've done?'

'Yes, let's,' Arthur agreed. He followed his mother towards the grotto, waiting while she paid the fee. They walked through a curtained doorway into a suddenly magical place. The lights had been dimmed and there was glistening white snow everywhere; elves wearing red and green costumes, and a small train with open carriages that children could sit in and ride around the large space that was piled high with brightly wrapped gifts. A big Christmas tree was decorated with strings of silver, tiny candles, and glittering glass balls. Drawings of Christmas things covered the walls and there was a lot of silvery tinsel stuff hanging down from the ceiling. At one end was a nativity scene with Mary, Joseph, and the baby Jesus in his cradle, surrounded by models of lambs and a donkey as well as a host of other animals, like rabbits, and cats and dogs, a dove, and some other creatures.

A man wearing a red suit and a white beard sat at the other side with a sack of presents beside him. A small queue of children was waiting to see him to receive their gift and whisper their wishes into his ear.

Arthur took his turn but refused to sit on his knee. 'I don't believe in Father Christmas,' he said. 'It's just pretend.'

'Don't you think there's any magic in the world?' the man said. 'Isn't there something you would like, something you want to whisper?'

'It won't come true,' Arthur replied, but he whispered something anyway and the man looked at him and then at Emily.

'Perhaps you'll get your wish,' the man said and handed him one of the wrapped gifts from the sack beside him.

Arthur thanked him and returned to Emily. She had been chatting to a lady with a small girl and was smiling.

'Ah, there you are, Arthur. Shall we go and buy something nice now?' She asked as she took his hand. 'I'll buy you whatever you choose. They don't have as many toys as they used to before the war, but I've been told they have some Meccano and a few trainsets.'

'I'd rather have some colouring pencils or a box of paints,' Arthur told her. 'I like to draw things.'

Emily looked down at him. 'Let's see what they have, then.' She noticed the package in his hand. 'Is that what Father Christmas gave you? Aren't you going to open it?'

Arthur looked at it, then nodded and undid the string. Inside was a picture book suitable for a child half his age with pictures of balloons and children playing.

'Oh dear,' Emily said and laughed. 'Not quite right for you, Arthur! I suppose most of his visitors are younger. You can take it to school, for the library there.'

Arthur nodded, slipping the little book into his jacket pocket. 'I knew he wasn't real,' he said. 'If he had been, he would have given me something I could read – an adventure story.'

'It was pretty in there, though,' Emily replied. 'I rather liked it – didn't you?'

'Yes, it was nice,' Arthur agreed. 'Thank you for taking me, Mum.'

Emily squeezed his hand. 'We'll buy your present and then we'll go to Lyons' Corner House and have a pot of tea and some cakes.'

Arthur nodded happily. He didn't mind what they did as long as they were together. It was what he had whispered to the man who pretended to be Father Christmas – that he could be with his Mum for always.

In Lyons' they ordered a pot of tea, an orange juice, and a plate of little cakes. There were some tiny ones with green marzipan wrapped round the sponge and cream on the top. Arthur liked those and Emily said he could have both of them. She ate a small slice of a jam Swiss roll and a piece of plain cake.

Arthur swung his legs under the table, watching as people came and went. There were a lot of mothers with their children, a lot of talk and laughter as small groups came in. Everyone seemed happy, chattering about what they were doing, and there was a relaxed atmosphere.

After they'd finished their tea and paid, they went out into the street, stopping to listen as they heard the sound of carols. 'It's the Salvation Army,' someone said and walked towards the source of the music.

'Shall we listen for a while?' Emily asked him and he nodded, holding on to her hand as a crowd gathered.

Arthur listened to the sound of the carols. The air was frosty and the light was fading from the sky, street lamps beginning to come on as they stood together. Emily's fingers entwined with his and she squeezed his hand.

'Go and put this in the collecting box,' she said as a lady in a dark uniform and funny-looking hat came round with a tin. She smiled at Arthur and shook her tin as he slipped his sixpence in. Then, as he turned away, he bumped into someone. Looking up, he saw it was a lady.

'I'm sorry,' he said but she smiled and shook her head.

'It's all right,' she said, glancing from him to his mother. 'I think we met on the seafront once – sheltering while we ate our fish and chips?'

Arthur nodded. 'You gave me sixpence,' he said. 'Happy Christmas!'

'Rose – my name is Rose Smith,' she said. 'Happy Christmas, Arthur.' She slipped half a crown into his hand and turned away.

Arthur returned to Emily's side. She hadn't noticed him talking to the nice lady. She was speaking to Ruby from the fish and chip shop.

Glancing down at Arthur she sighed. 'We'll have to go home now, love. I thought we might go to the

197

library and choose some books, but I have to work this evening so I need to get ready.'

'You never work Saturday nights! It's our time,' Arthur said, feeling the sting of tears behind his eyes.

'I have to. Ruby's mother is ill and she needs to stay and look after her. I'll come home as soon as we've finished.'

Arthur fed the chickens on scraps Emily gave him before she left for work. They clucked round him greedily and he left them to feed, carefully closing the pen when he left. His mother liked having the hens; they were good layers now and kept them in eggs so she didn't have to use the powdered stuff she disliked. He looked at the empty rabbit hutch, biting his lip to hold back the tears as he walked past it and into the house.

Going upstairs, he flopped across his bed, bored and lonely. It would be hours before Emily was back and he didn't have anything new to read. Feeling the hard edge of something in his pocket, he took out the book he'd been given in the Christmas grotto, opened it, and looked at it in disgust before throwing it across the room. He didn't believe in Christmas wishes; they never came true.

Tears stung his eyes but he knuckled them away. Getting up, he went downstairs to the kitchen. The door was wide open and the cat sat on the mat looking at him.

'Go away, you horrid thing!' Arthur tried to shoo it, but it came to him, winding itself around his legs and mewing pitifully, as if to say, 'I am innocent. Please feed me.'

'I hate you,' Arthur said but at another piteous cry, he fetched a saucer and poured some milk into it. The cat drank it all and sat washing its paws. Arthur sighed and reached out to stroke it. Swift as lightning, its paw came out and scratched the back of his hand, drawing blood and making him cry out in pain. 'Get out of here!' he yelled and kicked out at it. The cat avoided his foot and shot out of the back door.

'Don't come back!' Arthur shouted after it. His hand stung as he thrust it under the tap in the sink, tears on his cheeks. 'I hate you. I hate you!'

He sank down in a huddle on the kitchen floor, his body shaking as he wept. It had started out as a good day – but now he was alone again.

Emily was so tired when she got in that evening. The shop had been busy as people queued for their supper after leaving the cinema and the windows had steamed up with the heat. When she left the shop, she realised it was later than she'd thought, because of all the clearing up and cleaning she'd had to do without Ruby's help. It was bitterly cold, a few flakes of snow falling as she began to walk home, knowing that the last bus had gone.

When she got in, the house was dark. She snapped on the light and went into the kitchen, filling the kettle. Arthur wasn't in the sitting room so she went upstairs and found him in bed, curled up and fast asleep, his thumb in his mouth and his cheeks streaked with dried tears. Emily sat on the edge of the bed and then bent to kiss his cheek. She could see that he'd been crying and her heart caught. She felt a pang of guilt and regret.

She did love him very much and it wasn't right that he should be left alone so often.

'It wasn't meant to be like this,' she said softly, reaching out to touch his soft hair. 'It will get better. I promise you, Arthur. I'm not going to live like this forever. If Pete asks me to marry him, I'll sell the lease of the shop and we'll go with him. I might work sometimes, but only when you're at school. I promise you it will get better . . .'

She got up and walked softly from the room, the sound of Arthur's soft breathing bringing a smile to her face. She'd had a letter from the solicitor telling her that he believed he could proceed to court for probate in the next few weeks. He would need her to go up to town and sign some papers – and then everything would be hers.

Emily sighed. It was time things started to go right for her. She felt so very tired after working late and all she'd wanted to do was spend some time with her son and get ready for Christmas. As well as his colouring pencils and drawing book, she had bought him the book he'd wanted, *King Solomon's Mines* as a surprise, but she was too tired to wrap them this evening. She ached from the tips of her fingers to the top of her head and couldn't wait to get to bed with her hot drink.

CHAPTER 20

'That looks nice, Rose,' Harry said as he came in from work and saw that she'd put the Christmas decorations up. He sighed as he sat in his armchair close to a roaring fire, warming his hands in front of the orange flames. 'It's so good to come back to a comfortable home again.' He smiled up at her as she touched his shoulder.

'Tired, Harry?' she asked. 'You work so hard.' He was always later than her and often went in early to make certain everything was as it ought to be. He didn't get paid overtime, but considered it his patriotic duty.

'Has to be done,' he replied, smiling up at her and placing his hand over hers. 'Just been told we have to keep running over Christmas. That means I'll be working in the morning as usual, but not home until two – so we'll have a later dinner.'

'We'll have it at four,' Rose agreed. 'Do I need to come in for a few hours?'

'They'd like everyone to do a few hours, share the shifts. We'll be running at two-thirds capacity to give the women a chance for a break but we can't shut down because if we do it takes so long for all the safety checks when we start up again. If you could do the early shift from seven until eleven I'll come in with you but I'll be working later than you.'

'You always do,' she said and sighed. 'I'll be glad when this war is over and done, Harry.'

'We all will,' he replied. 'What's for supper?'

'Sausages, mash and buttered cabbage – well, margarine, but it'll taste fine with a bit of salt and pepper.'

'That sounds good,' he said. 'I'm hungry.'

'Me, too,' she replied and dropped a kiss on the top of his head. 'I'll make a pot of tea and then it'll be ready.'

'Thanks, love,' Harry said and leaned his head back against the chair.

When Rose returned with their tea, his eyes were shut and she thought for a moment he was sleeping but he opened them and looked at her ruefully.

'I don't know when I've felt so tired, Rose.'

She brought him his tea and sat beside him, feeling anxious. 'Are you all right, Harry? Not feeling unwell? Perhaps you should see the doctor?'

'Don't you worry,' Harry said and sipped his tea. 'I'm tough as old boots. I'm just tired because it's been non-stop work these past weeks. Mind you, I wouldn't change it. We're winning, Rose. There's a feeling amongst those that are in the know. There was a time when I thought the tide was against us. Had the fly-boys not stopped the invasion when they tried to break us, we would have been finished.'

'Thank goodness they did. I don't fancy having to learn German at my age,' Rose agreed and finished her tea. 'I can smell the sausages. If I'm not careful they'll burn.' She got up and hurried to the kitchen.

Harry chuckled, got up and followed her in. She'd set their pine table with a bright red cloth edged with holly motifs. 'We might as well get in the festive mood,' she said as he looked at it and grinned.

'Aye, why not?' he replied and gave a sigh of contentment as she placed a plate heaped high with mashed potatoes, cabbage and two sausages in front of him. 'That smells delicious.'

'It is better than the watery rubbish we got in lodgings and some of the cafés,' Rose replied confidently. 'I felt like telling our landlady why we were moving out but some of our workers still lodge there so I thought better of it.'

'I'm glad none of our stuff was lost in the fire,' Harry said and tucked into his sausages. 'I'm going to enjoy sleeping in my own bed.'

'Your big Welsh dresser is still there. I knew we couldn't get it in the kitchen so I asked them to keep it, as well as the extra chests of linen and the best crockery. We don't have room to set those blue-and-white plates of yours out here, Harry. We might as well leave them in store for now.'

'Good thinking. I'd rather not get rid of that dresser – it belonged to my grandfather.'

'That's what I thought. It looked lovely in your kitchen at home – but that was much bigger than this room.'

Harry nodded. 'I know I've let the house for now,

Rose, but I think we might sell and look for somewhere else to live after the war – move out to the country?'

'I know why you're saying it,' Rose told him. 'You're thinking we would be safe from Reg – but I refuse to be intimidated by him. I don't want you to sell your house just for me, Harry.'

'Reg doesn't frighten me,' Harry told her. 'But if he suddenly reappears in the neighbourhood it might make things difficult for us. Perhaps we should just take ourselves off somewhere.'

'We'll cross that bridge when we come to it,' Rose said. 'In the meantime we'll put Reg out of our minds. We're here for the next year or so, Harry. The work is more important than that man.'

'As long as you're not brooding over it?' He looked at her questioningly.

'No, I shan't let it bother me,' Rose told him and smiled, getting up to clear the table. 'Do you want to go out for a drink this evening, Harry – or just sit by the fire and listen to carols on the radio?'

'I'll sit by the fire,' Harry said yawning.

'Go on then. I'll be with you in a few minutes – and, no, I don't want a hand with the washing-up, thanks love.'

Harry nodded and smiled and went through to the sitting room. Rose washed the dishes, dried her hands, and went to join him. He was fast asleep in the chair. She didn't bother with the radio, so as not to disturb him. Instead, she got her knitting out. She was making a cardigan in pink wool for Alice. She had already made a navy pullover for Davey and would send them with some sweets and a ten-shilling note each for Christmas.

Rose smiled as her needles moved: purl one, plain one, slip two, purl one, plain one . . . It was a lovely lacey pattern and Alice would love it. Her heart twisted with love for the little girl and then, for some reason, she thought about the young lad she'd seen twice now, once in the bus shelter eating fish and chips, and then again at the carols in the street. Why did he look so sad? she wondered. He was better dressed than most London boys and she thought he must get enough to eat, because he didn't look thin or pinched in the face, but those eyes were so sad.

Rose sighed as she pushed the thought away. It was probably her imagination, just her own loneliness for a child – and yet she ought not to be lonely. Rose scolded herself mentally. She had a good, kind man, and a nice home. She ought to be ashamed of herself for wanting more when there were so many who had much less. She'd sent her sons and her daughter-in-law cards, as well as her grandchild, but she'd had no replies. Still, it wasn't Christmas yet so there was time.

'I thought you wanted to listen to the carols?' Harry asked, opening his eyes to look at her. He glanced at the clock. 'We can catch the last ten minutes or so . . .' He got up and switched on the radio, smiling as the sweet sound of a young voice filled the room with 'Away in a Manger'. Harry nodded. 'That's one of my favourites.'

'Me, too,' Rose agreed and put down her knitting. 'This is nice, Harry. Just the two of us . . .'

'Aye – but a young lad or lassie about the place would be nice, too.' He smiled. 'I haven't forgotten, Rose. Let's get Christmas over and then we'll see if we can start the procedure to adopt.'

Rose nodded. She couldn't say anything. Her heart was too full. How had she got so lucky?

Christmas Day was perfect as far as Rose was concerned. They'd both had to work for a few hours but after that they were able to celebrate. She'd managed to buy a decent-sized chicken for their dinner and an onion to make stuffing. It was ages since she'd seen onions in the shop and she'd pounced on them with glee.

'It's only one per person,' the shopkeeper had told her. 'We don't know if we'll get any more for a while but they're nice and big, just right for a treat at Christmas.'

Rose had picked the biggest one she could find. She used half of it for stuffing with some dried herbs, but the rest she saved so that Harry could have it with a bit of cheese for his supper.

Harry gave a sigh of pleasure as he finished eating his Christmas meal. 'That was so good, Rose. Roast chicken, potatoes, and proper stuffing, sprouts – and carrots just how I like them.'

'I wish I could give you Christmas pudding with brandy sauce, for afters,' she said, 'but all I could get was some cooking apples, so I've made apple pie and custard.'

'That will do me,' Arthur said and patted his stomach. 'If you can produce a meal like that with a war going on, I can't wait to see what you'll do when it's over.'

'Do you think it will end next year?' she asked hopefully.

'Can't say that, but I think we're heading the right way now. Mr Churchill is a good bloke but he didn't have the resources to win this war despite our

206

allies from Canada and Australia and elsewhere. The Americans have got a lot more money than us, Rose, and that means more fire power and more men.'

'It would be good if we could start moving against the Jerries instead of being on the receiving end,' Rose said with a sigh. 'I know we're bombing their cities but they started this horrid war.'

'I think we'll see a big push next year,' Harry said. 'I reckon the Allies are building up to something.'

Rose looked at him curiously. 'What do you know that I don't?'

'Nothing. Not that I could tell you if I did – but I know by the orders we're getting that there's a build-up of arms going on, and I reckon that has to be for something.'

'Yes, we've been getting more and more hours recently,' Rose agreed. She was aware that Harry knew a lot more about what was going on at the factory than she did; Rose simply oversaw her line of workers and checked safety, but Harry worked in another part of the factory where new weapons were developed. He had control over his department and would naturally be told of any new orders that had come down from the War Office. However, they were all signed up to the Secrets Act and Harry couldn't tell her anything, even if he wanted to.

'Anyway, that's enough of the war and work,' Harry said. 'Now it's my turn to surprise you, Rose.' He went to his work haversack and came back with a bottle of rich ruby port and a small parcel wrapped in silver tissue. 'Here you are, love. I know you like a drop of port and I don't mind a glass myself – and this is for you.' Harry offered the parcel almost shyly.

'Oh, Harry! You gave me an extra five pounds this week. I didn't expect anything else.' She took the parcel and unwrapped it carefully. Inside was a blue leather ring box. Her eyes went to him in surprise and then she gave a little gasp of pleasure as she opened the box and found a ruby and diamond three-stone ring. 'Harry! This must have cost a fortune . . .'

'I bought it from an antique shop in town,' he told her, smiling. 'We had a wedding but I never gave you an engagement ring, Rose. I hope it fits . . .'

Rose slipped it on to her left hand and held it up for him to see. It fitted perfectly and the stones flashed in the electric light. 'It's beautiful . . .' she breathed. 'I've never had anything like this, Harry!'

'Well, you have now, and when this stupid war is over, I'll be giving you a lot more things you've never had. I've been thinking, Rose. I reckon we should emigrate – go to America, or Canda, or Australia. Make a new life for ourselves somewhere.'

Rose stared at him and then laughed, her eyes shining with excitement. 'I've never even thought of such a thing, Harry!'

'Not after all the stories Davey told you about Canada? Wouldn't you like to see something different, Rose? I reckon there's a better life out there; the world is a big place and I've got a bit of money saved. We could explore, have some fun.'

Rose smiled at him. 'When we've won the war,' she said. Harry was yawning. 'Pour us some port, Harry, and take yours by the fire. I'm going to put these dishes in the sink . . .'

CHAPTER 21

Pete's visit was short; he came on Boxing Day morning, stayed to eat the lunch he'd provided; a large piece of beef, a tin of salmon, and an iced sponge cake. He'd also brought presents for Emily and Arthur. For Emily there was a gold locket on a fine chain and a bottle of Yardley perfume, and for Arthur there was a set of Biggles adventures books and a big packet of boiled sweets.

'How have you been doing at school, old chap?' he asked Arthur. 'And how's that rabbit?'

'School's all right,' Arthur said, his bottom lip wobbling. 'But Bella died – the cat killed her.'

'We don't know if it was the cat. It could have been a fox,' Emily said but Pete was looking at Arthur.

'That's bad luck, Arthur,' he said. 'I lost a dog I loved once – someone shot it. I think it was a farmer and he thought it was worrying his sheep. But old Pouncer would never have done that and it broke my heart.' He reached out and gave Arthur's shoulder a squeeze. 'I know it hurts – but it will get easier and one day I'll buy you a dog.'

Arthur shook his head, tears welling. 'I don't want it if it might die.'

'We can all die,' Pete told him. 'You have to learn to be strong, Arthur. Sometimes things hurt and we want to cry, but we hide our tears and slowly we heal inside. That's when we become a man.'

'Don't want to be a man!' Arthur had twisted away. Emily told him not to be rude but he'd run upstairs to his room, the tears dripping down his cheeks. Later on he'd gone down and apologised to Pete, as Emily said he should.

'I understand, old chap,' Pete said, looking at him with sympathy. 'We're still friends, aren't we?'

'Yes,' Arthur nodded vigorously. 'And thank you for my present. I love adventure stories.'

'You've got the first six. We'll add to the collection on your birthday.'

Emily was looking on smiling and Arthur sat down to a tea of salmon sandwiches and celery. It was delicious and he ate all his share as well as a slice of iced madeira cake.

That evening they played games until gone half past nine and then Arthur went to bed, but Emily and Pete stayed downstairs talking. Arthur was soon sound asleep, but he woke up when Pete knocked and came into his room early the next morning.

'I have to go now, Arthur,' he said and smiled as Arthur rubbed at his eyes. 'I wanted to say goodbye – and to promise that you'll feel better about Bella soon. One day we'll go and buy a couple of puppies together, when the war is over and you and Emily come to live with me in Yorkshire.'

'Are you going to marry Emily?'

'I hope so. There are things we both have to sort out, but if we did – would you be happy, Arthur?'

'Yes, I'd like that,' Arthur said and his smile wobbled. 'Do you have to go back and fight now?'

'Yes, I do,' Pete said. 'We've got to give them hell so they know not to do it again. I'd rather stay here with you and Emily, but I have to do my duty first.'

Arthur looked at him solemnly. 'I know. You're a brave man and – and I think I love you.'

Pete grinned and ruffled his hair. 'Reckon I might love you just a bit, old chap,' he said and got up. 'Now, you take good care of Emily for me.'

Arthur promised he would and lay back against the pillows as his friend left. No one had been as kind to him since his dad died, not even Emily.

The rest of the school holidays were much like any other time in their lives. Emily went back to work after Boxing Day. She didn't say a word about them going to live with Pete, but she seemed happier than she had been in a while.

Arthur spent the lonely evenings drawing pictures. He drew Pete from memory and when Emily saw it, she exclaimed over the likeness and asked if she could have it. Arthur said she could, though he'd have liked to keep it himself. He drew a picture of her too, but she didn't like that one or ask to keep it.

Sometimes, he took one of his new books to bed and read them. They weren't new; some had been inscribed to Pete for his birthday or Christmas from his parents and Arthur liked them even better because they had been Pete's. He felt it meant that his friend really liked him to give him something so special. Arthur didn't have one thing his birth parents had given him. He didn't remember being given anything much at Christmas by his parents, though he thought he might have had a wooden train, but it had disappeared after his father died.

A letter came a few days after Christmas. It was from Pete and it made Emily smile. She didn't show Arthur what he'd written but said that he'd said he hoped Arthur was well and enjoying his books. After she put the letter away in the dresser drawer, she called Arthur to her.

'If Pete asks me to marry him when my divorce comes through, we'll go to live with him somewhere,' she'd told him, looking thoughtful. 'But if he doesn't, I think we'll return to Canada. Not where we were living but perhaps more in the countryside. You'd like that, wouldn't you?'

'Yes, Mum. I like Pete too. He's thoughtful and nice.'

'Yes, he is,' she said and ruffled his hair. Arthur let her do it, even though he didn't like it much.

Arthur had given Emily a card and a trinket box for her Christmas gift. He'd made both of them at school and was quite proud of them. He'd painted a Christmas scene on the card and on the box he'd carved a bear with its cubs. The woodwork master had complimented him on his talent in making the box and Emily was pleased with it. She didn't have many trinkets but she used it for pins and bits on her dressing table.

Emily was working almost full-time at the shop now. She said the help was only temporary; the teenage lad who had taken her place on the counter had returned to school. Arthur went back to school, too, at the end of the holiday. He had made more friends now, but still no one who lived near enough to come round and play.

In January it was very cold and one day, when Arthur came home from school, he went out to the back garden to feed the hens. To his dismay when he opened the pen, he discovered that something had got in and attacked them – all three were dead, their throats torn out, just like his pet rabbit.

Arthur didn't cry. He went into the house and through into the sitting room, where he put a match to the fire, setting light to the kindling Emily had prepared that morning before they left. For a long time he sat on the floor in front of the fire, hugging himself, numbed by what he'd seen.

Why did everything he cared about die?

'I know you thought of them as pets,' Emily said when she got home and he told her what had happened. 'But I think we should eat them, Arthur. It only happened today and they've been out in the cold so they won't have gone off. I'll cook them all and give one to my neighbour next door.'

Arthur didn't argue, but when the meal was put in front of him the next day, he ate only the potatoes and vegetables. His mother ate hers and frowned but she didn't force him to eat the meat. He felt sick inside but still he didn't cry.

His mother gave two of the murdered hens away.

She ate the rest of the one she cooked for them but Arthur wouldn't touch it. He knew it was foolish. A lot of his friends spoke of keeping chickens in the back yard so that they could have chicken for their Christmas dinner, but he'd thought of his hens as pets. It would have choked him to eat them.

'Nellie said they thought it must have been a fox got in,' his mother told him when she came back from the next-door neighbour's. 'Apparently they've been scavenging in people's gardens in this cold weather.'

Arthur nodded numbly. He believed it was the cat which had jumped up on next door's wall and over the top of the wire netting. Emily said a cat couldn't have done it, but Arthur knew what he knew. That cat had it in for him and had done ever since he'd arrived.

They missed the fresh eggs and Emily grumbled about it. She had to use the powdered stuff she hated and talked of getting some more hens when she could, but Arthur hoped she wouldn't. He wouldn't pet them next time, he decided. It hurt too much when they died.

His feeling of being alone had intensified and sometimes now, in the playground, he just went off and sat by himself. Arthur was hurting inside. It wasn't just Bella or the hens, it was losing his father and his mother turning against him. He felt as if nothing was safe, nothing was stable. It could all disappear like a puff of smoke in a second. He knew Emily looked at him oddly at times, as if wondering what was wrong, but he couldn't bring himself to tell her. She'd cooked and eaten one of his hens and somehow it was a betrayal too far.

It was the middle of February when his life began

to get so much worse. The letter was waiting for Emily when they got home that afternoon. Arthur picked it up and gave it to her and then went into the sitting room to put a match to the fire. He'd just got it going when he heard a cry from the kitchen and ran in to see his mother sitting at the table, staring at her letter. There were tears running down her face.

'Mum?' Arthur felt a pang of fear. Emily didn't often cry; she got angry but didn't cry much. 'What's wrong?'

Emily didn't answer. The letter fluttered to the floor as she hid her face in her hands, her shoulders shaking. Arthur picked the letter up and read it; it was from Pete's parents.

Pete told us about his friend in Hastings and we felt you should know – our beloved son Peter was killed on active service just after Christmas . . .

Arthur was stunned. He replaced the letter on the kitchen table. There was more but he felt too sick and stunned to finish reading it. How could that happen? His friend Pete was dead! Arthur's eyes burned but he didn't cry. His grief was like a hard knot inside him, but he couldn't cry like Emily. His hand reached for hers, but she pulled it away. Arthur looked at her. She didn't want his sympathy, was too miserable to think that he'd lost a friend, too.

Arthur went back to the sitting room. He sat by the fire, hugging himself; it hurt so much but he wasn't sure whether it was knowing he wouldn't see Pete again or his mother pushing away his attempt to help her.

It was almost two hours later when Emily brought in a plate of sandwiches and a mug of tea. 'I'm sorry.

I didn't feel like cooking anything,' she said in a flat, emotionless tone. 'You'd best eat this and go to bed.'

'Mum, I'm sorry about . . .' She turned to look at him and he saw her eyes had gone strange. Arthur knew then that she was hurting inside just like him. He wanted to go to her and hug her but knew she didn't want his comfort.

'I wondered why there were no more letters,' Emily said but she was talking to herself, the way she did when she was upset. 'I thought he'd just been working . . . I never knew – I never knew he was dead . . .'

Arthur tried to eat a jam sandwich but it stuck in his throat. 'Can I take them to bed?' he asked and she nodded. He went to kiss her goodnight but she hardly noticed. Arthur took his tea and sandwiches up to his room. He placed them on the chest beside the bed and slipped into cold sheets. Shivering, he snuggled under the covers to get warm, letting his breath heat the air around him.

Pete wouldn't be coming to see them again. They wouldn't go together to buy the puppies. Arthur felt a cold knot about his heart. He'd liked Pete, felt safe with him. He'd hoped his mum would marry him and they'd all live together. Perhaps they would go back to Canada now . . . Was it his fault Pete had died, because he'd wanted to return to the things he'd liked? Arthur's eyes burned with the need to cry but he couldn't; it just hurt so much.

Eventually, he fell into an uneasy sleep. He was alone in a dark mist, running, always running but he couldn't get out of the fog. Branches clawed at him. He was in a thorny wood and his flesh was scratched and

216

stinging. He cried out for Emily but she didn't answer him. He was alone.

Emily sat before the fire Arthur had lit. Her head was in a whirl. She'd built so much on Pete's promises but the letter from his parents had said that he was to have been married. He was engaged to a girl he'd known all his life. Apparently, they'd found a letter from her to Pete in his things which had just been returned to them. Until then they hadn't known she existed.

Had Pete been stringing her along? Emily feared the worst. She'd been let down before – how could she have been so foolish as to believe him when he'd told her she was the only girl for him?

Her feelings of grief were tainted with doubt. Emily's first tears had dried and now she was hurt, bewildered, and lost. She'd based her hopes on a few flirtatious meetings – and yet Pete had seemed so genuine. He'd spoken more than once of a life together after the war, but he must have been lying if he was already engaged. Was it her? Was she impossible to love?

Emily's heart and mind were in turmoil. She didn't know what to believe, but even if Pete had loved her, as he'd claimed, he was dead.

What was she going to do now? She'd felt so happy. Despite not getting more letters after the one thanking her for Christmas, she'd been sure he would be in touch soon. He'd sent her a lovely card, given her beautiful gifts, and promised he would visit as soon as he could, told her he loved her. Told her he wanted them to be together. Emily had been content to wait. He was in the

RAF and he had his duty but he'd been dead all that time and she hadn't known!

Tears welled up and spilled down her cheeks. Pete was so young, so full of life; it wasn't right that he should be dead. Her heart ached for him and for herself. She had lost so much. She had no one but Arthur. Her head came up at the thought. Her poor little boy must be suffering, too. Arthur had liked Pete, because he'd been so kind to him. Emily had regretted afterwards that she'd eaten one of the hens – but it was so hard going without meat . . .

Squaring her shoulders, Emily knew that she had to go on for Arthur's sake. They still had each other. Once she came into her aunt's possessions, she would sell them all and go back to Canada. She'd made up her mind and couldn't wait to leave this miserable country. Nothing had gone right since she got here.

She got up and went upstairs to check on Arthur. She would tell him it was all right, that they would always be together and assure him that they would go back to the place he loved.

Emily saw that Arthur was asleep. His mug of tea and sandwiches were untouched. She bent her head to kiss the top of his head gently.

'I love you, my little one,' she whispered. 'It will be all right. I promise it will all come right soon.'

Arthur slept on. Emily smiled, picked up the plate and mug and carried them downstairs. She hadn't eaten anything. The sandwiches were a bit dry now but she would eat them, because it was a sin to waste food when there was so little of it in this country. She hardly knew why she had come in the first place, but then

218

remembered how lost and angry she'd felt, wanting to put all the hurt of Ken's betrayal behind her, to find him and vent her fury on him. Besides, her aunt had been grateful that she'd come and had left Emily everything she owned. It would be a new start for her and Arthur. All she had to do was wait until the lawyer said that it was all hers to do as she wished with.

CHAPTER 22

It was a bitterly cold day in March 1944 when the next blow fell. Emily had recognised the printing on the envelope the moment she got in from work that evening; it was from her lawyer and she felt excited as she tore it open. She read the contents and then stared at the page blankly.

> *Dear Mrs Henderson,*
>
> *I am writing to tell you that I have been informed that there may be another claimant for your aunt's estate. The position is not yet clear but I would be obliged if you could come to London on the fifteenth to discuss the matter, as it may now involve a lengthy court case. It is my personal opinion that you are the rightful heir but there are complications. I would like to discuss the situation with you in person so that you understand the situation and costs that are likely to arise.*

What did that mean? Emily's mind was a blank as she read it through several times. Was she her aunt's beneficiary or not – and what costs were involved? Her heart lurched as the words sank in and she realised that even if she won the case, it might cost a great deal of money, which might leave her with much less than she'd expected.

The fifteenth – that was tomorrow. She would have to let Ruby know first thing in the morning that she wouldn't be in that day and it was a school day. She couldn't take Arthur out of school. No, this time he must go to school as usual. She would be home again before he knew so it might be best not to tell him . . .

'Is something wrong, Mum?' Emily became aware that Arthur was looking at her anxiously. He was a sensitive child and soon picked up on her feelings so shook her head, tucking the letter on the mantelpiece behind the clock.

'No, it is just a letter from my lawyer,' she said. 'Nothing to worry about.'

She tried to talk normally as she prepared their tea of bread-and-butter pudding and a vegetable soup. Surely there was nothing to worry about, she thought as she asked Arthur about his day at school, though she hardly heard his answers. Her aunt's will had been clear, signed but not witnessed. It would surely be upheld in a court of law – wouldn't it?

After a while she became aware that Arthur had stopped talking and was looking at her in a way that made her breath catch. His expression was a mixture of anxiety and hurt that caught at her heart and she realised that he knew she wasn't listening to him when he talked about school. Perhaps it was best to be honest after all, because it would affect him, too. She went to the mantel and took the letter down, giving it to him.

'You'd better read that, Arthur. It's from the lawyer in London – and it means I might not get this house or anything my aunt owned.'

Arthur read it through and then looked up at her. 'What does it mean, Mum? If we can't live here, where will we go?'

'Back to Canada if I can afford it,' Emily said, frowning. Her wages from the shop were barely enough to pay the bills, feed and clothe them, and she hadn't managed to save more than a few pounds since she'd been here. However, there was the hundred pounds of her aunt's money they'd found in the cash box and she would hang on to it. 'Don't worry, Arthur. I expect it's just a mistake and it'll all be sorted out soon.'

'Are you going to London tomorrow?' he asked and she nodded.

'It's best you stay here this time,' Emily told him. 'It's a school day and I'll be home as soon as I can – probably before you.' She looked at him pleadingly. 'You don't mind, Arthur – do you? Please say it's all right.'

'You will come straight home when you get back?' He looked at her and she caught a glimpse of such worry in his eyes that her throat caught.

'Of course I shall, darling,' she said. 'It isn't something I want to do, Arthur, but I have to – do you understand?'

'Yes, Mum,' Arthur agreed. 'I know it's important to you.'

'To both of us,' she replied. 'If I get what my aunt left

me, we can have a nice life when we return to Canada, find a little house – and I'll get a job in a shop, but I won't work in the evenings. I haven't liked leaving you alone so much, Arthur. It wasn't my fault that Ken let me down. I brought you here to England, because I believed it would be a better life for us, but I should have stayed in Canada, found a house to rent and a job. I'm sorry . . .'

Arthur flung himself at her legs, hugging them and sobbing into her and she bent down, holding him tight and kissing him as she wiped away his tears.

'Don't leave me, Mum,' he begged and she felt the tears on her own cheeks as she kissed the top of his head. 'I love you . . .'

'I love you, too, Arthur.' She held him away from her and wiped his cheeks. 'Don't cry, my darling. I've been upset over – over lots of things and perhaps I neglected you, but I will do better in future I promise.' She stroked his back to soothe him. 'Will you be a good boy and go to school tomorrow for me, please? I promise I'll come back as soon as I can.'

Arthur gulped and then nodded. 'I'll be good – but you *will* come back?'

'Of course I will,' Emily said and smiled as she ruffled his hair, her eyes wet with tears. 'You're my little boy and I love you. I promise I will come back once I've been to the lawyer.'

'All right . . .' Arthur sniffed and rubbed a hand over his eyes. 'I'll go to school, Mum – but come back soon.'

Emily was thoughtful as she tucked Arthur up in bed and then went to bed early herself. She knew Ruby would complain about having to run the shop without her help but there wasn't much she could do about it. She needed to get this settled as soon as possible. Emily couldn't wait to go home to Canada. She'd made a mistake coming here to this war-torn country and had begun to feel trapped. If the fish and chip shop wasn't hers, she wouldn't go on working there, but she wasn't qualified to do much other than work in a shop. Emily couldn't type and she wasn't good with figures so it might mean she would end up in a factory or washing up in a café.

Tears stung her eyes. She'd counted on her inheritance – without it she would have nothing.

If only Pete was here, he would know what to do. Emily wasn't sure she'd been in love with him, but she'd liked him and thought they might be happy as a family. He'd really taken to Arthur and it could all have been so wonderful.

Why did he have to die? She pummelled her pillow in sudden anger. This damned stupid war! It was men who started wars and none of them could be relied on. Her tears came thick and fast as she regretted what might have been.

She lay for a while, tossing and turning in her cold bed. It wasn't fair! She thumped her pillow again in anger and then hid her face in it. Somehow, she had to keep her spirits up, she had to believe that things would come right – because poor little Arthur needed her.

Emily closed her eyes. She would do it somehow. She would make a home for them, even if it was in a dingy lodging house until she could save enough for their fare home and something left over to get them started again.

'So that is the position, Mrs Henderson,' Emily's lawyer said the next day as she sat in his office. 'I'm very sorry, but it seems there was a prior will, made through a solicitor. The money was left to a friend of your aunt's – but it seems she moved away a few years ago and they lost touch. The letter from your aunt leaving everything to you is dated after the previous will but it is handwritten and the other claimant's solicitor is questioning its veracity. His client once lent your aunt some money and, apparently, she says the will was made to cover the loan, that she is, in fact, owed a large sum of money, namely five hundred pounds.'

Emily looked at him in shock. 'I doubt my aunt's house is worth much more than five hundred pounds, Mr Baxter.'

'I would say it might be nearer a thousand, but the costs involved in a lengthy court case might exceed that sum. Your aunt didn't own the fish and chip shop, only the business, which may be worth a small amount for the lease.' He looked at her over steepled hands. 'Are you willing to take the case to court, knowing that even if you win much of your aunt's estate will be used to fight the case and if you lose you would have to pay costs?'

'I can't afford that,' Emily told him. 'I'm not sure I can pay you for what you've done already, Mr Baxter.'

'I'm not concerned with that – I can waive the fee in this case, but I am annoyed that this should happen when I know how much you relied on a favourable outcome.' He frowned. 'I have asked the claimant's solicitor to provide proof of this loan agreement. Had that not been in existence, I believe you have the better claim, Mrs Henderson.'

'So there is still a chance that it might be mine?'

'I would have to go to court on your behalf, and the decision would be made by a judge – but it's my belief that you would win. However, if the loan agreement is tied to the will and properly signed and witnessed, you might be required to repay it. I don't see that the whole of the estate would be forfeit.'

Emily looked at him in silence. 'I don't believe my aunt would have changed her will if she owed money to someone who had helped her, Mr Baxter, but I only have my wages and they aren't very much. I can't ask you to carry on with the case knowing that I may be unable to pay you.'

He smiled at her. 'In any other case I would probably have decided to let that be an end,' he told her. 'However, I am not satisfied that the other claimant is telling the truth – and, besides, I was very fond of Peter. He asked me to look after you, and I gave him my word. I shall continue to investigate, Mrs Henderson, and we will consider my fee should we win the case.'

Emily blinked hard, tears starting behind her eyes. She struggled to control them. 'That is so kind,' she said in a barely audible whisper. 'I don't know how to thank you. Even if we win, I may not be able to pay you.'

'Will you allow me to continue in your name?'

'Even a small amount of money would help,' Emily said in a choked voice. 'I had hoped for a new life for myself and Arthur.'

'Ah yes, your son,' Mr Baxter nodded. 'Peter told me about him – a bright lad by all accounts. Well, do I have your permission to proceed?'

'Yes, and if we lose . . .' She swallowed hard. 'I will pay you one day . . . somehow.'

He stood up and offered his hand. 'Please don't worry, Mrs Henderson. I shall do my utmost for you – I know Peter would have expected it of me. I will let you know if I consider that we should proceed to court.'

Emily clasped his hand and left his office with a little shake of her head.

Tears stung her eyes as she emerged into a blustery wind. Debris was whipping along the street and the bitter cold stung her eyes and cheeks. She rubbed away the foolish tears, feeling suddenly weary and defeated. All her hopes of a better life seemed to have vanished like a puff of smoke. She had nothing to look forward to and she would struggle to feed herself and Arthur if she had to take a menial job. Besides, she was so tired of working all hours and barely making a living. She was tired of being alone with no one she could turn to for help. She'd run from Canada thinking she might lose Arthur because she couldn't support him, and now, if she couldn't look after him properly, she would lose him anyway. In her desperate state of anxiety, she felt lost and so alone. How could she keep Arthur if she had nothing?

Why did everything have to go wrong? She'd believed for so long that Ken had loved her, but he was a cheat and a liar. Pete had begun to make her believe again, but he was gone and she didn't even know if he'd truly loved her. Her aunt's legacy had seemed God-given but now that was vanishing into the mist of uncertainty. There was no point in going on, She felt too tired and empty to think beyond the loss of all her hopes, for she did not believe the solicitor could help, even though he'd promised to try. Tears filled her eyes. Her vision was blurred as she stepped into the road and perhaps she never saw the delivery van that hit her, though one person who saw the accident, told the police that it looked as if she'd walked straight into its path . . .

CHAPTER 23

It was dark when Arthur got home from school and the house was cold; it's emptiness hit him like a blank wall, making his stomach tighten. He snapped on the light in the hall and dumped his school satchel on a chair by the hatstand, then went into the kitchen.

'Mum?' he called hopefully, but knew she wasn't there. The range in the kitchen hadn't been lit that morning. Emily had said she would light it when she got home. She'd promised she would be home early, but she wasn't here. Another broken promise.

Arthur went into the sitting room. He could manage to light the fire there; he often did it and he knew he could get it going with paper crackers that they made from newspapers, folding them into long thick strips and then criss-crossing them into good kindling. He made his paper lighters, crunching more newspaper to go underneath to help it catch, then placed a few thin sticks on top and then some small pieces of coal. He knelt on the floor, blowing at it until the flames lit, and then he put the guard in front and went into the kitchen.

He was hungry and thirsty, but he didn't like using the gas cooker and the range was cold. He got himself a glass of water. It didn't taste as nice as a mug of warm cocoa, but he drank it and then went to look for something to eat. There wasn't much in the pantry, just half a loaf, some margarine and a pot of jam that was almost empty. On further exploration, he discovered a bag of potatoes and some cooking apples.

Arthur took the loaf into the kitchen and cut himself a slice. He decided to take it into the sitting room and toast it in front of the fire. It was a bit of fun seeing it turn golden, and, when it was ready, he brought it back and spread it with margarine and a little strawberry jam. Eating hungrily, he wondered what his mother would bring for their supper that evening. Perhaps she'd stopped in town to do some shopping, he thought. She might even bring some fish and chips home, though they got a bit cold by the time she arrived and she always had to warm them through again in the oven. It was better when they bought them and ate them out of newspaper by the beach.

After Arthur had eaten, he retrieved his satchel and went upstairs; he took off his school uniform, folding it on a chair and putting on his comfortable old trousers and a pullover. Emily liked him to keep his school things nice, because she couldn't afford to buy more.

For a while he lay on his bed and did the sums his teacher had set for the class as homework. They were easy and he put his books away in the satchel, then took out his drawing book and looked at the picture of Emily. He thought it looked like her, but he'd drawn her as he remembered her on the days they'd gone

232

out with Pete, smiling and happy. She wasn't like that now, hadn't been since Pete died. For a moment he was tempted to take a pencil and scribble over her face, but he didn't. Instead, he turned the page and began to draw things he remembered from his time in Canada. A lake rippling in the sunshine, a bear and her cubs by the waterside and trees, tall and imposing, jewel-like birds fluttering in the branches.

He was intent on his picture and when he eventually looked up, he realised that he'd forgotten to make up the fire. It would go out and if Emily had to rake it all out before she could make a new one, she wouldn't be pleased. Running down to the sitting room, he was relieved to see that the coals were still red and smouldering. Arthur made it up and sat by it as it began to burn bright again. Looking up at the clock, he saw that it was almost nine o'clock. Where was Emily? Had she gone to work at the fish shop? She'd promised she wouldn't but perhaps she'd had no choice.

He fetched a cushion from Aunt Becky's chair and lay down, his hand under his cheek, curled up like a puppy. He was so tired and he wanted to cry, because Emily had promised she would come straight back and she hadn't. Yet something told Arthur that tears wouldn't help. He had to wait and be patient and she would come soon – wouldn't she?

The fire lasted until the early hours and then it went out. The room got colder and colder as the frost deepened and made patterns on the small-paned windows. Arthur woke up shivering and called out in fear.

'Mum – are you home yet?' he cried but the silence of

the house told him she wasn't. He'd closed the curtains earlier but left the light on. Glancing at the clock, he saw it was four in the morning and Emily wasn't home. He shivered as the icy fingers of fear inched down his back. He was alone in the house and suddenly every creak, every little crack, was menacing.

She wasn't coming back, ever. His dread had come to pass. Emily had left him alone. She didn't want him anymore. The tears were so close now. He knuckled his eyes to stop them, because Pete had told him you had to master your tears to be brave, to become a man – and he needed to be brave now. Arthur didn't feel very brave but there was no one to run to.

It was so cold but Arthur had used most of the newspapers and the coal the previous evening. He knew there was a small heap out in the coal shed. When it got light, he would fetch a bucket in. He wouldn't be able to fill it because it would be too heavy, but he'd bring as much as he could; first he would have to clear out the ashes and take them out to the bottom of the garden. Emily had started to make a path with the cinders. She said they might as well be used for something and she wanted a path by her washing line.

What if Emily never came back? His fears returned, a feeling inside telling him that something bad had happened. Had she just left him, because he was too much trouble or was she ill?

Arthur tried to tell himself that she wouldn't leave him alone if she could help it. Only the day before yesterday she'd promised things would get better, told him it wasn't her fault that she'd had to come here – she'd told him she loved him, but Arthur wasn't sure he believed her. People said things but didn't mean them. His real mother had promised she would stop drinking; she'd said she loved him, but she'd gone on drinking, drowning in a wave of self-pity that led to Arthur being sent away to Canada after she died. He'd been so frightened, but then Julie and Davey had looked after him and he'd loved his new home. He'd thought then that Emily might love him but now he feared she'd left him, because it was all too hard for her. He'd seen her change from a happy, smiling woman to one who was tired and sad, but he'd still loved her. Surely she wouldn't just go off and leave him?

What was he going to do? Arthur decided that he would go to bed, get under the blankets, and keep warm. When it was light, in the morning he would decide what he ought to do.

Arthur slept late and by the time he got up and washed his hands and face in cold water, he'd missed his bus for school. Emily would be cross with him, but it was her fault. Why hadn't she come home when she promised?

He went downstairs and into the sitting room to clear the ashes from the previous night. He had to make three trips down the icy garden. The hen coop was still there, forlorn, and empty, and Arthur shuddered at the memory of the slaughtered hens. It was odd that he hadn't seen that cat since then. If he did, he would kill it! A surge of anger went through him. He glared at some black birds, hopefully looking for crumbs.

'I haven't got anything for you,' Arthur shouted, sending them startling up into the tree at the bottom of the long garden.

Returning to the house, he patiently made paper crackers and laid his fire. He'd discovered a few bits of kindling in the coal shed and some old newspapers; when he fetched the coal, but there wasn't much of that; still, he manged to get the fire going. And he was so hungry! And he wanted a mug of cocoa, but he was afraid to light the gas, because it popped and Emily had told him it was dangerous if you left the gas on too long before you lit it.

He fetched the last of the bread and made himself a piece of toast, but there was hardly any jam. After he'd found half a pint of milk in the pantry but when he tasted it, it was sour so he put it on the wooden draining board and went to sit by the fire.

What was he going to do if Emily didn't come home? Arthur had a little money. He hadn't spent the money his mother had given him in London and he'd saved the half a crown that kind lady had given him at Christmas. She'd told him her name was Rose Smith. Emily didn't know he had that money, because the lady had put a finger to her lips so he'd just slipped it in his pocket: it was a secret and he'd planned to use it to buy Emily a present on her birthday.

Arthur was just considering whether or not he should go shopping to buy some food when he heard a banging on the door.

'Mum!' he cried, running to open it. His brief excitement faded as he saw who stood there.

'Where is she?' Ruby demanded. 'If she thinks she can leave all the work to me and go barging off to wherever she's gone, she's wrong!'

'Mum isn't here.' Arthur said. 'She went to London to see the lawyer and didn't come back last night.'

'I suppose she stayed over with her boyfriend,' Ruby snarled rudely. She slammed some keys on the table just inside the door. 'Well, I've had enough. She can open up herself when she's ready. I quit and I took my wages from the till – here's the rest of it. I've got a new job and I shan't be coming back so you can tell her that!'

Ruby slammed some notes and coins down on the table beside the keys and stormed off, leaving Arthur to close the door in dismay. Emily wouldn't be pleased about that when she returned – if she did? She had to, didn't she?

Was she with Pete? No, Pete was dead. Surely she wouldn't have stayed away all night? Arthur's thoughts went round and round in circles. He wanted to believe Emily loved him, but past experience told him that things changed.

The cold knot of fear in his stomach returned. He looked at the money on the table. There were three crumpled pound notes and as much again in small change – enough to buy food for a few weeks if he was careful.

Arthur took five shillings from the pile. He would only use as much as he had to, because Emily might need this money when she returned.

Arthur pulled on his school overcoat and took the key from the front door. There was a shop in the next road that sold bread, jam, and other things that he liked. He couldn't cook anything on the stove but he could make toast and perhaps he could boil a saucepan on the fire in the sitting room. Then he could make cocoa or boil an egg. He might even toast a sausage over the fire if he was careful.

Arthur thought of something and went back into the kitchen and found Emily's string shopping bag. Now what else did he need? Ah yes, the coupons. Most things were on ration so he would need those. Emily kept them in the dresser drawer. He looked and smiled as he found them. She kept all her important papers in here and he saw his own documents next to hers. They would need those to return to Canada when she sold this house.

He felt the key in his pocket, peeped into the sitting room and checked the guard was up in front of the fire, then returned to the hall and went out, locking the door safely behind him. He would buy sensible things that Emily liked too and then, if she came home, she wouldn't be angry with him for taking her money . . .

CHAPTER 24

'There's a letter for you, Miss Vee – looks like it came from England,' Aggie said as she brought it into the comfortable sitting room. The sun was shining in the window, making it warm and cosy despite the frosty air outside. The winter had been hard in Canada that year but the spring looked to be coming early. 'Mebbe it's from that agent you contacted in England.'

'Yes, perhaps it is,' Vee replied, taking it from her as her friend and long- time housekeeper looked at her curiously. Aggie lingered as Vee took the paperknife from her desk and slit the envelope. 'Yes, it is . . .' She read the letter eagerly and gave a little cry of pleasure. 'They think they've found Emily and Arthur! It seems that they're living in a seaside town named Hastings in a house that belongs to her aunt . . .' She folded the paper with a little nod of satisfaction.

'Well?' Aggie said. 'What are they doing about it then?'

'They're sending someone down to speak to Emily and discover whether she's all right or if she needs any help.'

'And?'

Vee smiled as she saw Aggie's impatience. 'That's it for now,' she said. 'I can't force Emily Henderson to return to Canada if she's happier there. I'm willing to offer her a home and a job – and I know Julie is anxious about Arthur and longs to see him– but it will be her decision, not mine.'

'That's not like you,' Aggie said with a sniff. 'They can't be doing very well over there the way things are with all that rationing and bombs and things.'

'No, I don't think they can,' Vee replied, meeting Aggie's eyes. 'I've given instructions that they're to be offered a home and job here – and that Arthur's friend Julie, from the ship, would like to see him.'

Aggie gave another sniff. 'I can't see why she did a bolt like that . . .'

'Apparently, she went to look after her aunt, who runs a fish and chip shop – or did. She has since died and it's possible that Emily may inherit the estate. There is some dispute over it, but her case is being fought, so she may well be independent and that's not a bad thing for anyone.'

'Mebbe she won't want to come back if she gets it.' Aggie's disapproval was clear now and Vee sighed.

'What do you think I should do that I haven't done so far, Aggie?' She raised her fine brows, a look that would certainly have quelled most men but held no fear for Aggie.

'Don't ask me,' Aggie grunted. 'You're the clever one around here – but I should've thought you might write a letter to her, and mebbe one to Arthur, telling him that Julie and Beth want to see him, and that you'll make sure he's looked after if they return.'

'Oh, you do, do you?' Vee smiled. 'What if I've already done that? What if I've told my agent that they are to be helped to return to Canada, if they so wish and it's possible?'

Aggie stared at her. 'Right then,' she said and nodded. 'I haven't got all day to stand here and talk to you. I've got work to do . . .' She stomped off, leaving Vee to smile to herself. That was a very good idea of Aggie's but she had no intention of telling her so.

She sat down at her desk and wrote a long letter to the agent she had employed, then checked her letter again. There was a London solicitor involved in looking after Emily's claim to her aunt's estate. Perhaps she would just drop him a line and let him know that she was prepared to pay Emily's expenses if she needed to go to court for what ought to be hers. She drew another sheet towards her and wrote her letter of instruction, sealed the envelope, and put the stamps on.

Glancing at the clock, she got up and picked up her letters. She would walk to Beth's school and bring her home and post her letters on the way. They might go to the ice cream parlour for a drink of pop and either ice cream lollipops or a chocolate sundae. Beth was very fond of those and Vee liked them too.

As she popped her letters into the posting office she smiled. How Aggie would crow if she knew that she had acted on her advice. It was quite possible that both Arthur and Emily were happily settled, but it was better to be safe than sorry and she would be happy to give Julie news of the little boy she'd mothered on the voyage from England more than three years ago now.

Now 1944 and that awful war still went on. If it

were not for that Vee would have taken Beth and gone over to see for herself that all was well. A shudder went through Vee as she thought of what might have happened to Beth had not Vee's brother Malcolm decided to bring her home to them. He'd been worried about Vee being lonely, for she'd never married again after her husband Bill's early death although it wasn't for want of suitors. Vee was an attractive woman, even now in her fifties, and wealthy, but no one could ever take Bill's place in her heart. It was her one regret – and his – that they'd had no children.

Seeing Beth run to her, a look of delight on her lovely little face at seeing her mummy, Vee knew that she had the child both she and her husband had longed for. Bill would be so happy for her. She smiled and embraced Beth as she ran at her and caught her round the waist. Beth had shot up this last summer and looked healthy and full of vitality. She was going to be a beauty and would have all the boys after her when she was sixteen or so.

'Did you have a good day, darling?' she asked as she hugged her daughter.

'Lovely, Mummy,' Beth said, taking her hand confidingly as they began to walk through leafy sidewalks towards the old town centre where the houses had a stylish grace that was lacking in more recent developments. The city was encroaching on virgin land and Vee didn't much like it. 'I'm in the running team now. I'm going to train on Saturdays and then I'll represent the school at the races at the summer sports meeting.'

'That's good,' Vee said. 'I know you can run fast –

Julie said you beat her to the canoe when you were up at the lake with them before Christmas.'

Beth nodded contentedly. 'Are we going up to the lake to see Julie and Jethro this weekend?'

'Yes, we've been invited to lunch. Julie says she has something to tell us.' Vee smiled to herself. She'd already guessed Julie's news but wouldn't spoil the surprise, but the thought of the young couple she cared for like her own becoming parents was both satisfying and exciting.

Beth skipped along beside her. 'I love Julie and Jethro, Mummy.'

'Yes, I know you do, darling. I'm very fond of them, too.'

Beth looked up at her. 'Have you heard any more about Arthur? Julie keeps asking whenever we see her.' She screwed up her face. 'I hardly remember him now. It seems so long ago since we came.'

'Do you ever wish you were still in England, Beth?'

Beth shook her head vigorously, 'No, Mummy. It was always dark where I lived but here it's light and I love it up at the lake where Julie and Jethro live.'

'Yes, it *is* nice there,' Vee agreed. 'We thought once we might have a house built on some of the land but we never did . . .' A little sigh escaped her because her husband's death had left so much undone, like the European trip they'd once planned to France, Italy, and England, too. She would probably never go on such a trip now. Even if the war ended soon, and the newspapers seemed to think it might happen, the places she'd wanted to see would be damaged and violated, perhaps taking many years to recover.

'I like living here,' Beth said as they approached one of her favourite shops. 'But I like going to the lakes for a visit.'

'Yes, I do, too,' Vee admitted, dismissing her foolish regrets. 'We have the best of both worlds, don't we?' She smiled to herself. One day, when Beth was finished school, maybe, just maybe she'd take that trip she'd always promised herself, but she would take Beth, too.

In the meantime, she would simply wait and see what transpired in England before telling Julie that Arthur might have been found. She wanted to give her positive news, not another maybe.

CHAPTER 25

His mother had been gone three days now and
the house was bitterly cold when Arthur got home
from school that night. He managed to find enough
sticks to lay on top of the newspaper he'd made
into crackers. He'd had to spend some of his store
of money to buy a paper, because there was none
left in the house. He could have torn some of Aunt
Becky's books up to make kindling for his fire but he
thought Emily might be cross if he did that, because
she wanted to sell as much as she could when they
returned to Canada – if they ever did. Arthur felt a
tingling at the nape of his neck. Emily wouldn't go
without him, would she?

Arthur felt very frightened then. What would he
do if she never came back? Surely, she would? She'd
talked to him about selling her aunt's things and
having enough money to get her own small house. She
thought she would still need to work but they would be
comfortable again; that was why she'd gone to London
to see the lawyer.

Arthur shivered. The cold knot of fear had been

growing inside him. Where was Emily? Why didn't she come home?

He knew she'd been upset over that letter about her aunt's property. It wasn't all as easy as she'd hoped but she'd promised she would come straight back. Why had she broken her promise?

Emily didn't always keep her promises. Arthur knew that. She always apologised when things went wrong or she just forgot, but she wasn't truly reliable. Arthur felt the sting of tears but blinked them away. He was too big for tears. He had to be brave and face up to what the future might hold. Pete had told him so. He had to act and think like a man.

If Emily never came back, what ought he to do?

He could tell his teachers at school, but he knew what would happen then. They would go to the council. Arthur would be put in a home and then they would send him away somewhere. If he thought they might send him back to Canada where he'd been happy for a while – but who would look after him?

He might be given to another family but he might just be put in an orphanage here in England.

Arthur fought the desire to cry. He hadn't liked the orphanage where he'd been sent after his first mother got sick. The woman who had looked after him there had been rough and she'd hit him several times when he'd wet his trousers. He hadn't meant to do it, but he was only a little boy and he was frightened.

He was older now. He didn't think he would wet himself now, but he didn't want to go to a place like that. Since his real mother gave him up, he'd been sent from one place to another and he wanted somewhere he could belong. Arthur's brow wrinkled as he sat by the warmth of his little fire and toasted a slice of the bread he'd bought. He had a slice of streaky bacon too, and he'd discovered he could lodge a small pan on the fire and cook it in its own fat if he was careful. He hadn't been able to buy butter but he used the fat from the bacon on his toast to make it soft and tasty and then folded it over like a sandwich. It tasted so good.

Arthur wondered what he would do when his dwindling store of coins ran out. Could he find work to do that would bring him in enough to buy his food? He wasn't old enough to do a proper job but someone might pay him to do errands or wash windows. He would need coal as well. He had some shillings for the electric meter but once they were gone the house would be dark and he hated being alone in the dark; the house was creepy at night, especially upstairs. After the first night alone, he'd brought pillows and blankets down to the sitting room and curled up near the little fire to keep warm.

Arthur wasn't hungry. He had a meal at school every week day and ate bread and jam most of the time when he was in the house. Sometimes he bought a couple of slices of bacon or a sausage, which he toasted over the fire. The fat from the meat made the fire spit and the room smelled of burning fat as the sausage blackened. Arthur didn't mind; he liked the taste of it, had always liked his sausage well browned. He was like his dad, who had always liked his a bit burned. Arthur's mum used to laugh at him over it – but she was different before he died, more inclined to smile than to shout at Arthur. That had started later.

Arthur felt wistful as he remembered the days when his father had been around to lift him on his shoulders and give him a bear hug or some sweets on a Saturday. His real mum had loved him then but she'd forgotten him in her grief for his dad. Was that why Emily had forgotten him now, because she was grieving for Pete?

Arthur wiped his greasy fingers on his handkerchief. He didn't much like washing in cold water and that's all there was now. After a while of just staring into the fire, he made it up with some small pieces of coke that were normally used for the range; it would smoulder a bit and didn't burn as brightly as the coal but it kept a bit of warmth in the room. When it was red hot, he would warm some water and make cocoa in a saucepan over the fire. It wasn't as nice as when Emily made it with milk but it was warm and sweet. The milkman had stopped leaving milk, even though Arthur had put the bottles out; he didn't know why but thought perhaps Emily hadn't paid him.

Arthur took a book from his satchel and settled down in his blankets and pillows to read. He'd fetched it from the library after school. It was warm in the library and he lingered as long as he could, because there were people and he hated the idea of coming home to this big empty house.

Sometimes, Arthur switched on Aunt Becky's wireless to listen to music or a serial called *Dick Barton, Special Agent*. It crackled a bit and had a strange whistle at times, but it was company. Unfortunately, it used electricity and he didn't dare have it on too long, because he was afraid his shillings wouldn't last.

If Ruby hadn't brought that money from the shop, he would have been even more anxious but he still had a nice little store of notes and coins. Surely Emily would return before he ran out?

She would, wouldn't she? She knew he hated being alone. Surely she would come soon?

Emily had been gone two weeks when one of the teachers stopped Arthur as he was going into the classroom and drew him to one side. He looked at him disapprovingly, his gaze dwelling on Arthur's greasy hair and dirty face.

'Why hasn't your mother washed your hair for you, boy?' he demanded to know, his hand gripping Arthur's shoulder, hurting him. 'She should be ashamed, sending you to school like this. Go to the cloakroom and wash your hands and face immediately – and tell your mother your clothes are a disgrace.'

'Yes, sir,' Arthur mumbled and ran off as he was released. The water was lukewarm in the school cloakroom basins, but it was better than the cold he had at home. Arthur scrubbed his hands and face with the soap that they used, but it smelled like tar and stung his eyes. He looked at himself in the mirror. His shirt was crumpled and the collar was dirty, but he'd used all three of his school shirts now and wasn't sure how to wash them. Besides, they wouldn't dry on the line in the back garden; they just froze and went stiff or dripped forever if it rained. Emily dried them above the range in the evenings when she couldn't put the washing out. He rubbed his scuffed shoes on the back of his long socks but they didn't look much better.

Perhaps he would try to polish them when he got back that evening.

Hearing the bell go, Arthur ran to his classroom. If he was late, he would get the cane on the back of his hand. It had happened twice now and it hurt.

His class teacher gave him a sharp look as he came panting in, but didn't call him out. Arthur sat down at his desk and knuckled his eyes as he felt the sting of tears.

'Cry-baby!' a spiteful voice hissed behind him. 'You stink, Henderson. Doesn't your mother know what soap is?'

Arthur kept his mouth shut and his eyes on the blackboard. It was a maths lesson this morning and one of his favourites. He felt a ping on the back of his head and then another on his ear. He turned his head to glare at the boy behind him. John Mickle was bigger than him and a bully and he'd got an elastic band in his hand, which he'd used to sting Arthur.

'Mum isn't home,' he said. 'She'll wash my things when she comes back.' Tears sparkled in his eyes, but he blinked them back.

'Dirty cry-baby! Mummy's gone and left him—'

'Stop it!' Arthur cried and hit out at him with his ruler.

'Henderson! Stop that immediately! Come here, boy.'

Arthur heard the master's command and got up reluctantly. He went to the front of the class. The master looked him up and down and frowned.

'Sit there,' he said, pointing at an empty desk. 'We'll discuss your behaviour later.'

A snigger from the back caused the master to look there suspiciously. 'Mickle, come here,' he said. The boy came reluctantly. 'Hold out your hand.'

'It wasn't my fault, sir! He hit me.'

'I saw and heard you, Mickle.' The master rapped his hand twice. 'Go back to your seat and do not be a bully. I do not like bullies in my class, Mickle.'

Mickle went off, but not before he shot Arthur a look that threatened revenge.

At break time the master called Arthur to the desk. His look was not unkind when he spoke to him. 'Is something wrong at home, Henderson? I don't think I've seen you come to school in a dirty shirt before?'

Arthur looked down as he lied. 'My mother isn't well, sir.'

'I see . . .' For a moment longer the master stared at him and Arthur was afraid he could tell he was lying. 'Well, when she's better, ask her to wash your things, Henderson. And it is always best to ignore bullies – do you understand?'

'Yes, sir . . .' Arthur hesitated. He was tempted to tell him that his mother hadn't come back from her trip to London, but he was afraid of what would happen to him. He liked his school. He'd had friends, though some of them had started to desert him recently because he smelled bad. 'Thank you . . .'

'If you need any help, you can ask,' the master said. 'We are strict but fair, Arthur. You should tell me if something is worrying you.'

'Yes, sir. I will sir.'

Arthur was glad to escape after school. Mickle had

given him looks all day, even though Arthur had been moved to the front of the class permanently. He hesitated and then decided to walk home. It was a long way but it would save a few coppers for other things. He could get a loaf as he passed the shop on his way.

He had turned the corner when they set on him, jeering, and hitting him. It was Mickle and some of his friends. They punched, kicked, and spat on him, tearing his jacket as they pulled and pushed him one way and then the other. Some coins fell to the floor and they pounced on them, stuffing them into their pockets before they ran away.

Mickle stopped a few yards ahead and looked back. 'That'll teach you, dirty cry-baby! Go blabbing to the masters and you'll end up dead.'

He turned and ran off with the others, leaving Arthur to stare after them in dismay, wishing he'd caught the bus. They didn't dare attack him outside the school gates for fear of being seen, but knew they could get away with it once they were out of sight.

Arthur swallowed hard and started walking. His school clothes were torn and he didn't have any others. In the morning he would have to wear the things he normally wore at home and then he knew he'd be in trouble for not wearing his uniform.

It was a long, cold walk home. The small amount of money he'd had in his overcoat pocket had gone, which meant he'd have to go into the house and get some more and then walk back to the shop for his bread. He put his hand into his pocket, searching for the key. It wasn't there!

Arthur hunted frantically through all his pockets,

but the key had gone. It must have fallen out when those bullies attacked him. It might have gone into the gutter – or one of them might have taken it.

Arthur felt the tears come now. He had no money. He couldn't get into the house to get what he needed to buy his supper and it was a long way back to where they'd attacked him. Yet he had to go. He had to look and see if he could find the missing key. Emily would be so cross with him if he'd lost it and it would cost money to have another made for him and she wouldn't trust him not to lose it again.

Torn by fear and misery, Arthur trudged all the way back to where he'd been attacked. There were no lights, but he thought he'd found the right place and went down on his knees, feeling for his key. His hands encountered muck in the gutter that smelled awful and a bit of broken glass, two stones and an empty cigarette packet, but no key. Just as he was about to give up, a glimmer of light from the moon, which had just come out from behind the clouds, showed him something that glittered. He grabbed for it. It was a half-crown coin and, as his fingers closed around its smooth edge, it felt like riches. He could buy something to eat! He decided he would walk down to the promenade. The other fish shop there would be open and he would buy a bag of chips, find somewhere sheltered to sleep and, in the morning, decide what to do.

Arthur settled down under the pier after he'd eaten his chips. He'd also bought a small bottle of pop, which hadn't left him much more than a shilling. As he wrapped his coat tighter around him, his back up against the wall of the promenade, Arthur knew that he was going to have to seek help. While he'd had the house and a little fire and enough money for food, he could manage, but now he had nothing.

He wanted to cry for his mother but he didn't have a mother. Emily had gone. She'd deserted him, or perhaps she was dead, just like his real mother. The knot of coldness settled inside him as he slept.

He was awoken by a rough hand shaking him. Blinking in the early dawn light, he stared up at the face of the man bending over him, recoiling in fright as he saw the scruffy beard and long hair.

'W-what?' he asked in a scared voice. 'I'm not doing any harm!'

'Nay, lad, don't be frightened,' the old man said. 'It's not often I have company down here. I just wanted to make sure you were all right.'

'Do you sleep here?' Arthur asked, reassured but still wary.

'Aye, most nights, when I'm this way. I travel about from place to place. Never stop anywhere long – they try to lock me up if I do.' He made a guttural sound in his throat. Arthur saw then that he wasn't as old as he'd thought, just dirty and unkempt, as though he'd been living rough for a long time.

'Don't you have a home?' Arthur asked.

'Aye, I had one until the bloody Jerries blew it to kingdom come and my bloody old woman ran orf with another bloke.'

'That wasn't very nice of her,' Arthur said, feeling sympathy for him. 'My mother didn't want me so

254

they sent me to Canada – and then my new mother brought me back here and – and she went off and left me alone.'

'That was bad,' the man said and looked at him. 'I had two sons once but they're grown up now and they side with their Ma. I'm on me own now – but when I catch up wiv 'er she'll know it.'

'She shouldn't have left you,' Arthur agreed solemnly.

'Yer right there, lad,' the man said and seemed to consider. 'Are yer 'ungry?'

'Yes . . .' Arthur swallowed hard. 'I was attacked by bullies and I lost the key to my house. I can't get back inside and I've no money – well, only a little.'

'Right then. We'll go to the seaman's mission along the road. They'll give us a cup of tea and a bowl of soup and a bit of bread, no questions asked. I used ter be in the merchant navy yer see.'

'Will they give me some too?' Arthur asked, getting up quickly as the man nodded.

'Yeah, and then yer can show me yer house. I'll see if I can get yer in, lad.'

'All right.' Arthur smiled at him. 'Thanks, mister.'

'Not a word to anyone if I do – right? It'll be our secret . . .'

Arthur nodded, feeling drawn to his new friend. He'd been frightened when he first saw him, because he was a big, rough-looking man, but he seemed kind and Arthur was hungry. The promise of hot soup and bread had made his stomach grumble. He wasn't sure what Emily would think of the big man getting into their house, but she'd gone away and forgotten him, so perhaps it no longer mattered what she thought.

255

CHAPTER 26

'It's got ter be our secret, lad, understand?' Reg had insisted when he'd broken a window at the back of the house, opened the catch and climbed through; then he'd unlocked the back door with the key that was in it and let Arthur inside.

'Yes, I won't tell,' Arthur agreed. 'But why is it a secret?'

'Because if the coppers found out they'd come and take us away. I'd be locked up for housebreaking and they'd take you away, lad. Put you in a home for kids, I reckon.'

'My name's Arthur,' he'd told Reg, nodding his agreement. 'They'd put me in an orphanage and then send me on a ship somewhere.'

'You can call me Reg,' his new friend said. 'Why would they put you on a ship, then?'

'That's what they did last time,' Arthur told him. 'I went to Canada but my new mum brought me back. This was her aunt's house but she died. Mum thinks it belongs to her now but she has to wait for the lawyers to say she can sell it.'

Reg nodded. He'd gone through to the sitting room, Arthur following behind. His eyes were darting everywhere as he took in their surroundings. The curtains were shut but he didn't open them or put a light on.

'Looks as though you've been sleeping in here, lad?'

'I didn't like it upstairs on my own. It creaks and there are noises in the attic.'

'Probably mice,' Reg nodded. 'Not much here of any value. Did the old lady have any jewellery upstairs?'

'I don't go in her room.' Arthur looked at him nervously. For the first time he wondered whether he'd done right to let this stranger break into the house. He had an odd little feeling in his tummy, as if he'd done something terribly wrong. 'If she has it belongs to Emily now.'

'Yes, but she ain't 'ere now and you've got to eat, lad. Yer mum wouldn't grudge us a few pounds if it meant yer were all right, now, would she?'

'Suppose not,' Arthur replied. 'Aunt Becky's room is on the left at the top of the stairs. Don't take Mum's things, will you?'

'Nay, lad. I'll just see if the old lady had anything worth selling . . .'

Reg left him alone and Arthur thought about his little store of money. Now that he was in the house, he could keep himself for a few weeks, but he wasn't sure whether he could trust Reg. He went to the old jar on the mantelpiece and tipped the money out, stuffing it in his pockets. Upstairs he could hear Reg moving around, opening drawers and searching. Something fell over and he heard the sound of breaking glass. Arthur sat down and waited nervously.

After about twenty minutes, Reg came down with some vases and a few silver trinkets. He'd stuffed some things in his pockets too, so they were bulging.

'Nothing much any good,' he told Arthur. Arthur didn't say anything. He just waited, frightened, because a man who would steal things might do anything. 'I reckon I'll take these to the pawnbrokers and see what I can get for them and then I'll come back. I'll bring some food. What do yer fancy?'

'Can I have fish and chips?'

'If I get a couple of quid yer can,' Reg said. 'Now, don't forget, lad. This is our secret, right?'

Arthur agreed. After Reg had gone out through the back garden, using the gate in the fence this time, Arthur looked at the clock on the mantelpiece. It had stopped so he wound it up, but wasn't sure what time it should be, until he heard the church clock strike ten. So he was too late for school. Besides, he wasn't certain he wanted to go back there after what those boys had done. It was their fault that he'd had to sleep under the pier and met Reg. He'd lost his key because of them; it was their fault Reg had broken the window and got in but Arthur had shown him the house. So it was his fault too and Emily would be so cross with him when she got back.

He regretted telling Reg anything. The more he thought about it, the more Arthur thought he'd done wrong, letting Reg break into the house. He'd stolen those things – things he said were not worth much – but they belonged to Emily now and she would be really angry with him for letting it happen.

Arthur sat alone in the house, waiting. He heard

the church clock strike eleven, then twelve and then one. Reg had been gone a long time and Arthur was getting extremely hungry. The hours crept by and then it began to get dark. Arthur tried to put the light on in the sitting room but the meter was empty and he didn't have a shilling. He found the matches and a candle and took it into the kitchen. There was no food in the house at all and the shops would start to close soon.

Just as he was about to go out in search of food, he heard a noise, a fumbling sound and then the back door opened. Reg appeared and he had a parcel wrapped in newspaper.

'I thought you weren't coming back,' Arthur said half-accusingly.

'I told yer I would; I 'ad somethin' ter do,' Reg said. 'I got one bit of fish and some chips. We'll share. I got them ter put salt and vinegar on but yer might need a bit more salt.'

'I think there's some salt in the pantry . . .' Arthur ran and fetched it. When he came back, Reg had divided the food. He noticed that his portion was much smaller than Reg's but made no complaint. Feeling ravenous, he ate the still warm food, swallowing it down without chewing.

'You'll give yerself the belly gripes,' Reg told him with a grunt. He ate his own meal and then looked around. 'Got any tea in the 'ouse, lad?'

'Yes, I think so and a little sugar, but no milk.'

'I'll make a cuppa, then,' Reg said. He filled the kettle and then lit the gas under it, holding his hands to the flames and rubbing them. 'It's a raw night, lad.

I'd make a fire but that's a sure giveaway that we're in the house. We've got a roof and I'll fetch some more blankets down to the front room.'

'All right.' Arthur thought it best to agree with what Reg said. 'I used to have a fire, though.'

'We don't need it – and we don't want lights at the front of the house. It's all right in here. No one will see the candle.' There were walls on two sides and a fence with a gate at the back.

'So did yer go to school while I was gone?' Reg asked and Arthur shook his head. 'Won't someone wonder why?'

'I don't care,' Arthur said with a touch of defiance. 'I don't want to go back there.'

'Suit yerself.' Reg shrugged. 'Only don't go opening the front door or letting folk know about me.'

'I won't,' Arthur promised but he wasn't sure he would keep his word. People made promises all the time but they didn't mean them. So why should he?

For three days Reg went out in the morning and came back after dark, bringing fish and chips, and once he brought a large loaf of bread. He never bought butter or biscuits or fruit, just the fish and chips they shared. It wasn't enough for Arthur but he dared not say anything. Then, on the fourth morning Reg looked at Arthur for a few moments in silence, before seeming to make up his mind.

'I've got somethin' ter do, kid. I ain't sure when I'll be back – or if I will. Anyway, yer can take care of yerself now, I reckon. Yer can get in the 'ouse by the back way, so I'll be leavin'.' Then he put his hand in his pocket and took out half a crown. 'That's fer 'elpin' me, lad. I hope yer mum comes back . . .'

Arthur swallowed hard and accepted the coin. He knew Reg had got a lot more for the things he'd stolen but it was no good worrying about it. Emily would be cross when she saw her things had gone, because Arthur knew they'd been taken, as well as Aunt Becky's few treasures. He'd been upstairs and tidied the rooms while he was alone and he knew Emily's few pieces of jewellery had gone from her dressing table. She hadn't had much, but there had been a silver bangle, a long chain with a locket, and a little gold brooch. Arthur felt guilty but he couldn't have stopped the big man taking them, even if he'd tried.

When they'd found the black tin box, there had been a lot of money inside. Emily had counted one hundred pounds in five-pound notes. Arthur didn't know what she'd done with it, but he knew it was the money to take them back to Canada. He hoped Reg hadn't found it, but he thought she'd put it in a bank so it would be safe. If Reg *had* taken it, they would have to stay here in this house until they couldn't anymore. Arthur didn't understand about wills or who was entitled to things – he only knew she'd gone to see the lawyer and hadn't come back.

'I'm off. Don't look for me to come back,' Reg said.

'Goodbye, then.' Arthur swallowed hard and held out his hand. 'Thank you for getting me back into the house.'

'That's all right, lad,' Reg said gruffly and punched his shoulder, but not hard. 'Mebbe I'll see yer . . .'

He went out of the back door and through the

garden, leaving Arthur alone once more. He returned to the sitting room and wound the clock, then checked his money and put on his overcoat. He had two pounds left. If he was careful that might last him a week or two but then he didn't know what he would do. When he'd thought Reg was coming back, he'd waited for him, but now he was going to go out. Arthur would prefer to wander about the town during the day, buy some food and come home when it was dark.

Leaving the house, he locked the back door, though it was easy enough for anyone to get in the broken window. Arthur thought for a moment and then hid the key under the rabbit hutch. He didn't want to lose it again and it was easier for him than climbing in the window.

He walked through the roads and lanes towards the seafront. It was even colder here, the wind whipping the water with a wild ferocity into frothy white crests that broke on the stony beach. Turning his collar up, Arthur headed for the library. In there he could keep warm for an hour or two if he was quiet and careful to stay hidden from the librarian. She was usually busy, replacing books or stamping them, but she seldom came right to the back of the library and he could hide behind the shelves. He knew that she liked to sit reading most of the time so all he had to do was watch out for her trolley and make sure he disappeared into the shadows if she started to replace books.

Arthur liked the smell of the library. Books had a smell of their own and sometimes he caught the fragrance of freshly brewed coffee from a café nearby. He never bought coffee or tea, though he'd been glad of the warmth when Reg made a cup of strong tea. He thought he might try heating some water for cocoa that evening, because he intended to light a fire. Reg hadn't wanted him to do it when he was there but now Arthur could please himself.

Arthur picked up discarded newspapers, bits of wood that had washed up on the shore and anything else that might burn and keep him warm. His coal had all been used up and the coke didn't burn very well. It took ages to light and needed more kindling. Once he saw some logs for sale outside a house and he bought as many as he could carry in his satchel for a few pence. The woman looked at him oddly and said he should get his mother to fetch some in a sack, but Arthur told her his mum couldn't afford a sackful and she sniffed in disgust, looking at him as if he was something the cat had dragged in.

Arthur knew he must look very scruffy now. He just wore a pullover over his shirt, but kept the collar inside so no one could see how dirty it was. His hair was growing long in his neck and it needed washing, but Arthur couldn't face getting in a tub of cold water. He did try to wash his hands and face, but the water was too icy to do more than splash himself and rub it off on a towel.

He eked his money out a few pennies at a time, always trying to buy the cheapest he could find, and living mostly on bread with a little jam. Now and then he bought two slices of streaky bacon as a treat, but sausages were too expensive. He longed for a big bag of fish and chips, and almost wished Reg back, even though he'd been scared of the big man.

All day, Arthur trudged the streets or the beach, trying not to loiter and be noticed. If he sheltered in the same place too often someone might let the man know who collected up truants and took them to school – or to an orphanage. Sometimes he wondered what he would do if the money ran out, but he knew that if he asked for help, they would send him away somewhere and he wanted to stay here until Emily came back. She had to one day, didn't she?

It was one night during the third week of his not going to school that someone knocked at the door at about five in the evening. Arthur couldn't open the door even if he wanted to. He heard the knocking but stood in the hall and shivered, afraid to call out, but when he sensed that whoever it was had gone, he ran to the sitting-room window and moved the curtain a tiny bit to look out. He couldn't be certain from the back view, but he thought it was his teacher, the one who had moved him to the front of the class.

He'd come to see why Arthur hadn't been in school! Arthur felt his tummy turn over. How much longer would it be before someone came to fetch him away? He knew it couldn't be long. He only had two shillings left in his coat pocket. If he didn't ask for help soon, he would starve, because Reg hadn't returned and nor had Emily. She'd gone away and forgotten him.

Arthur curled up into a ball on the floor by the pitiful excuse for a fire and closed his eyes, battling the tears. Crying wouldn't help. He didn't know what to do. If there was anything left in the house worth selling perhaps he could find someone to buy it for a few shillings but he thought Reg had stolen anything worth more than a few pence.

Hungry, cold, and miserable, Arthur eventually fell asleep. In his sleep his cheeks were stained with the tears he'd refused to shed while awake. Dreaming, he saw a woman hold out her arms to him to embrace him.

'You're home now, Arthur,' she told him, but before he could run to her arms he woke up, shivering and frightened. He remembered the woman but he hadn't seen her face. Was it Emily? Would she come back for him?

CHAPTER 27

'Well, they didn't say no,' Harry offered as they left the office of the adoption centre, where they'd been interviewed as prospective parents for an orphaned child. 'It's just a matter of checking and verifying that we're who we say we are – and that's a good thing, isn't it?'

'Yes, of course it is,' Rose agreed and hugged his arm. 'He seemed a nice man and very encouraging, didn't you think so?' It was still a lot of rigmarole and she couldn't see why they didn't just let decent folk get on and adopt the children who had been orphaned by the war. Goodness knows, there were enough of them. They hadn't been as fussy when they shipped the kids off to the country and Rose had heard of some of them being mistreated. Why the heck didn't they just get on and give a child a home and not bother about the red tape? She sometimes thought she might as well do just that; the country was in a mess anyway, loads of records having been lost to the Blitz. Who would ever know?

'Yes, I did,' Harry smiled as she joined the bus

queue. It was a bitter day and March seemed to be going out like a lion, the wind from off the sea front cut through his clothes like a knife, making him shiver. He caught the smell of fish and chips. 'Shall we get some?' he asked.

'What, from there?' Rose looked in the direction of the enticing smell. But she didn't much like the look of the shop, the windows steamed up and grimy outside. 'It's a pity that other place further down the promenade closed so suddenly. I liked the way they cooked everything and the fish was always fresh.'

Harry glanced at the shop, seeing the dirty paint, and nodded. 'Perhaps we'll give it a miss. Here's our bus, Rose . . .'

The bus slowed down and halted. Inside it was steamy with the warm breath of many passengers. Rose had to go right down the back to get a seat and Harry had to stand in the aisle. As the driver drew away, something made Rose turn and look out of the window. She saw a young boy staring in at the fish shop window and the hairs at the back of her neck prickled. She knew him! It was Arthur, the lad she'd last seen at Christmas with his mother, listening to the carols, but there was something wrong. He had an unkempt air about him, his socks falling down about his ankles and his shoes scuffed and dirty. She wanted to get up and go to him but the bus was moving away and there were people standing in the centre aisle. To get off she would have to ring the bell and upset a lot of people.

She let it go, wondering if it was really the boy she'd seen a couple of times, when they'd come into Hastings. If it was, something had changed. His mother had seemed a bit distant when they spoke to her, but she'd clearly looked after her son. He'd been healthy, his clothes clean and his shoes polished. She shook her head. It couldn't have been the same boy. She'd made a mistake . . . the feeling she'd had for him had misled her.

It was daft, really. Rose didn't know why her heart had been drawn to Arthur – the man with them had called him Arthur. She hadn't thought he was the boy's father. In fact, Arthur didn't look like either of them and his elfin face and blond hair made him seem angelic.

His hair – Rose felt a little jolt as she thought of the boy staring longingly into the fish and chip shop. It was greasy and it wanted trimming. Arthur's had shone and was neatly cut. The child she'd just seen had been neglected for a while and she wished she'd stopped the bus and barged her way through the passengers to reach him, but when they reached the next stop, she'd still hesitated, because surely the boy would have moved on, with or without his bag of chips.

'You're quiet, Rose?' Harry murmured as they got off the bus some time later. 'Something upset you?'

'It was just a kid staring in the fish shop window,' she said. 'He looked hungry.'

Harry nodded. 'I noticed him, too. I thought he looked a bit like a lad I'd seen somewhere before . . .'

'Eating fish and chips from the other shop, that night we took them to the bus shelter?' Rose said and nodded. 'I thought so too.' She looked at him thoughtfully, making up her mind all of a sudden. 'I'm going to take a day off tomorrow, Harry. I'll go to the shop that closed down and see if they've left a contact notice. His mother worked there. I remember the girl behind the counter was having a go at her and I've got a bad feeling, though I don't know why. I should've stopped the bus. I think that lad was in trouble.'

'Why didn't you say? I'd have stopped it.' Harry looked at her sharply. 'There's something about that lad, isn't there?' She nodded. 'Is it because he looks a bit like Davey Blake did at his age?'

'Might be,' Rose admitted, though she hadn't really thought about it. 'But mostly it's those sad eyes. That lad is crying inside, Harry. I've seen him a couple of times now and I'd say he's had a rough time, even if his mother does her best.'

'You take the day off tomorrow and the next if you need it,' Harry said. 'See if you can find him. I don't like the thought of any lad being in trouble.'

'You're a good bloke, Harry,' Rose told him, checking back her tears. 'Most men would say I was daft for even thinking things like that and they certainly wouldn't approve of me taking time off to go on a wild-goose chase.'

'I'm not most men,' Harry told her with a grin. 'I know you, Rose Smith – and I know you'll fret yourself to a frazzle if you don't find the lad so do whatever you have to.'

Rose stared at the closed noticed in frustration. It just said it had closed, nothing more, not a word of explanation or an address where the owner might be reached.

'Oh bugger!' Rose muttered. She rattled the door handle in the vain hope that there might be someone inside working but it remained securely locked. 'Now where do I go?'

'They closed down, missus,' a voice piped up behind her. Rose spun round to see a youth of perhaps fifteen looking at her. 'Ruby couldn't cope wiv just me and her when Emily didn't come no more.'

'Did you work here?' Rose asked and he nodded. 'I liked it – and I liked the new boss. Emily was all right. Strange she never come back after she went off to London. I dunno why she'd do that.'

Rose looked at him sharply. 'Did this Emily have a son – a boy about nine or ten years old?'

'Yeah, that's Arthur,' the youth said. 'Me and him got on all right when he helped me wash and peel the chips. I reckon they must have got fed up with the hard work and just gone off.'

'Did Arthur go to London with Emily?' Rose asked but he shook his head. 'I dunno, missus – but I lost me job. Ain't found another yet.'

'I'm sorry you lost your job . . .? I don't know your name?'

'It's Tom,' the lad said and grinned at her. Rose reached in her pocket and gave him half a crown.

'Cor thanks, missus.' She nodded and turned away. 'I know where the old lady lived until she died. I think Emily and Arthur lived there too.'

'You know?' Rose looked at him and he gave her a lopsided grin.

'Yeah. She used to ask me to do errands for her sometimes. It's Old London Road, just at the bottom of the hill. I disremember the number, but it's on the left as you get off the bus at the bottom. You can catch a bus over the road.'

'Tom, you are a good lad,' Rose said and gave him

another half a crown. 'I hope you find another job soon.'

'I shall if I try, so my mum says,' Tom answered and grinned at her. 'She wants me to try at a factory.' He stuck his hands in his pockets and went off whistling.

Rose crossed the road and stood at the bus stop until the right one came along. She boarded it and told the conductor she wanted the stop at the bottom of the hill and asked if he would call out when they got there. He gave her a ticket and nodded. Rose looked anxiously out of the window. She'd been lucky so far but her nerves were tingling and she'd got a prickle at the nape of her neck, always a sign that something was wrong.

She got off when the conductor called out and went to the house on the left next to the stop. It was modest compared to several in the road but better than the one she and Harry had rented. She lifted the large black-painted knocker and rapped it three times. There was an empty sound and she was sure there was no one in. Two empty milk bottles stood to one side, both dusty, as though they had been there a while.

Rose looked about her in frustration. She'd hoped against hope Emily would open the door and all her fears would prove groundless. If Tom had been right and Arthur's mother had gone to London and never returned, what had happened to him? Had Arthur gone with her or was he the boy she'd seen looking hungrily at the fish shop? If he was, she sensed that something bad had happened to his mother. Emily would surely never have gone off and left him alone? She hadn't seemed that sort.

As she stood debating what to do next, a woman came out of the house opposite and crossed the road towards her.

'Are you looking for Mrs Henderson?' she asked. 'I'm Mrs Rowe and I don't know her well. She keeps to herself, but I knew her aunt well.'

'I wanted to see if she was all right and Arthur,' Rose told her. 'I saw the fish and chip shop was closed and the lad that used to work there said Emily had gone off to London and never returned.'

'Is that where she went? I saw her go off dressed up but I haven't seen her since. I've seen Arthur a few times, not recently though – but I don't watch all the time. I have my house to clean . . .'

'You've seen Arthur leaving and entering on his own?' Rose asked. 'How long ago did Emily leave?'

'A few weeks ago,' Mrs Rowe said, nodding. 'I thought I must have missed her. She wouldn't go and leave a boy that age alone, would she?'

'I'm sure she wouldn't if she could help it,' Rose agreed. Alarm bells were going off in her head. She was convinced that the lad she'd seen staring longingly in the window of the fish and chip shop was Arthur and feared for his safety, and that of his mother. Emily Henderson hadn't looked the sort to just go off and leave a child alone, so what had happened to her?

'Could you let me know if you see Arthur, please? I'm going to give you my address,' Rose said. She scrabbled in her bag. 'I'm at work most days but a letter will reach me here.' She found a scrap of paper. 'Could I borrow a pencil?'

'Yes, come over and I'll find one,' Mrs Rowe said. 'Are you Arthur's granny?'

'Just a friend,' Rose replied, 'but a concerned one.'

Mrs Rowe nodded and Rose followed her across the road. She didn't invite Rose in but left the door open as she fetched a pencil. The hall floor looked highly polished and smelled fresh, everything spotless and neat.

'It's wrong, that's what it is,' Mrs Rowe grumbled. 'Leaving a lad of that age alone and going off to London, anything could have happened.'

'Yes, I agree,' Rose said, wanting to keep on her best side. 'But she may have got into trouble. I'm going to do my best to find Arthur and then I'll go to the police if his mother is missing.'

'You do that,' Mrs Rowe nodded and glanced at the paper Rose had given her. 'You don't live that far away.' She smiled. 'Let me know if you discover anything.'

'Thank you. Don't forget to let me know if you see Arthur, Mrs Rowe – and if you can, ask him where his mum is and if he needs help. I'll help him if he needs someone.'

'Right you are then,' Mrs Rowe said. 'I'll keep a sharp eye out for him.'

Rose thanked her, crossed the road, and stood for a moment after the door had closed. Then she saw a bus for the town centre coming and got on it. She would have a wander round the town, go as far as the fish shop, just in case . . .

'So your fears were confirmed.' Harry looked at her anxiously that evening when she told him what she'd discovered. 'Do you think she intended to desert him – or did something happen to her?'

274

'I believe something happened to stop her returning.' Rose held his concerned gaze for a moment. 'I think I should report it to the police, don't you?'

'Oh, certainly,' Harry confirmed. 'We'll go to the station this evening and give them all the information we have, Rose. If that child is living there alone, he needs help.'

'The funny thing was the house looked as if no one was living there. Some empty milk bottles stood outside and looked as if they'd been there a while. I can only wonder why they haven't been collected.'

'You think the milkman hasn't been paid?'

'Perhaps,' Rose replied, looking puzzled. 'It doesn't fit, somehow, Harry. She looked like the sort to pay her bills – and why any mother would go off and leave her son I just don't know.'

'Well, we'll report what we know to the police and see what they say.'

'Could we just check back to the house again and see if Arthur is there first? I wouldn't want to cause trouble for his mother or him if he's all right.'

'Yes, of course we can, love. Makes sense, because the police won't stir unless we present a good case – too much else on their minds.' He looked at her strangely and her spine tingled.

'What's that, Harry?' Rose gazed at him anxiously. 'Something I don't know?'

'Bit of an alert at the factory. You know we've been working on new weapons? Well, they think there might be a bit of espionage going on – and there have been some unexplained lights out at sea, which have them on high alert up and down the coast.'

'You think there are spies about?' Rose gasped. 'No, I know you can't tell me any more, but it gives me the shivers.'

'We had a fire alarm drill today while some experts went over the factory, but everything was OK. Might be just false information, but I know the local police are edgy and beach patrols have been stepped up at night.'

Rose felt a coldness at her nape. 'You think someone might try to sabotage the factory from inside? Surely none of our workers would risk such a thing? So many lives would be lost!'

Rose thought about the factory with its tiny windows high up that no one could climb through. There was an escape door at either end that opened wide to let the workers out, but in an alarm there would be pandemonium, and the workers could be crushed as everyone tried to escape. Sheltered in the woods from detection by enemy aircraft, it would cause an inferno should an explosion occur.

'It would be easy enough to do,' Harry mused. 'A small fire in the right place – or an explosive device – would be enough to destroy the factory although whoever did it would risk their own life.'

Rose nodded. 'I suppose there are some folk mad enough to do it.' A shiver went through her. 'Makes my flesh creep to think about it, Harry.' There were some bad folk about but it was scary to think she and Harry might be working side by side with an enemy spy.

'Well, don't,' he advised with a smile. 'We've stepped up security and there will be extra patrols around the perimeter.'

'Good. Besides, I've got other things to think about for the moment.'

'Arthur and his mum,' Harry agreed. 'You take a few days off to do what you have to do, love. I wish I could join you in the search . . .'

'You've got enough to worry about,' Rose told him with a shake of her head. 'We'll finish our tea and then we'll go back to the house. I'll put a note and some money through the door and tell Arthur where we live if he needs help.'

Harry agreed that the house was empty and didn't look as if it had been lived in for a while. The empty milk bottles hadn't been collected and he told Rose he really thought it must mean the bill hadn't been paid.

'Stands to reason: if he was still collecting money and leaving milk, he'd collect the bottles.'

'I should've thought he would anyway,' Rose grumbled. 'Waste of good bottles and I heard they were getting short – like most things.'

'We'll take them home and put them out with ours,' Harry said, slipping them into his coat pocket. 'The lad isn't here, Rose. We've knocked loud enough to wake the dead. Either she took him with her or he's gone off on his own.'

'Why would he do that, though? Even if his mother wasn't here, surely he would be better off with a bed to sleep in rather than on the streets?' She frowned as she looked at the lock. 'It's not a Yale lock so he couldn't have accidentally locked himself out.'

'No, but he could have locked the door behind him and then lost the key. You know what young boys are like, Rose.'

'Yes, that's true. We always left our key on a string behind the letterbox so ours could put their hand in and get it if I wasn't in when they got home – not that I did that much. Reg wouldn't let me work at the start, because he said it would shame him.' She made a wry face. 'I didn't bother when the lads were young but then I decided I'd do a few hours – after all, Reg was at sea most of the time. He gave me a smacking when he found out, but then he realised it gave him extra beer money so he said no more.'

'You like to work, don't you?' Harry looked at her anxiously. 'If you felt you'd rather stay home—'

'Don't talk daft, Harry,' Rose cut him off quickly. 'I like the chat and the gossip. 'Sides, there's a war on.' She popped an envelope through the letterbox. It contained five shillings and her name and address. If Arthur needed help, surely he would respond to her request to get in touch?

Harry nodded, his look of concern for her fading, to be replaced by a frown as he said, 'We'd best go to the police station then and report what we know.'

Rose agreed and they caught the next bus into the town centre, neither of them saying much. It was a bitterly cold night and the bus windows had patterns on the glass as warm breath met icy panes.

'A boy of about nine, fair-haired with fine features and sad eyes . . .' The police officer looked at Rose doubtfully. 'You can't tell me what he was wearing?'

'I only caught sight of him through a bus window and, as I told you, I can't be sure it was him – Arthur Henderson. His mother is called Emily and she went

278

to London to see a lawyer and never returned, so Mrs Rowe told me. She lives opposite and I think she watches her neighbours come and go quite a bit. She has seen Arthur since his mother went off, but not recently.'

A look of disbelief entered the officer's eyes. 'So you are reporting a boy you *think* may be on the streets and a woman who *might* be missing? That's a bit airy-fairy if you ask me, Mrs . . . Smith, did you say?'

'Yes,' Rose held back her impatience with difficulty. 'She worked at the fish shop that has closed down.'

'Well, I'm not sure what we can do about it, Mrs Smith. You haven't given me enough information to put out an alert – and you're not a relation, are you?'

'No, just a friend,' Rose told him. 'A concerned friend. I'm almost sure that Arthur is out there alone somewhere and he must be hungry, cold, and frightened.'

'Well, I'll tell the lads to keep an eye out for a lad with fair hair who looks to be in trouble – but they would bring him in if they spotted him anyway.' He saw the expression in Rose's eyes. 'I'll put them on the missing list, but we don't have the resources to search for every boy who decides to play truant. I suppose you have tried his school?'

'I'm going to try the schools tomorrow,' Rose said. 'I am very anxious, officer.'

'The most likely school is Mount Pleasant,' he said. 'You could try there – and I'll make inquiries myself at another school on my day off, which happens to be tomorrow. Let me know if he turns up safe and sound.' He closed his report book after writing a couple of sentences.

Rose turned and left, Harry following behind. 'A fat lot of good he was!' she exclaimed when they were outside in the street. 'I don't know what they need to make them get off their backsides and get out and search!'

'I suppose it sounded a bit vague to him,' Harry offered but frowned. 'They don't have the manpower at the moment, Rose. I'm not making excuses for him, and I'm sure he'll do what he can.'

'In the meantime, Arthur could be starving.' Rose looked annoyed and then sighed. 'I know, Harry, but I'm worried.' Her gut feeling was that it was urgent to find Arthur, but she couldn't explain why, to herself or anyone else.

'Do you want to go down the sea front, have a mooch around, see if we can spot Arthur?'

'Yes, please,' Rose said. 'I don't know where to start other than that fish shop, but I should think it's closed by now.'

'We'll have a walk along the front, near where we saw him,' Harry said. 'In the morning you can try some of the schools – start with Mount Pleasant – and then see if you get any information to go on from there.'

They hadn't seen him, even though they'd walked right along the front, looking in shop doorways and bus shelters. There was no sign of the lad they'd seen when they were on the bus. Rose had thought he might be in the amusement arcade but it was locked and dark, just as all the shops were. Even the fish shop window was blackened so that light didn't leak out and attract the attention of enemy planes.

They'd heard several planes go over as they were walking, but Harry reckoned they were Allied bombers on their way to a mission – quite a few of them by the noise they made. Rose shivered as she thought of the death and destruction they would rain down on homes and cities. Even if it was the enemy, it would still cause heartache and pain, and she didn't like the idea of it happening. All she wanted was to find a lost boy and go home and be safe and she was sure the women in those cities overseas felt just the same.

Rose was anxious as she went to bed that evening. Where was Arthur? Had his mother returned and taken him away with her, unbeknown to her neighbours – or was he alone, frightened, cold, and hungry?

CHAPTER 28

'You wanted to talk to someone about Arthur Henderson?' Rose had been standing at the window watching the children play outside and turned at the sound of the man's voice. He was tall and thin and wore heavy spectacles but looked to be pleasant enough. 'You are?'

'Mrs Rose Smith,' she told him, extending her hand. He took it in a firm clasp. 'I'm a friend of Arthur's family and I've had some disturbing news about his mother. I understand she went to London about three and a half weeks ago and hasn't returned.'

'That would explain it!' he said. 'I'm Danvers, by the way. Arthur is in my class for maths, history, and English. He's a bright boy, as I expect you know, and I've been worried about him.' He paused, then, 'He came to school in dirty clothes, shirt not washed, hair greasy, shoes not polished – and one of the boys made a derogatory remark. Arthur hit out at him with a ruler. I moved him to the front of the class and punished the other lad but Arthur hasn't been to school since. I went to his house a few nights ago but there was no answer – and yet I'm almost certain he was there.'

'I went twice yesterday,' Rose said. 'I thought I caught sight of him on the sea front but wasn't sure so I-I went to his house.' She couldn't tell him that she'd had to discover where Arthur lived, because unless he believed she knew Arthur well he would not confide in her. 'I went to the police but they didn't seem to think it was a case for investigation.'

'Perhaps they didn't realise he hadn't been to school for nearly three weeks?'

'I tried to make them see how serious it was, Mr Danvers. I've been looking for him and I intend to go on searching but the police merely made a note and did nothing.'

'I'm glad you have shown concern, Mrs Smith. I shall visit the police myself now and make my own worries known. I promise you they will listen to me!' He glanced at his watch. 'I must go. I have lessons – but if you could give me an address? If I hear of, or see him, I will let you know.'

'Thank you,' Rose said, feeling relieved that someone else shared her and Harry's concern. She wrote her address down on the little notepad she now carried in her handbag. 'I'm going to have another day searching for him, Mr Danvers, but then I shall have to go back to work. I will continue to check with the police and to look for him at weekends, but my work is important . . .'

'You're from London, aren't you?'

'Yes.'

'Then you'll be working at the munitions factory . . .'

He saw her face and smiled. 'Yes, I know it's all hush-hush, but most local folk know it's around here somewhere, though we might not know exactly where – but people talk and they recruited workers.'

Rose nodded. 'We all have to keep close mouths these days, Mr Danvers. You never know who is listening.'

'I've heard rumours there might be enemy agents about,' he said and nodded. 'I know a lot of people, and I hear things, but I do know most folk would be sharp enough to pick up on something like that – and I don't credit the rumours. Just a lot of hot air if you ask me. The time for an enemy invasion is past and the war is on the turn. It will all be over in a few months.'

'I hope you're right,' Rose said and smiled as she handed him her address and left.

She was thoughtful as she walked through the town and towards the sea front. Harry had said she could take as much time off as she liked but she knew it made things difficult, especially when the factory was at full stretch. Despite Mr Danvers' confidence, the war wasn't over yet.

Rose had been wandering about the town and sea front for some time when she had a prickling at the back of her neck, as if someone was following her. She turned sharply and caught sight of a large man on the corner of the street. Her flesh prickled, because despite his scruffy appearance and the beard she knew at once that it was Reg – her husband! He was here and that meant he'd followed her down. Someone must have talked about the location – unless it was just coincidence, and she didn't believe that. He'd come looking for her – for revenge. She tensed, thinking he might rush at her and give her a clout, but he just stood there.

He leered at her openly, standing there, daring her to say something! Rose felt hot and then cold, her stomach tying itself in knots. She knew that he was here to make trouble but the street was busy and he wouldn't want to be seen attacking her. No, he would wait until it was dark, hope to take her by surprise. As she paused, wondering which way to go to avoid him, he turned away and walked off.

She shuddered. He hadn't tried to hide so he was taunting her, trying to make her afraid. He would laugh if he could make her life a misery. Rose set her mouth firmly. If he thought she was going to hide from him in terror, he had another think coming! She would be ready for him now.

After a moment to catch her breath, she decided not to give up her search for Arthur and spent another two hours wandering around. She asked in the fish and chip shop if they'd seen a boy of about nine, a boy who might look dirty and untidy and they shook their heads, but when she was leaving one of them said, 'I think he might have been here yesterday. He asked what he could buy for a penny. I gave him a bag of crispies for nothing. He thanked me. Nice, polite lad – but dirty.'

'He's missing from home,' Rose told her. 'If you see him again, could you let the police know, please?'

'Well, I'm not always on the counter but I'll try . . .'

Rose left the shop, feeling that she was getting somewhere at last. Arthur was wandering around Hastings, she was certain of it now – but how one person alone was ever going to find him, she didn't know.

Harry looked at her that evening when he got home and saw the anxiety in her eyes. 'No luck then?'

'I went to the school and met a Mr Danvers. He's Arthur's teacher for some lessons and he said the other boys had been bullying him for coming to school dirty but then he stopped going.'

'That's boys all over,' Harry said, looking worried. 'So you were right, love. He's on the streets alone, he's dirty and hungry – but why isn't he in the house at night? Do you think his mother locked him out when she went off?'

'I would've thought she would leave him a key,' Rose said, 'but what do you think can have happened to her?'

'Damned if I know,' Harry said and then looked at her as someone knocked at their door. He was about to answer it, when Rose caught at his arm. 'Be careful. I saw Reg down the town this morning. He knew I saw him but then just walked away . . .'

'Rose . . .' Harry began but the knocking came again. He picked up the poker and went to the door. Rose waited in fear of a fight, but a moment later Harry was inviting someone into the house. His eyes met hers. 'This gentleman is looking for Arthur, Rose. He went to the police station to make inquiries because there was no answer at the house and the police told him you'd reported him missing . . .'

Rose looked at the man. He was dressed in a brown suit and cream shirt with a tie and had a Trilby hat in his hand. A quiet sort of man, one you'd pass in the street and hardly notice.

'What did you say your name was?' she asked suspiciously.

'Robert Carson, Mrs Smith,' he said and smiled. 'I'm a private agent and I've been hired by a Mrs Veronica Bittern of Halifax in Canada to search for Mrs Henderson and Arthur.'

'Are they in trouble?'

'Far from it as far as Mrs Bittern is concerned. Mrs Bittern wants to offer them a home and job if they wish to return to Canada – but more than that, she needs to know that they're safe and well. Arthur travelled out to Canada with a dear friend of hers and they're all concerned for his welfare – and that of Emily Henderson.'

'Mrs Henderson has disappeared,' Rose told him. 'Apparently, she went to London to see her lawyer about a month ago and never came back. I reported her missing and Arthur, I believe, is still in Hastings but living rough and I think he's hungry . . .'

'That's shocking news,' Mr Carson said, taken aback. 'I discovered Mrs Henderson's lawyer through some adverts in the newspapers, and I know she met him at his office. There was some dispute as to whether she would inherit much of her aunt's estate, because of a debt but he didn't know she hadn't returned to her son. I came down to visit them and tell them that Mrs Bittern has offered to help in any way she can . . .' He shook his head in disbelief. 'I cannot imagine she went off and left a child alone just like that. She must have met with some kind of accident.'

'That's why I reported it,' Rose said. 'I thought the police might check the hospitals but they haven't as far as I know.'

'I most certainly shall,' Mr Carson assured her instantly. 'And do you know anything at all that might help me trace Arthur, please?'

'He went to Mount Pleasant school until about three weeks ago. His teacher, Mr Danvers, says he was bullied for not having clean clothes. I don't suppose he knew how to wash them.'

'Probably doesn't have hot water,' Harry put in. 'If he's got a range like ours, he couldn't get it going.'

'We saw him near the fish shop on the front – the one that's still open. The one his mother worked in has closed; because she didn't turn up for work, I was told. He was there a few days ago but only had a penny for some crispy bits off the fish batter. The poor little lad must be starving . . .' She felt her throat catch with tears, because it wasn't just the hunger, it was the fear that lived inside that would be even worse. 'I've looked for him all over but couldn't find him, Mr Carson, and now I need to return to work . . .' She looked at Harry as he shook his head. 'Yes, I do, Harry. I know my job is important and I think it's pointless just wandering around the town. I don't know how to find him.'

'I might have a better chance,' Mr Carson said. 'It's my job and I shall look in places you wouldn't think of. It's door-to-door slogging work sometimes and a lady like yourself wouldn't know the right folk to ask. There are bound to be a few tramps living rough under the arches. I'll ask around and see what I can find out.'

'Thank you. I would be so grateful,' Rose told him

and the tears just came, trickling down her cheeks. 'I've been so worried. I don't know the boy that well but I took to him . . . he has the saddest eyes.'

'From what I've been able to establish he's had a sad time of it, Mrs Smith. His mother went to pieces after his father was killed in an accident. She neglected him and started drinking and they took him into care. After she died there was no one who might have had him so he was sent out to Canada. Mrs Bittern believes he was well cared for by Emily Henderson, at least until her husband bankrupted them and went off to fight to get out of facing his creditors. She lost her home and brought Arthur here to live with her sick aunt, but the aunt died.'

'Poor little love!' Rose said. 'Now Emily's gone off he must feel as if he's been abandoned all over again.'

'That's about it,' Mr Carson agreed. 'I think we have to find that child, Mrs Smith, and find him quickly. Believe me, I shall spare no effort in the search. You can leave it to me now.'

'You will let me know – and bring Arthur to me if he needs care? I would love to look after him.' She gave him a pleading look. 'You won't let them put him in a home again.'

'If and when I find him, I'll bring him to you,' Mr Carson said. 'You'll take care of him while I discover what happened to his adoptive mother and a decision is made about his future care.'

'We'd take him and love him, wouldn't we, Harry?'

'Yes.' Harry looked at her lovingly and then at Mr Carson. 'He has a home with us if we are allowed to keep him. We're looking to adopt a child and we've both taken to the lad.'

'That's wonderful news,' Mr Carson said, beaming at them. 'All Mrs Bittern wants is to make sure he's well and cared for.' He nodded to Rose and then Harry. 'I shall leave you now – and as soon as I have news of any sort, I will be in touch.'

'Thank you – thank you so much,' Rose said and Harry made a gruff sound in his throat.

After he'd seen their visitor to the door Harry came back and looked at Rose. 'So now you can tell me about Reg. Are you certain it was him?'

'Oh yes, quite certain,' Rose said. 'He knew I'd seen him and he smiled at me in a leering sort of way, and then he went off. The street was busy and there was a policeman further up the road. Reg dared not attack me there in broad daylight and I think he wanted me to see him, thinking he would scare me and make me worry about when he'll try to hurt me.'

'If he lays a finger on you, he's a dead man!'

'Please don't say that, Harry,' Rose pleaded. 'I love you and I don't want you hung or locked up in prison for the rest of your life. In London you had mates who would have made sure he disappeared, but if it happened here you might end up in a police cell.'

'If he attacks you, I'll do what I have to,' Harry said firmly. 'Hopefully, it won't happen. He might just try to torment you for a while and then go off somewhere.'

'Not Reg. He'll try to attack me when I least expect it,' Rose said. 'But I will *always* expect it! Oh, let's forget him, Harry. I don't want to think about Reg. Do you think Mr Carson will find out what happened to Emily Henderson and will he manage to trace Arthur?'

'He seemed pretty confident so I'd say yes.' Seeing

291

her face light up, Harry cautioned. 'Don't get your hopes too high, love. I hope and believe Arthur will be found but that doesn't mean we'll be allowed to keep him.'

'Surely we will,' Rose said, a note of longing in her voice. 'He has no one and we've been approved as adopters or foster parents.' A little voice inside her was defiant. If she got Arthur and he was happy to live with them, no one was going to take him away again. Be damned to their red tape!

'I know.' Harry kissed her. 'I want Arthur as much as you do, love. We'll just have to pray . . .'

CHAPTER 29

Arthur stood in the shadows and watched as the family entered the fish and chip shop then came out some minutes later with parcels of steaming hot food. His stomach clenched with the pain as he saw them scurry off and he thought wistfully of being a part of a family like that; mother, father, children, all laughing and happy in anticipation of an evening spent together.

He was convinced now that Emily had never loved him. Why would she have left him behind if she cared?

Only a tiny pinprick of light showed through a corner of the blackened shop window, but to Arthur it was a beacon. His stomach rumbled noisily and he longed for a packet of soft chips and some crispy bits from the fish batter, but he only had one penny left and he wasn't sure they would give him anything. One kind lady had given him a big bag of crispy bits for nothing, but a man had sent him off with a grunt last time.

'We don't serve the likes of you – clear orf!'

Arthur reluctantly turned away from the enticing smell. The streets were emptying fast now as people hurried to their homes. He wasn't sure what day it was or even what month, though it was still bitterly cold at night. Soon he would need to return to the empty house he hated so much. He would light a small fire in the grate, but there were no newspapers left or any form of kindling and only a few small lumps of coke. He had begun to use some of Aunt Becky's books; the ones he didn't want to read, like a French dictionary and a book about cooking. They didn't last long but he'd been able to heat enough water to make cocoa; it was a large tin but it was nearly finished.

Arthur fingered his last penny. Should be spend it on a bread roll or save it for tomorrow? Perhaps a mug of cocoa would be enough when he got home.

Every day he'd hoped that Emily would be there. He knew she would be cross about the things Reg had stolen, but it wasn't his fault. The big man had used him, pretended to be kind to get into an empty house and steal. Arthur understood that now. He'd thought he meant to help him but instead he'd pinched the things Arthur could have sold in time to keep himself in food.

Sometimes, Arthur wondered if there was anything Reg had missed that he could sell for a few shillings. Could he perhaps find a little job, or should he go to the school and tell his teacher the truth? The thoughts rolled round and round in his head and he wanted to cry but he was too cold and hungry, even though it hadn't been quite as cold that day and he knew it would soon be spring.

He left the back gate unbolted now so that it was easy to get in. His key was under the rabbit hutch as usual and he let himself into the kitchen. It felt cold and damp and he'd noticed dark mould appearing round the window ledges.

Arthur put some water into the small saucepan he'd found on the bottom shelf in the pantry and took it into the sitting room. He'd cleared the grate that morning and stuffed it with paper from his aunt's books and two tiny pieces of coke. Once the paper lit, he placed two whole paperback books on the top and watched the flames begin to lick into them. It was almost as good as his newspaper crackers. The coke was slow to catch but in the end it did, glowing red but not sending up a flame; he placed his water on to heat and waited. His tummy rumbled and he felt it cramp with pain. He was so hungry.

The smell of the warm cocoa was comforting and Arthur sat with the mug in his hands, sipping it slowly, making it last. For a while it helped, giving him a feeling of something in his stomach, but it didn't last long and then the hunger pangs started in earnest.

Arthur clutched at himself and brought his knees up to his chest, rocking back and forth. He was starving and so alone. His throat hurt and his eyes burned with unshed tears.

Why did no one care about him? What had he done that was so bad he was being punished?

After a while, he went upstairs to Aunt Becky's room. Reg had left all her clothes on the floor after he'd emptied the drawers. Arthur folded them and put them back. He didn't think anything in the chest would fetch more than a copper or two at the rag-and-bone yard. He'd passed it on his wanderings, because he walked miles every day now, exploring and looking into shops and following roads to see where they went. It was better than sitting alone in the house and it was too cold to sit on the beach.

Looking through Aunt Becky's wardrobe, he thought some of her clothes might fetch a few shillings at the second-hand shop near the market. He decided that he would select a couple of things and take them the next day, because it was his only hope of getting something to eat. Despite his hurt – and sometimes anger – that he felt towards Emily for leaving him, Arthur didn't want to sell *her* things in case she did come back one day.

He had just taken what looked like a piece of fur with a head and legs from a box on the floor and was trying to decide if it had once been a fox, when he heard a slight noise in the kitchen.

Arthur's spine prickled with fear, but then he thought it must either be that pesky cat come looking for milk – or Reg. He dropped the fur on the floor and went out onto the landing. There was definitely someone down there in the kitchen. He must have left it unlocked . . .

'Reg?' he called and went down the stairs, feeling his way in the dark, because he'd left his only candle in Aunt Becky's room. 'Is that you? Have you brought chips? I'm so hungry . . .'

As he entered the kitchen, the light snapped on. Someone had put a shilling in the meter and that someone was a man Arthur had never seen before. He stopped and stared, his heart pounding as the man looked at him.

'If you've come to rob us there's nothing left but some old clothes,' he said, suddenly defiant and angry. 'Reg took everything that was worth selling.'

The man looked at him and Arthur looked back. He was wearing a brown suit and a clean shirt and tie and he'd taken off his trilby hat.

'You must be Arthur,' the man said and sat down at the kitchen table. He took a packet out of his pocket and placed it on the table. 'I thought you might be hungry so I brought these – one is cheese and the other is ham.'

'Sandwiches!' Arthur stared at them and then pounced. He grabbed the cheese one and started stuffing it into his mouth, gobbling it down so hard that he almost choked.

'Steady on, old chap,' the man said gently. 'There's more food where I'll be taking you later. We'll get fish and chips if you'd like?'

Arthur swallowed hard. 'I'm not going to an orphanage!' he said, glaring at the stranger. 'Thanks for the food, mister – but I won't go to them places. I'll run away.'

'I wouldn't take you there, Arthur. I am taking you to a friend. Her name is Rose and she might be your aunty . . .'

Arthur was about to deny knowing an Aunt Rose when he remembered the lady who had given him half a crown after the carol service in town. She'd told him her name was Rose and she was kind.

'She might be . . .' he said warily, starting on the ham sandwich. 'Who are you?'

'My name is Robert Carson and I'm a private detective. I was hired to find you, lad, by folk who are worried about you. Do you know who that might be?'

'Who?' Arthur demanded. 'No one cares about me! Mum let them take me away and Emily-mum left me. No one wants me.'

'Do you remember Julie, Davey, and Beth?' Mr Carson asked and Arthur stared at him.

'From the ship?' he asked, feeling a little leap of hope.

'Yes, from the ship that took you to Canada. Julie is married to a nice man now and Beth lives with Mrs Veronica Bittern. It was Mrs Bittern who asked me to make sure you were all right – but you haven't been lately, have you, Arthur?'

Mr Carson's soft voice lulled Arthur's fear but he was still disbelieving. 'Why would she care what happened to me? Emily-mum said she loved me but she went off and left me here alone . . .' There was a break in his voice that he couldn't hide.

The man looked at him with sympathy. 'I'm sorry, Arthur. Sorry for all you've suffered, but Emily couldn't help leaving you. She had a very bad accident and she died . . . I discovered that recently. So you see, she didn't just leave you.'

'She's dead?' Arthur stared at him. His eyes filled with tears and spilled over. 'I thought she didn't want me anymore . . .' His voice wobbled and then he was sobbing. Mr Carson hesitated and then took him into a rough hug. He squeezed him tight a couple of times and then let go, stepping back.

'I think we should get your clothes, Arthur, even if they need washing, and take them with us. I'm sure your aunt will wash them for you.'

Arthur stared at him in silence and then nodded. He knew he couldn't go on living alone for much longer or he would starve to death. 'All right,' he said. 'I'll get them – there isn't much.'

He ran upstairs; it was easy now he had electric light again, and grabbed everything that meant anything to him – the books Pete had given him, his whistle, and his clothes – filling his school satchel and the bag he'd carried with him when they came from Canada. Arthur was still trying to understand what had happened. His tears had been reaction at being told the truth – Emily hadn't left him because she didn't care for him. She was dead and Arthur knew people died. His father had died in an accident and he'd carried that grief inside for a long time, but it had hurt even worse that his real mother had neglected him and then let people take him away. He knew she had been ill, because she'd died – but she hadn't wanted him and he'd loved her. It was the not-belonging that made him feel so miserable.

Remembering, he went to Aunt Becky's room and blew out the candle.

'I am sorry,' he said. 'I didn't mean to let anyone steal your things.' Then he left and went swiftly down the stairs again.

Mr Carson was looking round the house when he got back. 'Have you lost the front door key, Arthur?' He nodded. 'We'll take the back door key with us then. It will go to Emily's lawyer. I'm not sure who owns the house now – that will be for the law to decide.'

Arthur didn't answer. He didn't care about the house or anything in it. Mr Carson took his heavy bag and slung it over his shoulder.

'Would you like some hot food – or would you rather go straight to your aunt's house?'

Arthur considered. 'I think I've had enough for now,' he said. He followed Mr Carson outside.

'Good, it won't be too late when we get there if we go straight away. I have a car outside. Have you ever ridden in a car, Arthur?'

'We had a truck in Canada,' Arthur said, looking at him hard as they got into the car. 'Are you really a private detective? I read about someone like you in a book.'

'Ah . . .' Mr Carson gave a soft chuckle. 'I bet your private detective had a more exciting life than me. I usually just find people and collect incriminating evidence when a lady wants a divorce.'

'The detective in the book solved a mystery and caught a thief.'

'Not me. Just the boring domestic stuff. But sometimes it is really rewarding – like today.'

Arthur digested that in silence. 'Because you found me? Why did you come to the house tonight?'

'Just thought I'd try the back way,' Mr Carson replied. 'Who is Reg, by the way? You called out to him when I arrived.'

Arthur told him and at the end Mr Carson commented, 'Not a very nice man then, Arthur. I hope you learned a lesson from it?'

'I was sorry I trusted him.'

'Yet you trusted me?' Mr Carson shot him a curious look.

'You're a private detective – and you knew about Davey and Julie, and Beth – and – and my aunt . . .' Arthur crossed his fingers. He didn't have an aunt as far as he knew but he did so hope it turned out to be the nice lady . . .

CHAPTER 30

Rose was cooking Harry's supper when she heard the knock at the door. She called over her shoulder and asked if he would answer, her concentration on making sure a pan of fragrant soup didn't boil over. Meat was still scarce but Rose had managed to get a ham bone with quite a few scraps clinging to it and she'd put it in her big soup kettle together with lots of vegetables and stock and the smell was mouthwatering. Together with chunks of crusty bread it would be a filling meal, followed by baked apples and custard.

She heard the sound of voices in the hall but didn't turn until Harry's voice made her start. 'Rose, love, I think there's someone here you've been waiting to see . . .'

Rose turned and she gave a strangled cry of delight mingled with distress as she saw the child she'd longed to help, but also the state of him.

'Oh, Arthur love! Come here and let me hug you,' she said, because it was all she could think of. He came towards her, slowly at first, but when she dropped to her knees and held her arms open, he made a little mewing sound like a kitten and ran to her. Her arms enfolded him. She smelled of cooking and lavender and warmth, and Arthur buried his head in her soft breasts, his body shaking with silent sobs. 'Oh, my little love. I've been so worried about you . . .'

Arthur looked up at her, a mixture of hope and disbelief in his young face and in that moment, Rose understood how badly he needed love and reassurance. He would get it in abundance from her and Harry. In that moment she vowed to herself that she would do anything rather than surrender him to anyone – unless Emily came back looking for him. Even then, Rose would want to know why she had deserted him.

'Why were you worried?'

'Because you looked sad – and then I saw you staring at the window of the fish and chip shop, but I was on a bus and I couldn't get off.' Rose gave him another hug. 'I tried to find you, Arthur. I guessed something must be wrong and I did look for you several times, but I couldn't find you – but Mr Carson did.' She looked up at the private detective who was watching with an expression of satisfaction. 'Thank you so much, sir. Where was he?'

'At the house, but I went in the back way.' He looked at her uncertainly. ' His mother was knocked down in London and was killed and Arthur doesn't want to be put in an orphanage again. So, is it all right if I leave him with you? You *are* his aunt and uncle, aren't you?'

She didn't hesitate. 'Yes, of course, we are. We'll look after him.' Rose looked at Arthur and saw the apprehension in his face. 'I'm going to take Arthur upstairs and give him a nice warm bath and find something clean and comfy he can wear. Talk to Harry about things – and stay for supper if you wish. There's plenty of soup, and I've turned it down so it can just go on simmering for a while.'

'Come on,' Rose said, offering her hand to Arthur. 'Do you want a jam tart to eat before your bath?'

'Can I have it later?' Arthur asked. 'Mr Carson gave me some sandwiches – but I'd love some hot soup when it's ready.'

Rose nodded and took him through the hall and up the stairs. He'd lost weight these past weeks, because his clothes were too big, but he wasn't yet emaciated and she guessed he must have managed quite well on his own for a while. He was a brave lad and her whole being filled with love for him.

The water was lovely and warm and Arthur sat back in it but Rose gave him her soap and let him wash himself. He did so, seeming to enjoy it and scrubbing vigorously round his ears and neck. She washed his hair for him and rinsed it well. He'd obviously done his best to keep himself right, even though it had grown untidily and was greasy, and she was pleased to discover he didn't have the dreaded nits that were the bane of schoolchildren's lives.

When he was out of the bath and wrapped in a big warm towel, Arthur looked at her solemnly. 'Are you my new mum, missus?'

'Would you like me to be?'

'I don't know,' Arthur said and his bottom lip quivered. 'My real mum stopped loving me and they took me away and gave me to my Emily-mum – but I don't think she really loved me. She left me on my own in that house and went to London . . .'

'Did Mr Carson tell you what happened to her?' Rose asked and he nodded. 'So it wasn't really her fault, was it, Arthur?'

'No . . . but people don't keep their promises . . . they change . . .'

Rose rubbed his back briskly and then gave him one of Harry's flannel shirts to put on. It came down to his knees but she rolled up the sleeves and tied a sash from her dressing gown round his middle. She'd always been aware of Arthur's sadness and thought there must be more to his story than any of them knew.

'You're decent,' she told him with a smile, her voice gentle but firm. 'You've had a hard time, Arthur. And listen, some folk don't always keep their promises, but some do. I won't make you a promise I can't keep – I'll just say this to you, Arthur: wherever I am, you are welcome to be. If I am alive and can look after myself, I'll look after you. If the people who decide these things let me keep you, you will live with Harry and me for as long as you want to – and if they don't, I will come and see you wherever you are, and do whatever I can to get the care of you.' She was kneeling on the floor with him, looking into his eyes. 'Does that sound fair to you?'

Arthur looked at her hard. 'Why? Why would you do all that for me?'

'Because I like you,' Rose told him. 'And Harry and me want a young lad to look after. We like kids.'

He nodded solemnly. 'You're nice. I like you, too – you gave me money and smiled at me after the carols.'

'Yes, I did,' Rose agreed. 'I think Emily cared for you, too, Arthur – but perhaps things were difficult for her?'

'Yes, because Ken left us and we had no home and no money so we had to come and look after Aunt Becky but she died . . . and then Emily went away. Pete died too. He was Emily's friend, but he bought me a rabbit and some hens . . .' A tear trickled down his cheek. 'The cat killed them and Emily ate one of the chickens . . . Everyone I love dies or leaves me . . .' Suddenly, the tears he'd struggled so long to hold back came pouring out of him.

'Oh, Arthur,' Rose said, gathering him into her arms as he cried. She cried too, kneeling there, holding him to her, kissing his damp hair that was slowly beginning to curl where it dried out. 'My poor little love. I'm so sorry for all the nasty things that happened to you, Arthur. I don't think I'm going to die for a long time, because I'm strong – but I can't promise it won't happen. I can only say that I think we can learn to love each other. I think I can make you happy, my love.'

'I loved my rabbit. It hurt when it died . . .' Arthur looked up at her. 'I'm not sure I want to love anyone or anything again . . .'

'Well, shall we just be friends, then?' Rose said, looking at him. 'You don't have to love me, Arthur, even if I know I'm going to love you – but I hope you will learn to trust me as your friend.'

'Yes, I'd like to be friends,' Arthur agreed and for the first time since his arrival he smiled properly. 'I'm hungry now. Can I have some of that soup, please?'

'Of course you can, Arthur. We all will – Mr Carson, too, if he's still here.'

But Mr Carson had already left when they got down. Harry shook his head when Rose looked at him inquiringly and knew that he would tell her whatever had passed between them when Arthur was in bed and asleep.

Arthur ate two bowls of the delicious soup and a thick slice of fresh bread with a little butter, and he asked for a cup of cocoa when Rose said it was time for bed. She made it in a little saucepan with milk and water and frothed it up with a whisk and added a spoon of sugar.

Arthur drank a mouthful and gave a sigh of content. 'That's the best cocoa I've had!' he told her and drank it all as she tucked him up for the night in her spare bedroom.

'Will you be all right here?' Rose asked. 'Would you like the hall light left on so that you can see?'

'Yes, please,' he said. 'I don't like being alone in the dark. I don't like it when the wind howls round the eaves.'

'You're not alone now, Arthur,' Rose reminded him. 'Harry and me are downstairs – and we'll be coming up to that bedroom across the hall pretty soon, because we have to get up early. Harry has to go to work but tomorrow I'll stay here with you and we'll work out a routine. You'll have to go back to school. Your teachers tell me you're a bright lad.'

'I like sums and drawing, and making tunes on my whistle,' Arthur said sleepily. 'Goodnight, Rose. Thank you for helping me.'

She tucked him up, bent to kiss his forehead and

then went from the room, putting out his light but being careful to leave the landing light on and his door ajar.

Harry looked up from his paper as she entered the sitting room. 'All right, Rose?'

'Yes . . .' She sat down in her chair. 'He's settled for the moment but I think he's had a bad time, Harry.'

'She didn't look like the type to harm a child . . .'

'Not physically. He hasn't been beaten, but I think she might have been a bit careless. He's very insecure and I don't think it's just the past weeks when he was alone either. I think he managed pretty well until the last week or so. He's thin but not emaciated. No, it's more mental – fear of being left alone or deserted. It seems as though everyone or everything he cares for is either taken from him or dies.' She shook her head. 'He's hurting inside, Harry. I sensed it the first time I saw him and it's got worse since then. I think it would just about break him if they put him in an orphanage.'

'Then we must make sure it can't happen,' Harry said. 'Mr Carson is a decent sort. He says he doesn't see why he should tell the police he found Arthur; they weren't interested when he spoke to them – too busy with other things. He thinks he must tell Mrs Bittern that the boy is with us, but he'll tell her Arthur is with his Aunt Rose and Uncle Harry . . .'

Rose stared at him. 'So we just carry on and keep him, don't tell the authorities?' Hope flared within her.

'I suggest we wait for a while, see how things go.' Harry raised his brows. 'People disappear in wartime, Rose. Think of all the families that got separated in the Blitz – folk took in kids off the street then and thought nothing of it. No one noticed most of the time. I can't see why anyone would bother themselves. If they didn't while he was alone and in need, why would they now?'

'Most of the kids in London who got lost or orphaned in the Blitz were claimed by relatives, but the authorities couldn't keep track then.' Rose nodded. 'It's what I want, Harry, you know that – but the ration book and medical records . . .' Harry grinned, a light of mischief in his eyes.

'It's a funny thing, but Mr Carson handed over Arthur's ration card and his papers. They were in the kitchen drawer, apparently. He found them when Arthur was upstairs, packing his clothes. It's his job to be nosy and it seems Arthur used them a little at a time.' He handed them to her. Rose stared at them, not understanding for a few moments and then she looked up in stunned disbelief. 'It says here that he's Arthur Smith, born in the East End of London, the son of James and Molly Smith – the same name as yours, Harry!'

'Yeah,' Harry smiled. 'Smith is pretty common, so who's to know he isn't my son – or my brother's lad? Folk would have to get very nosy to prove it wasn't so, Rose.' He grinned at her. 'It's fate, Rose. He was brought to us for a reason. Mr Carson believes we're his aunt and uncle so why not run with that?'

'Harry! Could we? Dare we?' The thought of it sent Rose's brain whirling. She and Harry had already broken the law by going through a civil marriage ceremony when they knew that Reg wasn't dead. 'Supposing someone told on us?' Yet already she knew she was going to risk it. There was no way she was going to let them put Arthur back in an orphanage.

'Who's going to do that?' Harry asked. 'None of the women who came down from London know much about me. He'll be my nephew, not yours, Rose, if anything goes wrong. Besides, we shan't be going back to London – at least, not where we're known. I've had a good offer for the house. I wasn't sure if I wanted to sell but what is a house? We can go wherever we want once the war is over.'

'Oh, Harry. It's what I want but you could be in trouble . . .'

'What can they do to me?' Harry said. 'I adopted a child who had no home. Besides, there are going to be a lot of children needing homes when the war's over, Rose. Not just in this country but abroad. Think of all the misplaced children wandering around Europe. I've heard of a scheme where they're planning to bring some over here and find foster homes. I doubt if anyone will even know Arthur exists.'

Rose drew a deep breath. 'Mr Carson will tell that woman in Canada, but I don't see why she would bother if she knows he's safe. We'll do it, Harry – at least, we'll give Arthur a while to settle in and then we'll see. If he's happy with us then we'll just carry on as if he belongs to us; after all, we have his papers. If he doesn't settle then we'll ask him what he wants to do – and we'll abide by that.' It was the right answer, though she longed to keep Arthur with every fibre of her body.

'You're a good woman, Rose,' Harry said and smiled at her lovingly. 'I can't see him preferring to be sent to an orphanage to being with you.'

'Oh, Harry,' she sighed. 'I think he's been a very

unhappy boy. I just hope and pray that he can settle with us.'

'Amen to that,' Harry said and took her hand. 'I know how much it means to you, Rose – and you've taken to young Arthur proper, haven't you?'

'Yes, I have,' she agreed. 'I just want to make him smile – not just with his face but from inside. He needs to know he has someone to love and care for him – people who are not going to abandon him.'

'Well, he has a forever home with us if he wants it,' Harry said. 'He's a lovely lad and we'll do our best for him . . .' He thought for a moment. 'Once he's back at school, you'll want to be there for him when he gets home so we'll put you on a permanent shift from nine to half-past two, then you can pick him up from school. He'll feel more secure if you do that, Rose.'

Everyone who was fit and able was required to work these days, even married women, because of a shortage of labour caused by so many men being required to fight. Rose had been glad to do it, but she was relieved when Harry told her she need only do the one shift and she was lucky he could arrange it for her because recently many of the workers had been asked to do extra shifts. There was a big push coming and a great deal of ammunition would be needed for the armies. No one had been told officially, but the factory had been asked to produce more and the papers hinted at things being on the move, that Britain and her allies were going to take the war forward, to push against the enemy instead of just defending.

'I'll give him a few days before I take him back to

school,' Rose said, 'but I'll let them know he's all right and will be returning next week.'

'Yes, you do that,' Harry agreed. He smiled and nodded. 'Don't look so worried, Rose. It will be all right. You'll see . . .'

CHAPTER 31

Arthur woke in the night and lay for a while listening to the different sounds. By the shaded light in the hall passage he could see he was in a room that was new to him. He remembered being brought to this house the previous evening and being cared for by the lady called Rose. He felt warm and comfortable in the bed that was loaded with blankets and a thick eiderdown. He couldn't hear any strange noises and he wasn't hungry.

For a while he just lay curled up in his comfortable bed. He didn't feel frightened, but he couldn't help a little curl of uncertainty invading his thoughts as he tried to understand his life. Nothing seemed permanent. Everything changed. People came and went and Arthur wanted to be safe. He wanted – needed – a home of his own.

Rose had told him that she would look after him now – but could he trust her to keep her word? People made promises but then they broke them. He didn't think Rose had promised anything; she just said that she would be his friend if he liked and that he could stay with them.

313

He thought about her husband. His name was Harry and he seemed all right. Would he want Arthur – would he go away and leave them?

Arthur gave a little whimper and burrowed into his pillow. He hoped he could stay with Rose for a long time. She was kind and she had been looking for him. He liked her – but he'd liked Emily-mum, too.

She had died. She hadn't just abandoned him. Arthur wasn't sure if that made it feel worse or better. He felt tears on his cheeks. He was sorry Emily-mum died. He thought her life had been difficult the past year or so and he'd heard her cry a few times when she didn't know he was awake listening.

'I'm sorry, Emily,' he whispered. 'I didn't want you to die.'

Arthur wiped his tears and burrowed deeper under the covers. It hurt so much to lose people if you cared about them. He liked Rose and perhaps he would like Harry too, but he wouldn't love them. It hurt too much and Arthur didn't want to be hurt again.

Rose had washed some of Arthur's things and dried them overnight. In the morning they were ironed and ready when he got up. Arthur washed himself in the warm water she provided and came down for breakfast, which was toast and marmalade and a handful of dried apricots. Rose trimmed his hair out of his eyes, shaping it neatly at the back, as she had for her own boys when they were young, and then she took him shopping.

'We're going to buy you some new clothes,' she told him. 'I've got plenty of coupons and I don't need

314

anything, because I wear overalls at work all day. Would you like clothes for at home rather than school?'

'At home, please,' Arthur said. 'Do I need to go to school, Aunt Rose? I could leave and help you – come to work with you . . .'

Rose chuckled. 'I don't think you're quite old enough yet, Arthur. I have to stand and watch women packing things all day and sometimes I have to stop the line and repack a box that has been badly done.'

'Why?' Arthur looked up at her.

'Because it might cause an explosion if it wasn't packed properly.'

'Oh.' He looked at her anxiously. 'Are you in danger – like the soldiers?'

'Not if they do their work right,' she said. 'But we're all in danger when the bombs come, Arthur. Hopefully, this war will end soon.'

She looked at the shop ahead of them, holding his hand tighter. 'Let's see if we can find you a nice pair of long trousers and a jumper – what colour would you like?'

'Red,' Arthur said and a smile flickered in his eyes. 'Can I have long trousers, really?'

'Yes, I think so. Shall we see what we can find?'

'Yes, please!' Arthur pulled free of her hand and went to open the shop door, holding it for her to enter.

'What a polite little boy,' a lady behind the counter said. 'How nice to see such good manners. You must be very proud of your son, madam.'

'He's my nephew,' Rose told her. 'We want a pair of long trousers and a red jumper if you have it.'

'I think we have trousers, though maybe a bit long.'

'I can shorten them,' Rose told her. 'What colour, please?'

'We have grey or navy – or these dark green cord.'

'Arthur, which do you like best?'

Arthur looked at her and then the trousers. 'I like the soft ones . . .' he said hesitantly.

Rose held the cord trousers against him. 'We'll have these,' she confirmed. 'And the jumper?'

'We have navy, grey – oh, and this . . .' She took out a rusty-orange colour and showed them. It had a cable pattern with a V-neck and long sleeves. 'This would go well with the cord trousers. I'm afraid we don't have red, though.'

'What do you think, Arthur?' Rose asked. She held it up against him and showed him his image in a hand mirror that lay on the counter. 'Do you like it – or shall we try for a red one elsewhere?'

Arthur hesitated, then, 'This is nice, Aunt Rose. I'm happy with this one.'

'It will do for now,' Rose agreed and handed over the coupons and paid for their purchase. They left the shop together and she looked at him. 'Would you like a bag of chips to eat on the sea front or shall we go to Lyons' Corner House for an ice cream?'

'I'd rather have the chips,' Arthur said and looked at her shyly. 'You're very kind to me, Aunt Rose. Thank you.'

'I like you,' Rose replied. 'I want to look after you – if you'll let me, Arthur.'

He gazed at her for several minutes and then nodded. 'I would like to be your little boy, if that's all right.'

'Thank you, Arthur. I should like that very much.

Now I think we should go to your school and tell them you'll be starting again next week, don't you?'

Arthur was silent for a moment, then, 'I like school but there's a boy in my class and he – he set on me and I lost the key to Emily's house.'

'He won't do that in future,' Rose said. 'I'm going to work until half-past two, Arthur, and then I shall come and fetch you. I'll see you on the bus in the morning, but in the afternoon I'll bring you home. Is that a better idea?'

Arthur nodded slowly. 'He couldn't hurt me then . . .' He looked up at her seriously. 'Thank you, Aunt Rose. I should like that. I – I don't like being in an empty house alone.'

'Has it happened a lot, Arthur?' she asked. 'Even before Emily went away?'

'Yes . . .' He took a deep breath, shuffling his feet. 'She worked nights at the fish shop and the house creaked when the wind blew. I knew it was just the wind, really, but I was frightened . . .' His voice dropped lower, almost to a whisper. 'When . . . when my real mum was drunk the stairs creaked when she came up and sometimes she came and dragged the covers off me and started screaming at me because it was my fault . . .' Arthur gave a little sob and caught his breath. 'My fault my father died and I was still alive!'

Rose stared at him, her heart contracting with the shock, pity, and anger. How could any mother have done that to her child? To put such grief and guilt on a little boy! She bent down and looked into his big blue eyes.

'She shouldn't have said those things to you, Arthur,

317

because it *wasn't* your fault. Do you know how your father died?'

'An accident on the docks . . .' Arthur gulped back his tears. 'I couldn't have done it, could I, Aunt Rose?'

'No, you couldn't,' Rose told him. 'Your mother was ill and distressed but she was wrong to blame you. I'm sorry those bad things happened to you, Arthur, and I'll try to make sure they don't again.'

Arthur wiped his tears. 'I shouldn't cry. They call me a cry-baby at school and my friend Pete said men don't cry.'

'I can assure you they do sometimes.' Rose lifted his head to make him look at her. 'I'm crying too, Arthur. It isn't wrong to cry, it just happens because we're sad – and I'm sad for what happened to you, Arthur.'

He reached for her hand. 'Don't be sad, Aunt Rose, I'm all right now.'

'You will be,' she said and made herself a promise. He would never have reason to be sad again, if she could prevent it!

'Well, I think that is very smart,' Harry said when he saw Arthur dressed in his new cord trousers and rust-coloured jumper on Sunday morning. 'Do you like playing football, Arthur? Shall we have a game in the back garden, lad?'

Arthur stared at him, dawning pleasure in his eyes. 'Do you mean it? Can I, Aunt Rose?'

'Of course you can,' she said and smiled to see him happy. 'Go on and enjoy yourselves, the pair of you. Lunch will be ready in an hour and a half.'

She watched them from the window, chasing up

318

and down after the football Harry had produced. They played as equals, pushing and shoving, laughing, and joking, as the game pulled down all barriers.

After lunch they all went for a walk in the woods and Arthur darted ahead, picking up different things and exploring.

'So where did the football come from?' she asked Harry.

'It was mine when I was a lad. I found a pump and pumped it up for him.' Harry smiled at her. 'He's an intelligent lad, Rose, and he likes a good game.'

'Yes, I could see that. It made him happy, thank you for thinking of it.'

He nodded, but looked serious. 'I haven't said anything Rose, but yesterday we had an alert at the factory again. There was someone mooching about and they found a fire in the woods.'

'You don't think someone is really trying to sabotage the place? I mean, surely they wouldn't try to set light to it?'

'I would have thought they'd more likely try to blow us up,' Harry said and looked anxious. 'I really wish you didn't have to come back at all, Rose. I know you have to work but couldn't you find another, safer, job?'

'And leave you to go on working there? Some kind of wife I'd be, Harry! Besides, the hours you've fixed for me will suit us now. I doubt I could get such favourable terms elsewhere. I saw a job advertised in the fish shop, but I'd have to work evenings and I won't do that.'

'No, I wouldn't want that,' Harry said. He looked

at her ruefully as Arthur came running back to them. 'What have you found, lad?'

'I saw a snake in the bushes,' Arthur said. 'Is it poisonous?'

'Did it have V-shapes down its back, like this . . .' Harry drew a line in the earth with a stick. Arthur shook his head. 'Then it's only a grass snake. We only have one poisonous snake here, Arthur, and that's an adder. I think there are more in Canada?'

'Ken hated them, said to stay away from all snakes, because they were probably poisonous.'

'Well, that's good advice,' Harry told him. 'Did you like being in Canada?'

Arthur nodded. 'It was much nicer than where I lived before. I like it here, all right, though. The woods are fun and the beach is nice, even though it's stony.'

'Hastings is a nice place,' Harry agreed. 'Would you prefer to live in the country or the town?'

'The countryside,' Arthur said promptly. 'But . . .' His eyes went to Rose. 'Would it be with you?'

'Oh yes,' Harry said instantly. 'We have to work here now, because of the war, Arthur, but one day we'll be able to choose – all of us together.'

'Could it be in Canada?' Arthur said, tipping his head to one side as he studied their faces.

'Yes, maybe,' Harry replied, glancing at Rose. 'When the war is over we can talk about it again. How's that for an idea?'

'It's good,' Arthur said. 'Can we play football again, Uncle Harry?'

'I think it will be too dark when we get home, but if

we're up early and it's fine we might have a go before breakfast . . .'

'I think he's taking to us,' Rose said when they were in bed together that night. 'He was happy in the woods. And playing football with you . . . that's the first time I've heard him laugh.'

'Aye, he's a good lad,' Harry said as she snuggled into him. 'I'll be up early and get my breakfast, then I can play with the lad before I leave for work.'

'I'll make breakfast,' Rose told him. 'I'm used to early mornings, Harry. Just because you've spoiled me by bringing me a cuppa and letting me come into work a bit later, it doesn't mean I'll let you get your own breakfast.'

CHAPTER 32

Arthur was a bit nervous starting school on Monday morning, but Rose had him looking smart in clean clothes and at least the bullies couldn't call him names for being dirty. He was surprised when he took his place in class to see that the boy who had tormented him wasn't there. He looked all round the class but he wasn't to be seen. Feeling relieved, Arthur settled down to his work.

The morning went well. He got all his sums right and answered several of the geography questions correctly. At the end of the lesson the master called him out.

'Glad to see you back in school and looking better, Arthur. How do you know so much about Canada?'

Arthur hesitated, then, 'I learned when I was out there, sir.'

'When did you live in Canada?'

'Before I came back here, sir.'

The master nodded. 'And you live with your aunt and uncle now?'

Arthur hesitated an instant, then, 'Yes, sir. Uncle Harry and Aunt Rose.'

'Very well. I'm glad to hear you learned so much when you were in Canada. Off you go now and have your lunch.'

Arthur ran off. He didn't glance back or he would have seen the master staring after him in a puzzled way.

Lunch was toad-in-the-hole with mashed potatoes and cabbage. Arthur ate it, but couldn't help thinking that it wasn't as good as Rose had cooked for them on Sunday. She made lovely, tasty meals and her jam sponge was gorgeous.

After lunch they had sports and Arthur played football with some of the other boys. At the end of the games lesson, he saw one of the boys who had attacked him that afternoon after school and went up to him.

'Where's John Mickle?' he asked, emboldened by his new security.

The boy shuffled his feet for a minute and then looked at Arthur. 'His dad was killed overseas and his mum took him off to live with her mother somewhere. She has to work and can't look after him.'

'That's bad,' Arthur said. 'I'm sorry it happened to him . . . it's what happened to me once.' His fear had gone and he felt sympathy for John Mickle, even though he had tormented him, because he knew what it felt like to be sent away from home.

The other boy stared at him. 'I'm sorry I helped him hit you. He used to hit us if we didn't obey him.'

'It's all right,' Arthur said. 'I knew it was him.'

The other boy took something from his pocket and offered it. 'I picked this up and kept it for you but you didn't come back.'

It was the key to Emily's house. He took it and put it in his pocket and thanked the boy.

'It's all right,' the lad said. 'We might be mates now he's gone – if you like?'

'Yeah, all right,' Arthur agreed. 'What shall we play?'

The bell rang for end of playtime and they shrugged, running off to their separate classes. Arthur settled down as the lesson began. It was reading and the boys all read a passage from their books and then the bell rang again and it was time to go home. When Arthur left the playground, he saw Rose waiting for him outside the school gates. She smiled and beckoned and he ran to her eagerly.

'Did you have a good day?' she asked and gave him a red lollipop from her basket. 'Did the bully leave you alone?'

'He isn't here anymore,' Arthur said and told her what had happened to John Mickle's father.

Just as they were about to leave, a voice called to them and Rose stopped, looking round. 'Mrs Smith?' the master said again.

'Yes, Mr Danvers – you want to speak to me?'

'Just for a moment. Arthur, just wait over there while I speak to your aunt.'

Arthur looked scared but walked off to stand by the railings. Rose waited for a moment, then, 'Is something wrong?' she asked.

Arthur couldn't hear what was said but he saw Rose didn't look happy. She shook her head a couple of times and then her expression changed. He wasn't sure whether she was cross or worried. She walked away from the master and held her hand out to Arthur. He gazed up at her with anxious eyes.

'Is something wrong? Am I in trouble?' he asked.

Rose looked down at him. 'No, you're not in trouble,' she said. 'He was just asking questions about Harry and me – who we were and how we came to be looking after you.'

'What did you tell him?'

'I said Harry was your uncle – that you were his brother's son and we had taken you in now that your mother had died.'

Arthur absorbed this, then, 'That isn't true, is it? I know I call you Aunt Rose and Uncle Harry but it isn't true.' His eyes questioned her, seeking truth.

'No,' Rose admitted and he was glad she'd spoken the truth. 'Mr Danvers doesn't know that – and if I'd told him that we only met a few times before you came to live with me, he might have told the council and they might have taken you away from us, Arthur.'

'Would they put me in an orphanage again?'

'They probably would,' she agreed. 'I know it was a little lie, but it was worth it to keep you safe with us. Do you agree?'

'Yes, I do. I like being with you, Aunt Rose.' He held on to her hand tightly as they crossed the road to the bus stop. 'I don't want to go to that horrible place again . . .' All he wanted was a home to call his own, somewhere warm and comfortable, where he was treated kindly and felt safe. He thought he might have found it with Rose and Harry.

'You won't if I have anything to do with it,' Rose told him and Arthur smiled. He was beginning to think he might trust his Aunt Rose, even if she wasn't truly his aunt.

* * *

Mr Danvers didn't question Arthur after class again and things seemed to get better every day. He was happier than he'd been for as long as he could remember and the days and weeks seemed to fly by. There was school, then there was home with Rose every evening; at weekends they visited the beach and the woods and Harry played football with him and then taught him to use a cricket bat.

He knew that sometimes Harry and Rose talked in an anxious way, but it was usually about the factory or the new bombs that had started to cause devastation in London and other cities. People called them doodlebugs, and they were silent until they suddenly fell on you and exploded with no warning. For Arthur life had settled into a routine that felt right and proper and he began to feel as if he had come home at last.

Then, one day, Harry got a letter. He read it in silence and then exclaimed. 'Damn it! It's from my solicitor, Rose – the house has been bombed. One of those flippin' rockets. That means the sale won't happen and I'll get nothing – no insurance and no rent.' He looked at her and it was plain he was worried. 'We shan't be able to have our own house now, Rose.'

'Oh, Harry, I'm so sorry,' Rose exclaimed. 'I know how much it meant to you.'

'I don't give a fig about the house itself,' Harry told her, 'but it means the money is lost, Rose. We'll have to rent a house wherever we go now, love.'

'It doesn't matter to me,' Rose told him. 'We're all right here, aren't we, Arthur?'

'Yes, we're all right,' Arthur said, but he felt a

moment of apprehension. When Emily lost her house, she'd brought him here and then she'd died.

'Oh well,' Harry sighed, 'it doesn't change things, Rose. We'll still decide where we want to live when this is all over – and it can't be long now.'

The big push had begun and the Allies were on the march against the enemy, fighting through France, Normandy, and into Germany. Soon, the war would be over despite this latest flurry of defiance in the form of rockets that had been sent to put fear into the hearts of the British and other European peoples.

Arthur went up to Harry and touched his hand. 'Don't worry, Uncle Harry. One day, when I'm old enough to work, I'll buy you a house of your own.'

Harry looked at him and then laughed. 'Will you, lad? You're bright enough, I'll give you that – but don't you worry. We'll do just fine. You wait and see. Harry will come bouncing back again. I was never afraid of hard work and I'll make a good living for us, maybe take out a loan from the bank and get us our own house again one day.'

'Don't be daft, Harry,' Rose told him. 'We'll manage . . .'

What she was going to say then was never finished. A knock came at the door and when Harry answered one of the other managers from the factory entered the hall.

'You'd best come, Harry,' he said. 'There's a huge alarm on at the factory and we need you.'

Harry glanced round at Rose. 'I'd better go, love. You stay here and take Arthur to school. Don't worry about me – but I don't want you near the factory today.'

'Just you take care. I know you, Harry. No heroics!'

'As if I would,' he said and went out, leaving Rose to stare after him anxiously. Arthur moved closer to her, reaching for her hand. He had a horrid, trembly feeling inside, as if something bad might happen – something that would snatch away the happiness he was just learning to accept.

Rose looked down at him, as if sensing his fear. She squeezed his hand. 'Don't you worry, Arthur. Harry will be all right. He'll sort things out; he always does.'

Arthur looked up at her and nodded, praying she was right. He didn't want anything to destroy the safe world he had begun to build with Rose and Harry.

Arthur spent a busy day at school. He did well in his maths and English lessons, and in art class his work was held up to be shown off to the other pupils. He'd drawn some of the animals he'd seen in Canada and the art mistress was very impressed.

'These are very lifelike,' she told Arthur. 'You're a very talented boy. I hope you'll make use of your talent when you leave school one day.'

'Do artists get paid much, miss?' Arthur asked innocently and she gave him a strange look.

'Not unless they become very famous,' she said, 'but surely art is for art's sake, Arthur – isn't it?'

'I like to draw, miss,' Arthur agreed. 'When I grow up, I want to buy a house to live in with my aunt and uncle . . .'

'Ah, I see,' she said and smiled. 'Then you'd best make it your hobby – although you *are* very talented.'

Rose was waiting for Arthur when he left school.

She smiled and gave him a lollipop, as always, but she looked anxious.

'Are you worried about Uncle Harry, Aunt Rose?'

'Yes, I am,' she admitted. 'I've got a wobbly feeling in my tummy and I don't know why.'

'I get those sometimes,' Arthur confided, holding tight to her hand as their bus arrived. He let go as she motioned him forward and they sat in the front seats.

When the conductor came round, he looked serious, and Arthur heard him say something about a big fire over towards Bexhill. Arthur knew that Harry worked somewhere that way and he felt Aunt Rose stiffen beside him.

'Did you say there was a big fire near Bexhill?' she asked a little breathlessly.

'That way,' the conductor told her. 'They're saying it might be the factory they've got hidden away in the woods.'

Rose gave a little gasp but didn't say anything as he issued their ticket and moved on. Arthur pushed up close to her and she took his hand, holding it so tightly that he almost had to cry out but after a moment the pressure relaxed and she looked at him.

'It might be where we work, Arthur. I'm worried about Harry. When we get home, I'll go to the phone box on the corner and try to telephone him. I've got a number he gave me for emergencies.'

'Will you go there?' Arthur asked. She hesitated and then shook her head.

'No, Arthur. There isn't much I can do, especially if there is a fire. It will be utter chaos and I'd only be in the way. It's best I stay with you.' It was the answer he'd wanted but he knew that she was upset and he had to be brave for her sake.

Arthur took a deep breath, then, 'If Uncle Harry's hurt you'll have to go to the hospital. I shan't be frightened if you leave me all night – as long as you come back when you can.'

They had arrived at their stop and Rose got up, Arthur following her out of the bus. They stood on the pavement waiting as it drew away and then crossed the road into their house. Rose took her coat off and went into the kitchen. She put the kettle on and made tea, giving Arthur a cup of milk and a piece of treacle tart. She looked at him then, a slow steady gaze that made him feel safe, because he knew she was thinking of him, that she cared.

'I might have to go to the hospital if Harry gets hurt. He did once before when there was a fire where we worked – he was very brave and rescued other people.'

'I know you must go,' Arthur told her. 'I'll be all right here. This house doesn't creak like the one I lived in before. It feels warm and safe here. I can manage . . .'

'I know you don't like the dark.' Rose looked at him solemnly as she poured herself a cup of tea and cut a small slice of the tart for herself. She sipped her drink. 'You must keep the light on if you go to bed and I'm not here. There are plenty of shillings for the electric, Arthur, so you won't run out. And I'll come home as soon as I can.' She took another sip of tea. 'Besides, Harry may be perfectly all right . . .' Her hand trembled slightly as she picked up her slice of tart and put it down again. 'There was a time when I wasn't keen on Harry but I didn't know him then. I wouldn't want to lose him now . . .'

Her hand was reaching for the tart again but she jumped as a knock came at the door and Arthur saw the fear in her eyes – the kind of fear he'd known too often himself.

'I love you, Aunt Rose,' he tried to say but the words were only a whisper and she couldn't hear them because she was rushing to the door. As she opened it, a man entered.

'Mrs Smith . . . I am so sorry,' he said and Arthur could hear his words clearly, making his stomach clench. 'There's been big trouble at the factory. A small fire in part of the stores was put out and no one was hurt but everyone was moved away to safety. The army was rushing everywhere because the man who started it, a saboteur, had been seen. Harry was trying to get everyone to safety when a man came crashing through the trees with a huge knife he was waving around, threatening to kill anyone who got in his way. A woman tripped in front of him and he turned on her, but Harry wrestled him – he was very big and you know Harry isn't – but he's strong. They fought for a few seconds and then Harry gave a cry and fell . . .' The messenger paused for breath, then, 'The army officer arrived then and he shot and killed the saboteur.'

'What about Harry?' Rose cried. 'Never mind about that devil, what about my Harry? Is he dead?'

'No, but he is seriously hurt and they've taken him to the hospital. I've come to take you there.'

Rose turned but Arthur was there with her coat and

handbag. 'You must go, Aunt Rose,' he urged. 'I'll be all right here, I promise you.'

'Thank you,' she said and bent to kiss him. 'There's a fresh loaf in the pantry and you can have cheese, jam, or dripping for your supper, whichever you choose, love. I'll come home as soon as I can.'

'I know,' Arthur said and smiled at her. 'Go and see Uncle Harry – and give him my love.'

Rose hugged him, put her coat on, picked up her handbag and left.

Arthur heard the door snap to behind her and waited but the expected sense of fear, of being alone, didn't come. All he felt was anxiety for the kind man he had come to accept as his real uncle, no matter that it hadn't always been so. He and Aunt Rose were the best people he'd known for a long, long time. Arthur's dad had loved him, but he wasn't sure his mother ever had. However, love was in Aunt Rose's eyes every time she looked at him, and Uncle Harry was the same.

Arthur did something then he had never done except when he was told to in church. He went down on his knees and he prayed. He prayed to God that Uncle Harry would live and get better. He prayed that Aunt Rose would come back home with her eyes shining and a smile on her face, and he prayed that he would always be able to live with them.

CHAPTER 33

Rose hated to leave Arthur alone in the house but he'd told her to go and she'd known she must. If Harry didn't make it, this might be the last time she ever saw him. She must tell him how much she loved him, because she wasn't sure he knew how precious he'd become to her.

Ted – as she'd learned the messenger's name was – took her to the front of the hospital and asked if she wanted him to come in when he'd parked and wait for news with her. Rose had thanked him for bringing her but told him to get back to his wife, who had a small child, and must also be anxious.

'If you need anything, you know where to find me,' Ted told her and she lifted her hand and walked inside the large building that smelled of strong disinfectant the instant you entered.

She'd gone to the desk and asked for her husband, explaining he'd been stabbed in an incident, without giving the receptionist the details of it being a saboteur at the munitions factory.

She was advised to take a seat and wait. Half an

hour passed before a man in a long white coat came towards her. His expression was serious and her heart caught as he asked if she was Mrs Rose Smith.

'Yes, I am,' she said. 'Harry is – is he . . .?' She couldn't bring herself to say the word and let out a little gasp.

'Your husband is a very strong and a very brave man,' he told her with a smile. 'Fortunately, the knife was deflected by something your husband carried in his breast pocket and slid off into his shoulder. It bled a lot and he'll be in pain for a few days, but after that he should heal well. Had he not carried a silver cigarette case, he could have died.'

'That old case?' Rose whispered. 'It was my dad's and I gave it to Harry when we got married. He didn't smoke when he went to work, but it must have been in his breast pocket when he went rushing off this morning.'

'Well, whatever, it undoubtedly saved his life,' the doctor said. 'We've patched him up, Mrs Smith, and he's a bit groggy, but asking for you – so if you'd like to see him . . .?'

'Yes, please.' Rose was close to tears but tears of joy. Harry was alive and would be all right. 'Thank you so much, doctor. Thank you for helping my Harry.'

'It was a privilege, Mrs Smith. I've been told all the details, though most of my staff are not privy to the information. Your husband did a brave thing. Some would say foolish, but his intervention probably saved a woman's life.'

'It's not the first time he's risked his life for others,' Rose said and told him what had happened in London when the factory there had caught fire. 'Was anyone else hurt, doctor?'

'We had some women brought in for treatment because of shock and a few cuts and bruises where they got pushed over in the panic, but nothing serious. By the sound of it, there could have been a much worse result if the fire had not been quickly contained.'

'Yes. I heard on the bus it was a large fire but by the sound of things that was an exaggeration.'

'I believe there was a house fire near Bexhill,' he said and then stopped. 'Harry is in a private room, Mrs Smith – just in case – and we have a police officer on the door. We can't be certain the man they killed worked alone.'

'No . . .' Rose looked at him doubtfully. She nodded to the police officer and went inside alone. Harry was lying with his head back against a pile of pillows but as she approached the bed, his eyes opened and he smiled.

'Rose, love,' he said and lifted his hand. 'I'm sorry I gave you a fright. It was just instinct. I couldn't stop myself.'

'That's because you're my Harry,' she told him and bent to kiss him softly on the mouth. 'It's the way you are and I wouldn't have you any other way. I love you, Harry, but you did give me one hell of a fright.'

Harry chuckled and then winced in the same breath. 'Gave myself one if I'm honest,' he told her. 'It was a daft thing to do, Rose. The army was there and they acted . . .' His expression became grave. 'I swear I didn't know when I went for him, Rose, but it was him. It was Reg . . .'

Rose sat down hard on the chair next to the bed,

staring at him in shock. 'Are you sure, Harry? It doesn't sound like Reg – a saboteur? Why would he be involved with something like that?'

'Money? Revenge because the world treated him bad – or perhaps he hoped we were both working there and he would kill us both. You said yourself he looked at you as if he was ready to kill you, Rose.'

'Yes, he was – and he would, but with his fists or a knife maybe,' Rose said slowly and shook her head. 'I just can't see him trying to set fire to the factory. It doesn't sound likely to me.'

Harry frowned for a moment, and then nodded. 'I think you might be right, Rose. The fire started in the non-dangerous stores – just food stuffs for the canteen, overalls, tools, and that sort of stuff. I wonder . . .' A smile came briefly to his eyes. 'I wonder if Reg was camping out there, hoping to catch you alone when you left work at night, helping himself to the food . . .'

'He would've had a long wait; I don't work past half-past two and three other married women with kids leave with me.' She looked thoughtful. 'I reckon that's more what was in his mind, Harry.'

Harry nodded. 'He didn't know that you left early every day, Rose. He thought it was like the old days when he could bully you. He saw you in town that day and mouthed a threat at you. It would be just like him to steal government property while he waited to get his revenge on us.'

'Yes, that's more like Reg,' Rose agreed. 'Well, he got more than he bargained for this time – the army shoot first and ask questions later when they think they've cornered a saboteur.'

'They can't ask questions this time, because he's dead,' Harry said. 'No one else saw his face, so he'll be buried in a grave marked unknown, unless I tell them who he is . . .'

'Then let it happen,' Rose said and her expression was set. 'He's dead and we're free of him, Harry. You didn't kill him, the army did. There will be no coming back for him this time – and I'm glad. He was a bad man and he deserved what he got.' There was no regret or sympathy left in her for Reg, just a feeling of relief that he'd gone from their lives.

'Yes, he did,' Harry agreed. He chuckled and winced again. Rose raised her brows at him. 'I was thinking of all the kerfuffle he caused, Rose. The pandemonium and chaos because we thought there was a saboteur. I don't know how many times the army searched that wood and didn't find him . . .'

'I suppose he just used it when it got dark,' Rose said. 'I told you Arthur said a man helped him get back in his house when he was locked out and then stole everything he could find of value. He told Arthur to call him Reg and he was a big man so it could have been Reg Parker. It's the kind of thing he might do. He didn't harm Arthur – and he was always reasonable with our boys, but he took it out on me. That's why the boys squared up to him when they got older and then cleared off.'

'They haven't been home to see you since you told them he was officially dead, have they?'

'No,' she admitted with a sigh. 'I suppose they have their own lives now – and we have each other and Arthur . . .' She smiled at him. 'But they sent me a

Christmas card – and that's really all I need now I have you and Arthur.'

Harry smiled as he lay back and closed his eyes. 'You get off home back to our lad, Rose. I'll be all right here now.'

'If you're sure,' she said and bent to kiss his cheek. 'You rest now, Harry. I reckon you've done your bit. It's about time you gave up and took an easier job, love.'

'Maybe,' he said, but she knew he would stick it out, and perhaps it didn't matter because the tide of war was turning in the Allies' favour and it would surely soon be over.

Arthur was sitting by the range in the kitchen reading a book when Rose got in. He jumped up and ran to her, flinging his arms around her. 'Is Uncle Harry all right?' he asked, looking up at her eagerly.

Rose bent and kissed the top of his head. 'He's going to be soon,' she told him. 'He has a knife wound to his shoulder and it hurts but he'll be back with us soon,' she told him honestly and without hiding anything, because he needed honesty so that he could trust and count on her to keep her word.

'Good,' Arthur said and his eyes shone with happy tears. 'I'm so glad!'

'Me too,' she said and hugged him. 'I'm hungry. I don't know about you, Arthur, but I just fancy a bit of toast and dripping.'

'Ooh, yes please,' Arthur cried joyfully. 'Can I fill the kettle for you, Aunt Rose? I could put it on to boil for you if you show me how.'

'Yes, you fill it and I'll show you how to light the gas safely, Arthur. We'll get our supper and eat it together, because you have school in the morning, and I have to go to work.'

Arthur smiled at her. 'You must be very proud of Uncle Harry.'

'Yes, I am,' she replied. 'I sometimes wish he would think of himself more for our sakes – but I suppose he wouldn't be the man I love if he didn't do what he could for others.'

'He's a good man,' Arthur said, 'and you're good, too, Aunt Rose.'

'Thank you, Arthur.' She paused, then, 'You do know that Harry and me love you very much, don't you?'

Arthur nodded, and then he grinned. 'I reckon I love you, too,' he said and ran off into the pantry to fetch the crock of dripping.

Rose stood stock-still and waited, her heart beating so hard she could almost hear its thud. Had he actually said the words she'd longed to hear? Her eyes pricked with tears but she didn't cry.

Smiling as he set the crock down, she nodded. 'There's a good boy. Now fill the kettle and we'll have a nice cup of cocoa with our meal.'

Harry was looking annoyed when Rose went to visit him two days later. She'd taken Arthur to the library and left him there to find some books, telling him she would come and fetch him after her visit to the hospital.

'Would you believe it – the daft lot!' Harry said waving a newspaper at her. 'Look what they've gone and done, Rose.'

She took the paper and scanned the headline, before handing it back to him. 'It seems you're a hero, Harry – but then I already knew that so why shouldn't everybody else?'

'I didn't want a fuss,' he grumbled. 'All I did was wrestle him for a few minutes. Next thing you know, we'll have reporters camped outside our door.'

'What does that matter?' Rose asked. 'We have nothing to fear now, Harry. Reg is dead. He can't hurt us any longer – and we can marry again if we want one day, just quiet like – but I'm happy as we are.'

Harry nodded. 'I've had a visit from some influential people, Rose. I've been told I've done my bit for the war and I can retire on a pension now. They know my house was hit by a flying bomb and they said I can claim a house rent-free because of my devotion to duty . . .'

'And what was your answer to that, Harry?'

'I told them I wanted to carry on, but I've been thinking. If I don't need to work at the factory, I could look for a nice place somewhere we could maybe have our own little business.'

'That sounds nice, but what would you do, Harry?'

'I'm good with engines. I might start up a little garage in a village that hasn't got one, have a petrol pump . . .'

'Cars are getting more popular all the time,' Rose agreed. 'It would suit me, but you do what you want, Harry. All I need is a home with you and Arthur.'

'How is he?' Harry asked. 'It's a pity they won't let kids visit here.'

'I left him at the library. You know how he likes to read adventure stories.'

'Takes after me then,' Harry said and laughed at her face, because he never read anything but the paper.

'He told me he loved you,' Rose said with a little grin as Harry's face lit up. 'Now that really is a feather in your cap, Harry Smith. Something you can be proud of.'

'I know.' Harry looked at her in wonder, the sheen of tears in his eyes. 'I always envied you your boys, Rose – but now I've got a lad of my own to raise. I swear I'll make a good job of it. Arthur won't want to leave home.'

'No, I don't think he will until he's ready for a wife and one of his own,' Rose said. She looked at him consideringly. 'Would it matter to you where your little garage was, Harry?'

'No. I just want us to be settled and happy. Wherever you and Arthur want to be will suit me, love.'

'How about Canada?' she asked and saw him gasp with surprise. She hadn't been keen on the idea when he'd suggested it once.

'What made you suggest that?' Harry asked. 'I know Arthur says it's nice there but . . .' He was silent for a moment, thoughtful, then, 'It would be an adventure. Do you think we could do it?'

'We might, with some help,' Rose said and opened her handbag. She took out a letter, unfolded it, and handed it to him. 'Read that – it's from that Mrs Bittern, the lady who sent Mr Carson to look for Arthur.'

When he'd read it twice through, Harry looked at Rose.

'Why would she offer us a home and a job, Rose? She doesn't know us – do you think she wants, Arthur?'

'I wondered that the first time I read it,' Rose said. 'Then I remembered the names – Beth and Julie. Arthur mentioned them as being his companions on the ship going out there.'

Harry nodded. 'She says that they've been anxious about Arthur, and were glad to hear that he'd found his real family. Because she knows things are hard here and likely to remain so once the war is finally over, she says she would be happy to have us as her tenants for life and to give us jobs if we would like them – and she's offered to pay our passage out there.' Harry was silent for a few moments. 'It would give us a start, Rose – and I could look around and find a good place for my garage.'

'She sounds a really nice, caring woman,' Rose agreed. 'I know Arthur liked it there and he would enjoy seeing his friends but we can take our time and think about it, love. She said there's no hurry – and the war isn't quite over yet.'

'No, it isn't,' Harry agreed. 'Didn't you say Arthur mentioned Davey Blake as one of the children on the voyage with him? Why don't you take him down to see him and hear what he thinks of Canada?'

'Why don't we both go, Harry, when you come out of hospital? It's getting warmer and you need a holiday, even if you decide to go back and finish it out at the factory. Take a break, love, you deserve it. Let's have our first holiday together as a family.'

'Yes, why not?' Harry agreed. 'I'll need to go up to London at some point, too. The house was flattened, but the lawyer has told me that I can still sell the land it was built on – because our homes will be rebuilt, Rose.

The war nearly did for poor old London, but it didn't take the heart out of us, the people, and we'll build it up again.'

'You sound as though you'd like to be a part of it?' Rose looked at him hard. 'I thought you didn't want to go back there?'

'I don't,' Harry assured her. 'That's the past for us, Rose – but it doesn't stop me being proud of being a Londoner, born and bred.'

'Me too,' she said. 'We'd be safe to live there now Reg is dead, but I'd rather look further afield, whether it's in Canada or somewhere in England.'

CHAPTER 34

Davey and Arthur stared at each other and then they both grinned and gave a shout of joy. Davey ran towards Arthur, picked him up and swung him round and round as they laughed together.

'You're so big,' Arthur said when they stopped their rough and tumble to catch their breaths. 'I wasn't sure it was you – and you disappeared when the ship was due to dock.'

'I hid because I didn't want to go to a shopkeeper again. I had a lot of adventures, too.' Davey grinned at him. 'Come on, let's go down the beach. I want to hear your story, Arthur. My sister Alice is cooking with my aunt, but you can meet her later. Let's tell each other what we've been doing . . .'

Arthur looked at Rose. 'Can I, Aunt Rose?'

'Yes, of course you can, love. Harry and me will be at the house over there when you're ready – but you'll be fine with Davey.'

She watched as they went off together, then linked her arm through Harry's. 'Come on, I'll introduce you

347

to Davey's aunt and then you can talk to the boys when they get back . . .'

Davey looked at Arthur for a long moment when he finished telling him what had happened to him in Canada, and here in England, and then he nodded.

'You had a rough time,' he said. 'I loved what I did in Canada. I had fun with Bert. He taught me so much and I loved him. Corky and Rodie were all right, but not the same as Bert. I liked them – but I didn't trust them the way I did Bert.'

Arthur nodded solemnly. 'I think I loved Emily,' he said, 'but I wasn't sure I could trust her. You can't trust everyone . . .'

'No, you can't,' Davey agreed. 'You're lucky now. though. Rose is a good 'un. You can trust her and Harry. I didn't know him as well as Rose – but she was always the same. You're lucky you found them.'

'Yes, I know.'

Davey picked up a flat stone and sent it skimming over the waves, which were calm and gentle that morning. Little piles of seaweed had been left by the retreating tide and lay on the wet sand. Overhead the seagulls swooped and called, swirling through the salty air as a thin sun warmed their feathers.

'It's nice here,' Arthur said, selecting a stone like Davey's. He threw it but it only skimmed once before disappearing beneath the waves. 'Do you like being here?'

'Yes.' Davey nodded, selected another stone. 'You throw it like this . . .' He showed Arthur how to make it go flat so it skimmed the waves. Arthur tried again and this time his stone went further. 'I like it for now – but I want to explore the world one day and then I might go back and live in Canada when I settle down.'

'I liked it there,' Arthur agreed. 'It's nice here, though.'

'Yeah, when it isn't blowing a gale,' Davey said with a grin. 'Let's go back now and see what there is for tea . . .'

'I like it here,' Harry told Rose a couple of days later. He and Arthur had been for a walk along to the harbour and through the town. They'd seen the rows of drying huts where the kippers were cured and the fishermen's cottages. Lowestoft was a busy fishing port and it was nice to buy freshly-caught fish straight off the boats. 'I think Arthur does too. It's got a pleasant old-fashioned feel about it.'

'Are you thinking we could settle here?' Rose asked and his eyes met hers. 'Because Alice and Davey are here – is that what you're thinking?'

'It's an idea,' he said. 'You like their aunt and that means you'd have a friend.'

'Yes, that's true. I do like Marie – but you and Arthur have to be happy too, Harry.' She hesitated for a moment. 'What do you want to do, love?'

'I think I should finish out my job until the war is over – but if you wanted to settle here—'

'And leave you on your own?' Rose glared at him. 'You can put that right out of your head, Harry. If you want to go back to your job then that's where we'll go. We'll both see it out until the war is over – and then we'll decide. I think we ought to take Mrs Bittern up on her offer, even if we only go over for a long holiday.'

Harry nodded. 'You know your own mind, Rose Smith, and that's just one of the things I love about you.'

'So I should think,' she said with mock severity. 'So what are we going to do this afternoon?'

'The boys want to go fishing off the pier,' Harry said. 'Do you fancy coming, Rose, or would you rather stay here with Alice and Marie?'

'I'll come with you,' Rose said. 'I've promised Alice I'll help make her new dress but I'll do that tomorrow. This afternoon I'd like to be with you and the boys . . .'

It was breezy on the pier, the wind blowing in off the sea. Most of the pier was closed to the public but there was a small section of it that the locals used to fish from. It was actually part of what was supposed to be closed, but a part of the barrier had been taken down now that the fear of imminent invasion had passed.

They all managed to squeeze past, the boys in high spirits and Harry looking on proudly as he got their fishing rods – all lent by Aunt Marie – and the bait he'd bought that morning.

Rose sat on an upturned wooden crate someone had obligingly left and watched the boys enjoying themselves – all three of them. She thought she'd never seen Harry looking so happy or so relaxed. He was thoroughly enjoying his holiday. She wished that he had decided to take the opportunity to retire from his job, but it was his decision and she wouldn't argue. It was just good to relax and enjoy this holiday.

The afternoon was a success, even though all they caught was a couple of crabs and some tiddlers. They ate sandwiches and drank lemonade from a bottle and laughed all afternoon. At about half-past four the wind came up and it began to get cold so they decided to pack up and go home.

As they left the pier, they heard laughter and saw a crowd of women wearing daft hats and eating ice cream walking towards them. About to turn away from the day trippers, Rose heard a scream and then her name.

'If it ain't Rose – Rose P . . . Smith. It's Gertie!'

Rose nodded to Harry and the boys. 'You walk on. I'll have a word with Gertie.'

Rose stopped and waited as Gertie detached herself from the others and came to greet her with a tremendous hug. 'Wot yer doin' 'ere then, Rose?' Gertie demanded.

Rose smiled. 'I've finally persuaded Harry to have a holiday with the boys,' she said.

'I saw them – one of them was Dora Blake's boy Davey, wasn't it?'

'Yes. He and Alice came to live with their aunt when he came home from Canada. I visited them a few times if you recall.'

'Yeah – and didn't that go down well wiv some of the bitches in the factory,' Gertie said with a dry laugh. 'Who's the other lad?'

'Oh, that's Arthur, Harry's nephew,' Rose said without thinking. 'His parents died so we've got him now.' As she saw the look in Gertie's eyes, she realised her mistake. Gertie had known Harry's family all her life.

For a long moment Gertie looked at her. 'Never knew Harry had a brother,' she said and then nodded. 'Yer a good woman, Rose. I reckon I've got a big mouth and a rotten memory. Yeah, I remember now – there was an older brother who went away . . .' She tapped the side of her nose.

'Are yer comin', Gertie?' a loud voice shouted at her and she looked back and frowned. 'I 'ave ter go now, Rose. I'm glad you've got yer boy. You tell Harry I remember his brother real well if anyone asks . . .' She winked and went off to join her impatient friends.

Rose stood staring after her for a second or two and then ran to catch up with the others. Gertie's first words had struck fear into her. She was certain Gertie wouldn't betray her – but there might be others who would know the truth.

'Who was that?' Harry asked as they paused while the boys ran into the house. 'Londoners, weren't they?'

'It was Gertie Bright. Told me she remembers your elder brother well, Harry.'

'Bugger!' he muttered. 'We went to school together, Rose. Will she tell?'

'No, I don't think so – but there might be others who remember, Harry.'

He looked at her, and then he nodded. 'Then I think we need a slight change of plan, Rose.'

'What do you mean?' She stared at him anxiously.

'I don't have to go back to the factory. If you're willing to risk it, we'll accept Mrs Bittern's offer and be off to Canada as soon we can safely arrange it.'

'Oh, Harry . . .' she breathed. 'I thought you wanted to stay in England, maybe settle down here?'

352

'What I want is for us to be a family,' Harry said. 'I don't want to risk losing our boy, Rose. We might get him back, but we might not – can you take that risk?'

'No, I can't,' she admitted. 'I suppose we should have told the authorities in the first place and asked to be allowed to keep him.'

'Mebbe – and mebbe not,' Harry said. 'Arthur needed us, Rose. He needed a home and stability, and that's just what we gave him. I'll get in touch with my old mate Tom Simmons tomorrow – he's got lots of contacts on the docks – and see what he can fix up for us, even though it is still a bit risky. We won't be able to take anything but clothes and our papers with us, love, but if we have a few years over in Canada and come back no one will even remember us. And if we stay we can send for the rest of our stuff.'

Rose smiled and kissed him. 'You're right,' she told him. 'Arthur needed us and he has learned to love us – and so we'll go. It's as simple as that . . .'

CHAPTER 35

Despite some fears of attack from the sky or beneath the waves, Rose was mentally prepared and had everything ready in three weeks. All their furniture was to be stored for the time being.

Arthur had been excited when they told him the news, but a flicker of doubt was in his eyes as he'd looked at Rose. 'I will be with you when we live in Canada, won't I?'

'Yes, of course you will,' Rose told him. 'You're our lad, Arthur, and that's one of the reasons we're going – because it will be a fresh start for us all.'

Once reassured that nothing would change between them, Arthur couldn't wait for the day of their departure. He told Rose about seeing the bear at the lake and how it had wanted their sandwiches.

'Well, that was a bit scary,' she said, her eyes twinkling at him. 'I'm not sure I'd want to meet a bear.'

'Don't worry, Aunt Rose, I'll protect you,' Arthur said and giggled as she caught him and swung him off his feet.

'I reckon you'll need to,' Rose teased, a feeling of

happiness sweeping through her as she thought of the future that they could look forward to together.

The voyage was uneventful, not even a storm at sea to send them scurrying to their cabin. Rose felt a bit sick the first two days but Arthur and Harry were both fine. They spent a lot of time on deck and after a while she was able to join them.

There were a few other passengers on board. Most were returning home after a visit on essential business – only Rose, Harry, and Arthur were making the voyage with the intention of emigrating.

Harry made friends with one man while walking on deck and spoke of his hopes of setting up a small garage.

'Bob Jackson says there are plenty of small towns around where they don't have a working garage,' Harry told them one evening before dinner. 'He thinks it might be harder to get established in Halifax but he says there might be an opening in either Upper or Lower Sackville.'

'Lower Sackville is where Mrs Bittern lives, isn't it?' Rose asked and he nodded. 'We might think of settling there, Harry – unless you felt like going elsewhere.'

'We'll see what sort of a reception we get there,' Harry said. 'She sounded nice in her letter, Rose – but let's see how we get on when we arrive.'

Their arrival was expected, because Harry had sent a wire when he'd known their sailing date and someone was standing on the dock holding a board with their names on it. Harry spotted the man first and waved at him. As the man walked towards him, he saw that he walked with a pronounced limp, one of his feet dragging, but the smile he gave them was so welcoming that his disability was immediately forgotten. He extended his hand warmly and Harry gripped it.

'Welcome to Halifax, Mr Smith, Mrs Smith – and is that, Arthur?' His smile got even broader. 'I'm Jago and I'm married to Julie – do you remember her from the ship, Arthur?'

'Yes, sir,' Arthur said and his face lit up. 'She was so kind to me . . .'

'She is beyond excited to see you,' Jago told him. 'Julie's with Miss Vee up at the house waiting for you all. Beth is there, too. Miss Vee adopted her and they're all happy you've come.'

'We're happy to be here,' Rose said as Jago led the way to a large, slightly old-fashioned motor car. He held the door for them to get in.

'You'll be staying with Miss Vee until you find a house of your own,' he told them.

'This is so kind of her,' Rose said. 'We weren't quite sure what to expect when we got here. Harry spoke to the purser and he said we'd find somewhere to stay easily in Halifax but we'd rather be somewhere quieter . . .'

'Her house is in a nice area,' Jago told them as he glanced over his shoulder and then moved off into the flow of traffic. 'She lives beyond the old town, up in Lower Sackville – but there are quiet places to be found around here still, though the expansion is a problem. We have to protect our wild areas, Mr Smith, or we'll have none left.'

'Please call me Harry – Harry and Rose,' Harry said. 'I'm not sure we want to live in the real countryside – but a small town or village where I could set up an automobile garage.'

'You a mechanic?' Jago half-glanced towards him. 'I could do with one of those up at the sawmill. We have trouble with the machines sometimes and the boys are always needing to take their trucks into Halifax to get them fixed.'

Harry turned to look at him. 'I might be needing a job for a while, until I can get myself set up. Besides, I've been told we have to apply to become Canadian citizens if we want to stay for good.'

'True, but don't let that bother you,' Jago said and grinned. 'There isn't much Miss Vee can't fix and if she can't, one of her friends will know how to guide you.'

'She has already been so kind,' Rose said. 'I could hardly believe it when I first read her letter.'

'Miss Vee is a right decent lady,' Jago said. 'She helped me from the time I was a young lad and I owe her everything – but you don't mess with her. Not that you'd want to . . .' Jago chuckled softly to himself. 'Just wait until you see the welcome, she has lined up for you!'

When she saw the flags and all the tables set outside in the garden, the big banner saying Welcome to Canada, Arthur, Rose and Harry, Rose felt tears come to her eyes. It was like one of the street parties after the first big war and it seemed half the neighbourhood had turned out to greet them. Everyone had brought food – more food than Rose had seen in years – and it was all delicious.

Miss Vee looked very elegant in a grey silk dress and Rose felt a flicker of unease in her tummy when she saw her, but when she held out both her hands and smiled, her wobbles ceased. A young woman standing next to her gave a cry of delight and swooped on Arthur.

'You've grown so much!' she cried. 'Oh, Arthur, I am so glad to see you. Are you well? Are you happy?'

'Julie?' Arthur stared at her uncertainly for a moment and then smiled as she opened her arms and hugged him. He looked up at her. 'I wasn't happy back in England until my aunt found me – but I am now.'

'You must tell me all about it,' Julie said, 'but first come and say hello to Beth – you do remember her?'

Arthur went with her. Julie had looked very different, grown up, and it had been a minute or so before he really knew it was her but he didn't recognise Beth at all. She came forward shyly and held out her hand; they shook hands formally but then she smiled.

'I can't remember you very well,' Beth said. 'I'm glad you've come, though. Julie was worried about you.'

'I can't remember you either,' Arthur told her honestly. 'I know we were on the ship together but so much has happened and – you've changed. You look different.'

'That's because I'm happy now,' Beth said and smiled, still a little shy. 'Do you want something to eat? Aggie's made lots of lovely things. Come on, I'll show you . . .' She held out her hand and Arthur went with her, though he didn't take her hand.

'Well, it is wonderful to see you all,' Miss Vee said to Rose. 'This is my brother Malcolm and his wife Sheila.

Malcolm will take your cases up to your rooms. Would you like to freshen up before we eat?'

'Yes, please,' Rose agreed. 'I'd like to use the bathroom if I may.'

'Of course. I want you to feel at home here. You're welcome to stay for as long as you need, though I'm sure you'll want your own home.'

'We might have to use lodging houses for a while,' Rose said uncertainly. 'Our furniture is in store and it will have to be shipped out after the war when we find somewhere to live.'

'Oh, that won't be a problem,' Miss Vee told her. 'I could find you a house – and furnishings if you wish until your own arrives.' A frown entered her eyes. 'Emily Henderson put her furniture in store when she left for England and I understand she died there. Her lawyer told me of her intention to divorce her husband and she apparently left what little she had to Arthur so that means he is entitled to the furniture and personal things she stored and anything that remains from her aunt's estate once it's settled. Perhaps a thousand Canadian dollars, I am informed.'

'That money is Arthur's,' Rose said firmly. 'It will go into a bank for him and he can sell the furniture if he wishes or keep it.'

Miss Vee nodded her approval. 'Well, you can think about what you want to do when you decide where to settle,' she said. 'For the moment you have a home here with us.'

'That is so kind,' Rose said. 'I don't know how to thank you.'

'No need. This house is much bigger than I need.

I've been thinking I might sell it and find something smaller. Beth likes it up at the lake and Jago has offered to build us a house near him. I'm not sure yet but I might decide to move up there one day . . .'

'It is a big house,' Rose said, glancing around her. 'We had a nice one in London, but it got bombed. It was nowhere near as big as this, of course, but we were comfortable there.'

'You must have had a terrible time during the Blitz,' Miss Vee said, looking at her in concern. 'I can't imagine what it must have been like to lose your home and everything in it, just like that . . .'

'It happened to me,' Rose said. 'Before I was married to Harry – but his house was let out to someone else when it was bombed. It was one of the new rockets they're sending over. Fortunately, no one was in it and our stuff was in our new home.'

'Well, that was something,' Miss Vee said and then smiled. 'I'll take you up to your room – I've put you and Arthur next door to each other in case he gets a bit frightened.'

'He isn't keen on the dark,' Rose told her. 'I usually leave a small light in the hall for him. He had quite a bad time of it one way and another . . .'

'Yes, so I understand,' Miss Vee said. 'We'll talk about it another day, Mrs Smith – or may I call you, Rose?'

'I'd rather you did,' Rose replied. 'I've been called a lot of things in my life, mind, but my name is Rose.'

'Then that's what I'll call you – and now I'll leave you to make yourself comfortable . . .'

Alone in a room twice the size of anything she'd

been used to, Rose looked around in wonder. So this was how the other half lived! She liked the shine on old furniture and the gorgeous smell of perfume, which came from a huge vase of flowers on the dressing chest. Rose liked the way it was furnished; it looked soft and comfortable despite being a little grand in size. On the polished wood floor were rugs that glowed in jewel-like colours and the chair beside the bed was deep and squishy. Rose went through into a tiny cloakroom that led off the bedroom. It had a toilet and a washbasin and again it smelled like roses. She was washing her hands and face when Harry entered.

'This is all right,' Harry said. 'Nice folk, Rose. Malcolm told me there's a job at the store if I need it.'

'That's two offers already!' Rose exclaimed. 'I liked Jago. I think that might suit you for a while, Harry.'

'Yes, that's what I thought,' he said. 'It might be best to take a job for a start, I think. See how we feel . . .'

'Not getting cold feet, Harry?' Rose looked at him but he shook his head.

'I was thinking of Arthur. He seemed pleased to see Julie and he was getting on all right with Beth – but not the way he did with Davey. We'll have to see if he settles – if we all do.' He glanced around the room. 'This is nice, Rose – but I'd rather have our own place, even if we can only rent it for a while. I just want you and Arthur to be happy.'

'I like what I've seen so far,' Rose admitted. 'Let's see how Arthur feels once he's back at school . . .'

CHAPTER 36

Harry started working for Jago a week after they arrived. He came back the first evening and told Rose how beautiful it was up at the lake and on the Sunday they hired a little truck and drove up there to have a picnic by the lake with Jago, Julie and Maya, Jago's mother. At the end of the afternoon they took Maya home and she invited them in for a glass of iced julep. It was such a homely place that they all felt comfortable at once.

'Jago wants me to go and live near him,' Maya told them. 'He's cleared the ground for another cabin like his – but I'm not sure I could leave this place. It was my home when I married . . .'

'It's very nice here,' Rose said. 'If it was my home, I'm not sure I'd want to leave – though I see his point. It could be a bit lonely living here on your own.'

'I can walk into the town and the church,' Maya told her with a smile. 'And I have help looking after the animals.'

'I'd help you with them if we lived near here,' Arthur said. 'I love the woods – do you get any bears?'

'I haven't seen any for a long time,' Maya said, but seeing his face fall said, 'You never know when

363

one might come visiting and there are lots of small animals and birds in the woods. Jago cuts the trees for the logging but he plants more than he cuts so they'll be here for a long time to come.'

'Good!' Arthur looked at her. 'Do you know the names of the animals that live in the woods?'

'I might,' Maya said. 'Your aunt might let you come visit one weekend and I'll take you there and see what comes to us. Sometimes they come if you call them with your heart . . .'

Arthur looked at Rose and she nodded. 'If you're sure he'd be no trouble.'

'Oh, no, he's a kindred spirit. The folk of the woods will love him.'

Arthur gravitated to her, listening to her stories of animals Jago had brought home and nursed before letting them go free again. He was enchanted, asking so many questions that Rose had to laughingly put a stop to them.

'You'll wear Maya out,' she told him. 'I think we'd best get back, Arthur, or Miss Vee will wonder where we've gone . . .'

Arthur followed Harry outside, but, as Rose was about to leave, Maya touched her arm. 'What you fear will not happen,' she said. 'You are safe here.'

Rose stared at her, a tingling at her nape. 'What do you mean?'

Maya's eyes met hers in a deep gaze. 'You have a secret that worries you but there is no need to be anxious.'

'What has someone told you?' Rose asked, her nerves jangling.

'Only that you have a secret worry,' Maya said. 'I believe Miss Vee can help you. You should speak with her.'

Rose looked at her hard but there was no malice in her. Jago's mother was from one of the indigenous tribes of Canada and there was something mystic about her at that moment, as though she could truly see into a person's soul. She was certainly a wise woman and she'd been kind and generous. Rose decided there was no reason to fear her words, and so she thanked her.

She was thoughtful as she was driven back to Miss Vee's house. It was entirely possible that Miss Vee did know what troubled Rose. If the private detective she'd used could track and find Arthur, he could quite easily discover all there was to know about Rose and Harry.

It was the following day, when Beth and Arthur had gone to school, and Harry was at work that Rose found Miss Vee sitting alone in her parlour. She hesitated and then went in.

'May I join you?' Rose asked. She rarely sat in the parlour unless invited, preferring to help Aggie in the kitchen or go for walks to accustom herself to her surroundings.

'Yes, I wish you would,' Miss Vee said. 'I think we should have a little talk. Shall I ask Aggie to bring some coffee – or tea?'

'I'd rather just talk for a start,' Rose said and sat down in a chair opposite her hostess. 'It's very good of you to have us here, Miss Vee. We've had time to get used to things and think about what we ought to do. I've seen a nice little house not far away that's to rent and I'm going to ask if we can view it . . .'

'Good. I'm glad you've found something you like.'

Miss Vee raised her fine brows. 'Does that mean you've decided to settle here?'

'Harry's getting on well with Jago. He likes engines and he's happy enough. When his affairs in England get settled, he will have a bit of money and he might set up his own garage then, but for now he is content as he is.'

'And what about you, Rose?'

'I'm all right. As long as Arthur and Harry are happy, I'll be fine. I might look for a part-time job somewhere – I've done all sorts in the past, factory, or waitressing. I only want a few hours. I like to be home for when Arthur gets out of school.'

'Yes . . .' Miss Vee nodded. 'There is a job in our store if it interests you – but Malcolm is the one you should speak to about that, Rose. I leave those decisions to him.'

'He did mention something,' Rose said. 'It's very kind of you, Miss Vee. I'll speak to him and see if I'm suitable for what he needs. Harry says there's no need for me to do anything, but I'd like to help him get his garage.'

'Yes. It was unfortunate that his house should be bombed. The insurance doesn't cover such things – but the land should be worth something. There will be a lot of rebuilding when this wretched war is over. I believe the end cannot be far away now. I pray it is so.'

'We all do . . .' Rose sat for a moment, staring at her hands. 'Yesterday, up at the lake, we met Maya . . . she's an interesting lady . . .'

'Ah . . .' Miss Vee nodded. 'Maya is from an ancient people and she has senses and gifts that most of us do not.' She paused, then, 'Did she tell you something?'

'She said that I had a secret fear but I shouldn't worry because I was safe here . . .'

'Did she also tell you that I might help?'

Rose was silent. She did not know whether to confide in Miss Vee or not. She liked her – but could she trust her?

'Has it not occurred to you that Mr Carson is a very thorough man?' Miss Vee asked with a smile. 'I do know that Arthur is not actually Harry's blood nephew. Mr Carson investigated you both and told me that Harry Smith was an honest, brave man who deserved a medal and that you were a good woman who had done your best to find Arthur. He was unable to find a connection between you, so I must ask how you knew he was in trouble?'

'I only saw him two or three times,' Rose said, because there wasn't much Miss Vee didn't already know. 'He was with Emily and someone called Peter – a friend of hers, Arthur says. There was something about him – something that pulled on my heart. I thought he had the saddest eyes.' Miss Vee nodded her understanding. 'Then I saw him again after some months – and he looked different. His hair was long, his clothes were dirty and he was staring at the fish and chip shop in a way that made me think he was hungry . . .'

'So what happened then?'

'I was on a crowded bus. I couldn't get off but the look of him haunted me. I told Harry and I took the next day off to look for him. I discovered where he lived but couldn't find him. I went to his school and to the police but they didn't seem bothered. I suppose a lot of children went missing during the Blitz and they had a bit of a scare on locally. Harry and I went back to his house again but it looked deserted from the front. Mr Carson got in the back way and found Arthur there alone.'

'Yes, he is a resourceful man,' Miss Vee said. 'He discovered you had been looking for Arthur and he brought him to you and asked if you would care for him until a decision could be made about his future.'

'Yes, that's right,' Rose agreed. 'Perhaps we ought to have let the authorities know, but I wanted to take in a young lad who was homeless. I've two grown sons of my own but they have their own lives and Harry and me, we tried the adoption centres but they said no at first and then they were more encouraging, but they preferred younger folk as adoptive parents so we weren't sure we'd get Arthur. Besides, he was happy with us and we didn't want him upset.'

'So, after Harry was wounded and then given a discharge from his duties, you decided to take up my offer and come here?' Miss Vee nodded, studying Rose's face. 'You're still a little anxious, because you think someone might try to take Arthur away from you?'

Rose nodded. 'I know it's daft – and mebbe we did wrong but—'

'I think you did exactly as you ought, given the circumstances,' Miss Vee told her, her voice firm. Rose opened her eyes as she saw the look on her hostess' face. 'It is very much what I did when Malcolm brought Beth to me. I had no right to take her. Someone else paid for her passage out but they didn't claim her so my brother brought her to me. At first, I was reluctant but then I began to love her and I knew I could never part with her – so when someone tried to take her, I fought them and I won.' Her smile was one of triumph. 'I adopted my Beth – and you can do the same!'

'But will they let us . . .?'

'You will use my lawyer,' Miss Vee said in a voice of authority. 'I shall vouch for you, so will Malcolm, Aggie, Jago, and Hank. I do not imagine you will have the least difficulty, and if there is I will deal with it.' Her smile for Rose now was gentle and filled with sympathy. 'No one here wants to take Arthur from you, Rose. I wanted to see for myself that he was happy and that you were decent folk – and now that I know you love him and he loves you, I will do everything to make sure that he is yours legally. Please trust me, my dear Rose. I count you as a friend now and I will do all I can to make sure Arthur remains safe with you.'

Rose couldn't speak. She was too full of gratitude, relief, and happiness to get a word out, but at last she managed a croaky, 'Thank you,' and then the tears just rolled down her cheeks.

'Nothing to cry for,' Miss Vee said. 'I'll go and ask Aggie to bring us some coffee and cake. I'm sure you could do with it. I certainly can!'

Rose told Harry when he got home that evening and he grinned. 'I was going to suggest it to you, love. Things are different here somehow; the people are friendly, and it's a good life. Jago says we could have a cabin on his land if we wanted but I thought you might prefer to live a little closer to the town?'

'I'm not sure. I've always been used to the town, but it is beautiful up there,' Rose said. 'It wouldn't be too far – and you could teach me to drive, Harry.'

'Jago said he wants someone to help his mother. You liked Maya, didn't you?'

Rose stared at him for a moment. 'Yes, I did, and I'll be wanting a little job – but let's ask Arthur. See what he thinks . . . and we'll tell him he's going to be adopted so he's always ours, a part of our family.'

Arthur looked from Rose to Harry. 'Are you asking me if I'd like to live up at the lake?' he asked and his face lit with delight. 'Could we truly?'

'Jago was building a cabin for his mother but she refuses to move from her home,' Harry said. 'He offered me the chance but I wanted to know what you and Rose thought.'

'I'd love it!' Arthur said, the delight in his eyes telling them how much the idea appealed to him. 'Is it all right, Aunt Rose?' he asked, still uncertain it would happen. 'Will you like it up there?'

'I'll be happy if you are,' she said and he ran to her and embraced her, then turned, leaning into her as he looked at Harry.

'We could play football and cricket, go on the lake and swim . . . and it's so peaceful, Uncle Harry! Could we truly live there?'

'Yes, we can,' Harry confirmed. 'There's one more thing, Arthur. We're going to adopt you legally so you will always be our family . . . we'll be your official mum and dad then.'

Arthur's smile disappeared. 'Will I call you Mum and Dad then?'

'Don't you want to?' Harry asked and Rose caught her breath.

Arthur looked round at her and then back at Harry. Then, in a halting voice, he said, 'I had a dad and he died. I had two mums and they died . . .' A little sob escaped him. 'I don't want you to die and leave me. I'd rather call you Aunt Rose and Uncle Harry if it makes it so you don't die and leave me . . .'

'Oh, Arthur!' Rose's arms went round him and she hugged him, turning him to look at her. 'We just want to make sure you can't be taken from us, love. You can call us whatever you like, but we love you and we will look after you and love you for as long as we live.'

'You won't be alone again,' Harry promised and came to join them, putting his strong arms around him. 'You've got me and your Aunt Rose – and now you've got lots of others who care for you, too. There's Julie and Jago, Maya, and Miss Vee, Beth, Aggie and Malcolm, and Hank, and even Selmer. Everyone cares about you, Arthur. None of us would let you be alone and frightened or hungry. And soon you'll be big enough and strong enough to look after us. Do you believe me?'

Arthur looked up at him and the tears were gone. He grinned at Harry. 'Yeah, reckon I do,' he said and then laughed as Harry caught him up on his shoulders. 'Can we go and tell Jago now?'

'You can tell him on Saturday,' Harry said. 'How about we have a game of football before you go to bed?'

Rose watched as Harry carried their boy outside on his shoulders to the large back garden, listening to their happy laughter. She breathed a deep sigh of relief. Life was a funny old thing with its ups and downs. They had all been through some harrowing times, but at the moment it really couldn't get much better.

Read more about Cathy Sharp's orphans whose compelling stories will tug at your heartstrings.

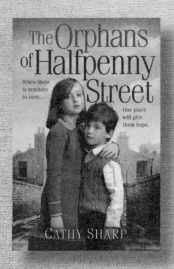

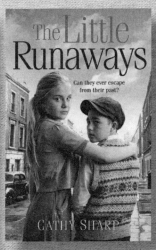

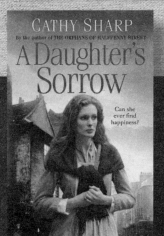

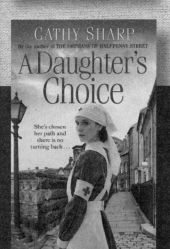

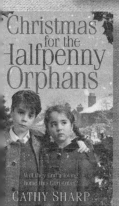
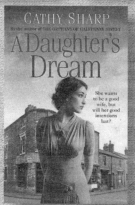
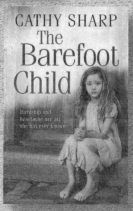

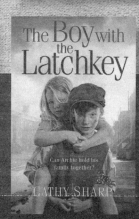

CATHY SHARP

THE BOY
with the
SUITCASE

**He must travel a
long road to find
his way home…**

'A story which touched my heart'
Glynis Peters

Available now

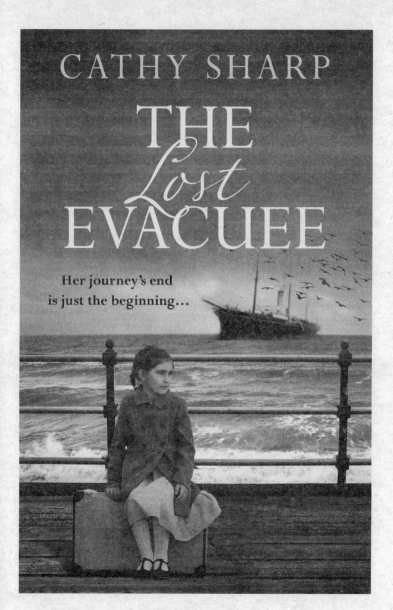

CATHY SHARP

THE
Lost
EVACUEE

Her journey's end
is just the beginning…

Available now